SWEET SPOT

LINTON ROBINSON

Copyright © 2009 By Linton Robinson
First Edition

Where used trademarks are acknowledged as the property of their respective owners.

1. Literature. 2. Mexico. 3. Baseball.

Sweet Spot
        / by   Linton Robinson
                p. cm.

ISBN 13: 978-0-9820467-2-2

adorobooks.com

In Collaboration with Bauu Press
Boulder, Colorado

Printed in the United States of America
ALL RIGHTS RESERVED

SWEET SPOT

LINTON ROBINSON

TUESDAY
FEBRUARY FIFTH

ANNIVERSARY, PROCLAMATION OF MEXICAN
CONSTITUTION

Carnival Calendar

Coronation of Queen of Fair, Salon Bacanora, 7PM
Presentation of Arts Awards, IMSS Auditorium, 9 PM

The reason why Marxism fails so often and so utterly, while the apparently similar PRI and Catholic Church have succeeded for so long, probably has to do with its tendency to motivate people through common interest and fear, rather than self interest and love, which are the forces responsible for world's biggest victories, most stable creations, and most appalling mistakes.

"Of Burros, Sticks, and Carrots" by Mundo Carrasco

Nexus, September 1999

I had seen the whole *bola* before and hadn't liked their looks. I liked them even less huddled up in the healing halls of Sagrada Familia with their muddy plastic sandals, grimy 'Señor Frogs' shirts, and cheap polyester pants. Especially the two big, rough-looking bricklayers who wore imitation Stetson *sombreros* instead of filthy baseball hats. They didn't seem to like my looks much, either.

I didn't know them as individuals, but I'd known the herd since childhood. They were The Poor. Not the *superpobres* picking scraps out of garbage dumps, just the typical working poor of Mazatlán. And not the sort of crowd usually allowed in the marble arches of *La Familia*. I had seen this very bunch during the campaign, filling the crowds when my boss – *El Candidato* back then – dragged us out to speeches in the lower class *barrios*. They were his wife's shock troops, Blanquita's bodyodor politic. To me, they represented something I'd left behind a long time ago. To *El Candidato* himself, they were a huge voting block delivered to him by marriage like a scabby dowry. To her, they were a flock of birds to be fed, a mass of grubby children to be nurtured and loved, a doting family to be embraced and protected. They belonged to her – and therefore to Us and His Campaign – simply because they worshipped her.

Which I could understand completely, I would tell you straight off that I only took the damn job because of Mijares. It wasn't reciprocal enough to be called love, but worship will cover it.

It had been like a religious experience to shrug myself awake and see her standing right there by my bed.

The moon was behind a thick bank of fog, but the beacon lights on the antennas up the hill were washing her body with a slow red pulse. I had to fight off the impulse to reach out for her, knowing it would look pathetic. Then I didn't care if was pathetic or not, but she'd moved to look out at my dirt-cheap loft's million dollar view. Of course, she looks just as devastating from the rear. She leaned over the railing, looking down at the Oldtown and bay. I got up and stripped off my shorts, started plowing around in the pre-morning dark, looking for pants, coat, notebook, light switch, anything. She turned again, and sized me up.

I was pleased that my dreams – and her provocative bendover at the rail, I suppose – had left me somewhat swollen and lengthened, but not stabbing out enough to look ridiculous.

She gave a glance and smiled, "Always nice to see old friends."

I stepped to the rail and looked out over the city, sensibly slumbering at four in the morning – though Chema's gamecocks would change that soon. I glanced down at the street and sure enough, Coyota, my neighbor's German Shepherd bitch, was sitting in the middle of the street looking straight up into my face. She's a peculiar dog. I said what I say every morning, "Coyota, go kill those damned roosters."

I looked at Mija standing beside me, sniffed her scent. I said, "Hey, look ..."

"I did look. But I'm not going to touch. Get your ass in gear, hero. This is a major *chingadera.*"

I pulled on a shirt and said, "How bad?"

"About as bad as it gets." Which showed she wasn't as omniscient as she thought.

"Did he get caught screwing some councilman's little girl?" I found some pants draped over my printer and pulled them on. "Or little boy?"

"No, he's become more of a homebody since he was elected. Supposedly beat the hell out of his wife."

Hardly news in *machista* Sinaloa. I looked up at her for the rest while tying my shoes.

4

"She's reportedly in the hospital, badly injured. Police have responded."

"Not just city cops, huh?" Or she wouldn't be here.

"No such luck. They did the normal response to the kids' call, ambulance and everything. But the PGR heard the kids report the bag of cocaine and pills on the table. That was what they were fighting about."

"*Federales*. Great. Well, sounds like time to earn our pay."

"Yours. I did my job coming over here to get your lazy ass out of bed. Why didn't you answer the phone?

"I couldn't hear it."

She looked around my little penthouse. Corrugated cement roof covering half of the four-meter square slab, a cement railing, nothing else but night sky. Nowhere to hide. She whipped out her cellular like an Old West gunslinger and punched a button. She listened a second, then gave me a look.

"Well, okay, *now* I can hear it, I'm awake."

She followed the muted beeps, which wasn't very hard to do. She looked down into the toilet and shook her head. "Thinking of quitting, are we?"

"I have quit. But nobody else knows about it yet."

"We'll keep it our secret for now." She started to stride out of the bath stall, but stopped and gave it a look. Not much to look at, just two brick walls, shoulder high, with a shower head and toilet seat.

"There's no curtain. No door, nothing. What do you do when you use the bath?"

"Same as anybody else, I'd guess."

"Can't your neighbors see you over here showering and shitting?" She waved her hand at the open space that surrounds my aerie.

Sure enough, if anybody from the surrounding mansions wanted to watch me pee, nothing would stop them. I never really thought of if before.

"They're all politicians and drug lords. They probably have funner things to watch than some *indio* take a dump."

"*Ay, Mundo. No te aguantes.*" She was back up to speed by then, with a last shake of her head before getting back to the problem at hand. "Let's get moving."She was out the door as she said it, tripping smoothly down the steep dark stairs.

Three flights down, out the gate, she handed me another cellular. She had three in her bag. I headed down the steep sidewalk towards the steps leading down to the Military Hospital. She was in her car with the motor on before she stuck her head out and called me back. "Just got another call, *mi chavo*. You'd better take your so-called car because it's a long walk to Sagrada Familia."

I paused a minute on the way over to my battered Safari. "Where's His Honor?"

"Down the toilet," she said, smiling. "But don't worry, we'll get it back for him."

He'd be in a drunken, coke-stoked dither at that moment, tearing around in his fleet of Suburbans jabbering to his bodyguards and *cuates*. But we'd be working on his image. I shrugged and went out to face the vanguard of pissed-off poverty.

But even my sympathetic comprehension of these poor urban peasants throwing themselves into the political machine out of sheer desperation and adoration didn't make me any happier to see them standing between me and my pretty urgent conversation with The Mayor's sainted wife. No surprise that it was the two big *abañiles* who stepped out to block my way.

And no surprise the way they cut me off at the perfect spot for their cronies to flow around and flank me, moving in like highly experienced brawlers. Two ugly customers with big, brick-coarsened hands and absolutely no use for my line of goods. I gave them my old ballplayer grin, buffed up by six months of working in politics.

"¿*Qué onda, compa*? Is this where they brought *Señora* Varedas?"

The one with the blue shirt spat about an inch from my shoes. I assume he didn't miss on purpose.

"¿*Y 'aste', quien es?*" he growled, "*Compa*."

Saying *'aste'* for 'you' instead of *usted* was like a nametag, "Hi, I'm a Hillbilly."And sneering the "Buddy" on the end of it probably meant he wasn't going to ask me to autograph some old scorecard. But you have to go through the motions.

"I'm Raymundo Carrasco, deputy of the Mayor's office ..." *Ay,* already they didn't like it, maybe I shouldn't have promoted myself up from Press Relations. "I'm supposed to see if Sra. Varedas is all right, if she needs anything."

"She's gotten enough from the Mayor tonight, *wey.*" He stepped right up in front of my face to say it, as big as I am and a lot rougher around the edges. "Why don't you run back and tell your *culero* boss to come down here and talk to me himself? See if I'm as easy to beat up as a delicate flower of a woman."

They couldn't even talk about her like she was a common noun. And I'm here representing the guy alleged to have choked her half to death and banged her head on the floor. Wonderful.

"Look, *amigo.*" I tried, "I'm just a working stiff like you. I've never even met Varedas. I have no idea what happened. They told me to come over here, so I have to, you know? Anything I can do to take care of her, help her out, that's what they told me."

He seemed to take the notion that I'd just told him a pack of damned lies, which in fact, I had. I had a very good idea what had happened to Missus Mayor – Mijares had spelled it out on the phone while I drove, then put me through to the hospital. I'd also lied about why they jerked me out of bed and sent me over there. The main priority wasn't exactly fluffing her pillows, it was to assess her mood and even, if miraculously possible, shut her up. She had a soft spot for me for some reason.

The bricklayer said, "I see your work. I see your nice clothes, your rich dad, your expensive barrio. You think you own us, can push us around. Me, I doubt it."

"My dad was a *peon* for the railroad, *wey.*" I didn't mention that he rose to track crew boss and union rep. "And I grew up in Ferrocarril, which if you've ever been out of a bar long enough to notice, is not exactly the *barrio de luxo.*"

I established my working class origins; they established their working class muscle by crowding in on me, starting to push me back and forth. The big mason stayed right in front of me, his partner just behind my right shoulder. Didn't know I'm a switch-hitter, apparently. But not much of a fighter. It always seemed pointless to me. One of my college coaches said I lack the "God-given killer instinct." So I smiled and tried to talk sense. But the big masons had the perfect argument against that sort of notion.

The guy behind me hit first, a very hard punch that numbed my right shoulder. I swung around to defend myself and the leader of the *bola* kicked me in the small of the back, punching me right into his partner, who used my momentum to put a spectacular bruise on my forehead. I wouldn't have gone down, but the rest were crowding and tripping me. I fell on my hands, but they were kicked out from under me and a lot of feet started kicking my face and stomping my ribs. I did a sudden roll to my left, sweeping into a forest of feet and knocking a few of them down over the top of me. I did a power pushup, jerked my feet under me, and saw an opening. I plunged through it, a sort of staggering controlled fall, and broke through the pack. There were two nuns at the top of the stairs, looking appalled but not entirely sympathetic. The Church is also fond of Blanquita, especially her work with hospitals and hospices.

But they were enough to stop the Army of the Poor from running up and kicking me down the steps or just gobbling me up. I looked back at them from the top of the steps, twenty very angry men practically in rags. I couldn't really hold anything against them.

I said, "No hard feelings, *muchachos*. Tell Sra. Varedas if she needs anything at all, not to hesitate to call room service."

The biggest *albañil* stared at me for a moment then started laughing. His sidekick joined in and immediately the whole bunch was laughing in the high spirits of victors condescending towards a loser who's a good sport about it. Nobody could ever say I'm not a good fucking sport. I turned around with what shreds of dignity you muster when you're bleeding and rumpled and have just been kicked around like a dog. And defended by nuns. They were still laughing when I stepped out the front door.

I got to my car just as two black Suburbans with opaqued windows blasted into the parking lot and burned off an inch of tires just stopping. His Honor's bodyguards finally figured out where she was. Good job, you clowns. There were about four guys in each vehicle, stereotypical beef wearing Ray-Bans at night and starched *guayaberas* hanging over their ornate pistols. Half of them also had UZI's and M16's. I grabbed a towel out of the back seat and mopped up a little, thinking, "Good luck, Mister Mayor, Sir. I'm bruised and dissed just for working for you, let's see how you come out."

In fact, I decided it would be fun to see exactly that, and walked back to watch through the big glass front doors. The phalanx of *guardespaldas* was confronting the rabble. My bodyguards can lick your bodyguards ... family spat by proxy. I had a press box view of what happened. The Poor had taken the top end of a double-header and were up for the closer. The Mayor's Men had guns, but had apparently been ordered not to use them. Even a bungling moron like Hizzoner Frederico Varedas could figure out that shooting up poor constituents in the Sacred Family Hospital would not play very well in the theater of public imagination.

This time there was no clever blow from the rear, and the nuns had sought retreat elsewhere. The *bola* of working wounded just piled into the big mercenaries and started flailing away. Some threw bottles. I even saw a chair fly into a bodyguard's head. They pushed the forces of Order back to the steps, then tumbled them down and threw them out the doors. Then they kicked them into their Suburbans and battered the Suburbans as they drove off. I was back in my Safari by then, with the engine running. I flashed the winners a two-fingered victory salute and they laughed and waved at me as I left the parking lot – just as a car with a press sticker from *Adelante* drove in. Silvio Rodriquez arriving a minute too late, as usual. With the Press already buzzing around the smell, I was glad to be out of there. Those poor are no joke in a fight, but the press is really a pain in the ass. My former colleagues might smell better, but they fight dirtier. I realized it was my first combat on the side of The Establishment.

Because I have to be honest here. My obsession with Mija was overpowering, but there was more to my career shift than just that. I wanted to be part of the Power Show I used to just write about. I wanted to get up in the engine and drive, or at least shovel the coal. I wanted to belong to it all. Which is another way of saying I wanted it all to belong to me. And, of course my desire to belong to Mija had the same overall goal. I still can't believe that I didn't realize it would be like trying to ride two crazy horses at the same time. The job was essentially The Establishment; meaning the establishing of structure. And Mijares was essentially Anarchy; meaning the reduction of any structure to the most minimal, indistinguishable components. Working for the new mayor's party to be close to a neo-Marxist rebel. It's not all as crazy as it might sound here in Mexico, which was ruled for eight decades by something called the Institutional Revolutionary Party. But crazy enough.

Mexicans get confused when people criticize nepotism. Who would be better to have working for you than family? It's especially non-applicable in a system dominated by the PRI, which may be a machine in the political sense but is organically a family, or at least a clan.

"Chariots of the Godfathers" by Raymundo Carrasco
Los Angeles New Times, March 29, 2000

Three very cute *chiquitas* work in the Public Information office at City Hall, all three fluttery but efficient. They help compensate for the general air of battered decay. The whole *Palacio* is shabby and dirty even by the standards of a Mexican city. The building itself is arrogantly ugly, squat and shabby with the flaking cement painted a drab off-color Mijares once called, Diaper Contents Yellow. The opening to the courtyard is cluttered with noisy families waiting for paperwork, tables selling schoolbooks from the State press, and even booths hawking appliances, raffles, and cellular phones.

The courtyard is open and bare, with a pathetic cement fountain shaped like a bicycle horn where pigeons peck at cigarette butts in the stagnant water. The paint is peeling, tiles are missing. Heaps of chairs and musty cardboard boxes full of files are stacked up under the balcony, sometimes blocking doorways. A Civic Information booth lies on its side below the split stairway leading up to the balcony running around the second floor. It's a *porqueria*, the best translation I can come up with for "piece of crap". On the other hand, it might not be a good idea to have public buildings look much nicer and more luxurious than what the voters have to live in.

The Public Information office goes well with the general air of neglect and underfunding. Compared to publicity offices at the Arizona State University, for instance, it's a dirty broom closet that could use a hose-down and exterminator. They've got us on the second floor, rear corner, diagonal across from the Mayor's office. I take comfort from being as far as I can from the scene of inaction. Two rooms, aging computers, press clippings, morgues, the three info-cuties and one mean old hag who files everything. Mijares, as Director of Public Information, gets one room, which she paid to have painted an interesting shade of rose. I get a special Press Relations desk, army-colored metal with only one drawer left.

None of the cute *info-chicas* got too interested in nursing my bleeding face and ripped suit when I dragged in at eight. Neither did three or four people who don't work there, but seemed to be helping the *info-chicas* stand around avoiding eye contact and hiding smirks. As soon as I walked over to my desk, where I could hear what was going on in Mijares office, I saw why. Daddy had dropped by for a little anti-social visit. And was chewing her butt off.

You can expect family political spats when the patriarch is Donaldo Gortari y Guzmán, secretary of the local PRI machine, and his daughter goes rad-chic to work for the scruffy PT organization – barely what you'd call a Labor Party. But he'd brought it down to City Hall for all to enjoy. And since the *info-chicas* are terrified, awed and despised by Mijares, they would be enjoying it the most and suffer for it later.

I went over to the door where I could hear everything said, unapologetically eavesdropping on my boss/desire object. I never made any secret of being totally absorbed by anything and everything to do with Mijares. I could focus my entire perception and intellect on whether her eyebrow actually grows in such a graceful curve, or whether she has skillfully sketched it like she did back when she shaved her head.

Now she flaunts a glossy black mane that most women would probably want to throttle her for shaving off. Or just for being too perfect and letting them know she knows it. What she's done with the rest of her various hairs I don't know – and even thinking about it leads to sweats, flameouts of fancy and throbable cause.

Her *papi* was laying into her about her stealth campaign to reverse the decision to widen Avenida Sabalo through the tourist zone. One of those infrastructure things that are so stupid they are almost inevitable, and so profitable for the power structure nobody even thinks about bucking them.

He must have found out what she was planning when some of his captive editors at the *Sol del Pacífico* got a look at the preliminary papers she'd been circulating to more sympathetic press members. She'd probably also been working up support from powerful Councilmen, who would of course be his friends and sycophants. And would have told him what she was up to.

"It's necessary for healthy growth," he was saying.

Raised Mijares for twenty-five years and still thinks you can argue with her logically.

"The hotel zone is so choked nothing can move," he continued. "Tourism is a major industry here, and you can't keep an industry running without modernizing the physical plant."

"By tearing out all those little sidewalk shops and restaurants that help make your cement Disneyland out there attractive to tourists? Who don't drive cars, by the way. Oh, but I forgot, all the big hotels and restaurants are set back far enough they won't lose their facades or seating area, will they? And there'd be no profit to be made for people with construction companies and city contracts, would there?"

"Growth is inevitable, you have to plan ahead."

"It's not inevitable. Acapulco isn't growing much anymore, is it? They drove their tourists away. You have to control traffic, not bow down to it. If you go to six lanes, they'll fill up in a year. Then what? Eight lanes? Twelve? Get rid of the sidewalks, have a car-only embarrassment like Brasilia?"

"What do you know about Brasilia?"

That would piss her off. Know-it-alls just hate running up against people who know more. She may think *Internacionale* but she's never been that far from home.

He saw her smolder and pressed on. "And what do you know about business? Or government for that matter?"

"As a matter of fact, I work for a government. At this very moment – didn't you see the signs on your way in?"

"A government that works for me, my friends, the people you sneer at. So what are you doing?"

"I couldn't explain it to you in a thousand years."

"Oh, I doubt you could explain it to yourself. But what I don't want is you explaining it to *Don* Filiberto or anybody on his committee. I want you to keep your nose, and your overly available little ass, out of this thing."

"This office ..."

"No! This office has nothing to do with construction or lobbying. If I hear of you trying to personally influence this thing one more time, you're going to regret it."

"Well, the convent and the boarding school and the stress camp didn't work. What else do you think I might regret?"

"How about having to get by on what this so-called job pays you?"

Ooo, that would have hurt. Lefty rebels hate to be reminded they are living on daddy's ill-gotten capitalist gains. Her dad had a good sense of when to make an exit, too. He left her fuming on that one and surged out, almost bumping into me.

He looked like he was going to roar like the cinema lion, then smiled and greeted me warmly. With his broad tiger's face, his tailored one-button suits everyone thinks of as 'Armanis' and in his case probably are. He called me, "Raymundo." He can switch from chewing ass like a pit bull to slathering on hearty regard without touching the clutch. He's secretary of the semi-omnipotent *Partido Revolucionario Institucional* so he's used to it. Even more so now that the PRI lost their eight-decade monopoly on Mexican government and actually have to win votes instead of just rigging everything up. But it still left me with a heightened sense of self-esteem I hoped to hold on to while facing the slavering jowls of the working press over lunch.

At her desk, Mijares was seething; nostrils widened, face flushed, nails digging into her elbows as she leaned against her desk and hugged herself like she might explode into flames and fragments. One look at her and I felt like my crotch might do more or less the same thing. I swear her ears were laid back like a dog's. I wanted to push her right back on the desk and pitch into her on the spot – after applying a gag, restraints, elbow pads and the other safety equipment you'd need for taming a wild beast in the

14

process of psychic implosion.

So, instead of taking appropriate action, I just said, "Press in at two?"Mijares likes to deal with them in the early afternoon, when they're mellow and sluggish from the free lunch and cheap booze at Lo Peor. The last thing we need on our hands is a hungry, peevish, sober press corps.

She gave me a hot, slightly crazed look then a full-body shiver as she banked the rage inside and morphed back to a mere gorgeous human female. She focused me in, noting my wounds and abrasions, but also refraining from nursing or fluttering. She gave me her smile. Which is like saying the sun gave you some light. Her acceptance and beauty washed through me like the dancing radiation of life. Getting Mijares' approval is not like pleasing other people, who are often basically nice. Mijares is not nice and her genuine smile is hard to win. Which by itself would make it worth going after, even if it wasn't such a breathtaking explosion of everything the human eye and heart have been created to applaud.

She said, "Great job with the First Martyr, Mundo. I'm impressed."

That was her usual nickname for the Mayor's wife, but aside from that I had no idea what she was talking about. I grunted ambiguously, looked stern and deserving.

"As soon as Blanquita called that talk show bitch at *Radio Mujer* every other reporter in town had it. There just isn't much they can do it about it right away," she said. "So her cronies over at *Hora* probably won't even get a scoop, poor dears. But it's wonderful, however you did it. Not only denying rumors that hadn't even started yet, but blaming them on propaganda from political enemies. I couldn't have scripted it better myself. You're too much."

This was all news to me, though nothing's supposed to be news when you're in the news business. Later I found out that the First Batteree's denial of the beating had been broadcast on "Woman Radio" at about the time I was driving back in from Sagrada Familia. Drivetime newsbreak.

I shrugged manfully and said, "Her loyalty to her husband and his political position takes priority over her personal difficulties."

She nodded, "Good line. Just so we don't let anybody get too specific about what those difficulties are." She'd bounced back from her early embarrassment with no more residuals than a cat recovering from a fall. Back in the more accustomed huntress role.

She took another look at my face and said, "Looks like you had to go through the Army of the Unwashed to get to her?"

"Under that grime, odor, and combativeness, they're as human as you or I."

"Well, thanks for the above-and-beyond, Mundo. I appreciate a man who'll bleed for me." She fixed me with one of her searching glances, which I would have turned into a strip search with the slightest encouragement, and asked if I'd had my ear to the keyhole while her father was in. I gave the kind of shrug that admits no guilt but defends against no charges.

"And he hasn't even heard about Our Man punching out Blanquita, yet. I can't wait for him to come rub in what a low class thug I'm working for."

"Populist thug," I said, "Alleged punching. As yet unconfirmed, officially denied, and probably mere oppositional propaganda."

"Keep saying that," she muttered, "You're going to need it. Have a nice lunch."

The word *hogar* is not completely equivalent to the English "home". We don't speak of a "home office" or "home town". Mexicans can say, "*Voy a casa*," but not "I'm going home," when returning to their native country. *Hogar* is a hearth, a family. A single man can have a *casa*, even a *mansión* or *hacienda*, but not an *hogar*.

"Home for the Holidays" by Raymundo Carrasco
"MazSpeak" Column
Mazatlán's Pacific Pearl , December, 1998

Well, lunch would come soon enough and the prospect wasn't appetizing. Since I was bleeding, disheveled, and having One Of Those Mornings, I decided it would wait until I'd readjusted *un poco*. Go home, shower, change clothes, do a little first aid – I'd given up on any flutter/coo therapy – and ditch my car. I'd much rather walk than drive, especially in the downtown, and one thing I like about the *Palacio* job is that I can walk to work. If I need to go somewhere out of the downtown I do it the third world way, by taxi. Or the Mazatlán way, in one of the fiberglass, open-air, rolling jukeboxes we call *pulmonía*s, because they're a good way for tourists to catch pneumonia.

It's a bad idea for a lower hierarch like myself to leave a car at city hall anyway, since there is no parking lot and the reserved spots on the streets are jealously guarded. In fact, as I got in to my old Volks Safari I noticed a city pickup full of M16-toting cops with that frustrated, looking-for-parking look focusing the tow-the-sucker stare on my battered Safari with all the lame paint jobs.

The first time Mijares saw my Safari she called it *El Vehiculo Ridiculo* but it suits me. These old Safaris are getting hard to find, probably because they have lousy steering and vulnerable body structure – you might remember the similar model *Vocho* sold in the United States under the name, 'The Thing'. An early owner gave it a coat of camouflage paint, accentuating its boxy resemblance to a Nazi staff car. Then another previous owner accepted money from Boots cigarettes to paint their logo on both doors and the sloping front snout. So it's sort of conspicuous, and has

17

proudly earned the name everybody but Mijares calls it: Das Boots.

I wound it up the slope of Cerro Neveria – Icebox Hill to gringos for some reason – the rackety motor complaining on the steep stretch of Calle Pedregoso. I went through my mooring ritual of banking the wheels to the curb, wedging a rock under a rear tire. More than one car has gone down this hill without the stabilizing counsel of a driver. I glanced up at my building, two stacks of studios fronted with arched porches and divided by a gigantic, sprawling rubber tree, and waved to my gringo neighbor Grady Clevell, strumming guitar on his balcony. People used to call it The Tree House, but lately I've been hearing it referred to as Twin Towers. I unlocked the gate and zig-zagged up three flights of stairs through the tree. Getting home is an uphill chore.

I first moved in on the ground floor, then up into the place where Grady lives now, then on up to my current aerie when I worked out a deal with my landlord, Pablo, to convert the roof into living quarters. I keep moving into higher and smaller quarters. I'll probably end up in a nest in the tree.

I stepped onto the roof where I live, slammed the balky iron door, and felt the usual relaxation and exhilaration hit me. No windows, no walls, just me and the sky and the sea. The water puts everything into a different perspective. Which might make a good motto for Mazatlán. Like I do every time I come home, I stepped over to the railing and spread my arms out wide to embrace my view of my town.

Watching the water and sky from my roof can completely change how I feel about the day. It doesn't look so much like Northern Mexico from up here, more like a poster of the French Riviera, Olas Altas Cove churning with trapped and funneled surf, the fishing boats and bathers on the beach, the domed mansions of Cerro Viggia tumbling down to the curve of seawall, and behind them the hunchbacked sugarloaf of Cerro Crestón topped by the Second Highest Lighthouse In The World. Or The Hemisphere, or something. What matters is the semi-superlative. Sometimes a few of the Largest Tuna Fleet In Mexico putt past the little string of decorator islands. All embroidered by wheeling gulls, hovering frigate birds, stuka-cruising pelicans and even a dolphin or two.

It's a mood-altering outlook at any time, and sometimes most beautiful under bad conditions. Storms whip the surf into a foamy filigree, like a green and white Arab carpet. The big waves blast into the point, showering spray as high as the top floors of Colegio El Pacífico on the cliffs above. Clouds look better than clear blue when the sun starts tipping off the edge, painting them garish Mexican colors and swirling patterns of light across the sky. I drank in the muted impact of the view and the rolling rhythm of the waves then took off my scuffed clothes and stepped into the shower.

When I say stepped into the shower, it's misleading, sort of like talking about "inside" my apartment. Can you be inside something with no walls? My landlord put up a corrugated cement ceiling and walled the space off from the stairwell. I ran a waist-high banister around the edge and added what are technically a kitchen and bath. The kitchen is one of those square cement scullery sinks Grady calls Mexican Maytags, a little refrigerator, and a propane tank powering a two burner stove that regularly tries to kill me. The bath is an open stall with a toilet and showerhead. Since I am at the same level as the cisterns that give any semblance of water pressure, I can only shower by turning on the pump that fills the cistern. I get a slightly pulsing shower, and only when the electricity is functioning. The bed is a concrete platform with a mattress on it and the table and chairs are white plastic with Pacífico beer logos – *Toma Pacífico, Nada Mas!* The closet is a rod between the bath stall and the rear wall. I keep my clothes in an old ice chest, and books piled up on the refrigerator. *Mi casa es su casa.*

It's very cheap. It's also the greatest place I ever lived and I hope I never leave. Everybody raves about the view, but there's more to it than that. The breeze comes through and cools it off during the brutal heat of summer and fall, the light just swarms in all over the place and the night sky is right there to touch. There's a sort of audio view as well. I am never out of the sound of the waves, hearing their changing moods. It does something good to me in my sleep. At night I hear the bark of seals on the islands. The treetops around me are full of birds and during the day I hear a constant concert of calls, helped out a little by the baying of dogs and Chema's damned gamecocks. I would never have a stereo up here, much less a television. Much, much less. Fortunately Grady, downstairs, and the old Guatemalan widow on the ground floor, feel the same way. Though Grady will sometimes play guitar and croak Grateful Dead songs on his porch all night if the mood – or a hit of *sinsemilla* – should strike him. It's my roost, up here. My home in the sky. In Spanish, *el cielo* means both sky and heaven.

I went to the railing and stood there naked, air-drying and examining my face wounds in the mirror taped to a beam. Not so bad, after all. I could stop the bleeding, not much chance of infection, especially after I splashed them full of Arricife after-shave, but they'd be impossible to cover up or hide. Kind of like my famously protruding ears. Something to be ignored and moved past. I looked good enough for government work. Mijares once told me I look like I was designed to be beautiful, but somebody slipped up in manufacture. Lumps and dents and the ears. I just shrugged and said, "*Hecho en México.*" It's what we say when something breaks or falls apart in our hands – "Made in Mexico." It's part of the national self-denigration that doesn't quite balance out our rabid patriotism.

The bruises all over my body were darkening and stiffening, but I could conceal them. I put on a clean suit, brushed my hair, and touched up the hurried shaving job I'd done in the wee hours. And felt a lot better. After all, I had gotten to watch the Mayor's asshole bodyguards get shoved around, Mijares had been impressed – however undeservedly – by my handling of the wife situation, and she had stood right here in my bedroom, touched me in my sleep. Amid the erotic punctuations I was putting on that, I suddenly wondered how she'd found me ... and how she'd gotten in.

I was heading out when something caught the corner of my eye. I looked around a minute before I spotted it, up on the top floor of the abandoned Freeman Hotel, a slabby piece of fifties ugliness that sticks up out of the historic bayfront like a bad tooth. Huge letters, bright red paint, 'MicroBio'. Damn that little shit! God knows how he managed to get up in the Freeman with his spray can, but that's what he's all about. And now I'll have to look at his name every day, like he'd managed to tag the inside of my house. This graffiti plague is a bad enough blight on the town – an ugly, demeaning infection from the drug gang culture of the United States – but now it's starting to move in on historic buildings and dance right in front of my eyes.

And this punk MicroBio is the worst yet, trying to deface more area than the legendary Poema, whose scrawled name can be seen all over the *municipio*, but is currently unable to defend his status because he had his hands smashed by a shovel in the hands of an angry building owner who stayed up all night for a week to catch him tagging a new repainted wall. Staining the wall, we call it.

I was furious. I started to retrieve the phone then stalled out, wondering who I would call. The Freeman? The editor at *El Debate*? Mazatlán Vice? I looked out at the bay and didn't feel so great any more, as though his paint had stained not just my view, but my life. What was I doing working for this town when I couldn't even keep it from being marked up like a latrine wall? Then I remembered Mijares was up to her luscious ass in alligators, and I might get another chance to bleed for her, so I headed for the door.

"This isn't over yet, Germ," I snarled at MicroBio as I slammed the iron door and skittered down the stairs. I was trying for a Batman villain effect, but probably sounded like a disinfectant commercial.

One of the main reasons for business failure in Mexico is what I would call *Cantinitis*. If a man plans to open a business he first brags about it to his friends in the local *cantina*, and ends up committing himself to something bigger and grander than he originally might have planned, or that makes any sense. Once he has stated his plans to have the biggest dance floor in the state or a motel with mirrors on every ceiling or a fleet of a hundred trucks, he can't reduce the scale, cut the price, or trim the frills without losing face in front of the only people whose opinions really matter—his drinking buddies. It is not economic pressure that creates failures here, but peer pressure.

"Why Mexico Isn't Japan...Yet" by Mundo Carrasco
Mexico Business Report, August 1996

The first time my father asked me what I actually did over at the *Palacio* to justify my paycheck I told him, "Mostly just have lunch."

He nodded solemnly and said, "Sounds a lot like the union."

But it's a major part of my job, possibly what I was actually hired for, other than to hang my fading athletic stardom on the party banner like a brass badge. My job title is Press Relations and those relations take place mostly in the confines of a shabby downtown bar called Lo Peor, meaning The Worst, which is pretty close to the truth. Closer than we denizens usually get, since so many of us are journalists, politicians, and lawyers. They will even serve gringos. It's an invaluable no-man's-land for city government, a place where elements ranging from powerful to downright criminal can come together. It's where a lot of the governing, at least as much as people are aware of, actually takes place, not to mention the formation of opinion and what we might call the Truth. Not a place you'd want to be caught dead in.

I take a two hour lunch there every working day, and I always walk through the cool, dim bar to sit in the Salón Elizabeth Taylor, a glassed-off area with extra fans that was named shortly after the owner put up a huge hand-tinted photograph of La Taylor at about age twenty five.

The other photographs in the Salón and the rest of Lo Peor are a sort of museum of Mazatlán political history, with a few of the region's artistes, like Lola Beltran, Pedro Infante, and Los Tigres del Norte, thrown in for good measure. The Salón is connected to the rest of the establishment by a glass door that only regulars have the nerve to enter during the lunch hour, and a window that passes through from behind the bar so Chuy can serve us directly without sending his waitresses into peril. When not mixing drinks or setting up beers, he lounges at the window, participating in the conversations of the elect, if not always elected.

Moving from the working press – if it should really be called such in a country where nothing like that really works – over to the City Hall crowd didn't alter my status within the group all that much. The first reporter to stroll into my first official press conference greeted me in the usual friendly/profane manner, then realized I was running the thing instead of sitting there trying to sabotage it. He gaped. "You're bullshitting me!"

I replied, "Not until everybody else gets here," which went the rounds. I might not be welcome in the newsrooms anymore, but I'm still part of the *bola* at Lo Peor, where the news really gets written anyway.

Not that I didn't know they were going to pounce on me as soon as I got my drink. They started licking their lips as soon as they saw me through the dirty glass. Wolves smiling over crippled meat. Well, sometimes the sheep just have to kick wolf ass. And that, as I've mentioned, was what I got paid for. I went through the usual handshakes, flesh-poundings and insults while I waited for Chuy to hand a bottle of Dos Equis through the window. It's an unwritten rule here that you don't attack anybody until they have their drink. They may need it. If only to throw at you.

Eusebio Andrados, every bit the rising young legal star in his Dockers and rep tie, did a double-take on my face, "Wow, Mundo. Where'd you get the decorations?"

I solemnly intoned, "In the struggle against poverty."

"Well, you'd make a lovely first lady."

Half-hearted chuckles, then Beto Aznar, a typical *Sol de Pacífico* hack/drunk, stepped up. "I suppose this means they'll recall all those PT stickers."

Damn, I'd forgotten them, all those yellow banners with the red star and big red stop sign, STOP the Violence, Corruption, and Impunity! One out of three isn't bad. Hell, it's over .333.

I gave Beto a pitying look. "I should have assumed you'd try to reduce ungrounded rumors about a man's domestic difficulties to a political issue, Beto. Working for an opposition party like you do." That would derail him a little. The national *Sol* chain is wholly owned by the PRI, one of the more blatant examples of their casual approach to running the country outright. They aren't pro-PRI papers; they are actually full-bore propaganda sheets. But their employees hate reminders of the fact.

"Don't start knocking the *Sol* again," Beto growled. He's known to get nasty, obscene, and violent when he's had a few drinks. His propensity for going off on people whenever his blood/tequila ratio destabilizes has led to suggestions that he just might be an alcoholic, which he denies vehemently. Says he's just a social drinker.

"You don't mean the 'Sol-d Out', do you?" put in Major Tom, one of two gringos present in the Salón. A tall, white-haired stringer for UPI, Tom is the envy of all dirty old gringo men because he shacks up with a tight young aerobics instructor. He's also an ex-paratrooper and gym rat at sixty-two, not intimidated by Beto's potential tantrums.

Lorenzo, smug in his linen *guayabera*, Vuarnets and city hall sinecure, snickered, "How could they sell out? They're already owned, branded, and impregnated."

Raging, Beto swung back on me. "Ridiculous. Who could be more owned, more of a ridiculous puppet, than your fat little *cocodrilo* mayor?"

I think of him as chubby actually. But it's hard to deny the accusation of him being not a crocodile, but a *cocaína* fancier. In fact, a fanatic of any intoxicant that should come his way.

I just said, "Well, of course he's a servant of the people."

"Servant of the *narcos*, you mean!" Beto was getting worked up. Might have had a toot or two earlier himself.

25

"Who are you claiming spent all that money on his election? The parties, the rallies, the subsidies ..."

"Actually, I heard it was Borrego and his little clique," Eusebio chimed in, "Rich hotel owners, old families ... wait a minute, aren't they all PRI people?"

"That has nothing to do with that little idiot!" Beto turned back to me, "How can you defend such a disgrace to the office, Mundo? To the city itself? He doesn't even have a public school education."

Harsh judgment from Beto, crammed in *liceos, collegios,* and private universities.

"Hey, he got through a year at *Secundaria Hidalgo,*" Lorenzo protested. His old junior high, too, but he shouldn't have mentioned it.

Beto gave him a sneer, "Like I said. No education."

Major Tom rolled a tortilla around a wad of *ceviche,* then licked the edge like he was rolling a cigarette instead of a taco. "He could have been stupider. Slugged her before the elections."

"And saved the city from puppet rule by a drug-dazed, drunken fool." Beto gave me a wide-eyed, challenging stare, "What kind of government is run by a talk show host, anyway?"

Before I could open my mouth, Tom spoke laconically around his *ceviche* taco, "A shockjockracy?"

Eusebio loved it. "A mediacracy, perhaps?"

"It's pronounced mediocrity, isn't it?" Lorenzo said, then flaunted his in-house connection to the topic. "It hardly matters. He never shows up at the office anyway."

Tom spread his hands, "Then how much damage can he do?"

"Ask his wife's surgeon," Beto snapped.

"You can't cover this one up, Mundo," Carlos Estrada, my old beat-mate from *Noroeste,* said in a sad way. "The talk shows are all over it, even *La Poderosa* and *Radio Ranchito* have cut the music to chat about it. Maybe you should try to spin it, make up a new motto, The family that abuses together confuses together."

"Cover up?" I asked, wounded to the core, "This is the New Government here, Carlito. The post-PRI approach. No corruption, no impunity, everything transparent."

Transparent is the new watchword in Mexican politics, meaning things get done in the open, not in secret. Santa Claus is catching on down here, too. Chuy popped through the window like a jack-in-the-box to set down fresh drinks.

"I can see right through that transparency shit." He paused a beat, then added, "And impunity can't touch me either." Then popped back out of sight.

"But..." Eusebio went on, trailing it out in one of his slick lawyer techniques. Taking the floor. "But, aren't we getting off the general topic here? Did Varedas or did he not sock his old lady? Also maybe pound her head on the floor? Put her in the Military Hospital last night?"

"That's exactly what I heard," Carlito blurted, disgruntled to get upstaged by information from somebody who was not even a journalist. "Isn't that sort of what the press conference is about, Mundo?"

"It might come up. But didn't you hear that Sra. Varedas denied those rumors?"

"Oh, well, that's truly surprising. Do you think she might answer a few questions about that?"

"Cut the crap, Carrasco," Beto snarled, "We're all going in there in an hour. What are you going to say about your boss turning his sainted *vieja* into a punching-bag?"

Showtime, folks. I took the Fourth Deepest Breath In Mexico and swung away. "Okay. Number one, so far we're dealing with rumors and hearsay. We don't yet know what happened."

"Oh, you're going to be like that?"

"How are you going to be? Run with rumors, then find out you were misinformed in contradicting Blanquita in her tearful defense of her husband?"

That kept them quiet long enough for me to proceed to, "Sr. Varedas is an easy enough target, all right. But he's just started in this job. Coming up from The People to a complicated position of honor. You might consider giving this guy a break, or at least a sporting chance. He thought he was bigtime because he started hanging out with bigtimers."

"Big time *narcos*," Beto muttered.

"Big time *PRIistas*," I said, like a teacher making a

correction. "High rollers. But now he's 'it' and it's blowing his mind."

"Not to mention his nose," Eusebio snickered.

"And who do you buy your stuff from, Sebi? Beach vendors? He's been attacked, made mistakes, had a tough time. He's adjusting. You shouldn't take his peccadilloes as proof of guilt on something like this."

"Mundo?" Uh-oh, it was Carlos' calm, solemn voice. I nodded at him.

"Have you ever met this guy? Ever spoken with him?"

The truth was, I hadn't. He'd met with very few City Hall people, actually. Preferred to spend his time partying with big shots and zipping around in his fleet of Suburbans coking out with his bodyguards and *cuates* from the old days. Like he was doing right at the moment when I could have used a little help cutting him down off the cross, the fucker.

"I work for him, Carlito. I'm trying to cut him some slack. All I ask you to do is look at what I'm saying here, ask yourselves if it makes sense." And it did, too. That was my credibility with them. I didn't feed them official bullshitburgers here at Lo Peor, I only put my case in terms that were mutually acceptable and beneficial. Down at the bottom of things the new media in Mexico are aware that their relationship with government is symbiotic. In other countries, I couldn't say. It would have been easier dealing with these guys in the old days – meaning prior to 2000 – when the parties just paid them off for good reviews. But then my job wouldn't have existed, would it? Oh, and one more thing, "Look, kick him when he's down, you have to live with him for three years."

I don't know what they would have said to that, because that's when Chuy stuck his head in the bar window and said, "*Oye, cabrones. Escucha La Ley.*"

Then he turned up the radio he listens to under the background rumble of *banda* music out in the main bar. "Listen to The Law" would sound almost biblical if *La Ley* weren't 86 AM, the most obnoxious radio station in town; once home to Varedas' old talk show, in fact. I suspected I wouldn't enjoy it much today. Sure enough, out came the spoiled tenor bleat of my boss telling Gaspar de Hacha and his *siesta* hour listeners all about how it wasn't precisely his fault that he'd beat the bejesus out of his wife. He sounded completely shit-faced. Of course we Mexicans don't use crude gringo expressions like shit-faced. We would call the condition *bien pedo,* meaning 'really fart'.

I was extremely gratified by the glances my former colleagues threw at me as he sniveled and blustered through a complete confession. When he tacked on the baroque embellishment that like all men, he socked up his *esposa* when necessary but he didn't do it every day, Chuy stuck his head through the window again, looked at me and cracked up. Well, they can't blame us for screwing up when the Mayor confesses to domestic violence on the airwaves. Not that somebody won't get around to trying. But I was stunned. I don't think I'd ever heard of the guy admitting the truth before. I could feel my neck pulling in and dick shrinking. Christ, they sent me to shut *her* up?

All eyes were on me when Chuy turned the radio back down.

I stood up and said, "I think I just heard the Call of Duty."

Beto smirked, "That's a shame, because I think the toilet is already occupied."

It was the second time that day I'd retreated from a bunch of people laughing at me. I missed the nuns.

You hear a lot recently about the concept (never really tested in this country) that political freedom can only function when accompanied by freedom of the press. What you don't hear as much, though it may be more important, is that democracy also requires a press that is intelligent, professional, and open. Governments don't have to work very hard to censor a press incapable of uncovering facts or presenting them properly.

"The New, Improved Corruption" by Mundo Carrasco
Proceso, May 1999

I was standing right there, watching the whole conference, but it was somehow less real that what I later saw on television. I'd never seen Mijares on camera before and it was impressive. I don't see any point in trying to describe Mijares for you. She is incomparably beautiful, so what would I compare her to? Should I list the perfect lips, gorgeous nostrils, precious toenails? It's easy to describe ugly people or pretty people with a few substandard features. It's easiest with people with one big flaw. I could mention ears, for instance. But there is a quality of beauty that makes it seem not only easy but inevitable for everything to be beautiful and hard to imagine anything being less than a perfect pleasure. Maybe that's why beauty makes us feel good. Unless there's something wrong with us.

But on camera she was something else entirely. She shimmered with media cool, like a slab of dry ice on a hot sidewalk. Every color of her outfit – apparently stored in her desk or car with 'Break Out In Case Of Emergency' stenciled on it – was perfect for pickup, as if dyed to match TV phosphors. Her makeup was a little too much for live viewing, but on camera turned her into the Goddess of Truth and Innocence. I even noticed a dark streak between her already pronounced breasts, giving them an even more emphatic enunciation. Dangling, stripy earrings framed her eyes in a parenthesis of moiré buzz. She sizzled like a blank white screen, was as bottomless as dark glass. She had their number, but good.

We'd only had about twenty minutes to brainstorm a strategy to cope with our boss tossing us to the wolves, then we had to open the gates and invite them in for wolf chow. It took Mijares about two to decide that she would handle the questions instead of me. No argument from my side. For one thing, if Mijares thought it would be a good idea for me to sing them torch songs in drag, I'd probably have done it.

Also, she would probably be better at this than I would, a woman, more formal distance from the reporters, and a nastier disposition. Besides, fielding questions on this one was the last thing I wanted to do. Mijares seemed to be looking forward to it. Her other change was that we would not appear in the room until the press was there and getting restless. Then we'd make an entrance. Again, right up her alley. She had them eating out of her cleavage until Rocío decided it was time to make her move.

I had spotted Rocío earlier, as usual around the edges of the press ranks. Still cute as a kitten in a basket, but tougher and more mature in her clothes and bearing. I gave her a big smile. I'm still extremely fond of her.

She stoned me off. Ah, well. It wasn't *just* one of those things where the cute rookie falls for her dashing mentor, but it wasn't *not* one of those things, either. I like the name Rocío, and always thought it fitted her. Dew, a sprinkle of diamonds laid down by the night, life-giving water without the impact of rain. Wake up in the morning and she's lying there like a light coat of moisture, fresh and sparkling. But burned off by the sun as the day heats up.

Basically we fell out over my pursuit of gringas. You can snicker if you want about the way we third world Romeos chase trophy blondes, but you just might not understand. Men who live in a world where everybody has dark skin, black hair and black eyes – and I'm talking about the vast majority of the human race – see the *güeras*, the fair Eloi women, as an enchanting distinction, like creatures stepped from fairy tales. Men are attracted to women by their beauty, and there is a beauty in golden or red hair that just doesn't exist in most countries and races. Coppery curls against white cheeks or pink nipples, eyes like clear blue or green lakes that you can see into and catch the dance of

32

light in the depths – these are rare qualities in this world.

And they are all, I realized at some point, recessive genetic characteristics. It would be possible for enough of us horny, dark-skinned men to wipe them out in a century or two. I hate to say it, but it's probably not a bad idea for Swedes and Danes and Irish to want to keep their blonde girls to themselves, an endangered species, their limpid eyes as vulnerable to the world as any other beautiful clear ponds. Meanwhile, I chased them around Mazatlán, enjoying their rarified treasures as well as their chatter about the North where I lived some very intense years.

I wouldn't have bothered telling Rocío any of that, of course. I told her whatever was necessary to get her calmed down and back in bed, and into the protégé status that did her a lot of good, to judge from her presence here today with no other *Noroeste* reporter in sight. I will say that as soon as she moved up from researcher to getting by-lines on news stories, she dumped me cold. And this, I seemed to have started dating *Mexicanas* more than tourists the last year or so. Much I traveled in those realms of gold, but the dark hills of home also have their appeal.

Anyway, there was little in my sweet experience of Rocío to prepare me for what she popped on Mijares. She timed it perfectly, in a sort of lull in the questioning, when Mija had things pretty well in hand. She stood up, delicate little thing in *prepa* skirt and sweater, and innocently asked, "But hasn't Sra. Varedas always told women to report all domestic abuse and stick by their accusations?"

Mijares was offhand, but earnest, "I think we'd all consider that good advice."

Rocío moved on in, "But she is denying this attack."

"Alleged attack. Since she was there, we should at least listen to her account."

"So you're saying she was telling the truth and Varedas is lying?"

Well all right, Rocío. She'd been pretty soft-spoken and maidenish when I first worked with her at *Noroeste*, not that promising. But now her question got the entire press corps staring at her and put Mijares on her mettle.

"I'm saying that you should respect Sra. Varedas' integrity. And I also wish you would respect her privacy a bit more. She didn't ask to be a public figure, you know."

"You give up some privacy when you make statements on the radio."

"She was trying to protect her name and family by denying rumors. That's hardly an application for the circus."

"So the Mayor's confession is not true?"

"I haven't had a chance to talk to him because..."

"But both of them talked to radio stations."

Mijares ruffed her off with, "We'll know more when we've had time to sift these things out."

She looked for another reporter to point at, but everybody seemed to be enjoying Rocío's line of questioning more than their own.

"Why would he admit to something he didn't do?"

"Again, I'll know more later. If you people would have more patience in your questioning, you might find that people had more answers for you."

She made a choppy hand gesture, cruised ahead full speed.

"I can tell you this. Sr. Varedas has been under extreme strain, especially with all the negative press he's been treated to since taking office, trying to carry out the people's will in a new and sometimes hostile environment. This is a simple man from humble origins, and he has been feeling guilty and confused. He was drinking with some friends last night ..." she smiled understandingly at the men. "The Toluca game, which I suppose a lot of you also watched. He might have blurted out anything in that state."

Rocío was on that one like a slow grounder to the mound. "So when the Mayor makes statements to the press, we should first ascertain whether or not he's too drunk to be believed?"

Mijares gave her a stare for a short beat, then quietly said, "I think if a troubled person, obviously the worse from drink, calls up a reporter outside of working hours and raves about family problems, it would be responsible to check out the whole story before dashing off to get it on the air in time to scoop the competition."

The reporters took that from her, like a mom's gentle scolding. Rocío, of course, already had her mouth open when Mijares moved in on the mike a little and cut her off in the bud. "One thing I would say, I like the idea of a politician who admits his shortcomings, instead of denying them, don't you?"

That stopped them for a second.

Rocío bounced back, though. She was coming along just fine in her new job. "So you are saying that Sra. Varedas is truthful in denying the attack that Sr. Varedas is courageous enough to admit took place?"

Mijares squared around to face her directly, looking right at her. There was a slight clearing of the intervening space as reporters turned to look back and forth between the two of them, the way people make way before a bar fight breaks out.

Mijares' voice got a little lower and a lot sweeter, "What I'm saying, honey, is that nobody yet knows exactly what took place and I would hope that the press wait until facts are established before reporting them."

Rocío stood up, faced her with shoulders back, "You are sure you don't mean, 'before they are fabricated'? Sweetie?"

Ah, yes, Rocío was no longer the little ingénue she looked. All of a sudden everybody was aware that Mijares, despite the surface glitz and charisma, was not that much older. And that Rocío did not at all mind playing hardball.

Mijares gave her a blinding grin and said, in a voice perfectly pitched to render what she said an inside joke as well as dead serious. "Well, if somebody is going to be fabricating facts, we'd rather it be the family involved, not outsiders."

Rocío couldn't find a way around that one, just shrugged and said, "Yes, I would imagine. And you will let us know, won't you?"

Mijares leaned towards her a little, humoring her, "You'll be the very first, kid." Her eyes swept the room, obviously asking for more questions. Questions from different people, that is.

A male reporter from *El Debate* said, "Could we get footage of the fight for the sports segment?" Getting everything back to the Mexican wink-nudge on such matters.

I could see Mijares smile victoriously, but if you didn't know her you'd have missed it.

Rocío turned to him, blinked sweetly, and said, "Fuck your mother, you *machista* pig." She slammed her notebook shut. "Maybe *that* would make the sports page."

The reporter looked around, shrugging and raising his eyebrows. Mijares caught his eye and made a dismissive gesture. She mouthed the word, "Women," and everybody laughed. Rocío walked out with her hand over her head with middle finger raised. It's a gringo gesture that really caught on in Mexico during the last election.

I suddenly understood why old Lermanez had become liberated enough to let a woman cover politics: unlike the men, she was immune to Mijares. And she'd come a long way. Baby. Rocío had made it out of the Society section without selling out her feminist principles. Mijares is also a feminist, of course, but a different kind. What she is about is manipulating people, getting her way, engineering consent. She's found the ultimate expression of that talent in Mexican politics and you can just see her licking her lips. Getting scuffed up by a *beibidoll* like Rocío would piss her off big.

She had turned her back on the press after ending the conference, but now that the cameras had left, she came over to me, patting her hair and preening.

"Was I good?"

"World class. But you had home field advantage. She might take a rematch."

She gave a disgusted snort, "In her dreams. Who *is* that little bitch, anyway?"

"Rocío Linares Espinosa. She's moved up into my old job at *Noroeste*."

"Where's she been? I don't remember seeing her during the election."

"She did some interviews with Blanquita for the *Sociales* and *Gente* pages, nothing that demanded your attention. She's been in before, just never caught your eye. This was the first time there was a woman's issue for her to get crunchy about. She's murder on abuse of women."

"Christ." Another angle flickered across her eyes.

36

"You know her, then?"

"Pretty well, actually."

"Fucked her maybe?" The shadow on her face deepened. "*Still* fucking her? I'd better not find out you'd ..."

"I thought romancing the press was my job description."

She started to say something, but I stepped up close to her, right into the perimeter of her aroma. I said, "You know you're the only woman I want, Mija."

She gave me a tired glance, moving off into emotional middle distance "You're saying that like it's a joke, Mundo. The trouble is, it *is* a joke."

"Maybe it would be funnier if you started taking it seriously."

"Maybe you should start taking everything seriously."

"Such as?" Women are always big on serious, but seldom specific.

"Your job, your life, the world, the body politic. That stuff."

"If I did, I'd bore you."

She smiled and shook her head, each flip of hair a tinkle of silver bells down my spine. "True. But see, it's only a game if there's a prize. If you win or lose. You don't care if you lose. You just want to see how it comes out."

"I always hope for a mutually beneficial result. Greatest good for greatest number, you know."

She shook her head like I'd just blown a math problem on the blackboard. "Very noble and charmingly naïve, Mundo. But getting back to the *prensa,* we've established that I did good, Rocío Whoever did good. How about you, Mundo. How'd you do?"

"I listened attentively, took notes, didn't pick boogers with the camera on me."

"And yet we expect so much more of you. I shouldn't have been walking into any ambushes out there with the mikes and cameras running. Should I?"

"Not in a ideal world. But I don't see what ..."

"Exactly. You were hired to manage the press, the feed them our opinions, to massage them into something we can work with. That's what I expect you to do."

Well, as Grady says; Duh. She went on, enumerating the reasons they'd brought me on board, including my alleged influence with my former colleagues. That and they figured you could lead me around by my dick, I thought. And they were right. I found myself wanting to slap my hand across her mouth to shut her up. Better yet, my lips.

I just turned around and walked off. As I stepped out onto the balcony, I saw Rocío talking to two of the *info-chicas,* but she looked right through me. She used to worship me so much it made me uncomfortable, before I became a minion of the Antichrist. I went to my desk and spent a few hours calling up reporters to schmooze and trying to get hold of old contacts who might know where the hell the Mayor had gone. At six I hung up the phone and walked out without speaking to anyone. My problem was that I was surrounded by smart, hip, educated people, experienced in the complexities of politics, sex, power and intrigue. What I needed was input from somebody uneducated, simple, and down-to-earth. And I knew exactly where to go get it.

If you like the idea that linguistics reflects sociology, you'll love exploring Mexican slang. For instance, what would you predict for a society in which the world *padre* means not just "father", but also "cool" or "swell"... while *la madre,* meaning "mother", is also a barely printable slur?

"Significant Others" by Mundo Carrasco
"MazSpeak" Column *Pacific Pearl,* March 1998

I usually drop in on my old man after work because I prefer Los Polluelos A. C. to the *Sindicato* hall itself or even the big open-air bar out behind it where he usually eats lunch. He prefers taking his after-work beers over at the athletic club with actual workers and sportsmen, not with his fellow Union stiffs. As soon as I came in the doors he stood up and started walking towards me. He seemed to sense that I wanted to talk to him, not sit there getting my back slapped and beers poured into me by every aging jock in the place. Hitching up his big cockfight belt buckle, strutting in the cowboy boots he'll wear right into the grave. As soon as I learned enough about sex to get over the realization that *my own parents,* of all people, had been initiating this grotesque performance, I started wondering if my *papi* took off his boots while he was doing it.

He walked up and shook hands, then pulled me up against the silver conchos on his leather vest for a quick *abrazo.* I stepped back and looked at him for a second. He doesn't get old, doesn't erode, just gets sort of burnished. The Indian facial bones move up underneath the skin, his hair gets glossier, his eyes get more bottomless. I suppose a lot of people study their parents for clues to where they came from ... or more important, where they're going to end up. I don't have to look very deep into my father to see myself, how I am going to look. He's very obviously Tarahuamara tribal stock; tall, slim, and ropy. I'm taller yet, but also more solid, maybe because my mother was of the Kora. I'm bigger in the upper body, probably just from playing baseball instead of *futbol,* doing strength training in college. The face is almost like a mirror, but twenty years in the future. Looking at him, being twenty years older doesn't look all that bad. Not that I'm in any hurry.

He still has that slight strut that works so well with his cowboy wardrobe. The stance of a man who came up from dirt to be somebody. And father other somebodies who moved even further on up. Hand built from gandy-dancer to respected official.

He said, "Shall we get a table, *Conejo*?"

"Well, *Jefe*, it'll give us a place to set our beers." We walked towards the back. I'll be 'Rabbit' as long as he lives, he'll be 'Boss' as long as I do, I suppose.

Polluelos is an actual athletic club, not a drinking society like some of them, although the only sports you'd see in the big, low clubroom are beer-drinking and sipping Tequila and watching televised athletes sell beer. So there were plenty of handshakes and *abrazos* and loud recognitions of the, 'See, I *know* the guy!' kind as we threaded through the long, low room full of tables covered with bottles and tacos, but when we sat down, back by the trophy case, they left us alone except to take our order for a couple of *medias* of Pacífico and a kilo of chopped pork *carnitas*. They appreciate celebrity at Polluelos, but they take it in stride.

My dad sipped from his bottle and looked up at the glass case full of trophies, and a big framed shot of the youthful Mundo punching out The Big Hit, *El Batazo*, down there in Columbia. He waved a hand at it and said, "Baseball. Where did I go wrong with you, *Conejo*?"

"Probably buying that television," I had a different answer for it every time.

He nodded solemnly. "That was when the whole country went wrong."

"I thought it was the privatization."

"You going to get me started on that?"

"God, I hope not." Which was starkly true. Not only did the 'neo-liberal' privatizing of the trains lead to the loss of passenger service, but it was a violation of every stereotyped retro-socialistic totem of Mexican political thought. Nothing I wanted him to pound in for about the thousandth time. Hell, I could read it every stupid day on any given editorial page. So I looked way up at the top of the case, at the older, smaller, faded, photo of a young stringbean with big hands and airplane ears wearing soccer shorts and holding a trophy while two old farts in *guayaberas* smiled and touched his shoulders. I pointed at it with my chin: I pick up a whole closet of hick mannerisms when I'm around my old man.

"*Jefe*, do you ever wonder if that guy went wrong somewhere? Might have handled it a little better?"

He leaned back and tipped his white Resistol back on his head. Still has all his hair at fifty-two, and none of it gray. The teeth will need some salvaging pretty soon, though.

"Cheap cup for such a major tournament. Yeah, I've wondered about that. But not for a long time. I've done okay, everything considered." As close as he would come to telling me he was pleased with the way his family had turned out so far.

"But when I did wonder about those things," he went on, "Like should I have immigrated to the North, should I have taken a shot at the pros, should I have coupled up with somebody other than your mother, should I have turned down this whole damned *Sindicato* nonsense – I always came up with the same thing, that I worried about that crap at the time I did it. You worry about it once, then it's over and you move on. You know what happens when some *tarado* throws a switch when a car's only halfway across?"

If I couldn't have figured it out, I'd have had to fall back on the dozens of times I'd heard the story. But before it had always been high comedy, laughing at that *burro* Alvarado who thought so much of himself before pulling the ultimate switchyard screwup. But this time it wasn't comedy and wasn't about Alvarado.

"The front truck is already on the main line, the back truck gets switched to the spur and you have a situation on your hands. I've always wondered how long a train could keep moving like that if the tracks stayed parallel. But if both lines went the same place, you wouldn't need a switchman, would you? So you end up with a bit of a *desmadre*."

41

I've pictured it before in Technicolor, that caboose trying to stretch, then rolling sideways and tearing itself apart until it derails the leading car and trips the air brakes. But always before with other images, Alvarado's smug face freezing in horror as his showoff move backfires, or the men inside yelping as they bounce around their cabin. This time there was only a slow motion close-up of raw destruction, a house on wheels rolling over and over, strewing it's own wreckage between the two tracks. I said, "I can see how the car might look back on the situation with some regret."

"Alvarado did, anyway. You know a lot of this wouldn't happen if trains could drive themselves."

Dad's distaste for engineers and switchmen was long-standing, but I knew who he meant, all right. Enough of the damn railroad metaphors.

"How can you pull your own switches when you're in over your head, *Jefe*?"

He gave me a quick look I'd seen before. Quick scan for the fingerprints of crime, vice, debt or dissolution.

"Like crazy about a woman, for instance," I said. That's a funny thing in Mexican macho *cantina* culture. In a way, the man's in control, takes no crap from any broad – but you just listen to the songs on the *fonola* and they're all about men being misled and betrayed by women. The ladies might not get a lot of respect around here as human beings, but nobody slights their destructive capacity.

"One of those women you never bring by the house?" He was semi-serious. "The house which is still, your mother wanted to be sure you know, in the same place you left it."

I smiled. Same old Mom. Same as everybody's old Mom.

Then the old man got serious again, which he's more cut out for.

"Let me ask you one thing, *mijo*. Before this woman took you by your ... emotions. Was your life on the right track at that time? Were things going well for you? Did you feel proud and well-occupied?"

"Have I ever before come to an unlikely source like yourself for personal advice?"

"Ah. And now, you are involved with this woman, how are things going?"

I did a sort of grin, "Have I ever come to you for advice before?"

"So. What do you think?"

Damn. As usual, the old guy says nothing and you've been told. "Why is it always so simple with you?"

"I'm a simple man."

"No wonder you played *futbol*."

My father motioned for another round of beer, seconding my motion to close out the topic. Then he said, "We saw you on the *tele, Conejo*. "

"Saw me, when?"

"When that woman was explaining how Varedas didn't punch out Blanquita."

"Oh, yeah. You know, that woman?"

"The one who talked to the reporters?"

"Yeah. That's the woman."

"*Hijo de la...*" My old man seemed to sort of go out of focus a little. He raised his beer bottle, put it back down, looked over towards the soccer game on the television. "Then, you know ... God knows what you're going to do."

I leaned forward, "*Ay, Papi*, you should see her." I had to get somebody to get the picture on this thing. "Naked, laughing ... you should see her. I ..."

He looked grim and worried all of a sudden. "Think about prayer, *Conejo*. And condoms."

I saw him catch himself, not make the sign of the cross. Like that might help. Maybe a silver bullet. Right between my *cojones*.

"You're more than a bunny, now, *Señor* Stud. And she's more than a hawk. Just remember, rolling stock doesn't stretch. Not for long."

He still likes to punctuate his proclamations by strutting off to the bathroom. While I waited, I looked around Polluelos, remembering when I thought it was the finest place in the world, where big, tough grown-ups made much of my victories in the *Infantiles* or *Juveniles* leagues and I would sit quietly behind my father and know he was proud of me. I leaned my chair back in the approved local fashion and stared at the picture of *El Batazo*.

To anybody else it looks like a kid in a Venados cap with a baseball wrapped halfway around his bat. But at that moment I saw a young man standing on a very steep and brittle peak that pitches off quickly in every direction. It was my high-water point.

I had the best seat at the full banquet of life, eating the rich red meat, as my father used to say. And at that very moment, even while I was still hearing the cheers, and sucking up the free dinners and drinks, and slopping around in the sweet cream of the women ... it was coming apart, already starting to drift off in the wind with all the juice and smell and love of it burning away. I look back to a year when it all got over with, to a month or so sucking up the congrats of a grateful people, to a week of sheer hilarity, to a day of all days, finally down to that moment of impact.

There's an infinitesimal moment when a baseball reverses its direction. It's a violent time, the ball flattening itself around the bat like a fat tortilla as it tries to hold together in the conflicting forces that are distorting it. But there must be, theoretically, some point when the velocity the pitcher put on the ball is in exact balance with the murderous force the batter is applying to it, a sort of secret silence like the center of a rotating disk that they tell us is motionless. A timeless period of balance before everything goes into reverse. The sweet spot.

I don't doubt that The Hit, although it didn't make any highlights clips on American TV, fanned new fire into my old scouting reports from Arizona State. Three months after the entire Venados club surged out of the dugout like an ocean swell and broke over me in a spray of manlove and bruises, I was wearing an Angels uniform and sitting on their bench.

I've never been able to get anybody to believe this – maybe The Prof – but that year in the Bigs was a letdown; a blur to me now, coated with fine gray dust like the old pewter trophies in the case. Oh, the spectacle was glorious. Kid from Colonia Ferrocarril hitting Manhattan nightclubs. The world's greenest grass, the world's whitest lime. Air-conditioned carpeted locker rooms and road trips in Boeings. The women were incredible. So was the money: I made over half of my total life income in that one year, and bought my parents the new house that my mother hates but won't say so. And the pitching was fascinating.

But I didn't even get to bat once a game. Not at all if we were winning. Like most pinch-hitters, I was never on the field with a glove. I sat on those plush benches and watched other men, better than me, clobbering and fielding the ball. In the end, I sort of gave up on the Majors. Even before they gave up on me. It's hard to explain, but I didn't know who I was up there. I was playing for big bucks, big cameras, big stakes, big ego. But see, I had played for Mazatlán. For my *barrio*. For my father's union, his friends' club. Once I played for Mexico.

In Anaheim I was either in it just for myself or playing for something so huge I couldn't distinguish it from The World Economy. My runs were scored for the organization, for the sponsors and advertisers, for Lite Beer from Miller – not *Pacífico, Nada Mas* – and local affiliate stations. The big time just didn't measure up.

I was never going down in the record books, never going to be a 'great'. I didn't really have that much passion for the game, just for the few minutes I stood in the box and unwound on the ball. It wasn't enough. Or was too much. Most likely, it just wasn't me. There had been a time when I was me – and much more than that – and it made everything else look a little pale. And that moment had lasted no time at all. Theoretically speaking.

I watched my father coming back through the room, a man with boys' games comfortably in his past. I had to wonder if I could get there. After he sat down I told him I'd been thinking of quitting my job at the *Municipio*. He thought I was nuts.

"The *perridistas* have lost their edge," he said, "Just intellectuals any more." Startling words from a guy weaned on leftism and a scarred veteran of Labor. "If I was younger I'd go with the PT myself, speaking as a workingman."

"I don't care about the parties, *Jefe*, I'd just go back to journalism."

"*Periodismo*? I thought you were over that crazy crap. What sort of man sits around all day writing stuff, especially that garbage the papers print? And why do they talk that way, so ... I don't know ..."

"Flowery?" I suggested. "Purple? Yellow?"

"Purple? Yellow? Christ, you're infected, too. They must just make up all those weird words they use."

"They're just Spanish words."

"Bullshit. I speak Spanish, everybody does. Did you ever hear anybody call killers, *sicarios*, ever? Or somebody who gets shot is an *acribillado*? Where do they get that? Why not just call a doctor a *Medico* like people do, instead of *galeano*? You're sure those are real words?"

"Well, maybe not as real as other words."

"See? That newspaper crap isn't the real world, it's some perverted shadow of it."

"Now that I can agree with completely. But you think politics is better."

"Okay, got me there. But let's just say it's a better opportunity, a man's kind of activity. What it is, you run things."

"Or get run by things. Maybe even run over by things."

"Look, you ever try sending a gang of men out to do something without naming a leader? They'll screw around all day and never get anything done. You put a boss on the gang and they get it handled."

"That doesn't sound very socialistic, *Jefe*."

"All I'm saying is, being a leader is a good *chamba*, pays well, fills a need. Takes the right kind of guy. You could do worse. And you work at the *Palacio* instead of tearing around all those lunatic places trying to get your dick shot off."

Outside, we crossed the street to Zaragoza Park, standing by the white-painted tree trunks lit by the circle of light from the round tower, where the chess club was pushing pawns around.

He stared at my head and said, "You still got that *méndigo* ponytail? Why don't you just braid it so you'll look like your mother?"

"I like to show off my ears." That got him. He's proud of his damn wingflaps.

He grumbled, "Shit, you could see those Carrasco ears even if you were wearing a clown wig and a pilot helmet." He stepped over to a flowerbed and spat, then turned to me. "You should come out to the house, *Conejo*."

"Tell *mama* I'll be out as soon as Carnival is over. Or you could bring her in, see one of the parades, the fireworks Friday ..." I knew that wouldn't happen.

"Oh, you know, she thinks Carnival has gone too far these days. Thinks Mazatlán is too violent and crazy anymore."

"Well, there's something to that."

"But you know, I wish you would go into that little room, you know – where she keeps all your junk."

All my trophies, that is. And the journalism awards, and the old clippings, and pictures, and caps from old teams, and okay, all my junk. She has the walls of what was supposed to be her walk-in closet lined with the scraps of my life, and even burns two little candles in front of it like a shrine. She hides them when I come, though, because she knows they creep me out. My old man always ignored the whole thing, or laughed when it was brought up. I couldn't think what to say about him wanting me to go see them.

"I don't know why I said that. It's just that, it's public record, you know. Of what you are. You're somebody, Raymundo. More than just somebody. I guess I'm saying to look at all that and what it all meant to all those people and just don't ever sell yourself out too cheap." Embarrassed, he grabbed my shoulders, gave me a shake, and strutted off to find his old pickup. I stood there and looked after him nodding my head. I knew what he meant. What I didn't know was, how do you decide the fair price for your love?

WEDNESDAY
FEBRUARY SIXTH

DIA DE SAN TEOFILO

Carnival Calendar

Coronation of Children's Queen, Salón Bacanora, 11 AM
Flower Games, Venados Stadium, 7 PM

Calling land invaders *"paracaidistas"* is funny, in the cute/cruel capital city manner, but it misses the deeper point. They appear suddenly overnight like paratroopers, but they don't float down from the sky, they spring up out of our national soil, like mushrooms. They claim the right to occupy federal lands, but their presence goes deeper than that. They are the indigenous, the original, they are what all of us were before we found homes.

"The Habitat Habit" by Mundo Carrasco
Proceso, May 1997

They came in just before dawn. Some of the women were awake. But the men and children were still asleep in that still, chill time of the last of the night. There was no electricity in the settlement, and candles are dangerous in shelters made of cardboard and scrap wood. Cooking and washing would wait until daylight, the water supply was in steel barrels at the edge of the sprawl of hovels and it was not really safe for a woman to walk the paths of the warren in the dark. The men who lived there were no worse than average, but they drank too much.

Also, it was damp and unhealthy outside after dark, dank with unclean mists off the estuary. In the wet season the water would come up into the area where the squatters lived and the brackish backwater would be full of sewage, industrial waste, rotted fish, and chemicals from the coffee plant. There were good reasons that people were not allowed to live in *Infiernillo.* But summer was months away and to these people that was a distant future. They had moved to the mudflats known as 'Little Hell' because where they came from was worse and there was nowhere else to go.

The organizer who had led them there like a modern day Moses relied on politics to protect them. It is always politically disastrous to throw poor people off land in Mexico, particularly government land. No political act could clash more harshly with the revolutionary principles that guide Mexicans' view of our nation. But with *Infiernillo* he had miscalculated, it was illegal for habitation because it was uninhabitable.

The organizer also counted on politics to make his area viable, to turn it into a home for his flocks. He would dole out the vote of his people slowly, trading it for light, water, streets, and basic services until the squatter camp became a *colonia* like any other, bound and protected by allegiances and old-fashioned symbolism. But he had also miscalculated the character and composition of the political structure. Since the end of the PRI's monolithic power, governments were shifting and grinding like the breakup of an ice sheet and it was the peasants, the Mexican *mujahin*, who would fall into the cracks. But even so they should have been safe in their beds.

Most of the people were awakened by the screaming of women, then of children. The police came in two lines, arranged in a shallow *V* and moving towards the water, trapping the squatters who ran from their shacks. They made no attempt to remove anybody peacefully, left them no options but to be herded like game. Moving through the *"cartonlandia"* like an army of fierce insects in pure black clothes, they were faceless and formless behind heavy flak jackets, steel-toes boots, lead-reinforced gloves and helmets weighted with mirror visors. All had heavy, shoulder-high, black staffs. Each hovel they came to they smashed; kicking in the flimsy doors, breaking down the walls with blows from their staffs. They had guns and tear gas, but wouldn't need them. Smashing into small, dirty places where families slept huddled together like mice, they beat those families – kicking them, slapping them, grabbing them up and throwing them out into the paths full of panicked people. If anybody resisted, they beat them to the ground, three or four policeman standing around them and swinging the staffs down like threshers. They beat men for standing up, they fondled women for being half undressed, they slapped babies for crying, they kicked children for howling in fear. Ten minutes into the attack, the bulldozers arrived.

Ninety minutes later, a community where four hundred people had been living on the tideflats was nothing but a mudpie scarred by the treads of heavy equipment and littered with the shabby little detritus that people keep in their homes. The dwellings had been reduced to a slick of trash fouling the water. The people had been herded together, marched out to the street, and told to disperse. Nobody was ironic enough to tell them to go home. They dwindled off into the night with what little they had on them. It is hard to say where they went, just as it was hard to say where they came from. The organizer had been identified and driven off in a police van, his family crying after him but restrained by big men in black with mirrored faces. It had been a brutal lightning war against the poor and the poor had lost the war and what pitiful scraps they owned. The bulldozers lumbered away and the police withdrew, leaving only a handful of armed marines to prevent crime, violence and looting.

Imagine that you've just taken over command of a ship on the high seas, with storms ahead. You inspect it and find rot everywhere, with the crewmen conspiring to hide the rot while they are undermining timbers and hardware for sale in port. You have few repair materials on hand and the crew will almost certainly steal materials and tools unless guarded so closely they might mutiny – and can you really trust the guards? Pulling out rotten beams will only cause other, less corrupted timber to collapse as well, removing old fittings will cause their rusty counterparts to crumble away. Slowly you become aware that it is only the rot and rust that is holding the ship together. Eventually it will sink you all, but for now it is all you have. What do you do? More specifically, how do you avoid becoming agent, protector, and eventually accomplice of the rot?

"You Beat The Machine! So Why Aren't You Rich?"
Raymundo Carrasco, *Mexico City News,* October 2000

I was a little late sauntering into the courtyard of the *Palacio Municipal.* Don't laugh about the name being applied to this decaying shambles; it's what every city hall in Mexico is called, even if it's just a shack. When Galardéz stopped me on the stairs I had no objection to being even later – I had a feeling it wasn't going to be a great day at work – even working in a Palace. He was taking bets, a complicated pool on Varedas making it through his term. A helpful touch for our generally Titanic-class morale, if Galardéz had been on the Titanic when it was going down, he'd have taken bets on getting rescued. The odds on our *Alcalde* serving his whole three years were pretty long, with nine to five against him making it through the summer. I declined, mostly because I hate to bet against myself and didn't feel confident enough to wager on the home team. For some reason it's illegal and corrupting to bet on your athletic team, but perfectly okay to bet on your political party. Galardéz trotted out a few side bets, even a 'ghoul pool' on him being assassinated. He wouldn't be the first Sinaloa mayor to get shot out of office.

I wasn't all that partial to Galardéz and he was smirking too much.

I said, "It's not whether he gets killed, it's who does it. Want to make book on that?"

He smirked more, "Nah, it'll end up like Colosio or whatsis name, Kennedy, *everybody* did it."

"Well, I certainly wouldn't bet against that proposition." I stepped around him and continued up the stairs and around the arcade to my workspace. As soon as I got to the door I was swept into an eddy of mild hysteria and forced optimism – evidently during the night police had forcefully evicted the land invaders from *El Infiernillo* and our favorite mayor's name was being mentioned. I heard a radio in the background, Consuelo Arguelles from *Radio Mujer* interviewing a little girl who seemed less concerned about being homeless than about having her doll trodden into the mud by police boots.

While the kid sobbed, *Señorita* Arguelles said, "Mayor Frederico Varedas Eduardez promised the poor homes, work, and security, now he throws the jobless out of their miserable hovels. He promised an end to violence, now he beats his wife and crushes a little girl's doll into the earth." She left it hanging with no punchline, her trademark style. She gives you space to draw the conclusions she just set you up for.

Xochitl muttered, "Thanks a lot, Conchita. And *muchas pinches gracias* to Woman Radio." Her language surprised me, but I could get behind the sentiments.

Loli, another *info-chica*, said, "I think we just lost the Children's Crusade."

Mijares stepped out of her office.

"We haven't lost anything, you twit. We haven't started to fight yet." She saw me at the door and beckoned to me, then turned back to the *chicas*. "So let's start fighting, shall we?"

The girls quickly bent over terminals and telephones, frowning in over-acted concentration. I have to say that Mijares' methods maintain a high level of productivity in her office, better than any other city office. Without her whiplash management style the *chicas* would spend all their time lunching, doing their nails, and calling all their friends and paramours. Personally, I enjoy her uber-Fuehrer mode – she looks smashing when she's cold and commanding, like a chromed sportster machine gun. And I don't have to take it to heart, you can't intimidate an employee who's already thrown his phone down the crapper. Or discourage a suitor who has gotten nowhere for two years and can't get out of the rut.

I walked across to her, but she was already moving towards the door, towing me outside with her. As soon as we were through the door – and I could imagine Xochitl's grimace behind us – she was filling me in on the boss's latest public relations triumph and what we were damned well going to do about it. I wished I taken a number in the pool before the odds shot up. As she strode through the archways she finished her terse wrap-up and turned to look at me, playful/predatory. "So what would you do first, Mundo?"

"Buy the little girl a new doll?"

Her eyebrow did a little lilt that made me want to french her whole face.

"Very good," she said, as if amazed at a spark of intelligence, "I hadn't thought of that."

That didn't exactly amaze me. I tried to imagine the little Mijares – oops, the little Monserrat Gortari y Guzmán – with a beloved doll.

"Actually I was being facetious. Did you ever have a favorite doll, Mijares?"

She smiled. "Not really. Just Barbies. When I was a baby I only liked horses and bulls. Drove my mother crazy. I still have those stuffed bulls and horses in a glass case. So what else would you do?"

I thought about it a minute. I might have some luck with the newspaper people, but the damn radio is completely out of control. The PRI always preferred buying people in to stamping them out, but when it came down to it, it was always easy to choke off somebody's supply of news print – much more common form of censorship than the more mediagenic bombings and shootings and wrecking of presses. If need be, you could always shoot a few columnists.

But radio, particularly talk radio, is a lot harder to do much about. People call in and talk ... how many of them can you go shoot? You could lock up the host, but any twit with a microphone could replace him. You can jerk their license, but that is an involved and very public process. Lots of radio news people handle leaks by having callers blab the material on the air then letting everybody else comment on it. To a media fireman, a newspaper talking smack about you is like a building on fire. But citizen radio is like a wildfire springing up everywhere and burning down coal shafts. It's journalism without journalists, like native drums or the horizon-wide speech of whales. It's a pain in the *culo*. What we needed to do was punt.

So I said, "Appoint a board of inquiry."

She laughed, "Excellent. A committee. That's where we're going right now. Our Brother is setting up a committee to investigate the blame for rousting the invaders."

Our Brother is Ibaes Tirado Alemán, head *regidor* of the *Municipio* – equivalent to a city councilman, or a sort of county congressman. The *Municipio de Mazatlán* is actually what would be called a county in the North, but combined under the city government. It's a hand-me-down from the feudal colonial system. In many, many ways. Tirado doesn't have any seniority, having come in with the current *Partido de Trabajo* administration, and the PT does not have the majority of *regidores*, but being in the mayor's party makes him second in command. There is no vice-mayor anywhere in Mexico. There are no vice-governors. Mexico doesn't even have a vice-president. This leads to some extremely tricky succession politics, but nobody wants to have anybody around who could automatically fill your shoes just by blowing you out of them.

Tirado is a tall, thin, concave sort of man. He wears gold wire-rimmed glasses and combs his thin hair straight back. In a suit he looks every inch the distracted history professor at the *Universidad Autonoma de Sinaloa*, which he is. In humble work clothes he looks like an academic arts scion fallen into dissolution, but he prefers to wear the clothes of the laboring classes, like Castro in his army fatigues. He might be called 'Old Left' in the United States, an *aficionado* of the Revolution, Marxism at its most hammer & sicular, an unpopular populist. He married wealth, generally an excellent position from which to appreciate the advantages of poverty and hard work.

He writhes with pleasure at a worker, especially a rebellious, commie-style worker, calling him Brother and will drive you up the wall with that comradely crap. It's probably why he joined the all-red-flag-and-no-rudder Labor Party in the first place.

He was well into that mode when he decided to appoint a board of inquiry into the roust of the *paracaidistas*. Decided to do what Mijares had already decided would be done, anyway. Just because it made sense didn't mean it would have been done. The Mexican tradition would have been more towards ignoring it or buying somebody off. The press, the judges, anybody. Not the poor themselves, naturally. But this is the "New Mexico". The renovated republic, not the one with Santa Fe and Navajos and stuff.

"We have to remember and live by what we promised in our campaign," he was intoning, staring around the room full of worried officials and flunkies. "*Primero los pobres*. And I would also say that The Workers Come First. Always. The working poor are exactly and precisely who we serve and who we protect."

Same speech, different day.

"Then we need to find out who ordered those men into the Infiernillo," I said, speaking as one of the senior flunkies. "Let's start questioning cops. I can round up some eyewitnesses easily. *El Debate* has put up a few families out at the Hotel Venado, saving them for their stories."

"More than we've done for any of the poor, I might point out." That was Rogelio Alvardo, ranking *regidor* for those commie-wannabe Perridistas. We'd tried to limit the meeting to PT faithful, but Rogelio just horned in and there was no way to throw him out.

"But we will, we will." Tirado was deeply wounded by being one-upped on compassion and solidarity. Especially by the party he abandoned to join the PT. "We've arranged land for their settlement, building aid, water trucks, representation."

In other words, co-opting them into a nice little solid pro-PT community. Which was going to be quite a trick as long as they believed that the Mayor's party had screwed them over. The inquiry board had been named and wheedled over, Mijares and I successful in making a change or two in its membership. They paid a lot more attention to us when they were in a jam where press reaction could determine the accepted explanation of events.

I took a deep breath, saw Mijares frown, but spoke anyway. "They already have representation in government. Us. They voted for everyone here except those of us you hired to help you represent them. We have to find out who did this to them and why."

Mijares' look became a cynical smile at that point. She didn't buy my sudden populism. I could hardly believe it myself, but there it was. This wasn't just politics; it was also a crime with victims. So it had a bottom, and I had resolved to get there.

Nobody else was particularly moved by my convictions, but I'd spoken the meeting's bottom line and nobody was sorry to see it break up. People stood, closed briefcases, picked up coffee cups. Mijares caught me at the door, walked with me to the rail around the walkway. She was enjoying my proclamation, but also mocking it. I wouldn't have had it any other way.

"So how long will it take you to find out who ordered that attack, Mundo? Since you're suddenly so hot on The Poor Come First."

"A lot less time than that committee will take. It's actually pretty easy, all you have to do is want to know."

"Oh it's easy to find things out. But when you find out, then what do you do?"

"Take it to the committee. If they drag their feet five minutes, I'll go public."

"Mundo, you're supposed to be managing public information, not releasing it."

"I don't really care about that, I just want to find out."

"As long as you remember who's paying your salary."

I gave her a fist salute. "The Fucked-Over Come First."

"True." Smiling at me like the clap of dawn. "But first we have to fuck them over."

The more you know about individuals who exercise political power in Mexico, the more it becomes obvious that many – probably the majority – of them are homosexually active. Married, fathers, but sodomizing young men on the side. This is an open "secret", the question that is never discussed is, "Why"? I've come to the conclusion that it represents two aspects of the arrogance of power. On the one hand, it demonstrates that the practitioner is above all laws, morality, and convention, recognizes no barrier to the powerful man's lustful prerogatives. Also, it both exercises dominance at a very basic level and extends it into an area where the boundaries are being pushed. Women are no challenge to a rich, powerful man – and no demonstration of what he is capable of getting away with.

"Bedfellows Make Strange Politics" by Raymundo Carrasco
Desnudate, October 1995

After the meeting petered out and the secretaries had tip-tapped away to write it up, Tirado buttonholed me at the rail. We could hear the beginnings of the protest outside; the poor gathering to be heard, mysteriously equipped with hot lunches and bullhorns. He twaddled around in his usual academese, trying to figure out how to tell me to route all announcements to him without coming out and saying to cut Varedas out of the loop. Sergeant Garcia was standing by the rail, watching the front gate and listening to the rising clamor of the protest meeting outside, when he suddenly stiffened up like a bird dog, fixating on something down in the courtyard.

Actually, his name is Sgt. Reynosa, but all the other cops call him *Sargento Garcia* because of some obscure past incident. We picked up on it when he got assigned to security here at the *Palacio*. He's got the thatch of black hair and thin mustache of the *Zorro* buffoon, and he's big, but there's not much resemblance. He's not one of the usual uniformed idiots standing around the doorways in a daze, he's a real cop, requested for the *Palacio* post because he's one of the best shortstops in the city leagues as well as a brutal, wily *futbol* wing. We've played against each other several times, including a quarterfinals championship game my first year in high school. His last year, and not before time: he must have been nineteen. We fell into jockly camaraderie from the first day I took the job, chatting at his open-air desk down in the courtyard.

His intense attention made me follow his stare, aimed at a tall young man who'd just come in through the milling rabble and thin cordon of security officers. He was a good looking kid with wide shoulders and an actor's mustache, dressed better than most people you see around the Maz city hall. He moved with the smooth, easy grace of a dancer or athlete. He looked around, obviously unfamiliar with the layout, started up the stairs on the south end of the building, then looked around again, trotted back down, and started up the other stairs, which would lead him right by us.

I glanced at Reynosa for a clue to his interest but just then Tirado, who had realized I wasn't paying him any attention, saw where we were looking and blurted, "What the hell is *he* trying to do?"

Without breaking his concentration, Reynosa said, "Whatever it is, he wants to do it with a gun."

I couldn't see any evidence of that, but cops are cops. Reynosa took Tirado by the shoulder and, so gently that it didn't look like he was doing it, shoved him into the conference room and told him to stay. I waited for him to pull out his radio or whistle, but he started moving towards the corner of the balcony where the kid would have to pass to get to the conference room. He glanced at me and I fell in behind him. I have no idea why he wanted me with him or why I followed. The guy's a sergeant's sergeant.

He stopped directly in front of the Public Information office, where we'd placed a file cabinet out on the walkway to gain more room inside. He pulled out the top drawer of the cabinet, narrowing the lane of passage. He cut his eyes to a position by the file cabinet. I started riffling through the drawer. He stood behind me and started talking about the civic basketball tournament, using big gestures and a lot of movement. The pistol-toter walked up slowly, looking at numbers on doors, glancing around like a visitor. I still didn't see any gun. Later Reynosa told me it's not the gun you see with amateurs, it's the way they de-form their attention and posture around the weapon.

As the guy came by Reynosa was shaking his head in disgust, backing away from me and gesticulating. His pistol flapped at his hip as he made the motions of shooting lay-ups and blocking the shots. The *pistolero* moved up steadily, but edged around to his right. Reynosa made clumsy dribbling moves, saying, "Like this, like this, like a damn girl," and almost backed into the guy, who side-stepped right over to the office door.

At which point Reynosa spun around and blocked him right through the door, hard enough to bounce a cabinet inside. Reynosa was right there to grab the rebound, stepping through the door and going for a chokehold. The kid was faked out of his jock – so was I, actually – but was cool and quick and came back fighting off the grip. Reynosa pressed in relentlessly, too close for the guy to go for the gun, wherever it was, but the kid did a tricky slip and shifted back on his hips, turning Reynosa and letting him slide past to the door. Reynosa was immediately on him, backhanding his guard away.

I stepped through the door and kicked down into the back of the kid's knees, which collapsed him and caused him to throw his arms back for support. Reynosa got his throat in his powerful hand and it was all over.

As soon as the kid grabbed his choking wrist, Reynosa shot his other hand inside the kid's stylish jacket and came out with a slim automatic pistol. I closed the office door, grating it loudly on the floor and shivering its thin glass. The lead *info-chica* was staring wide-eyed, hand poised fetchingly on her picturesque bosom, but I gave her some sort of smile and at least she didn't scream.

Reynosa said, "Stay where you are, keep calm, don't watch." Then he picked the kid right up off the floor and threw him into Mijares' alcove, where he hit the wall fairly unanimously and started to slide down. Reynosa caught his wrist, spun him into the wall and pulled a wallet out of his hip pocket, then gave him another pirouette and slammed him down into Mijares' chair.

I stepped in, closing the door. Reynosa handed me the gun, pulled his own over-decorated .45, and stuck it right into the kid's mouth, pushing his head back against the wall.

"You aren't required to speak, but I'd advise it. We get commendations for shooting guys who sneak in here with guns and I'm short of my quota."

The kid raised his hands in a surrender gesture and Reynosa pulled the gun out of his mouth but kept it right in his face. He looked at Reynosa, then at me, and said, "Oh, wow. Are you Mundo Carrasco?"

"Who else would it be with those ears? Dumbo?" Reynosa snarled, "But *con permiso*, we're a little more concerned about who *you* are. Apart from..." He flipped the wallet open and read from the voter card, "Gustavo Lazares, failed *pistolero*."

"You can call me Tavo."

"Gustavo, Tavo, *Asesino*, Shitbird, whatever. Actually that isn't really bothering us as much as ... say, what was it we were wondering, Mundo?"

"What he's doing here?"

"Oh, right. Thanks. Yes, what the ..." Reynosa's voice rose to a roar, "... FUCK ARE YOU DOING HERE, you stupid little *hijo de la chingada*?"

"Tavo" blinked in surprise at that outburst so Reynosa clarified a little. "I can blow your damn head off right this minute and nobody would ask any questions. If you want to talk me out of that, start with why you walked in here carrying a gun."

"It's hard to explain. Basically I just wanted to talk to Frederico Varedas."

"Around here we do that with telephones, not pistols."

"Well, I wanted his full attention." He looked back at me and said, "Mundo Carrasco. I can't believe it."

Reynosa stared at him a moment, so furious I thought he was going to lash his face with the pistol. Then he started laughing. "Incredible. He's serious. He just wanted to walk in and have a little chat with the Mayor at gunpoint." He grabbed the *pistolero* by the hair and shook his head, "Are all your mama's kids that smart?"

The kid's eyes blazed into rage and the muscles in his upper body snapped tight. I instinctively covered him with the gun I'd just been holding loose up until then. He spoke to us both, almost spitting. "Your fucking animal boss raped my little brother. Did you two help hold him down?"

Reynosa saw it then, or at least that part of it – the kid's face left no doubt he wasn't lying. He said, "Ah. Well, okay. I'm sorry for the crack about your family."

The kid shot him a look. "I notice the idea that he raped somebody didn't cause a flicker of surprise."

Reynosa put a little weariness into his voice. "Do you know how many people make sexual allegations against public figures?"

"This one's true and I can tell you know it."

"I don't know a damn thing. And I'm not saying I blame you for coming here to kill him. I might do the same thing myself."

"I didn't come to kill him."

Reynosa reached over and took the gun from me, held it up, and waved it back and forth. The kid lowered his head.

"Okay. No point kidding myself. I probably would. But that wasn't my idea."

Reynosa flicked an eye towards me. "So whose idea was it?"

"No, I mean, I just wanted to ... I don't know. Confront him, get him to admit it, I guess. So people would know."

"That would help your brother?" I asked him. "Having everybody know?"

"No. I mean ... I just couldn't stand the idea of him using somebody like that, then getting away with it. Maybe not even remember it ... he was really coked up and drunk."

Reynosa sighed, "¿Cuando no?"

I leaned towards him confidingly. "I hate to tell you, but admissions don't mean too much, either. Maybe in the Church confessions count, but out here ... I think I could print confessions to murder on the front page and nobody would even pay attention."

Tavo leaned back in the chair and blew out his breath. He closed his eyes. "So what happens to me now?"

"We give you back your gun and show you the office," I said, "But we can't pay you more than about a thousand pesos."

He leaned back against the wall and stared at me, then at Reynosa, who was also keeping a poker face. And covering him with his huge automatic. Then he gave a slow, shaky smile and started to laugh.

"Ah, you got me."

"Well no," I pointed my thumb at Reynosa, "He did. Which is a lot worse."

"And what I've got you for, leaving your business with the mayor out of it for the moment," Reynosa said, deadpan. "Is possession of a medium caliber firearm. Very serious offense, actually. You'd have been better off holding heroin."

"You ever try to blow anybody's balls off with heroin?" He was still shaky, but hanging in there.

"Well that does it," Reynosa said. "Obviously an over-educated wiseass. We'd better just let him go."

"Sounds good to me," I said. "Speaking as an over-schooled wiseass myself."

"Is that gun registered or identified in any way? Used in previous crimes?" Reynosa asked him.

"Not at all. It's completely illegal. I stole it from my father."

Reynosa nodded. "Excellent." He stuck it in his hip pocket.

He immediately grasped what we were doing for him, and knew he'd hit a million-to-one shot. He started to thank us, but Reynosa was gruff.

"Oh, you're still going to jail. While we figure out just what to do about you. Check out your story. But you won't end up facing the kind of charges the gun carries. You know, deadly weapon, suspicion of conspiracy to murder, that sort of thing."

"Well, if there's no gun," he said. "What evidence are you holding me on?"

Reynosa stared at him, dumbfounded, then burst out laughing. "Got me."

"*Al contrario*," he said, standing up and sticking his hands out for handcuffs.

Reynosa said, "Let's just walk out like this, not create any gossip. Ready?"

He nodded and turned towards the door. Then he

paused and turned back to me. "I suppose this would be a bad time to ask for an autograph?"

"Jesus Christ," Reynosa groaned, "This guy must be a professional luck pusher. I can't believe I'm even thinking about shining on a weapons charge without a *mordida*."

"I was pretty shocked you didn't bite off a little bribe. Those cool boat shoes, at least," I said.

"Yuppie idiot. Nice move on his knees, by the way."

"That's what we mean by press cooperation with authorities."

"I thought that was when you rigged things up then get outraged about them."

"Oh no, that's called participation in news events."

"Well, I'm hauling him over to El Cereso. Why don't you give Our Brother the news that he isn't going to be assassinated." He clumped towards the door, escorting the kid subtly but with total control. "See if you can break it to him without making it sound like he's not fully involved in the solidarity of assassination victims."

As it turned out, Tirado didn't seem to care one way or the other about the fact that nobody was scheduled to burst in and blow him away. He nodded vacantly when I told him that we'd interviewed the suspected armed intruder, but nothing had come of it. He didn't look at me, just said, "What was the real situation, Mundo?"

"I'm sure Sergeant Reynosa can confirm my report." He waited, looking down into the courtyard. "The kid was from Guadalajara. He came to confront the mayor with a personal grievance. Probably would have dealt with it violently. Reynosa took him into custody pending investigation."

He nodded twice, then said, "And what was that personal grievance, Mundo? And please don't embellish, varnish or edit. I want the truth."

"He said Varedas raped his brother."

He froze, stricken. I saw his knees tremble, but he caught himself on the rail.

"Oh my God," he muttered. "Oh my God how horrible."

"Everybody seems to assume it's true. Almost expected."

He quaked, his face pale, "No, Mundo. Nothing that bestial is ever expected."

"I hope not. I work for him, too, you know."

"True," he said, "We're all in this together."

The last thing I wanted to hear.

The People (and their betrayal) are such an icon of the neo-crypto-post-Marxism of Mexican political rhetoric that it has become hard to sort out who they really are, that we should be so mindful of them. They are more than The Poor, obviously not The Privileged. They are not Me, certainly not You...they end up being Those. My favorite commentary on The People was by Susanita, friend of cartoon favorite Mafalda. She reacted to a "Power To The People" graffiti by saying, "Yeah, great. And get your power all full of orange peels and used diapers and empty bottles and *chorizo* wrappers."

"Them, The People" by Mundo Carrasco
Commentario, May 1995

"What was that campaign slogan? 'Women and Children First', wasn't it?" That from Carlos Estrada, my old beat-mate from *Noroeste.* He was stroking two fingers up and down the condensation of his glass, like he always does. His jowls sagging down on his chest as he spoke into the glass instead of the company at Lo Peor.

"It was 'The Poor Come First', actually," said Major Tom. "But he kayoed his wife before he got around to clobbering the financially challenged."

"One more shattered political promise," Eusebio chimed in.

"So you can see that!"Beto yelped triumphantly. "He kicks them out in the street, beats up their women and children."

"A lot of effort for a fat little puppet?" I said. "Didn't you call him that?"

It was fun to watch Beto sputter. "He ... the police, you *pendejo* ... how can you..."

"Easy for you to say, Beto," I cut in, "If the police do anything around here it would have to be because the Mayor told them to, isn't that what you said last summer?"Or course he'd said exactly the opposite when they were investigating a four-cop death squad during the watch of then-mayor Rafael Lima, a PRIista. He took a deep drink, recharging his batteries.

67

"You know what I'm saying, here, don't you?" I put it as an open question. "About the wife-beating rumors, I have no idea. If anybody gets anything concrete, bring it to me and I'll get you statements. But this thing about rousting the squatters is a fact, the only question being who is responsible."

"I don't think I know any responsible people," said Andrados, our most venal young attorney.

"Any innocent people, either," muttered Beto.

Carlos saw where the lines had been drawn, and what would be forthcoming. He asked me, "So will there be a press meeting after lunch?"

Before I could answer, Mocho focused back in and blurted out, "Hey, why did that Mijares piece reschedule the *prensas* for after lunch, anyway?"

It was always "that Mijares" or "that Mijares chick", never just her name, much less her real name.

"She doesn't want to face you guys when you're hungry. You might jump us and started tearing our flesh with your teeth."

"Not a bad idea. The Mijares broad," Andrados muttered judiciously.

Actually, a fabulous idea. Done tastefully and in moderation.

I wrenched my head back to the matter at hand, "No, I don't think we need a press conference on this one."

Beto was immediately out of his seat in full pugnacity. "No need? When the jackboots of..."

"Beto," Carlito said, "Do you have any idea what a jackboot is?"

When Beto glowered in silence, he went on, "Mundo's right, on this one. We can get hundreds of interviews out there on the highway. Those people aren't going anywhere – that was the problem in the first place. We can collect no comment statements from the cops. What is the *Palacio* going to tell us? They hate poor people? They were taking a piss when it happened and have no idea? Write your own story. Or at least the PRI's own story."

Beto resumed sputtering, but I cut in again. "No formal announcement." Mijares had decided that very quickly, given me a pep talk and rushed me off to Lo Peor while she turned to her phone for higher-level damage control.

"I will make a statement on behalf of the *Palacio*, here and now, just for you. Will that do?" I gathered the surprised nods and said, "The statement is as follows: *Think!*" I paused, then added, "You *babosos*."

There was a moment of silence, not particularly reverent, then Juan Carlos Astores – generally known as Mocho around *El Debate*, spoke up, "That's asking a lot, we're journalists."

A crackle of snickers and outraged epithets went the rounds.

"So you'd rather a bunch of numbnuts *politicos* did it for you?" I asked. "Seriously, *compadres*, the radio and TV people are supposed to be simpletons. City evicts, Mayor is city, Mayor is on shit list, ergo Mayor evicted poor."

Beto gave an elaborate shrug. "Q.E.D."

I went on, "But you guys have the time, not to mention the brains, to think things out instead of just reacting. First question, why in the name of your nasty old mama would the mayor do something so stupid against the only people who like him?"

"Oh he's a pretty stupid guy," Carlito said.

No argument with that. So I hit Ramón D'Alba with it straight. He works for the tiny, scabby *Hora*, but he's sharp. "Ramón, what did you guys say about the invasion in Jabalíes last fall?"

"Well, you know, the usual ..."

"I remember your column, how these things can't work without the collusion of the power structure, trading them public land for partisan votes."

"Well, of course."

"Then does it sound like a good idea for Varedas to screw his biggest bloc of voters – who cost him *nothing* and are totally loyal? In order to clear out the estuary, which means absolutely zip to him?"

"Not particularly."

"On the other hand, there are a lot of councilmen, out-party *regidores*, who hate his guts, not to mention a lot of cops. It would be really easy to set that into motion. You look at what happened, it's pretty shrewd. You might even think they're taking advantage of his domestic problems to take a shot at him when he's already weak and politically vulnerable."

Mocho looked thoughtful. "Shrewd, eh? Well that rules out any PRI stooges."

Beto bridled immediately, forgetting that he'd always denied his stooge status. "The revolution doesn't need clever timing, history is on our side."

"Yeah, your backside."

Before Beto could yell, "*¡La tuya!*" Eusebio, prototypical out-party *regidor*, horned in with, "Care to name any names, hotshot?"

"So far just the concept," I said. "Although since you bring it up, yours has been mentioned."A complete fabrication on my part although it's possible, Sebi being a known PAN member.

"*What?* You listen to me, *cabrón...*"

"Hey, hey," I said, placatingly, "I didn't say anything about you. Just heard you mentioned as a possible. That's how these stupid rumors start. Which is why you should all think about this a little."

"Why," snapped Beto. "So you guys can use us to whitewash this outrage and smear somebody else with it?"

"What I'm saying is this. We will see the bottom of this thing. You can't send a hundred cops and two bulldozers out in the middle of the night without leaving some fingerprints. They've already appointed a board of inquiry."

"A rubber-stamp alibi club, you mean," Beto said.

"Not really. It will include people from several estates, including the press."

Carlito gave a world-weary smile and said, "Who from the press?" He could already imagine which payoff-fattened editors and broadcast execs would be picked to go along with whatever findings might be found.

"You for one." I said, which knocked that world-weary smile right off his face. I savored the next line like a connoisseur, "Your mission ... If you choose to accept it."

That created a major moment. Everybody looked around at each other, stared at me, belted down shots. A first for our administration. The inclusion of press had been Mijares' idea, Carlito had been mine. They respect him and he's pretty objective.

I drove on. "So when the truth does come out, where will you be? If you gangpile the Mayor, you're probably going to look like dumb sheep in a day or two, and it will be pointed out. You can be very sure of that. And you will have pissed off the poor, the majority of voters, and the administration itself. On the other hand, if you get thoughty about it, push for a probe, look for motives, start fund drives for the displaced, decry the lack of accountability, you end up looking smart and statesmanlike ..."

"And piss *everybody* off," Mocho said.

"Hey," I asked, "Isn't that why you got into this line of work in the first place?"

Beto, in a rare moment of insight, said, "I don't need a fucking newspaper to piss everybody off."

Carlito said, "We can't all be naturals." He took a drink, then said, "And what if it turns out Varedas actually did order the roust?"

"Then you dis him with dignity, since it was all proven by investigation."

"And you look like horse's ass."

"Won't be the first time. But I'll tell you this. If Varedas did this, I'll quit."

That quieted the room. You don't often hear people put their jobs on the line in Mexico: jobs are hard to come by. And you never hear of anybody in the press or politics getting that involved. It would hold them a few days. I meant it, and they knew it.

Carlito gave me a look. "How about His Honor? If little Frederico will quit, too, you've got a deal."

Beto stared at him, "A deal? A deal! What deal?"

Carlito ignored his missing the joke. "We do our jobs responsibly, we look good, we feel good. What more do you want?"

Mocho said, "So, Carlos, you going to take the appointment to the investigation?"

Carlito said, "You want to know what happened, don't you?"

Beto said, "I want to *do* something about what happened!"

Mocho swung around, pushing a finger into his face.

"Any asshole can act without knowing why. Our job is to tell people what they don't know. Print what you want, you damn whore. You always do. Which is why your paper looks foolish and nobody buys it anymore. They aren't buying any of the crap anymore, did you notice?"

Beto blinked, unused to anyone else being the aggressor. "The people ..."

"The people are an idiot," Mocho snapped. "And you help keep them that way. Have you ever heard of an investigation like this before, of having somebody like Carlito on it? Things are changing in this country since your *padrones* lost the election. People might have to start thinking for themselves."

"And if they do, what are they going to think about you?" Major Tom tossed in.

Beto looked around, holding his glass in front of his chest. "If the people want to think for themselves, we'll be glad to show them how to do it."

Everybody laughed and Beto showed a smile as if he'd intended – or even understood – the joke.

Mocho said, "Exactly. We reflect the people's opinion; we just reflect it first."

"If we didn't respect their views we wouldn't give them to them," Rosete, from *Canal 7*, chuckled.

"Sure," said Major Tom, "If speech were free, would newspapers cost six pesos?"

"That's why Jefferson and Juarez preferred newspapers over government," I said. "They're cheaper."

"Is that why you prefer government over newspapers, Mundo," Beto said. "Because they aren't as cheap?"

I laughed. "Come look at my office sometime. Tell me who's cheap."

"*Beto* is going to tell you who's cheap?" Eusebio snorted, "He's putting salt in his beer so it keeps foam longer."

"No, look at his pants," Mocho laughed, "The man is an expert on cheapness."

Carlos had been sitting quietly since I'd brought up the inquiry post. Now he said, "There is one thing fishy about this *Infiernillo* thing."

"A main characteristic of tide flats." Mocho reached

for the saltshaker himself.

Carlito gave a thin smile, "No, look at this. Where do these people usually invade? Federal land, so they can say it belongs to the people and dare them to do anything about it. Or land belonging to someone the government has decided to screw."

"You're right,"Eusebio said, "Once an invasion is settled in and the politics is locked up, the guy might as well kiss his land good-bye. Like Barros' piece out on the Culiacán road. What is it now?"

"Grupo Zapata," Beto offered. "A solid community now, not just speculation."

"There's nothing speculative about it," Carlos muttered. "Barros thought he could jump parties and buy his way into the Power Commission. Now he thinks different."

I saw where Carlos had been going. "But who does it serve to move invaders onto public land like that? Uninhabitable land? What were they thinking?"

Carlos gave a deep sigh and signaled for another Tequila. "I don't know. But it sounds like you've set it up for me to have to find out. Thanks a lot."

"So you get another big scoop and a more accolades and *obsequios* from your admiring colleagues. And end up doing Mundo's work for him." Mocho was laughing. "It's beautiful. Did you think it up, or *Señorita* Nose Cones?"

"Also doing the work of the administration, don't you see that?" Beto just knew there was something wrong about it all. "They're just stalling, trying to get out from under the obvious guilt for this outrage."

"Yes, it's an outrage," I said. "And I want to find out who ordered it. So does everybody in town, except the ones who did it. If you want to call that shot before anybody knows anything, be my guest."

He did, too – "Mayor Evicts Poor and Infirm". But that headline ended up sitting on the stands beside several more that raised questions and offered suggestions. I wave my wand across still waters and they churn dark and confused. An inquiry is a hundred questions, which raise a thousand answers, which engender ten thousand questions.

But I was pretty sure Varedas had not ordered the

cops out there to the estuary, and believed that who did could be determined, at least to my satisfaction. Unfortunately, I was also coming to believe that he had clobbered his wife. And I just couldn't get around the creeping suspicion that he had, in fact, raped that kid's brother. You don't carry a gun into a building full of cops over nothing. I had a growing feeling that what I was going to do, I was going to walk out of Lo Peor and not go back to work.

Carlito moved over beside me and spoke quietly, "I'm glad to see you worked up about something like this, Mundo. Since you left the paper, the stuff you write in your column ... there's something wrong with it. It's like a pornography of corruption. "

"That's what people want."

"But do they have to have their noses rubbed in ..."

"No, that's what I want."

He studied me a moment, sadly. "It's a sort of cynical cover-up, really. Makes people feel it's hopeless. Everything you write seems to paint the city in a depressing light, like we're sinking. You know what I mean?"

"I know and sympathize. Are you familiar with a writer called MicroBio?"

"*That* little cocksucker!"

So whatever I think about graffiti, people read it and know your name. Carlito drew away and I thought that maybe playing hooky from work should be permanent. Probably, as a matter of fact.

"Soccer" might have come from Scotland, but the Mexican obsession for *"futbol"* is rooted far back in native soil. The great Mayan cities were centered on huge stadiums for the ancient ball game of *Ulama*, a perverse game in which the ball could be struck only with the hips. *Ulama* legends, such as that losing teams became blood sacrifices and that winners were made into kings, are hard to verify, but not all that inconsistent with *futbol* as practiced in Latin America today. The first time an American soccer team defeated the Mexican national team in match play, a local sportswriter said, "Eventually the gringos will even beat us in *Ulama*." The remark was wryly quoted all over town, testimony to the North American drive to conquer areas that don't even interest them, and the way they buy off world talent, tainting world athletes with "Americanism". But I wonder if the result isn't the conquest of the United States by foreign enthusiasms. Would it be so bad for Mexican pride if the gringos became big fans of *Ulama*?

"Ulama Rama Ding Dong" by Raymundo Carrasco
Inside Sports, April 1996

Athletes generally don't go in for quitting, but I have done it before and know when it needs to be done. And one of those times is when you've been signed by a bad organization. On my way home from Lo Peor I paused in the main public square, Plaza Republica. There is a little nook carved out of the bushes behind the kiosk, with a circular bench. For once there were no giggling lovers in there groping, so I walked back into the shade and sat down, scanning the Plaza while I thought things over.

There's a plaza in Mexico City they call *Las Tres Culturas,* but here we have *Los Tres Feos,* a plaza lined with some of the ugliest buildings in town. The chipping block of the civic *Palacio* faces the Post Office, a staggering work of ugliness, as if Albert Speer had grown up in a communist slum and had his sense of proportion surgically removed. And right in front of me, one of the ugliest and most slipshod cathedrals in Christendom. The concrete blocks and cheap facings weren't tacky enough for the neo-chingadero style, they had to put neon crosses on top and always leave one of them burned out. I sat there pondering my decision under the glazed gaze of institutionalized ugliness.

I should explain a few things. It wasn't just my self-inflicted enslavement to Mijares that made me a good bet for this job, my shot at the big time. I was uniquely qualified because to the press in this town I carry a sort of an aura around me. Many of them dream of transcending this provincial town surrounded by cows and narcotics, hitting the big national beats. They lust after national awards and recognition. Not to mention foreign blondes. They wish they spoke English and had seen New York. They wish they knew if they could have walked away from an international athletic career for the pursuit of truth. They wonder if they could do all that and still be one of the guys – not realizing that I never really wanted to be anything else. But above it all, there is a gleam of trophies, flickering highlights of one sweet swing, the cheers when I stroke out another win for my employer.

So, in a way, I got the job the way I got everything else in my life ... by swinging a bat. My life is a history of swinging in the right place at the right time. Showing up on big dates. For openers, I was born in 1968, a number that will resonate through Mexico for generations. Not the Olympics, the government massacre of students and protesters in Plaza Tlaltelolco. It was a defining moment, and made the Kent State episode in the United States look like a tea party. Much closer to the events of Tienanmen Square in Peking. I've seen the year of my birth painted on walls my whole life.

I was born with my dad's size and reflexes, then had them refined by a lifetime of coaching. Women like my big Indian looks well enough. My height, my broad shoulders and strong legs. The hawk-like nose, the eagle eyes, even the wingspan ears. Hell, sounds like I was put together in a bird factory. Big hands, big feet ... you know what conclusions they draw. They like the loose stance, the easy grace, even the chewing gum. All just factors of growing up on the diamond. I guess you'd say my bat brings me my women, like everything else. Pitchers are the glamour boys, but it's always outfielders who get the women. Marilyn Monroe didn't marry Whitey Ford, she picked a slugger. And, come to think of it, a writer. I've got it nailed. All I need is to find a movie star sex symbol and I'm on the family track.

My father sacrificed to send me to a *collegio*, a private prep school where I could learn English and typing – prepare for a good-paying job, have a shot at being somebody. But I later found out that a lot of those expenses were quietly paid by alumni, who liked to go to games that their old school won. And we did win, like little heroes. I graduated in the class of 1984 – another famous year – then it was another sort of unofficial scholarship to the *Universidad Autonoma de Sinaloa,* which we write as UAS and pronounce like "Wass". Team captain, record-breaker, big stud on campus, I could have stopped right there and been remembered and favored by the city's elite.

But when Arizona State offered me a full ride to transfer there my last two years I jumped at it. America! *Gringalandia!* Yow! I joined a team that was already headed for a conference championship and helped slug them into two straight appearances in the College World Series. My first year we lost to Louisiana State in the quarterfinals – don't look at me, I hit .600 for the series, with nineteen runs knocked in – and my final year we blew out Texas to win the whole enchilada, partly thanks to an explosion of hits and extra bases from 'Ray' Carrasco. Right place, right year. I spent my life on winning teams, and never developed the taste for playing with losers.

Unlike UAS, they wanted me to major in something at ASU. Quite a few of the jocks took journalism, hoping for announcing careers after the hoped-for jock careers were over, so I did, too. Besides, I've always loved gossip. I couldn't have stumbled onto a better meal ticket for back home in Mexico. My senior year I did an article about Latino scholarship recruitment that ended up reprinted in something called *Mother Jones.* I did another one on the use of drugs in college sports programs, and kept selling them. I went to the magazine market just as Latinos were becoming fashionable. Over the next few years, playing in the pros, I sold articles on the politics of the Caribbean Series and the impressions of a young Mexican hitting the major leagues, which ran in *Sports Illustrated,*. who wouldn't have bought a cup of coffee from me if I hadn't been a jock. You see what I mean about this?

I was scouted a bit for the majors but was homesick for Mexico and showing another trait that turned out to be life-long, a lack of big league vision. So I signed with the Mazatlán Venados. Small-timer syndrome you might say. But you know, I didn't want to play in Fresno or Durham, I'd wanted to play for the Venados since I was a kid sitting in their bleacher section with my dad. I didn't dream of hitting in Candlestick or Fenway or The Bronx, I always fantasized playing here in Venados Stadium, wearing a Venados cap with the pissed-off deer on the front, riding to Culiacán or Navajoa on the big team bus, which I considered the coolest vehicle in existence, much more than a space lander, Maseratti or Stealth Fighter. Maybe hitting the cycle in the *Caribe* series or some such. Being a home-town hero. And it turned out I signed on with them at exactly the right time to become a National Hero.

The *batazo* might have happened in a microsecond, but it was a culmination of things coming together to bring me to that point in time. Winning the league, Ramirez joining the team late in the season, that left-hander coming down from the Mariners and able to cope so well with Venezuela's big bats. Events built one on another almost like a conspiracy. Leading to the peak. It wouldn't have been much of a hit if there hadn't been two outs in the bottom of the ninth with the Mexicans trailing by a run. Looking back on it, it seems a little eerie. At the time it just seemed like Real Life. The Big Hit was just two RBI's, really. But they came at a time that been decades in the making.

At that point, I didn't write news; I *was* news. They wrote about me nonstop, I could have sold an autobiography in a *chilango* minute. At the age of twenty-three. But I went to the States, did the Big Time for a season. Then I quit to come home. Time-outs are part of timing. The Small Time is still Time.

I didn't see any point in rejoining the Venados after playing for the Angels. And I was getting seriously interested in journalism – as good a *chamba* as any for a twenty-something pro washout. I got the job at *Noroeste* without even an interview, I called the editor to ask his advice on following a journalism career and he hired me on the spot, over the phone. My training at ASU and sales to big-time American publications gave me a tremendous advantage over the local competition, but I think my batting had a lot to do with the job offer. And not just historically speaking, the fortunes of *Noroeste*'s team in the *Liga Periodista* are jealously promoted. Lermanez, the owner, would take a win over a scoop any day, and a city league cup over a Degollado prize.

But I also kept doing magazine work 'by moonlight', as they say up North. *Millenio* pissed me off with a gassy expose of drugs in sports – how the athletes abuse them. I went straight to *Proceso* with the idea of how the *teams* abuse drugs ... and how many teams are owned and controlled by *narcos*. They went nuts over it. Six months later, following up on tips from some Tarahuamara relatives up in Creel I did another little *obra* on narco-culture's influence on tribal youth that ran in *Nexus* and won a national journalism award.

So narcotics turned out to be my beat, and later similar *macho* subjects like smuggling and illegal firearms. It fed on itself. I was so famous for it that the *narcos* liked me and would tell me things I couldn't believe they would say to anybody, much less a reporter. After awhile I figured out they liked publicity, thought of themselves as folk heroes. Which some of them are. I went to Tijuana to write about the Arrellano cartel, Sinaloa boys who made good, and met Blancornelas, the most famous investigative writer in Mexico, striking out from behind his troop of federal bodyguards.

I went to the borders of Guatemala and Belize, drank with gunrunners and traffickers in human lives. I didn't need bodyguards, they liked me. They remembered what I did and gave me drinks and girls and cocaine. But it was starting to lose its zip.

I suppose I could have pulled on my safari jacket and gone to Colombia, or even more ridiculously, Afghanistan. There might have been an article or two over there on drugs and firearms, do you think? But what would I know? Who would I be? I'd be as absurd as those American reporters, coming in here to write about the cartels or Chiapas; 'penetrating the local cover' in forty-eight hours, less commercial time, for their breathless reports. Understanding Iraq because they were stupid enough to stay on a roof during a rocket attack. I ended up quitting the Big Time again.

And, again, I found out I was more interested in Mazatlán than the World. In 2001 – continuing my penchant for red-letter years – I left *Noroeste* and got out of the international violence business. When *El Debate* offered me a column, I realized it was what I'd always wanted – a forum to shoot off my mouth about anything that caught my eye. *El Mundo Segun Mundo* became an opportunity to penetrate my city, and to try to help it become a less worse place, not only a lever, but a place to stand. I make ends meet doing sports and 'think pieces' for national magazines and getting a big kick out of it. My most recent sale was to an American magazine about the theology of chiles. I became the undisputed superstar of the city leagues and started working to improve my fielding. At the age of thirty-four. Trying to keep my eye on the ball and get my fingers under the edge. What I'm finding is, it's not so much skill as just paying attention.

Once I realized I was an incomplete ballplayer, I also realized that I was an incomplete writer and started working on that. But in a Small Time sort of way. I didn't care that much about the Big Tent, I just like slamming the ball, like hanging around the dugout with a bunch of big, rough, quick guys who respect me. But I can get that anywhere. I don't even really need top pitching to have fun. If the guy is slower or wilder, it just allows me to compensate, or to place my hits more elaborately. I'm not dueling with pitchers out there, I'm dueling with fielders. It doesn't do any good to poke a ball into the deep outfield, right into a glove. It's fun to hit it of course, but what fun is it to be out?

The same thing applies to my writing. Being a big fish in small pond suits me just fine. Women, adulation of kids, that flash of recognition when I walk into a place. Hey, the slugger. Hey, the smartass columnist. It took me thirty-four years to arrive at the place I was born. Then Mijares snatched me right into the small-change version of the big time. I handled the job just fine, then it was time to quit.

   With that decision made, I got up and walked out of the leafy bower, out under a beautiful red-streaked sky. A couple angled in to claim the love seat, the girl shy and giggly, the boy swaggering and unsure. I headed up the steep sidewalk of Angel Flores to pick up Das Boot and head out, once again to the Stadium. But not to play ball ... to worship a Goddess. I arrive, I win, I quit. I just never seem to learn.

The Flower Games have nothing to do with the Flour Games of the past century...the English pun is definitely a co-incidence. At *Carnaval* time the poor of Old Mazatlán divided, apparently at random, into two gangs and pelted the rival gangs with eggshells filled with flour and dyes. The practice was condemned and steps taken to eliminate it, but without much luck: it was just too much fun. I wish they still had them today, actually: splashing people with dye would be a lot more fulfilling than painting on buildings. And because it was fun and didn't really bother the victims, it was impossible to control or eradicate. If you think I'm hinting about drugs, prostitution, and alcoholism, you're right. Controlling Carnival is easier conceived than accomplished. These days it's in order, not through authority but by the simple exercise of commercialism. It continually amazes me that people fail to solve the world's problems with guns, clubs and prisons when it's so easy and effective to bring things in line merely by putting them on a paying basis.

"Games In Masks" by Mundo Carrasco
Phoenix New Times, November 2001

Everyone agrees it was one of the most beautiful Flower Games ever. I was totally knocked out, wide-eyed as a little kid. Aside from the big fireworks show, the Flower Games is my favorite part of *Carnaval,* and the most beautiful. It's hard to compare it to anything I saw in the United States, sort of like a coronation combined with a Super Bowl halftime, Olympics opening, and Las Vegas show – but with a unique tropical taste. The Games are held in the Venados Stadium, but it's not for the common people, it's for the *Mazatleco* elite. In fact, it's an event for a goddess.

The entire idea of Flower Games is backwards from your normal stage spectacular, even though it's put together by professionals from Spectaculare, who do routine extravaganzas for hotels and conventions. It's not about people up on stage entertaining the audience. It's a presentation to the queen, and the common subjects in our seats are part of the entertainment for the beautiful, freshly crowned Queen of Flower Games who sits up there on her throne and receives it as her regal due.

The odd thing is that it makes for better entertainment, in the same way that Catholic spectacles are more entrancing to the flock because they aren't *for* the people, but for God, Jesus, and the Virgin. Flower Games are a dedication that goes beyond the quaint Carnival conventions of royalty and starts to look like worship. Which finds fertile ground in Mexico, where even popular Catholicism has evolved into a virgin goddess cult.

Flower Games requires more preparation and devotion than any other event, even the parades. Decorators, dancers, musicians, choreographers, and special effects experts plan, rehearse, and bicker for months in order to throw one huge multi-media bouquet into the lap of a teenaged virgin. It's absolutely ridiculous. It's absolutely gorgeous.

As the stadium filled up, people in their fine best suits, gowns, and *guayaberas* circulated among the chairs set up in the outfield, chatting, making impressions on each other, and eyeing the huge stage and towers in the infield for hints of what was to come. I pushed through to the bar for a drink, then walked along the edges of the seating area and the orchestra pit out around the pitcher's mound. The security cordon was even stronger than at most coronations. The drunks and the press get out of hand at these things and have to be herded like delinquent goats. I was glad to see that the line of staunch guys in their very best uniforms looked up to dealing with kamikaze photographers and microphone-bearers.

The fancy VIP stand was squarely over second base and filling up with Personages of Very Importance. Conspicuously empty was the ribboned-off front row where the Mayor would sit in a satin sash while he and his party watched the show. I thought it pretty unlikely that the First Lady would show up, and His Honor was always a good bet to no-show. It was going to be a big crowd this year, even with threats of rain. People were even taking seats up in the grandstand. I stood in front of the celebrity pen for a moment, admiring the romantic gingerbread of the coronation podium – a towering round platform to support the queens and princesses, tiered and sculptured like a giant wedding cake from Panama Bakery. Turning back to scan the crowd, I saw Palomina in a dazzling strapless gown and a mask/headdress of white dove feathers. For a minute I thought she might be part of the Games, then I realized she was arm-candy for a stocky bullet-head wearing movie-prop, black western wear from The Heroin Cartel Collection. Ringed in by Senor *Traficante* Chic and four big bodyguards also dolled up like NarcoMariachis, she looked like a white dove herded by Rottweilers. She caught my eye and gave me an elaborate wink. I smiled but didn't wave into the wolfpack.

I'd known Palomina professionally since she was about eighteen, which is to say I occasionally stop by to watch her dance naked on the stage, tables, and laps of various venues. She might just possibly be the Best Naked Dancer In Mazatlán, and I always got a kick out of talking to her, often while paying three or four dollars for her to straddle my lap naked and chat with me lightly for the over-amplified duration of *Una Bomba* or *Hotel California*. Not very mercenary for a lap dancer, fun company, and fairly fabulously formed for sitting naked on your lap. She was a honey-colored girl with the exotic eye shape that is one gift to Mazatlán from our Chinese community. A *blonde du guerre*, you might say, but she is *artiste* enough to extend the bleaching to all areas, thus presenting no glaring contradictions to paying customers. She always seemed partial to me, affectionate and demonstrative beyond the call of duty. Probably because she's a baseball fan: she once did a dance on my table swinging a plastic bat while wearing only a Venados cap and a metallic gold jockstrap with the club's deer logo sewn on it. Anyone trying to cop a feel got a swat from the bat. A fun kid. Amid questionable companions. Like so many of us these days.

I had to hand it to Spectaculare; they outdid themselves in 2002. Instead of relying on local dance troupes – who aren't exactly chopped liver, themselves – they had brought in the cream, the National Company. The Angela Peralta Theater Chorus was handling the vocals, backed up by the entire State of Sinaloa Symphonic Orchestra. They started out with a dramatic splash of lights and flares and a big bash of symphony, but I noticed that the Mayor's row was still empty. The music and lights continued to clamor during the speeches leading up to the coronation. Five lovely girls wearing thousands of dollars in clothes, makeup and hairdos waited to find out which one would end up going down in the annals with a roman numeral after her name. My money was on Fabiola: she had the looks, the money, the family, the blind obsession. I'd met her before, and she is remarkably unremarkable in person, nothing to catch the eye. Her face is round, bland, almost featureless, a blank space onto which beauty can be painted. Meanwhile, the candidates awaited the decision, quivering in anticipation of what they'd crammed for all their lives. And the Games began.

The main event was stunning. The musicians whirled the dancers, in their intensely colored costumes, into complex patterns that spun them in closer and closer to the center of the stage, where they joined to create a tropical flower, a perfectly formed and exactly colored Dionaea. More dancers, dressed as bees with gossamer wings, circled elaborately in towards the Dionaea, which opened to receive them, then closed with the bees inside. The orchestra and chorus made much of this pause, then the flower reopened to reveal the queen inside. Right over home plate, I noticed. And sure enough, it was Fabiola.

In case all this sexual innuendo was lost on anybody, the queen's emergence from the fertilized flower triggered an explosion of skyrockets behind the stage, lighting up the night above the grandstand. The orchestra went nuts trying to compete with the sound, the chorus hit an extended crescendo, and the dancers writhed in an artistic orgasm. Blew me right out of the box.

The new Queen ascended graciously to her throne, a solitary bride on top of the big white wedding cake, and started receiving the adulation of the court. She stood there in front of a backdrape of colored fire, a night sky full of prophetic comets streaking her name across the heavens. At her feet was a sea of people, an orchestra performing for her pleasure, beautiful dancers saluting her beauty, armed men at her protection and command. It might make quite an impression on a twenty year-old kid. But it's been my experience that rich, beautiful young women learn to accept that sort of thing as their due.

The winner of the poetry prize read his poem to her, and she seemed to be listening. Unlike the rest of us. The winner of the painting prize unveiled his winning canvas, presenting it to her in spirit. She took it all with *noblesa*. She would end up sitting there accepting our adoration for over four hours, after having been at a round of balls and parties before, and expected to grace several more afterwards. Since people always look to journalists for dirty little inside secrets, I'll present you with one: most of the princesses and queens have learned to wear diapers under their gowns. It's not easy to drink champagne and be in the public eye for hours at a time, especially wearing clothing that takes a trained team to remove. I could make some subtle reference here to the realities that lie beneath the glorious facade of the worship of virgin queens, but for once I will trust you to do that yourself.

There was a short intermission before the second part of the pageant; a presentation of the entire opera *Carmina Burana*. I braved the mob at the nearest bar to grapple a drink for the road, then cruised by the security troops again, confirming that the Mayor had never shown up. But there was somebody sitting in the front row of his box; a golden-white dove. I walked over in front of the stand and leaned on the rail in front of her. She likes that sort of thing, was indulging herself while her escort and his *guardespaldas* were yakking with their fellow *narcos*.

She looked at me and pouted a little. "Mundo, am I or am I not better-looking than those little princess bitches?"

It didn't require any gallantry at all to say, "Absolutely. *No cabe duda.*"

"And more talented?"

"No comparison." Totally true: she'd been through The School on a dance scholarship.

"And sexually desirable?"

"Does the Pope crap in the woods? Does a bear have ships?"

"Then why don't I get a sash and tiara?"

"You get what you pay for, don't you?"

She sighed melodramatically. "Where did it go, the pure

worship of beauty?"

"To the highest bidder, I think."

She glanced at me, was assured I hadn't meant it like she might have taken it. Apparently she's less comfortable with her table dancer self-image when playing princess. It's amazing how far the queen obsession extends.

"I think I can get behind just selling the crowns off, more than all the 'right family' crap."

"Too clean for Mexico. What fun would corruption be if there wasn't family tied into it somewhere?"

"And the whole family thing turns out to come from corruption and selling out. Why don't they just use screwing contests to choose their sex symbols?"

"Who'd be the judges?"

"Somebody who would only vote for a virgin. I haven't seen you lately, Mundo. Down at work."

Her work, she meant. My obsession with Mijares became a dull ache over the last two years, and I'd gone with other women, enjoyed watching them, touching them, doing whatever you call it when you feel loving but it's not Love. I just hadn't enjoyed it as much as I had before meeting Mijares. But after working with her every day – seeing her, smelling her, being close to her; the same infatuation has come back full strength and other women tend to look like cut-outs, shadows, remains.

I said, "You know, problems at work."

She gave me a faint smile. "I'll bet. You should come by to say hello anyway, Mundo. All the girls miss you."

I miss me, too. But I made a note to stop by and have a drink with Palomina. I might be somewhat immune to her looks for the moment, but I like hanging out with her. She's very *simpatica*, what we call *buena onda* – meaning something like good vibes. Too good for me, apparently. Too good for my own good.

Which was what seemed to be on the mind of two big bodyguards who finally noticed her absence and that she was talking to a man who was not their boss. Who was at that moment drooling all over some debutante in watered rayon, but even so they wouldn't let his interests, even in a *bimbo du jour,* be compromised by the attentions of an outside male. They were heading over side-by-side, as alike as two draft oxen. I told Palomina I should probably be running along. Any minute they were going to start singing opera.

Getting to the exits was like swimming against a riptide. Everybody was getting back to their seats, most of them liquoring themselves up against the onslaught of Western Culture. On top of her spun sugar castle, Queen Fabiola III was smiling and waving, reigning and deigning as her loving subjects subjected her to another few hours of musical tribute. I wondered if she was wearing diapers, or perhaps the increasingly popular catheter. I wondered if she'd had as much pleasure as she could tolerate. I certainly had. Driving home, I thought of Palomina and made a note to call the Carnival offices and mention a few favors.

In Olas Altas, and especially along the Paseo Centenario and Paseo Claussen, it's hard not to see Mazatlán as a confrontation of stone and sea, an accommodation between object and force. The islands are islands because of the level of the sea, the bays have their shape because of the obduracy of the stones. The beaches are made of stone ground fine by the sea, but the sea deposits them only where the land creates the opportunity.

"Pearl of the Pacific" by Raymundo Carrasco
México Desconocido, November 1996

The excesses of *Carnaval* only make me appreciate my apartment that much more. Leaning on the cement railing, I could see the delicate white lines of surf start to form out in the darkness beyond the tawdry lights along Olas Altas, swelling as they moved in, the humps of wave behind them picking up streaks of color from the billboards, booths and neon circuses that had been built along the sidewalks for this one week. When they slammed into the rocks at the north end of the seawall, the spray took on glints of CarniColor, like a film projected on rain. At the south end, the combers slugged right onto the crescent sand beach.

One of the cool things about Olas Altas beach is that it moves back and forth with the seasons, the perfect natural symbol of a tourist economy. In summer the swells from the south pile the sand on my end of the beach, leaving only a pile of boulders at the foot of the stairs on the south end. The winter waves peel the sand away and pile it up to the south. The same cycles erode the beaches out in the tourist zone, but here the rocky points of the Bay trap the sand and it just sloshes from side to side as if in a big pan. Or as Luz wrote in one of her inimitable open letters to *Viejo Mazatlán* magazine, "Like a restive child in bed, snuggling close to one parent, then turning to hug his blankets up against the other." The contrast between the eternal cycles of the sea and the momentary chaos of human diversions couldn't have been drawn any clearer. I turned away from the view and opened up my office for the night.

Wherever else I might be working, my true office is a big watertight ship's locker turned on end against the only wall of my apartment. It's a heavy, shoulder-high box of gray metal with Navy markings overlaid by stencils from the MazTuna fishing fleet and now mostly covered with my collection of clippings, headlines, and journalistic esoterica. It was a good find, with waterproof gasket all around and heavy-duty hinges and hasp. An incredible pain in the *nachas* to hoist up here from the street, but well worth the trouble. When I swing the hatch open it's like a metal closet with a cluttered bulletin board inside the door. The shelves are *huanacaxtle* planks I sawed and sanded by hand, then oiled to bring out the beautiful reddish woodgrain. It protects my papers and jury-rigged word processor from moisture and bugs – and my files from theft and espionage. When I type, my toes keep playing with the big hex nuts that hold it down to studs embedded in the concrete floor.

The heart of this engine of fearless modern journalism is a battered, discolored, old portable computer with the KayPro marque, held together mostly with electrical tape and curses. It has no CD-ROM, no Windows, no mouse, no cam, no hard drive, no color monitor, no visible letters remaining on the keyboard. But it lets me write ASCII files on an ancient shareware program, then copy them to a floppy disk for transport to the office. The floppy disk drives don't really fit the holes left by the old five-inch drives, but that's what they invented duct tape for.

Actually I despise computers. When I first realized that I would be incapable of going back to using a typewriter instead of a word processor, I was filled with depression and self-loathing. The great journalists all used typewriters, Shakespeare and Cervantes wrote their masterpieces dipping feathers into bottles of ink. What a wimp I turned out to be. But there's no way I would go back to having to retype whole pages to eliminate one error, to any of those pre-cyber horrors. This might be the very essential nature of corruption, it's not the motivation of evil, it's mostly just accommodating ourselves to a convenience that we used to look down on, but accept the benefits and now can't live without. So I turned on the machine and prepared to write my weekly column for *El Debate*.

An hour later, I hadn't written a thing. I just couldn't come up with anything interesting. By some very careful agreement, I can't deal with city politics, and the national political scene has lost its appeal to me. In the year since the PRI was voted out of the presidency, I had felt a loss. There was no longer an evil force to be struggled against, nothing to boot up my indignation and crusader complex. From now on the corruption will come from us, ourselves. Not that the PRI was exactly imposed by outer space aliens.

Or, it suddenly hit me, maybe it had nothing to do with politics at all, maybe it was just me. At thirty-four I seem to have suddenly gotten enough distance and baggage to take a look back, enough perspective to frame things up. I have reached That Age. And the perspective, insight, and wisdom I have finally accumulated basically suck.

It seems to do more harm than good. For one thing, I have been noticing – reinforced by any glance around my small, wide-open, Spartan apartment – that men who reach this age without having a woman in their lives don't do very well. I don't think it has to be anything permanent or all-inclusive. What it needs to be is steady. You need to hit about .600 or better. She's mostly living with you, or at least you feel that 'this is my woman', people see you as a couple. With any luck, she is capable of handling your finances for you. She wants you to be good, to succeed, to be happy with yourself. She feels that betraying you would make her less happy with herself. That is the basic situation as I see it.

Women might have an entirely different analysis of what it takes. But of course, being women, they are not going to tell us what it is. Probably not even an analysis at all, just that they feel a certain way, or within certain brackets for an acceptable amount of time. I think maybe they only have to go about .270 to hang with something. Then again, people have told me that it's not even a woman that makes the difference, that what a man needs to continue into manhood, to keep on growing, is children. Maybe that's so. But maybe growing and maturing is not what I want. I look around and don't see much point in it. It's kind of like, if I can get on first, I'll start thinking about second and third, then about getting home.

Naturally, Mijares does *not* fit this scenario at all. And not just because she's not steady and she's not mine. She's all loose flame, red noise, and free fall – the things that scare babies from birth and enchant the feral tribes of youth. She's a broken power line swinging around in the wind, striking showers of sparks off the cars and buildings; the sort of thing kids stare at, and can't understand why their parents won't let them stay and watch. She's that few seconds between losing control of your car and slamming into something solid. I don't need her at all, but of course I have no choice but to move towards her; my mouth and eyes and veins and nostrils blown open, my hairs standing erect, my breath oppressed, my heart bailing out, my brain choked down to a dull reptile throb. Love is a disease. She's the only known cure.

All thoughts seemed to lead me to her, like a labyrinth. I gave up on corralling an article. I hooked my old Yucatan hammock to the rings in the support pillars and lay there staring out at the stars. Something about Mijares seems to kick up a sense of my own mortality. She is so perfect it's impossible to imagine her aging or even changing. But the rest of us do. Is there a specific point where you stop growing and start declining? Stop being born and start dying? When? At thirty-five, half of the time the Bible allows you? Is there a stopping of direction at that point; one of those timeless moments when the reversal takes place and your skin and bones shift their destiny towards dust? Do you feel that moment, your own high-water mark? A shiver down your limbs, the world silent for a moment? Or is it like a solstice or eclipse that can happen when you are asleep, or unseen in broad daylight, or on the other side of the world?

Swinging lazily, I could feel a strong sea wind moving across me and I could hear what it was doing to the waves down below. I concentrated on that rhythm, looking for a larger pattern, until it rocked me to sleep.

THURSDAY
FEBRUARY SEVENTH

DIA DE SAN RICARDO

Carnival Calendar

Children's Parade, Olas Altas Avenue, 9 AM
Queen of Carnival Coronation and Pageant,
Venados Stadium, 6 PM

Mazatlán suffers from *reinitis*—Queen-craziness. I'm sure New Orleans and Rio de Janeiro have similar levels of neurosis, hysteria and grim infighting over their pre-Lenten royalty, but here it's more like a part of life, the same cultural impulses that lead to the deification of the Virgin of Guadelupe, and the obsessive overdressing for *quinceañera* parties that announce the nubility of fifteen year old girls. *Reinitis* is a pathology that has been explored but not completely understood. I suppose for men it's a good solution to the virgin/whore dichotomy, since a Queen can be either if she so deigns—while girls just want to be queens. And we men quickly learn that treating them like queens is the quickest way to get them to act like whores.

"The Royal Scam" by Mundo Carrasco
Viejo Mazatlán Magazine, September 2000

I snatched a little time out to swing by the Children's Parade on the way in to the *Palacio*. I figured that it doesn't hurt to be late to quit. And if one look at Mijares swindled me out of quitting again, what the hell? The day before I'd covered up an outrage and faced a lone gunman. Things at the office could only get less stressful and more normal. Right?

I hustled down the stairs to Angel Flores, which was already blocked by cops and parents' cars, and came out onto Olas Altas just as the first entries rolled by. I'd promised Pablo I'd be sure to wave to his kids in their moment of grandeur and I've found it best to keep promises made to landlords. But in fact I've always thought the kids' parade is one of the nicest of the Carnival events. Just kids, you know; every kid who wants to can come out here and parade down the street just like the elected officials, crowned queens, and hired mummers.

Mazatlán loves parades; it's one of our main civic vices. All Mexican cities have a few parades a year, especially around Carnival and Independence Day and the First of Spring – but here we have parades every few days. Any pretext will do.

There are two main Carnival parades, but also a dozen or so just to show off the candidates for every queen and princess opening. Every high school votes for several queens a year, and each election deserves a parade, with cute teenaged girls hanging off pickup trucks and all their friends moving through the crowds with buckets to collect money for charity, whoever turns in the most money gets the crown. But they all get the parade, maybe even with a few skyrockets. All the colleges, sometimes even individual departments and programs, also have their days in the sun.

There are motorcycle parades, when cops escort leather-jacket members of Olas Altas or *Los Rucos* gangs, growling and farting their noisy bikes along the Malecón. There is a parade for the Juvenile Talent Competition. A Halloween parade. Any number of religious processions, with robed penitents carrying banners of Christ or the Virgin while marshals move them along with bullhorns. There is a re-enactment of the arrival of the Spanish actress Angela Peralta in Mazatlán a hundred years ago, another tracing the routes of the old *aguadores*, barrels they used to roll through the streets to sell drinking water. The *pulmonía* drivers have their own parade, one of the oddest and most seriously taken. There is an annual parade of public vehicles – and every fire truck, police car, street repair truck, and garbage collector has a siren and uses it.

My favorite is the Fat Queen parade, in which the obese girls get their shot at a tiara and anybody who doesn't bottom out the springs of their decorated car has a chance. I've never found out who sponsors the *Reina Gorda* thing, and it appears at random dates, unpublicized, by spontaneous acclamation. Most of the parades are unknown unless you happen to be standing there when they roll by. When the Port Authority bought a big shipment of heavy equipment, there was a parade through the whole town, people waving and throwing confetti from the hoods of huge forklifts, haulers, steamrollers, bulldozers, and cranes.

But mostly you just see a big line of cars and light trucks decorated with balloons or big, indecipherable banners, always topped with groups of happy people waving, throwing things, and basking in the bewildered attention of people just trying to go about their day, but happy to get in the mood. And they always have police escorts, with flashing lights and yowling sirens that set every dog in town howling like a chorus. I suspect that all it would take would be driving five pickups very slowly with girls sitting on the roofs and a swarm of cops would join up to escort you just because they like doing it.

Mazatlecos will honk their horns – usually custom versions that play music, sirens, wolf-whistles, or peculiar cartoon bleats – seconds after a light changes, immediately if somebody slows down to avoid running over an old lady, constantly during any traffic jam; but are strangely tolerant of parades blocking their progress. It seems that they just follow quietly, maybe acquiring a layer of waving girls as they creep along, thus becoming part of the parade.

This one was like that, car after car loafing by with kids sitting on top of them, little boys frozen and shy in their suits, crowns and vague costumes, the girls living out their dreams. They waved the standard 'window wiping' princess waves as they went by, smiling in their finery and cheap tiaras. Between some of the cars and pickups, an odd collection of commercial vans pumped out music to help them promote their tostadas or bottled water or chicken dinners. There were a few simple floats, mostly from private schools, and several marching bands playing military music on drums and trumpets. A few *comparsas* tripped by, costumed dance troupes like the Brazilian samba schools but mostly dancing to cowboy polkas from *banda* recordings. Clowns, mimes, jugglers, balloon wranglers and general oddballs pranced between the vehicles.

My favorites were squads of girls approaching their teens, not playing music or dancing, but just marching along wearing uniforms of short, swingy skirts, clingy tops, knee-high white boots and little military caps. There is nothing quite as beautiful and charming as a little girl just as she starts to bloom towards womanhood. My thoughts on pre-teen cuteness were disrupted by a voice behind me, speaking English, "Pedophiles' paradise, huh?"

I could tell without turning around that it was Grady, my downstairs neighbor and, as I've told him, my token gringo companion. I said, "Are all old gringos sick and dirty, or just you?"

"I ain't the one staring at the training bras, amigo," he replied, shouldering in beside me. "I'm just too old to rock and roll and too young to die."

"Is that a classical allusion?"

"Jethro Tull."

"Hmmm, Dickens, right?"

"Classic Rock." He broke into singsong, "Watching the pretty panties run."

"Don't drool when you sing, it's not classy."

"But it's hip. Sort of retro punk grunge deco-dent."

I speak pretty decent English, but whenever I talk with Grady, things twist off into alien gibberish like that. Probably a dialect of Dinosaur. In Mexico, *los dinosaurios* are the old-school PRI guys, the evil feudal barons of national politics. In the United States, apparently, they are guys who play rock and roll past the age of twenty-nine. Easier to live with, and less ideologically damaging.

Grady has lived here for years, leading a nameless oldies band that fans at the Puerto Viejo restaurant call The Grady Bunch. Himself on vocals, guitar and harmonica, especially when he gets on a Dylan jag; a pretty Canadian singer, Mexican bassist, German rhythm guitarist and blues freak, French pianist, and a drummer I think escaped from El Salvador.

Grady's face is patchily bearded, ravaged and deranged as Joe Cocker's, but he projects the look and feel of Jimmy Buffet with his Hawaiian shirts and trademark white Panama. When he plays *Margaritaville*, he ends up drifting off into Allman Brothers or Grateful Dead licks. He likes to turn it up and shake the place. According to him, he's not a Parrot Head or Deadhead, he's a Thunderhead. He's got great job credentials for working in Mazatlán, he can sing in English. He's told me he wishes he'd come to Mexico sooner in life, working steady, paying $90 a month for his view apartment, playing tennis at the Muralla sports club for $60 a month instead of the sixty a day it would cost him up in Seattle. "You don't have to be that good down here," he keeps saying, "Just have the equipment." But actually he's pretty good.

Pablo's old Thunderbird lurched by, covered in paper rosettes and smiling children. Grady and I waved frantically until we were sure his two brats had seen us and waved back. His snaggle-toothed four year old girl tried to toss us a piece of candy, but it hit another kid in the ear and he pelted her with gumballs until her older brother socked him on the head. So much for my community responsibilities.

I was just turning to hurry to work when I spotted a black convertible without any adornment except for an achingly lovely twelve-year-old girl in a red satin gown sitting on the rear seatback with a *ramo* of red roses cradled in her arms. She was so beautiful she stopped me in my tracks. For an instant she caught my eye and I waved to her like a loyal subject. She turned slightly as she trailed her hand back away from her mouth, wafting me a kiss as lingering as a vapor trail.

I watched as her car moved by and up the street. Grady, in a soft voice, said, "Future Carnival Queens of Mazatlán."And she might be in a few years. She has the looks, even the regal quality. On the other hand, who knows if she has the right parents? Like real royalty, Carnival queens don't just pop up through the ranks on looks and talent. They tend to be of the right family, and they have to pay their way.

Americans always react negatively when they find out there are financial routes to queenhood. Typically, they expect even Queens to be chosen democratically, and that to have heredity, much less inheritance, involved with it is corrupt and un-American. Like looks and talent aren't inherited. Actually it works out pretty well, and I would recommend the system to the Miss America Pageant, and even to the electoral system ... if it's not already in place. Candidates for Queen and Princess at any level in Mexico, from grade school to the Third Largest Carnival In The World, have to raise money for charity. Whoever pays most to help out gets the crown, plain and simple and no recount necessary. This doesn't mean that the queens are always those with the richest daddies, either. Their friends and supporters raise money for them, often stopping traffic to pester motorists with little cans and baskets for donations. A very popular girl in a small town or *barrio* can bring in more than a rich *papa* might care to donate just to see his little girl wearing a tiara and sash.

101

In Mazatlán there was a period when Queens were chosen by whoever collected the most bottle caps from a certain soft drink bottler that redeemed them for a few centavos each. When I tell Americans that the first Asian queen won because everybody in Mazatlán's large Chinese community chipped in caps for her, they seem somewhat mollified. Apparently the corruption of democratic process with money is not so bad if it promotes minority representation. As usual, Americans find that the relationship between corruption and democracy is more complex than they imagined.

Not that historical perspectives make it nobler to ogle a bunch of kids in costume. Maybe Grady's right and we're all just dirty old men from the time we quit being dirty little boys. Just as I had the thought, Grady grabbed me by the shoulder, snatched an earphone out of his ear, and stuck it in mine. I listened to the tinny voice of the announcer, then handed the plug back to Grady. Frankly, I didn't know what to say, or what to think.

He said, "I didn't think they'd actually *kill* the son of a bitch."

I said, "I've got to get to work."

So much for the workplace being more normal than yesterday. Maybe there'll be gusts of scattered normality in the late evening hours. As I hustled through the Shrimp Bucket sidewalk tables I heard Grady singing again, "Meet the new boss, same as the old boss." He sang the same song after the PRI's historic defeat last year; it's called, *Don't Get Fooled Again*. By a group called Who.

One thing that amazes me about the American penal system, at least the way they portray it on television and movie screens, is that they always threaten the drug dealers they are arresting with being anally raped in prison. They never seem to consider that the *narcos* might be the ones who perform the rapes, not receive them, but what makes me wonder is the idea that a justice system would offer sodomy by peers as the ultimate deterrent punishment.

"See Where Drugs Get You?" Raymundo Carrasco
Chamuco May, 1998

"Oh, they didn't just shoot him," Sergeant Reynosa chuckled. "No, *Señor*. You don't just don't gun down the mayor of the Second Largest Port In Mexico like he was some garden variety drug lord."

"So they shot him with protocol and he got to grabass a cute *chiquita* in a sash while they used a big ceremonial gun?" Nothing jump-starts the workday like hearing how your boss got killed.

"Might have been that way. Before they tied him up like a market pig, strapped him over a table, sliced him up with a scalpel, and stuffed his pecker in his mouth."

"Have you ruled out suicide?"

He narrowed his eyes shrewdly, glanced around, and dropped into a heavy, confidential purr. "I never rule out anything."

"Good thinking, Clouseau. I assume you have a list of suspects by now."

He reached in a drawer and pulled out a telephone book, then tossed it onto the desk in front of me. "That's just a partial list. We're following up leads."

"You work fast."

"I could work faster if I could learn to rule anything out."

"Like drinking on duty?"

"I wouldn't consider a couple of shots of Cabrito on an occasion like this."

"Well, not that I was offering them, over at Lo Peor around two."

"Sounds good to me," Hector Osuna said, sidling into the courtyard and over to the security desk. "We could consider it a sort of unofficial wake."

Osuna, the new Medical Examiner, is a waspy little jerk with an academic manner who might as well have embroidered 'Couldn't Make It In Mexico City' on the white lab coat he wears everywhere. I liked our old ME better before he got gunned down for mentioning that a powerful *narco* had AIDS at the time of his murder, a wiry, balding jock who played infield and basketball in the Intermedico league. Osuna didn't play anything but angles, desperate to work his way back to Mexico City. Like all *Chilangos*.

"I'm trying to remember what to ask coroners after media circus killings," I told him. "You know, just in case any questions should come up."

"I thought you might want a few facts when the press jackals swarm in. Sorry, I keep forgetting you're a sort of jackal emeritus." Yes, he's got that famous *Chilango* charm. "Time of death, about midnight. Body discovered around six, following anonymous call. You know all that from the Sergeant here, I assume."

"How about cause of death?"

"In the immediate, not historical, sense? Hard to determine exactly. It might have been all those pistol rounds in the extremities. From his own gun, by the way. Sort of symbolic, wouldn't you say?" He paused. "Shooting himself in the foot, I mean."

"We got that," Reynosa growled.

"Oh. Good. You never know. Anyway, it probably wasn't the various slices of flesh hacked off the body, but that can be more traumatic than you'd think, especially when some of the slices were originally intended for reproductive functions."

"Listen, maybe you should do the press conference. Those guys could use a little entertainment."

"Oh, I think my wit is over the heads of the mass media. But back to causality. Pounding the skull into a jellied lump would have done it, but we're wondering if he was still alive enough to truly benefit from that experience. The repeated stabs to the buttocks, back and thighs couldn't have helped, but my money's on the cauterization.

Putting myself in the killer's place – which I'm increasingly finding so enjoyable that I might have to seek some sort of counseling – I might have wanted our future ex-Mayor to get the full enjoyment of that perverted little opus, but I doubt he would have survived the shock in his weakened condition."

"Cauterization?" I could see Reynosa was interested in that one, too.

"Oh, that's right, you don't yet know about the *piece de resistance*. Probably token resistance by that point, I would think. If you allow somebody to strap you over a kitchen table naked, don't act surprised when their intentions towards your apertures turn out to be self-serving and even catastrophic."

"Can we go back to cauterization?"

"A medical circumlocution. Translates, in this case, into anal penetration with a cylindrical – or tubular, I suppose – foreign object, hot enough to fry meat on contact. Violent and repeated, let me hasten to amplify. Do you need it spelled out more graphically than that?"

"Last of the red-hot buttfucks."

"Yes, I imagine you would have to put it in terms your readers could understand."

"They're not my readers anymore."

"Oh, of course. These days you'd want to word things so the lay audience couldn't possibly understand them."

"You've been a big help with that. I can't wait to slip 'cauterized' into a press release."

Reynosa shook his head over it, "Cauterized, huh? Where I went to school we didn't have many rules, but that would have been one of them. You don't go around buggering folks to death with hot dildos."

He's always pulling that folksy *barrio pobre* stuff. But he lives in Playa Sur now, married to a pretty dentist, and sends their kids to the *Liceo*, not public education. I assume they honor the same rules against fatal pederasty as his working class schools.

Mijares stalked down the stairs, glancing under the balcony as she passed. She cut back and stepped into the shade around the desk, giving me a semi-scowl. About a 4.5

on her grimace-meter. "What are you doing down here?"

"Trying to avoid an office full of people going out of their minds and trying to share it with me. The Sarge grabbed me on the way in, brought me here for police briefing. And forensic." I bobbed my head at Osuna, who was giving Mijares the benefit of all his examination skills. I'm sure he was just burning with suppressed lust to incise her liver and weigh her entrails. The guy probably talks into a tape recorder during sex, reporting items of clinical interest.

"Good," she snapped. "Press comes in at three. We've been doing the leaks – could have used your help. But for now we've got a command appearance with Our Brother. His office, ten minutes."

You can't understand the Mexican Day of the Dead in terms of Halloween. The little frosting skulls are not to be shivered at, not even put on and tried for fit, they are to be eaten. Death as daily bread. *El Dia de los Muertos* is not Christian, doesn't involve dealing with the fear of death, it's about eating. It's just the day when the dead come back home to visit. The dead can't ever be gone; they are your family. Therefore they will always be you, until you are dead yourself. So you invite the dead to come share your table. And what's really commendable about the dead – they accept.

"A Day in the Death" by Raymundo Carrasco
Arizona Highways, November 1997

"Nothing is all that clear."

Which could have been Elias Tirado's personal logo, or even epitaph. He was lecturing us like a fuddled classics professor, leading the meeting the way the glummest mourner leads a funeral procession. The Mayor was allegedly dead and things looked reportedly glum. Or so it would possibly appear.

But one thing you had to forgive him for dithering over was the question of who would succeed Frederico Varedas as the titular head of The Pearl Of The Pacific. The more you poked at the question, the vaguer it got.

"As the leading *regidor* of the elected party, I will surely be confirmed for an interim period of ..."

"Thirty days," Mijares supplied.

"Thank you, my dear. During that period more permanent decisions will be made. Since our late Brother Varedas had not served three months, there is the possibility a new election will be called."

"A constitutionally stipulated possibility, at that," Mijares said, cloaking her obvious contempt with a deadpan delivery.

"Unless a majority of *regidores* can agree on somebody from an elected post to take over the Mayor's job."

Fat chance, I thought.

"Otherwise," Tirado droned on, "There is the possibility that the Governor, or I should say the State government, can simply decide to appoint a new mayor, as they would do if this tragic death had taken place more than ninety days after the election."

I was learning a lot. The whole city was learning what happens when you've mislaid your mayor. When foreigners are aware of the Napoleonic basis for Mexico's laws, they always focus on things like the accused bearing the burden of proving his innocence, or the lack of right to open trial or confronting accusers. Few get a peek at the Byzantine labyrinths of the power structure itself. Even citizens rarely take the time to try to unravel it. Because it's just a façade, what actually happens is that the big machine hidden back behind the ornate cathedral does what it wants to.

With Tirado's burble as a soothing background, I sized up the chances, and who would want what. *Nobody* in the room wanted a new election. If you were sitting here at this table today, trying not to yawn in Tirado's face, you were In. And those In seldom desire to be Out. Well, I did, but that also seemed to have gotten uncertain since Frederico had gotten his seat vacated for him. The idea of the *regidores* from six parties, including some loose change from the *Convergencia* and *Barzonists*, settling on a mayor acceptable to all was as likely as a bunch of alley dogs deciding to give a bone to the most deserving among them instead of ripping throats over it. Less likely, actually: there are always more bones.

Meanwhile Mijares, *Señorita Anarchista,* would have a big investment in keeping the status quo. The Governor was of the PAN persuasion, and Panistas would boot her right out after probably embroidering a scarlet ampersand across her *chi-chis.* It was difficult to imagine Tirado achieving similar stature in any conceivable government.

On the other hand, he was talking to me and I didn't know what about. "... something, something, Srta. Gortari and Sr. Carrasco." I had a feeling I hadn't had since school, daydreaming into a question, fighting the urge to look on somebody else's desk for the answer. And, as usual, it was the little teacher's pet who came though with the answer and saved my butt by making me look stupid.

"Of course, Sr. Tirado," she said primly, "We would both be glad to accept the challenges this brings us."

Oh, no! Not a challenge! I nodded solemnly, and realized that the whole thing meant I still had a job. As interim mayor, Tirado couldn't make big changes, but he could sure dump his PR employees if he wanted to. Especially me, essentially a non-civil service after-market accessory. But he wasn't going to. Worse, he was counting on us. Thank you Sir, I'll rush right over to Lo Peor and convince those press chumps that the rumors of death are exaggerated and Varedas is still in office. How would anybody know the difference?

But anyway, I still had a job. Mijares gave me a cool look, then patted my lower thigh under the table, which had the same effect as plugging it into a wall socket. My eyes rolled over and my underwear got suddenly tight and tangled. Yessir, Sr. Interim, I am up for the job.

"The city ... the people ... need each and every one of us right now more than ever before. Doing our jobs, working for our ideals."

I stared at him like a wide-eyed dog, willing myself to pay attention to his bullshit and not my raging erection or Mijares' aroma.

"I know much of what happened has confused you, made you question our mission here," he droned on. A less tumescent man would be snoring again already. "Working under these conditions ... I will say it ... under our late mayor, might have caused many of you to have doubts, to become cynical."

Or increased the stock of pre-existing cynicism, I thought.

"I have asked myself on more than one occasion – and I trust this will go no further than this room – 'Can you work for a deplorable man and still retain your own integrity?'"

Oh, good question. I had been avoiding answering it myself. But I didn't have to worry.

"There is no reason to side-step such a question. The government is an extension of the people. We are members of a team, cells in vital organs. We do not share the blame if another player or another cell fails in their duty. We all must just do our best. And we must all shoulder extra burdens, make the greatest efforts to serve this city in spite of such bad influences, and to rid the city of negative elements when we can; even if the negativism is only a part of our own attitude."

No problem, boss. Just keep talking long enough so that I can stand up without everybody reading my mind. Which, of course, he did. There's nothing like the solidarity of brotherhood to wilt an unrequited woody.

And he didn't let up, even when the pep rally had nodded out and everybody was sleepwalking back to their desks to shoulder additional burdens. He cut off my escape and beckoned me over to a corner. Mijares cut her eyes at me as she left the room, an eyebrow of caution, a shadow of smile, a hint of scent, a waste of erection. Naturally, he wouldn't get to the point.

"I feel sorry for Brother Frederico," he said piously. "He really didn't belong in all this. He was just used, picked up the way you pick up a pen or hammer. He was nothing but a tool."

You said it, I thought. Actually, Xochitl said it first. About five minutes after the first time she went into his office by herself.

"... to put his errors behind us, to start forgetting, letting things heal over." He was back into full drone. Listening to him long enough, I could forget my name. My ears could heal over.

"That's why I want you to do something for me, Mundo. Go over to El Cereso and release that boy who came after Frederico with the gun."

"I don't have authority to ..."

"I've already signed his release, but they'll hold him until you go there to talk to him. Tell him I have forgiven his crimes and he should do the same. And tell him to go back to Guadalajara to avoid future trouble here. Who knows who will make decisions about him next week? If he has no money, call me then drive him to the station. I will arrange for his ticket. I see no good that can come to the city if he stays here."

I had to agree with that, and was glad the *pistolero* was getting sprung. He seemed like too promising a kid to

110

have his life ruined so young. Plenty of time for that later. I bowed my way out of Tirado's presence and escaped the room. He might have still been talking when I left. Or it might have been the air conditioner.

I dropped by Public Information before heading to the jail. Mijares was gone, but had left detailed suggestions for my session at Lo Peor. I walked around the desks, using my bluff, manly dugout persona to buck up the *info-chicas*. Only Xochitl asked me what we should do. I told her, "Tell them they can look at the body for fifty pesos apiece, but nobody better grab any snapshots or souvenirs. Anyway, the main item is already in a jar of formaldehyde, and on its way to the state museum."

"They cut it off?" Little Yazmin would believe anything, "That's so sad, because that was about all there was to the guy. A dick with hands."

"Don't forget the nostrils. From what I hear about the *item*," Xochitl gave her an arch look, "they wouldn't need a very big jar."

"Is that all that's important to you women?" I asked, "Size? It makes us feel so cheap."

"Well, you also have to take into account the firmness." Xochitl posed prettily behind her cleavage. Jesus, Mijares isn't around for a half-hour and they're all over me. A comforting thought, I guess, but ... you know. God forbid I should get involved with anybody at the office.

At El Cereso, I found Tavo Lazares in a holding cell, sitting on the cement bunk benches with a few skinny, huddled addicts. I snuck a look around for telltale bloodstains, but mostly just saw grunge. He was rumpled and had a few scrapes, including on his knuckles, but looked in good repair if not exactly ecstatic. It might have been the smell of the place. I called his name as the jailer opened the barred door and he took one look at me and flopped over backwards on the bench, laughing softly. The turnkey who'd led me to the cell looked at me quizzically and I shrugged.

Tavo got up and walked over to the door as I scanned the cell – alert by habit for local color and possibly reportable abuses and scandals.

He said, "I don't believe it. Rescued by Mundo Carrasco."

Two of the junkies looked up at that, then lost interest.

When he was outside the door I handed him his possessions, including belt and shoelaces. He stashed away what stuff they had left him and said he had left his money at his brother's apartment and was hot to blow town as quick as possible.

I asked him, "How did they do all that graffiti in there if they take everything away from you?"

He shrugged, "The guys seemed to have plenty of matches and cigarettes. They set fire to their arrest papers and write their names in smoke."

The cell walls and ceiling were a single squirm of graffiti, but one caught my eye. It was a negative graffito, rubbed out of the mass of competing names, it said, "Micro-Bio". I was pissed.

I turned to the jailer and said, "You had him and let him *go*?"

He gave me the same look he'd given Tavo, and I quickly said, "Sorry, it was about an author I know."

Tavo said, "Come on. I want to get out of this town," and hustled us the hell out of there. In the taxi, I told him I could spring for his ticket back to Guadalajara, since I had never heard of anybody walking out of El Cereso with any of their money in their pockets.

He told me he wasn't leaving town. "I just said that for the audience. You think somebody will talk to the jailer?"

I hadn't thought of that, but thinking of it made me nervous. I told the driver to take us to La Puntilla. We walked through the tables and beckoning waiters to take seats right over by the water, looking down on the surrounding rabble of fishing *pangas* and tourism catamarans. We had a great view of the gilded Virgin de la Puntilla, ready to bless any fishing fleet that might happen to chug out of the estuary into the chop of the open Pacific. I ordered a Corona, he got a Pacifico and lifted it towards the twin towers of the brewery a mile down the waterfront. Then he reached out to clink it against my bottle.

"Incredible," he said. "You were such a hero to me when I was a kid, playing in the *Juveniles*. And now I'm grown up and you pop in and spring me from jail. Shouldn't you be wearing tights and a cape?"

"I was just the messenger. The new acting mayor had you released. And invited to see charming Guadalajara at your earliest."

"The acting mayor?"

"Actually the previous one was sort of acting, too. But somebody more efficient had your same idea. He's dead."

He nodded absently at that, as though it didn't surprise him. "Good thing I had an alibi. Disturbing the jailers' sleep while defending my honor."

"So Brother Tirado thought it would be best for everybody involved if you would just disappear."

He stared at me for a moment. "Tirado?"

"Elias Tirado. Interim Mayor, *Municipio de Mazatlán*."

He drank some more beer, looking out past the slick green water to the shacks tumbling up the shaggy mound of *Isla de la Piedra*. "Well, fuck mayors. I'd rather accept you as my personal savior. I can't tell you how much I admired and looked up to you when you were playing."

"Sure you can. Make it completely embarrassing."

"No, seriously. I can't begin to tell you. Believe me."

"So where did you play? Sorry, I don't remember seeing you."

"*Ciencias del Mar*. Nobody made a big deal about teams from Marine Sciences."

I laughed. "*Ciencias del Bar*?"

"You know," he said, smiling, "The famous scholarship to study *ballenas*."

Trite but true. A *ballena* is a whale in Spanish, but in Mazatlán it's universally understood to mean a liter bottle of beer because of the whale on the label of the Pacífico quarts. Everywhere else in Mexico a liter bottle is a *caguama*, meaning a sea turtle. We seem to find something highly jolly, maritime and yo-ho-ho about big bottles of beer. Probably reflecting a deep-seated need to drown.

"But secretly, you were more interested in baseball than drinking. What position?"

"What else?" he grinned, "A pitcher."

I laughed. "Of course. And my natural enemy."

"Just a student of your behavior."

I took a few more sips myself, wondering how to proceed. Finally I said, "Look, since you're a pitcher, maybe I can spare you the windup. I want to ask about your brother. Is he, you know ..."

"A *puto?*"

"Well, yeah. I wouldn't have necessarily put it like that, though."

"Was he a *joto, lilo, ave rara?* Is that your question?"

"It was. I'm sort of losing interest."

"I don't think so. He was a little effeminate, sexually backward, but I don't think he was queer. He's having some doubts in the matter now, of course. But, why do you ask ... because if he got it, he must have been asking for it?"

"No, man. Just wondering ... about the impact of it a little. And also if Varedas might have known that and figured ..."

"No, actually, I'm the *joto* in the family."

Whoa, caught me on the change-up. "What? You ... you're serious?"

"Didn't think macho ballplayers went that way, huh?"

"Actually, I always thought pitchers were a bunch of cocksuckers. Plate umpires, too."

He nodded emphatically. "We can agree on the umpires anyway. Blind cocksuckers at that. They give you fucking batters every *pinche* break, just because they can't see anything moving that fast and don't want to admit it."

"The politics of the game. What's getting to me is the game of politics. Do you remember the *Juego Limpio* campaign? I just happened to think of it."

"Of course. I believed in that completely, you know. The whole Clean Play campaign, pure sports, pure bodies, the fellowship of sportsmanship."

"Me too. It was a mistake to try to make national politics conform to those ideals."

"Maybe you should have stuck with baseball."

114

"Nah, I'd just have been one more player not quite good enough for the Bigs."

"But you *made* the Bigs!"

"But not for good. Making it, but not for keeps, is a recurring theme in my work. Not to mention my love life."

"Don't mention yours and I won't mention mine."

"I appreciate that. But you know what it really was? I just couldn't go become a gringo. I don't really know why. I'm just a *nopalero* at heart, I guess."

"So to keep from being second rate you played for the Venados? Not even the Mexican big leagues?"

"Are you kidding? The Venados aren't second rate. They're the team, hombre. Don't you remember that? You're playing in the *Infantiles*, thinking you're better than a couple of the older guys in the *Juveniles*, and trying to get your *papi* to take you to the Venados games to see the *real* thing, dreaming of hearing your name over the loudspeakers there, everybody you know waving and screaming *Oles*? That was the show, you know. I guess I just never grew out of it."

"There should be a Peter Pan League."

"Good idea. With Tinker Bell for the umpire."

"Tinkerbell?"

"You know, *Campanita*."

"Ah, yes, my favorite fairy. But I grew out of that."

I leaned back, relaxing a little. "So you'll probably grow out of revenge, too."

He gave me a hard look that didn't sit well on his handsome boyish face. "Oh, there's still room for improvement. My brother wasn't cruising for what he got. He wanted to get into politics, to move close to ... you know, to *it*. But I think he got sort of served up to your boss. By a sort of procurer system that sucks people in and fucks them, then walks over them."

I was starting to share that view. "So what can you do about it?"

The hardness in his face crystallized again, with a sharper, feline quality that was a little scary, especially from such a pretty, soft-spoken kid. "Punish them."

I said, "How, by confrontations at pistol-point?"

He stood up suddenly, and walked over to the rail, staring down for a minute at the boys swimming in the mucky water, diving for tourists' coins. He shook his shoulders and sat back down, his face back to normal. "I think I've decided pistols are a bad idea. But confrontation is not. The truth, face to face."

"There are a lot of faces in The System. At least two per capita."

"Well, if I get started right now ..." but he was smiling.

"You scientific types are always so naive about the real world," I said.

"Well, for a guy who played a kid's game for a living, you seem to have some ideas about *El Mundo*."

I leaned over and touched his shoulder. "Wouldn't it be better to just confront Everybody all at once?"

He was interested but hadn't gotten it yet, so I said, "*Todo el mundo*, kid. What do you think 'Mass Media' means?"

It takes a while to see it, but the *machista* fixation on women stems from a deeper factor of Mexican masculinity, Mexican men are uncomfortable around women. And much more uncomfortable around women not yet dominated. It's one reason why men always congregate outside at social gatherings. Squatting in the yard, standing around a pickup truck, hanging out on the sidewalk. Because inside it's all full of women. The male Mexican is a family man who is terrified by women and children, a passionate seducer who would rather be with his male friends. We relax in one-sex cantinas, where the only women are waitresses or whores. Once a man has mounted a woman, she recedes into his comfort zone, one example more of fixation fading to indifference as rapidly as the lust of a stallion is spent.

"Machismo for Beginners" by Mundo Carrasco
Slate Website, November 1996

"You know, Varedas didn't really have a whole lot of charm."

"No, but he had warmth up the butt." Beto and Mocho cackled like two street *payasos* and slapped each other high fives.

I was just sitting there waiting for it to blow itself out. Not that I hadn't been enjoying the last half-hour of *humor negro*. I wished I could use some of it in my column, but then, so did they all. Newsmen are at their best, which is to say worst, especially in the Lo Peor, when doing material they know they could never print. Besides, for once there was nothing to cover up. And with the mayor dead, my conviction to quit had greatly diminished. I didn't have to quit the mayor; he'd quit me. *Sobres!*

Major Tom said, "Yeah, Fat Freddy got burned again," but I had no idea what he was talking about.

"Well, it hardly matters," Carlito said to me, all earnest and serious, "He's no longer a sitting Mayor."

Mocho just about fell off his stool.

I kept a straight face, too. "Well, at least he got that hemorrhoid problem all ironed out." I picked that one up from Sergeant Garcia, but they all loved it. Mexicans don't have quite the twisty genius for sick jokes that Americans do, but we're closing the gap rapidly these days. The psychologists and sociologists all say it's a subconscious way to insulate against shock and belittle fear, but actually I think it's pretty much a chance to be funny, maybe shock a few people. Nobody around the Lo Peor, though.

Major Tom asked me, "Is it true the Mayor was born in Esquinapa but reared in Mazatlán?"

Beto came on with, "No, but he was a week behind at the office."

Eusebio frowned, "What the hell does that mean?"

"A weak behind," Beto wheedled, "W ... e ... a ... k."

Mocho shook his head, "But what does that have to do ... I mean, what's the point?

"Oh, fuck off."

I thanked them for the outpouring of sympathy and quiet dignity we expect from the working press during difficult times. And promised that the authorities would get to the bottom of the matter. Which touched off hilarity far out of proportion.

"Send 'em to the hot seat, will they Mundo?" somebody yelled. "Stick them in The Hole?"

So much for restricting forensic information. I will say, though, that nobody leaked the item in print or on the air. It got around the bars and grapevines, but we'd already used up all the easy jokes. That's another big reason why people become journalists. You always hear it first. And are egocentric enough to think that matters.

Suddenly the whole room went quiet, as if somebody pulled the plug out of the frivolity machine. I glanced at the closest faces, followed their gaze to the door. Rocío Linares was coming through the door. She had a double tequila in her hand. *¡Hijole!*

Rocío walked into the Salón Elizabeth Taylor like a strong swimmer striding into the surf. Making eye contact all around, making much of looking for a seat. Nobody leaped up to offer her one. She walked up to table where I was sitting with Carlito and Major Tom and said, "*Permiso?*" And well she should ask. Major Tom, being gringo and less aware of the unwritten, unspoken, and now flagrantly unobserved prohibition of women in *cantinas*, pulled a chair over from Eusebio's table and she sat down beside me, took a sip of her tequila, and lit a cigarette. A harsh, unfiltered, working-class Delicado.

She looked around and said, "So what's the difference between Catholic birth control and the Mayor's retirement plan?"

Nobody spoke, nobody much moved. I felt attention bearing down on me, You screwed her, you get rid of her. I turned to her and smiled – I always smile when I look at Rocío actually – and said, "Welcome to No Man's Land."

She didn't return my smile. "Looks more like No Women Land to me."

She had managed to get higher in her field than any woman in Mazatlán had ever gotten, and now she was going to push her luck. I was liking her better all the time.

I said, "Well, most women have more self-respect than to come to a place like this."

"Oh, I respect *myself*, all right. Most of the time," flicking a cold eye my way. "Is there anybody else here I should respect?"

I looked around, "Let me think a minute. How about Carlito?"

She laughed out loud, which surprised me and made me think this wasn't going to go very well, after all. Then she said, "Just kidding! I have a lot of respect for all of you. The press guys, anyway. Why do you think I went into newspaper work?"

Carlito seemed to pause a minute, like poising for a dive, then said, "Hunting for a top-grade husband?"

She didn't snag on her feminism for a second. "Oh please. Who respects husbands?"

"Nobody I ever married," Carlito muttered. He's on his third wife and it's not looking good.

"I've been doing some thinking," Rocío said softly, which got leery attention. We knew she was capable of it, just doubted we would like what she came up with.

"I'm a member of the press in this town, and I'm young and new, but I'm a colleague. I do what you do, I know what you know, I go where you go."

"See you next week in the Venados' locker room, in that case," Ramón cracked. One reason he remained with *Adelante* is that it lets him cover sports as well as breaking news. He thought the idea was funny, but if he'd played ball in the Bigs, he'd have known the joke would be on him. In a decade or so.

Rocío stopped his grin with a glance and went on, "I've realized that a lot of what happens in this profession happens here. So I decided I should be here."

Hard to argue with that. And hard not to pass the word that we would start meeting at Ramses instead. But Beto plunged into the breach.

"This is a *cantina*," he stated. He was only fairly safe grounds there, but abandoned it immediately. "This is a place for men. Just because they let you cover city hall doesn't make you a man."

"Neither does a clumsy haircut, Beto." And he does get rotten haircuts, too. "Look, how long have you been writing?"

"Over twenty years." He stuck his chest out and straightened his head.

"So you can read, too?"

"Listen, *Señorita* ..."

"So you can tell me what this says?" She flipped him a small metal badge with a pin on the back. Beto picked it up gingerly and looked at it, it seemed to be a realtor's name pin. He said, "Century Twenty One."

"Congratulations." Rocío said. "And welcome."

She turned to me and asked, "Mundo. Will you have a press conference on this?" Everybody else had just assumed we would. And play it for all the breast-beating and solemnity we could.

I told her there would be no meeting. "We've already got releases out to all of you. You can pick them up at my office or wait until the messenger brings them to yours. By four. Ibaes Tirado Alemán, as head regidor, will assume the duties until a successor is appointed by the Governor. Any statements from us will focus on the city's future, if you catch my drift."

"Not on regrets for the loss of a brutal, wife-beating, rapist addict?" Once Rocío makes up her mind to get in the water she doesn't ease in, she jumps.

I said, "I think the quality of our loss will be understood and appreciated."

"But you do kind of wonder who might have killed him, don't you?" Mocho teased, "Just a little bit?"

"We're on the edge of our seats with suspense. We are driving the police crazy with questions. I assume you will, too. Talk to *Teniente* Camacho, *sub-comandante* of Homicide. He'll be in his office all day and will also issue reports to you directly."

"I think I'll go see Camacho right now," Rocío said, finishing her drink and standing up. "See you guys tomorrow."

Nobody said any different. Mexico has gone through more change in the first two years of this century than the last decade of the old one. You end up just laying back and wondering where it's all going. Like the old guy on the Hector Suarez show used to say, "*¿Que nos pasa?*"

As she pulled open the glass door, Carlos called across the room. "Hey, Roci."

She turned to him, head cocked expectantly.

"So what's the difference?"

A cloud blew across her brow and her eyes tightened up as she started to speak.

Carlito said, "You know, Catholic birth control or the Mayor's retirement clause?"

She gave a victory smile that was both tough and touching. She'd been asked a question, called by a familiar name. Interest had been expressed in what she had to say. Which was, "Both ways you get it up the butt, but if you're the Mayor you don't have to pretend you're enjoying it."

She stepped out the door to friendly, if not overwhelming, laughter.

As soon as the door closed Beto said, "I don't get it."

Eusebio said, "You ever wonder why?"

Everybody watched her walk along the glass wall towards the exit. Including all the guys out in the main room. She didn't give them a glance. One of the waitresses scowled and turned her back on her. The other one held out her palm for a high five, then laughed out loud.

Chuy popped his head through the service window, scanned us and sneered. "You guys are having women in there with you now? What are you, a bunch of faggots?"

Mocho said, "That was no woman, that was my competition."

Chuy, with that flat voice of prophecy we've learned to respect, said, "I think she'll be back."

Carlos nodded slowly. "Yeah, she probably will."

Chuy shrugged. "*Me vale madre.* She probably doesn't tip, either," and popped back through his hole in the wall.

The door swung open again and we looked around, but it was Ramón D'Alba from *Adelante.* He beamed at us and said, "Hey, I've got a hot tip on the Mayor."

"So stick it!" we chorused.

So they are moving the *"Zona de Tolerancia"*, the notorious "red zone", out of Colonia Zapata because the neighbors voted that they no longer want it there, where it has been since before there were any neighbors. Maybe that makes sense, but where are they going to move it? Should they take out an ad, only prostitution-friendly neighborhoods need apply? And what purveyor of flesh is going to be confident in investing in a new *burdel* when the whole thing can be tossed out at any time? One lesson in the virtue of tolerance, the police, who make money off prostitution, have permitted what the voting citizens, who pay to support it, now prohibit.

"El Mundo Según Mundo"
Noroeste May 2000

I don't normally leave work tense and irritated, but it's not every day that your boss is sodomized to death. I assumed that things could only get mellower, but decided to drop by the Altazor Café anyway. Couple of beers would do me good. I sat at the smallest table on the sidewalk, screened slightly by the Bacardi umbrella and ficus tree. Joaquín had barely brought my Dos Equis when Palomina slid gracefully into the other chair, graced me with a wide-eyed smile and ordered sangria. She reached under the table and gave my thigh two sharp pats, like you would pet the ribs of a big dog. We sipped without saying anything, and I felt a lot less tense. She opened a copy of the café's little newsletter for the intellect and skimmed the articles. She snickered, showed me a headline that said, "Varedas Must Go!" I rolled my eyes upward, smiling.

From behind me, somebody said, "Prophesy in print, no?"

Luz Ibarrez strode up beside the table. She leaned down to accept my kiss on her cheek, then motioned to Juaquín for another chair. She was wearing her everyday Boho Collection, elegant hippie stuff topped off by a selection from her apparently endless collection of shawls, stoles, and *rebozos* – a slubby Peruvian alpaca *gavan*. What North Americans would call a *poncho*. Well, actually, what they persist in calling a 'Pancho'.

She was bubbling over with her usual blaze of positive energy, plus a very unYogi-like delight in the ex-Mayor's misfortune.

I broke into her glee, "But the PT will still be in control. They'll still have the same budget. And maybe they will now actually be able to get things done."

"Ah but they won't have his genius for destruction, that was an individual gift. What do you think would have happened to the arts festival with him in charge? The man's idea of culture was *banda* and table dancing."

The thought passed through my head that I see more table dances than ballet performances myself, but Palomina went on red alert at the remark, demanding, "And what's wrong with table dancing?"

Luz leaned back and studied Palomina the way she would examine a new backdrop for her flamenco academy's recital. "You were at The School a few years ago, weren't you?"

Palomina, very surprised, nodded, but she still had her nostrils widened and her tits at present arms.

"Yes," Luz went on, "I saw your recital. I thought you were very talented, but not sensual enough for Bizet. Perhaps you have compensated for that."

Palomina was equally prepared to accept compliments graciously or lash out like a flame-thrower, but didn't quite know how to deal with that one. She tried a neutral corner. "There isn't much income in ballet these days." You could sense she would welcome a fight, but wasn't yet sure if it was appropriate.

Luz did her thing, hosed her down with stark positive radiation. "Exactly. Where is the funding for performing arts ... when they can spend thousands on hiring rock bands to play at the marathon?" Palomina nodded, warily.

"But you," Luz rolled on, "Are working. Still dancing."

Facing down the intense, culture-vulture gaze, Palomina said, "I dance at Ramses."

That's where the big bucks are in table dance, she had told me. She makes less than most of the other girls because she doesn't do blow jobs in the private rooms, but still makes over two hundred dollars a night in a country where the minimum wage is under four dollars for a ten hour day.

Luz surprised her by saying, "How very nice. So few dancers manage to continue with it after school. It's wonderful you're earning a living through dance. May I ask you?"

Guarded, "What?"

"Are you still enjoying the dance? Are you excelling in it?"

Palomina thought a long time. "I am definitely excelling. Absolutely. I change my mind every day whether I still enjoy it or not." She paused, looking around the Plaza. "But I am sure about one thing."

"Yes?"

"I like dancing naked in front of men a lot more than I liked doing ballet in front of all those frigid twats and their bored husbands."

Luz didn't blink. "Then you are still dancing and are happy. You don't know how lucky you are. Do you have any goals to work for?"

Palomina looked at her for a moment. "I'd like to dance ballet on the stage at the Peralta, naked. Just for the art of it."

I said, "Now, that might get me to the ballet."

"That's what you go to Ramses for, Mundo," Palomina said. "It's not about full-contact to you, you like to see bodies move, look good, don't you?"

"Well, who doesn't?"

"I could go on and on." She leaned toward Luz. "I like dancing naked. I think it should be like that, not in those stupid little skirts and tights. There is something very pure about it, very Greek."

Her body is sort of between a ballerina's and a stripper's, buxom, but very slim, tight and hard. She likes to get fairly interpretative up on the stage at Ramses, fans, feathers, wings. She likes to get up on the brass poles and whirl around like the Pampamtla Fliers. I suddenly saw her on a Carnival float, wearing only feathers and wings. It would be wonderful.

I said, "I thought the naked Greek thing was gymnastics?"

125

She scoffed, "Big difference."

I think Luz could handle the corruption of dance to sex better than comparing it to gymnastics. For whatever reason, she suddenly stood up and said, "Ciao."

She leaned over to kiss my cheek, then quickly did the same to Palomina, who was too surprised to react one way or the other, then started away, waving to other tables.

Palomina spoke up enough for Luz to hear her, "You know what, though?"

Luz stopped, turned and came back to the table, giving her the full, rapt attention. Palomino said, "I think you'd find my dance a lot more sensual these days."

Luz beamed, and with no trace of sarcasm or condescension said, "The things that don't destroy us make us more brilliant." Then she was gone, cutting through the crowd like a marlin.

Palomina looked at me with a simmer of complicity, two conspirators undercutting the sweet reign of Truth and Light. "Just a couple of sinners sitting here drinking the devil's milk."

I beckoned Juaquín. "Another round, if you've milked the devil lately."

He nodded briskly, "We have switched suppliers, we use the Whore of Babylon now."

Palomina sipped the last of her sangria and looked serious. "Mundo, do you enjoy your work?"

"In other words, Are We Whores?"

"Yeah. In other words."

"Hell, we can afford to be."

She said, "Can we?"

I'd been thinking that over a bit, myself. I asked, "If you meet a man you like and take him to bed, does that make you a whore?"

"My mother certainly says so."

"But what if, afterwards, he gives you money?"

"Instead of before? Is that what makes the difference, if you're sure of payment?" She was smiling, enjoying where it was going. She doesn't think things on her own, just does things. One of the reasons I like her.

"No, I think it's whether you would do them

126

whether you got paid or not."

She frowned at that, "Well, then I guess I qualify. I love to dance, but you can't be as expressive sitting on somebody's crotch. You've heard how I'm lacking in sensuality."

"So you work in too close because you need the money, and I do because I need to know. I'm just too curious. Not technically whores, that's us."

She said, "I used to be curious myself. About men, you know. Now I think I know more than I need to and you know what? After you find it out it just doesn't seem very interesting after all."

"Once you girls get what you want, you lose interest in us?"

"Wouldn't you?" She looked impish, then suddenly turned serious, "You know, I tried straight-out whoring a little, Mundo. And spare me your shock, okay? I've left all that school stuff a long way behind. I wanted to see what it felt like, sort it out from lap dancing. And there is a difference about what I'm doing, what the men are doing. Lap dance is a shared thing, something men do together. I almost never get single men in there. Whoring is the opposite; the man is totally, completely alone. I'm not even there, myself."

"So maybe that's what makes it whoring or not? Whether or not you're really there?"

"Good working definition."

"How about when you're not working? A recreational definition?"

"Easy, the whore is the one who gets fucked."

"No, both do, don't they? But the whore gets the money, the customer gets the satisfaction."

"What if I'm satisfied with the money?" She looked straight into my eyes.

"Then you're just lucky, I guess."

"Well, there are worse things than having to charge for it."

"Such as?" I really wanted to hear this.

"Having to pay for it." Well, she had a good point there.

"How about," I asked, "Having to crawl for it?"

127

"Oh I don't see that as a problem at all. Men beg for it all the time. So do women. One way or another. The difference is, men can stand rejection and we can't."

She opened the newspaper and peered at me over the edge of it. "Anyway," she said, "How would you like a freebie? Every man's dream – free loving from a non-technical whore."

"I'd appreciate and admire it," I told her, reaching over to pull the paper down so I could see the small, delicately downy cleft of her upper lip, "Even knowing I'm unworthy. But I'm serious, Mina, this thing with Mijares has got me in the grip, you know? I just can't really even focus on other women until it burns itself out."

She was staring at me, so I shrugged and said, "Well, I'm sure it won't last."

"Which, her or your feelings for her?"

"Either or both. How would I know? All I know is right now, right at the moment she's standing there in front of me, I just light up. I sizzle. She cooks my goose, and there's no limit in sight."

"*Chin*. Mundo, that's so romantic." She said it teasingly, but there was an undercurrent of wistfulness that surprised me. She must have seen it, and she blurted, "I just like sitting with a man who isn't trying to wander his hands up any convenient orifice."

I shrugged to match her blasé pose, "I just haven't found any of them convenient."

She smiled, and looked at me awhile, shyly. "No, really, Mundo, I wish I could get in on something like that. What would you call it ... devotion?"

"Renunciation. Like in the song, *Esta dulce y total renunciación.*"

"*Solamente Una Vez*. So you only have that sweet surrender once in your life?"

"Well, he had a lot of famous lovers, didn't he? Agustín Lara?"

"So they say, but maybe he only really gave himself once. Maybe I'm like that, too, Mundito. One offer only. You're passing up a spectacular chance here, I have to tell you."

"Don't rub it in."

"Well, I won't ask you again. I don't really measure up to her, anyway, do I?"

I looked at her and for just a second saw something like the gold glitter of mica flecks in the surf, saw something inside her shyly peeking out of her eyes, her features momentarily softening around it, framing herself for a brief flicker. What I saw was, she is a lot like me. And she measures up just fine. But I was not in love with her, and the peepshow shut down for lack of proper response. One more sacrifice on the altar fires of Mijares.

"I guess I shouldn't be surprised that you'd pass up a chance like me," she said, looking down at the paper. "You're passing up on Mijares, too, aren't you?"

That took me aback, all right. "It's more like she's passing up on me."

She looked up and smiled. "Good place for one of your old movie lines. 'Then she's as big a fool as you are.' How's that?"

"Not bad at all. So what can I do?"

"Stop mooning. Walk in and grab her. Let her know who you are, for Christ's sake. Save her life and gallop off or swing through the trees with her in your arms. That works every time."

"I doubt if she'd take my personal call."

"Then kick in her door and clutch her to your manly chest, you *tarardo*. Don't you pay any attention to the love scenes? Just ask yourself what Pedro Infante would do. Or better yet, Clark Gable."

She'd caught me out there. I'd always idolized and identified with Gable. We have the same wide shoulders and big ears. I'd even experimented with a similar mustache, but gave it up. Just clean-cut through and through, I suppose.

She said, "You could practice it on me. Hey, you're a *macho Mexicano*, since when do you care?"

I gave her a heavy-lidded stare and said, "Frankly, Harlot, I do give a damn."

She reached out and patted my cheek and said, "Damn."

There's no real secret to hitting .400 for the season. I tell the young would-be sluggers all the time, but they don't pay any attention. Here it is again, never swing for the fence. You want to do just enough to get on. That's all batting averages are about, making it to first base.

Mundo Carrasco, interviewed for *Beisbol Hoy*, April, 1992

Beachview space right on the Malecón seems like an odd place for Wild Pitch, but there are still vacant lots in the middle of the five mile curve of boardwalk so why shouldn't there be a batting cage? The wide, paved seafront walkway was the giant step in Mazatlán tourism's march north to the Promised Land. First there were the big hotels, the DeCima, the Hacienda, classy high-rise for the New Maz. Then smaller, motel-type places as the fifties and sixties progressed. The Aquamarina, the Sands/Arena. And dozens of little places, cheap view of the waves across the street. Little *palapa*-roofed seafood shacks right on the sand. A bracing stroll with your choice of wave height along miles of tropical beach.

Then the Malecón reaches Valentino's, the glittering white Disney castle lit up on its rock thrust out into the sea ... and it's all over. From there on out, hotels are right on the beach and it's a tourist trap, gringo style, so the Malecón will probably never be totally built up. I suppose it helps *El Profe* a little that he's right where passing vacationers can see him, haul their brats in for some batting practice. But location isn't much of a factor when most of the business is ball players: college, civic leagues, even pros from the Venados come in to tune up.

I come in to tune down. Somehow the beers in the Machado hadn't unwound me much and had left me feeling like a complete chump. Wild Pitch is my real relaxation, my drug of choice. It's the place where everything makes sense and I understand exactly what I'm doing. The place where it's okay to lash out and hit something. There are no incidents or egos here, the machines spit the balls out at a nice, regular place. If they slam out into the netting at the same regular pace it's because of you, nobody else. If not, you can work on it. A man needs something like this, I think, and I'm lucky to have such a place where I can concentrate totally without a worry or thought.

Some people play golf to relax. Or so they say. I've tried golf. After one round I am so relaxed I feel like wrapping the clubs around somebody's head. It's just so stupid ... what is the point of it all? Driving is okay, but pitching and putting and all that standing around sort of crap is just too tedious. Make the little ball roll slowly into the hole. Talk about business. A woman's game, I'd say. A rich woman's game. Makes you bitchy. Bashing balls makes you calm, cool, and languid. Maybe a little horny.

Gabriel, the kid who runs the place for the Prof, went and got the little star-shaped wrench as soon as he saw my car pull into the lot. He could tell I wasn't into a lot of chatter, just handed me the wrench and went back to selling tokens to some slightly drunken *gordos* from the Z Leagues who were fanning so hard in the seventy mile an hour cage that they needed insurance against attacks by Don Quixote. They kept peering at me through the chain link of the two cages between the fast lane and slow lane. I used the wrench to reset the forty mph machine up to ninety-five, a nice, easy workout. Mexican macho keeps grown men from using the slow machine, and little leaguers don't show up late at night.

I clobbered the machine for three tokens' worth of balls, and was about to set it up to a hundred when the door squealed open. It was the Prof, stepping in to pick up my bat and take a few swings. Moves smooth for his age.

He said, "I could tell who it was just by the sound of the bat." Bullshit, of course, he could tell by the sound the machine makes when you torque it up. And the death rattle of Das Boots' engine dieseling. He'd been up over the office watching me work out.

I shook hands with him and tapped the bat, "The *Nacionál* sent me all the way to Bogotá and all I got was this funky old bat."

He shook his head, "That thing should be in the sports museum. I'm surprised you still have it. Of course you still have all of it, don't you? The laser eyes, the high-light film swing."

132

"Not really," I said as I set the *pichadora* at a hundred mph and hit up two more tokens, forty balls firing out into the dark and twitching into the netting. The Prof stood there watching with his hands stuck in his rear pockets the way he used to, his elbows sticking out like a gamecock's wings. He was still tall, lean and scuffed-up looking, maybe stooping a little now – if you looked you'd still notice the shoulders. The disapproving vertical grooves seemed deeper, but they'd always been there.

When the token expired he said, "No, you've still got it, kid. Every bit of it. Like watching classic newsreels. I tell people you hit .550 your first year in school and nobody believes me."

"Too bad I was such a rotten fielder, huh?"

"Used to drive me out of my mind. But what was worse, the University hires me away out of the pros because I was such a damned wizard batting coach, and the first blue chip player I get, turns out he was *born* knowing how to hit .400. And can't be taught to field. So you'll be playing for the *Palacio* this season, I suppose?"

"No, probably in the *Periodistas.*"

"Sure, help *El Debate* get another championship?"

"I don't know, *Profe.* Maybe on the Lo Peor team, or back with Polluelos. That new coach at '*Bate* is nuts."

He nodded, the eagle on his faded old UAS cap making three quick dips. "Estevez," he said, like he was naming something lamentable and probably contagious.

"He's bunt happy. Signals bunts five times in an inning. In the Bigs they don't bunt five times in a season. This tells you something."

"Ah, you just like to hit away. And you can't take coaching. Hell, if anybody oughta know. City Hall has some good players lately, I think they're about due."

"They've asked me to suit up. Sent me up a shirt with my name on it, like it was all arranged. Then they applied a little pressure – but I guess that's what city hall is all about."

"Except in real life, the pressure works."

I pulled off my glove and helmet and the Prof motioned towards the stairs at the back of the open shed where they kept their gear, counter and snack machines. I tossed the helmet to Gabriel, who also picked up the glove I'd set down to count out money for a soda. When he saw the Angels logo woven into it he dropped it like it was hot. I scooped it up and followed the old guy up to his personal lair above the shop, where nobody goes without an invitation.

It's a lookout, I guess you'd say. A rooftop shelter where he can watch the batting down below or the waves out to the West. Just an open-ended cement box with a collection of beat-up furniture and memorabilia. Two chairs, one low table, an old sofa; frankly, I think he lives up there. And the walls are a sports museum in their own right, but a history so personal nobody could guess at the significance of a quarter of them. Brass cups from university, various professional leagues all over Mexico, local leagues, bats, balls and hats hanging everywhere. If you ask, he'll tell you about them, but it's not really so much a museum as a scrapbook.

He sat down and tugged at a soda "So how's it going, Carrasco? Are you okay? I mean, are you happy?"

That surprised me. A lot. The coach was not a man to get familiar, much less philosophical. "Well, you know, I haven't really thought about it..."

"Well, I have. I've been thinking about you a lot, too. You were the greatest I ever coached and you reached some real peaks. The only UAS player to ever play in the Big Tent. Leading the Pacific league for so long. Bogotá. And now you aren't even playing. At what, thirty-two, thirty-three? Working for those jackasses down at the *Palacio,* playing against amateurs in the city leagues. What am I saying? I guess I just wonder if it's okay with you, if it bothers you."

"No, it doesn't, *Profe.* I just like to play, and I still play. And I have a real job. And you know, I left it all on good terms, on my own. I didn't get jerked around. I can see how you might ..."

"Can you?"I was surprised again at the bitterness in the flat voice and the tough, flat face. "I could still be coaching, could still be bringing home the cups. They kick me out for somebody younger and more aggressive, and what have they done since?"

"Went to the finals this year." Just to keep him going.

"First time in six years, and they lost in the first round. Just because a guy played for Arizona, does that mean he knows how to run a team? And why can't Mexicans think about anybody besides Arizona? The Diamondbacks, the Raiders, the Mavericks."

"They're confusing baseball with *futbol*."

Which was just what he wanted me to say, of course. He snapped, "Exactly! You can't have a speed-up offense in baseball, dammit. You can't 'attack all over the field' or whatever new cliché they have at the moment. You recruit speed and teach basics. Build defense and coach the bottom end of your batting order until you don't have any *burros*. And now I'm sitting here running this sideshow and coaching little league."

"Hate to tell you, Coach, but I agree with you."

"And what do you know?" Incredible. I've never seen him angry off the field. "Why were you team captain at UAS? Because of your hitting. You never had the slightest concept of teamwork."

"And you're going to tell me I still don't."

"You've got that right. You only understand batting – one man against an entire team. You never gave a damn about the score." He seemed to realize how mad he'd gotten and suddenly calmed down, the pepper going out of his eyes. "See, players care about the next hit, the next pitch, the next catch. But the team has to care about the score." He sat back and sipped his pop, looking down with his cap shading his eyes.

I said, "*Profe*, I've been wondering about that. Somebody was just telling me I can't really win because I don't care if I lose. You saw me, what do you think?"

He nodded rapidly, "No question about it, I saw that on you the whole way. I'd say it's why you didn't make it in a league where they have designated hitters and wouldn't have cared if you couldn't catch the clap. You just didn't care who won. You didn't even care if you scored, did you?"

"Of course I cared if I scored. That's the whole point of getting on base."

"No, all you cared about was getting on. Getting a hit. After that you went to sleep."

"Hey, I stole some bases."

"With your speed, you'da been a punk if you hadn'ta. But did you really give a shit? I mean really?"

"No, I guess not." It was the first I had realized it, and it didn't seem to hurt much.

"You'd be happy if all games ended in ties. You just live to hit the ball. Everybody else is killing themselves to win and you're out there stroking yourself off. Signing programs."

He suddenly looked up, right at me, "No, I don't mean it like that. One thing I always had to hand you, you weren't a showboat. The fame and fan adoration meant nothing to you. Me, I have to admit it meant something to me. A lot, in fact."

We sat there for awhile, listening to the surf broken up by the rhythm of balls slamming into the fence or being hit into the nets. It's like a sort of slow-mo techno-trance music. Soundtrack of my old coach's life.

Suddenly he said, "Know something, kid? I do like working with the *bambinos*. It's really something how much you're shaping their playing futures. Hell, just keeping them from getting injuries later ... that alone, you know. And I like having Wild Pitch, guys like you coming by here, being respectful. I don't let it get me that often. I guess I just need to keep learning not to care about all that stuff."

He took another sip on his soda, then got up, walked over to the edge and dropped it into an oil drum down below, a sort of satisfying clatter. He turned around and looked at me and said, "And I think you need to learn to start caring about it. Eventually there has to be something that you give a damn about winning or losing. And when you do, God help you."

Many of the symptoms of being *chileado* – essentially an over-dose of *capsicum* – are identical to the effects of adrenaline or fear. It might be hard for a non-initiate to understand why anybody would voluntarily afflict themselves with the sweating, the pounding pulse, the bulging eyes, the desire to cry out. *Aficionados* of *chile* understand completely. The essential effect of fear for life and limb is not bodily changes, but mental changes, the concentration of attention. Adventurers use fear of death to spice their experience of life. In Mexico, where so much of the culture and consciousness revolves around skeletons and blood, it is understood that the Gods are bloodthirsty, that life not spiced with death would be as empty as a dish without *chile*.

"Argumentum ad Capsicum" by Mundo Carrasco
Chile Pepper Magazine, January 2002

I had a drink or two with the Prof, something he doesn't do very often, though I've heard he was a wildman when he was young. He still thinks of himself as 'in training' and probably will for his whole life. We talked about some new studs on the Venados who he thought might move up with a little proper coaching. And his own career, which I think was pretty remarkable. He was the real thing – a class act, a champion of many seasons. I had been a flashy article but ultimately just that, a flash rather than an enduring beacon. Thinking of it in those terms, I stopped by the Caliente Book for a few drinks on my own. I don't know why I find a betting parlor relaxing and introspective, but I always have. In a way, the thirty silent screens showing races and games, the mutter of betters and takers and losers, has the same effect as the surf, timelessly timely, changelessly changing.

In the movies a guy sits down to a few solitary drinks and suddenly Gets The Picture, sees What A Man Has Got To Do. And just occasionally it happens in Real Life. I was sitting there staring at a pack of dogs pounding feverishly around the track when it started to get a little unreal. They don't have jockeys to spur them, they don't get paid, they don't catch the rabbit, it's not even a real rabbit and dumb as they are, they have to know that. They're tearing their hearts out just for the win, pure and simple. Idiot animal instinct. Bred from trying to be first to get to a bitch. And it hit me. I do have something I care about winning, am not equipped to accept losing. I care about it deeply but spend a lot of time pretending not to. I decided the renovation of my soul demanded that I go to Mijares and either get into her pants or out of her hair. Take my straight shot with the other hounds. About time, I thought. About fucking time.

Since it was after midnight and I'd had those drinks I mentioned, I drove straight into the private sculpture park her parents call home and strafed right over the lawn. You don't see a lot of big manicured lawns in Mazatlán, and maybe that's why. It didn't seem strange that I wasn't challenged by bodyguards. Or that her door was open. At that point it wouldn't have seemed strange if there'd been a glowing pink doormat and a rising swell of soundtrack music. I stepped into the mausoleum where she lives.

I'm not being cutesy, her home was a smallish, Moorish-domed, marble mausoleum. Her grandparents, numbered among the few families that literally own Mazatlán, bought an old private cemetery and set up housekeeping there. It's like a small park with life-sized Greek deities, several lovely chapels, and a private bluff with a cross on it that's a sort of public landmark sitting on private property. I don't know what they did with the bodies that were in the cemetery. Since Fate had opened her door to my mission, I walked right in on what was happening.

The big guy in cowboy shirt and boots had his hand covering her entire face and most of her head, like palming a coconut. His other hand was tearing off her skirt. She had a violet thong on under it, I noticed. The even bigger guy with the Hawaiian shirt and shiny bald head was holding her from behind, one elbow around her throat and the other twisting her arm up behind her. The goon ripping her skirt off heard me and turned, loosening his grip on her face enough that she saw me too. The hundred-kilo skinhead giving her the chokehold grinned at me and said, "Join the party, Slugger, you're also invited."

I have a keen appreciation for those few sweet occasions when I know exactly, without any doubt, what I should do. I turned around and ran the hell out of there.

The less huge of the guys, the cowpoke, came right after me and he was fast for his size, only a few paces behind me when I got to my car. There would have been no chance at all to get in and start it. But fortunately all I wanted was my imported Louisville Slugger, laying right on the back seat. Reggie Jackson model, victorious relic and scarred veteran of international play.

I snatched the bat out and came around, already putting my trailing foot down and turning my hips into the stroke. He got his right arm up, which didn't get him much more than a shattered elbow instead of a mushed face. I would have gone for his knees next, but he fell down on them, trying to claw under his left arm with his left hand. I didn't need any demonstrations of what he was reaching for. I just spun on the balls of my feet and swung back hard the other way.

I hit a whole game from the other side of the plate once, on a bet. I went two for five. I think I could hit .250 lefty if I had to. It was the damnedest sound I ever heard, something that will stick with me a long time. No clean, solid crack of the bat on this one, fans. It was like crunching a meat eggshell full of fruit – Satan's *piñata*. His face splattered all over me. I remember gritting my teeth and saying, "*Guacala!*" If you'd heard what I heard you'd have known what I knew: the guy was dead as the Argentine Peso.

I turned back to the house, and the two-meter baldie was filling up the whole door, even overflowing a little. He gave me a comforting smile, then pulled out a big automatic pistol and fired it at me. I fell back away from him as he raised the gun, and sort of waved the bat up in front of me as an instinctive, protective, waste of effort.

Suddenly the bat almost jumped out of my hands and there was another very memorable sound, which I calculated, after an appropriate delay, to have been the bullet imbedding itself in my bat. I lowered it with my hands really stinging, and looked at the bullet buried in the grain. Then I looked at the Big Guy and he burst out laughing at me. I must have had an enigmatic expression.

He was still smiling as he walked by me. He tucked the gun in his waistband and applauded softly. He said, in pretty good English, "Base on balls, *chico.*"

I stood there hanging onto the bat while he grabbed the belt of the guy I had knocked out the park for good, picked him up like an empty suitcase, and walked out to the street, where a black Suburban with opaqued windows had been parked without my paying it a great deal of attention. The rear door opened and he slung the dead man inside, then stepped in himself. He stuck his head out and yelled, "*Jonron!*" which is how we spell home run down here, and flashed me the two finger Peace sign. Then the door closed and the Suburban sort of hulked away like a partially mollified bull. There had been at least two assault rifles visible through the door, but nobody shot at me again, which I appreciated. I have a feeling machine guns are harder to hit than big league pitching.

I stared after the Suburban, stunned, then remembered Mijares. I ran inside, holding the bat across my chest like a firearm, having a pretty good idea what I would find. And there it was, a tangle of naked, bloody legs sticking out of a broken cabinet. I ran over and knelt beside her, cursing and praying at the same time, which is an ambiguous attitude, now that I think about it. I've seen her look better. I touched her throat, searching for a pulse. Her head lolled back loose and her eyes opened, straight up at me.

"Lower," she said, "And to the right."

Her voice was harsh and hoarse, almost as if somebody had just been choking her within an inch of her life. I collapsed forward, my head falling between her breasts. I touched my lips to her stomach, threw my arms around her hips and pulled myself into her, whispering thanks into her belly.

"Much better," she said, "But lower yet."

I had her propped up on the sofa, covered up a little, the blood mopped off her face. I was working automatically, shocked by the fight – if that's what you'd call it – and by her proximity and condition. She seemed dazed, and kept closing her eyes and drifting off, but not seriously damaged. Thank God, the blessed Virgin, and *la chingada madre* my prayers and curses had paid off.

140

She put her hand on my wrist, pulled it away from staunching her nosebleed. Completely conscious, she stared at me like she'd just found me under the sofa cushions. "Do you know what I thought when I saw you there, then you turned and ran away?"

"That I had more sense than you thought?"

"I doubt that. No, I was loosing my grip, getting very dreamy, and I sort of heard myself talking in my ear, soft and matter of fact, you know? Saying, 'Well, there goes the only man you could ever really count on.'"

"Sort of depressing, actually."

"Especially since I realize that it's true. You're the only man I can trust or believe in, Mundo. All the rest just want something from me."

"So do I."

"No. You want everything. There's a difference." She took my face between her hands and stared at me. "You've always been there for me, no matter what."

"You just never let me screw you enough to get tired of you."

"Stop it, Mundo. You came back and fought two men with guns and rescued me. You're my hero."

"Doesn't the hero usually get the girl?"

"In the movies, yes. In reality, not that often." She paused a beat and moved my hand down to her breast. "But in this case, absolutely."

I froze up completely, just staring at her with my gears jammed and burning. She laughed and said, "Better nail it while you can, Mundito. Apparently there's a bounty on it." She grabbed my head and pushed it down between her breasts, down into her fragrance and startling body heat. "Weren't we about here?"

"No, lower," I said. "And to the right."

"Okay, but don't neglect the left one."

You have probably figured out by now that I'd made it with Mijares before, but I won't bore you with the wealth of luscious and fascinating details. But this time was very, very different. What I had known before was a sort of full-contact posing session. She likes to show off what she's

141

got, likes to cherish heart-stopping tableaux, likes to impress you. And likes to pleasure herself. That's about it. Enough to keep my tongue hanging out for two years, but not really a grand passion, much less conquest.

There on her sofa – bruised, mussed and starting to bleed again – she was another story. She clung to me like the only raft on a stormy midnight sea. She gulped me down like a last meal for the condemned. She stared into my eyes, she sought my approval and pleasure, she blazed and beamed and billowed out like windy curtains. She gave me her body, her love, her complete and undivided. I felt religious about it, like a knight-errant who stumbles upon the Holy Grail on the bus home from work. I don't do this romance stuff very well, but it's no exaggeration to say that my life was split into two parts, all those antics prior to being made love to by Mijares and the far more meaningful events that came afterwards. Other than that, I guess you'd have to have been there. In plain jock talk, she fucked my fool head off and dropkicked it to the moon.

I knew better than to try to tell her about it. She *had* been there. When I was under control enough to speak I just said, "So it's true what they say, how the threat of death sharpens sexual response."

She was laying on her side; wrapped around me, stroking my stomach muscles, and breathing onto the sweat on my throat. "Isn't it supposed to a be mechanism to replenish the race?"

"I'm not so sure," I said. "Maybe a brush with death whets our appetite for death, is all. And sex is the closest they let us come to killing somebody."

"Not to mention the closest we can come to dying."

But I'm not sure I agreed. I woke up at in the back of Das Boots, parked in a clifftop pullout off the Paseo Centenario. I lay there listening to the waves and the birds, staring into a sky that was just too completely blue and deep for me.

FRIDAY
FEBRUARY EIGHTH

DIA DE SAN LUCIO

Carnival Calendar

Naval Combat Re-enacted in Fireworks, Olas Altas Bay,
10 PM

The main reason that religion is worse than politics is that political parties think that everybody in the country should think their way, but churches think that everybody in the Universe should think their way.

"Rendering Caesar" by Mundo Carrasco
RioDoce, February 12, 2000

The ice cream looked pretty good. But why was he eating it on a bench in front of the library, all the way across Plaza Leones from the petitioners and hacks hanging around the pay phones in front of the PAN offices? Belisario Macias de Barros is a lifetime politico, evolved to the point where he can hardly exist in any environment but an air-conditioned, smoke-hazed office or a black-windowed Suburban. And suddenly he decided to slide over to a low-class grocery store to buy an ice cream cone and eat it on a public bench in the sun? Not likely.

But there he was, instead of inside the huge new headquarters the PAN moved into about five minutes after their man Fox became the first non-PRI president since the Revolution of 1910. It gives them room for their huge *Partido Acción Nacional* sign. I suppose they don't simply use PAN so people won't mistake them for a bakery. And I didn't mistake bumping into Beli Macias on my daily route to work as a co-incidence. This guy is not a 'Man of the People' by any stretch of the imagination.

That's what I sort of like about PAN, actually, they're the only party that doesn't try to act like they care about the People, the Poor and Helpless. They are unabashedly conservative and Catholic. All these leftist revolutionary parties posture and preen while the poor get poorer, acting out adolescent rebellion while quietly manipulating their scams – and here's one party that wants to be Mom, wants to make us be responsible and go to church and clean up our rooms. Which might, in the long run do the poor and helpless more good. Or not: we're just finding out. But it's refreshing having one single non-leftist party, and incredibly refreshing to have them in power for awhile.

145

The fact nobody else has been in power all this time is one problem with all those leftist, People-Oriented Parties, especially in Latin America, they tend to turn into Marxist dictatorships, or polite versions of the same thing. So I guess you'd say the PAN pisses me off less than most political parties. So far.

He was, of course, surprised to see me. Pleasantly so. I went through the hail and well-being stuff then tried to slide by, "Have to get to work. God forbid the press should start thinking for themselves."

He moved subtly to keep me from edging past, saying, "Hey, I'm a *politico*; maybe talking to me *is* work."

I usually find it that way. Especially when I'm floating along in golden pink clouds of rapture, tingling with the charge of love, sex and wild surmise. Alternating with shudders of nausea at the sharp sting of blood on my hands.

He caught my look and said, "All I'm saying, let's talk for a minute. I don't think it'll be a waste of what they're paying you. Buy you an ice cream?"

Well, that's one of my soft spots, and there is a lot of good homemade ice cream for sale in Mazatlán. I got a cone of *chongos marranos*, being forcefully careful to pay for it myself. I licked the burnt milk flavor as we walked to a shaded bench over by the lions in front of the ridiculous round library by Frank Lloyd Wrong. He sat at ease, leaning back and crossing his legs. He had adopted the less formal, agribusiness style of dress that Fox brought in. I could tell he would have liked to have the tall, rangy Fox pose, but he's short and beginning the sort of belly that a lot of men suddenly take on at forty. He's not a strike force personality, he's a functionary with a round face marked by cares and minutia. I complimented him on his gleaming boots.

"Hey, this is Sinaloa," he grinned, "There's still a little cowshit around." He lifted one boot for a better look at the sheen that turns lowly cowboy accessories into acceptable business wear. "They were so shocked when Fox wore these to his inauguration, but now they're even fashionable in Spain."

I made admiring sounds and he finished off his cone. "I haven't seen you much since you changed jobs. You know, I just have to think you were doing this community more service as a writer than you are now."

"Well, I can see how you might. Fierce rivals that we work for and all."

He laughed at that, like I'd called a mosquito rival to a cougar. On the other hand, a mosquito or two can probably drive a cougar nuts.

"Actually," he said, "I always thought of you as more like one of us."

"Me? As a super-Catholic? As a defender of the rights of industrialists and nationalists? Where would you get an idea like that?"

"Oh, we aren't exactly a Catholic outfit ..."

"Just picked that blue and white logo at random, right? And the rest of those *Guadalupana* trappings?" Before Fox, people said that the highest official of the PAN was the Virgin of Guadeloupe.

He chuckled. "I'd say that we tend to favor a spiritual overlook on national doings, not a sectarian identity. But how important is that anyway, other than something to tease me about? You talk about defending the rights of the rich and powerful, what are you doing now?"

"Trying to help keep the administration together ... maybe trying to figure out who killed my boss. Hint, hint."

Because one thing I'd figured out was that the attacks on Varedas and Mijares were not co-incidental. Whoever killed him was after her for some reason involving his life and his death, and the only way I could protect her, and my new relationship with her, was to find out who was behind it and try to defuse it. Christ ... Mundo Carrasco, Private Eye.

Macias said, "So you're still more journalist than political animal, I see."

"Those are the warring poles of my soul. But it's not really an angel/devil sort of thing."

He was eyeing my ice cream. That's *politicos* for you. "More like a war of angels? Michael vs. Lucifer with three opening bouts in the German Evers Arena?"

"More like, What flavor of shit do you prefer?"

"Well, speaking as a political animal myself, that's worth learning. Not that it doesn't change every time you think you've got it figured. Still, I wish you were working for us. Instead of against us."

"Me too. I wish you'd won the election and hired me. But I probably wasn't on your list, was I?"

"Why, for all the service you've given our party in the past? Damaging our publicity during the elections?"

"Hey, I backed you most of the time when I wrote for *Noroeste*."

"And don't think we weren't thrilled by your approval. When we could get through the sarcasm enough to figure out who you were making less fun of. But now you're experienced. Probably too experienced to think this ridiculous thing you call a labor party is going to win again in three years."

"I'm a jock. Three years is a long time. I just play it one game at a time, you know, just try to pitch in and help out. Just use my God-given talents for the benefit of ..."

"And in politics, the next game is the election," he cut in. "Well, hell with it. I'm not trying to recruit you, here. Just tell you we always thought you had good stuff."

"So, did your hit team pop off Varedas?"

"And anally rape him while we were at it?"

"Well, you know, I thought of the Catholic/pederasty connection. What the cops call *modus operandi*."

He threw back his head and laughed, "That's just for little altar boys, dummy. Varedas was too corrupted to merit priestly 'intervention'. We just killed him, then Satan came by later to bugger his own."

"Now that's the info I need. What about motive? Opportunity? Current whereabouts of Satan?"

"Who would have better motive than we do, if you want to get serious? What the hell is your PT? A non-entity created and funded by the PRI for one reason."

"To split and confuse the leftist vote and piss off those pinko intellectuals in the PRD."

"They didn't have to worry about the PRD, certainly not up here in cow country. But us PANistas, now. What if we get a majority in congress, too? Then the PRIstas won't be just waiting for the *revancha*, they'll be locked out but good. We'd have won if Borrego and his cohorts hadn't bought it up for that ridiculous marionette. And you see the same thing all over the country. You set the PRI back, they mutate into little aliases and start undermining you under assumed names."

"It used to be easier to know what was going on before you guys single-handedly overthrew the one-party dictatorship," I said. "For which you have our eternal gratitude, by the way."

He shrugged off the eternal gratitude of the People pretty lightly. "That's the trouble with New Worlds. They end up bringing a whole bunch of New Problems."

"Let's get back to how you killed Varedas. I just keep thinking that's pertinent."

"We killed a lot of people just by winning the election. Do you know what I mean by that?"

"Sure. *Caciques* in places like Chiapas suddenly don't have federal police support around and nobody cares what happens to them. *Narcos* suddenly lose their impunity and get shot down by the cops who used to work for them."

He nodded. "Investigators close in on suddenly unprotected files, careers are ruined, wrists are slashed. Death by official neglect."

"Which has nothing to do with Varedas. He was nobody before, he's less than that now."

"No, that one was a little indirect. But we killed him as sure as if we'd pulled the trigger. We didn't know it would happen that way. Murder, even indirectly, is a sin."

"So ..." I pondered, "You gave information."

He didn't know whether to be pleased or disappointed that I'd figured that one out. "We found evidence that there were more strings on the puppet than anybody had supposed. The PRI string, and the rich *hoteleros* and the *narcos,* they are normal and don't get tangled up. But what we found was direct lines leading out to some very disturbing sources."

"More disturbing than *priistas*, drug lords and Boss Borrego? *Caramba.*"

He gave a worldly shrug. "Repugnant to you, but like I say, normal. And you know it, of course. But it's not so normal to be under the influence of you know, striker types. Which means, as you appreciate if so many others don't, *Zapatista* types."

Whoa. That was heavy, and had implications I really didn't care for. It's one of those obvious but carefully guarded truths that the Zapata 'army', the EZLN, is not really the spontaneous white pajama-ed peasant uprising that it suits everybody to believe it is. And it's fashionable to see the strike that paralyzed the *Universidad Nacional Autonomo de* Mexico for a year as a student expression.

Actually both of them were cold-blooded political manipulations by entrenched leftist groups, power plays that bloodied everybody involved except the rich men and pampered kids who instigated them. Anybody who has any doubt that the *huelga* at UNAM and the *Zapatistas* in Chiapas have the same source just needs to read the endless official documents, demands and exhortations the two movements produced. It's like they were typed out by the same guy. Using two fingers and a limited, post-Marx vocabulary. I'd had dealings with the *Consejo General de Huelgistas* and had not been enriched by their acquaintance.

"Once you're on it, it's a pretty blatant string, leading from local influences, up to *huelgistas* at the UNAM, *dinosaurio* funding, crypto-commies, armed rebels in the hills. Destabilization for the hell of it."

"So you just dropped that information in the laps of the PRI and let nature take its course? And obviously you wouldn't mind having people read about it in the newspaper."

"Not just information, stone cold evidence. Wired straight to the man. Very direct influence, we might say. Irresistible."

Aw, shit. "You're talking about Mijares, aren't you?"

"*Si, Señor*. Little Monserrat, black sheep of fine *priista* families. Your boss. Varedas' whore."

I was so distracted by the sudden buzzing in my head and my guts falling out of my ass that I don't really remember replying to that one, but at some point I crushed my ice cream cone. Macias eyed the dripping mess regretfully. "Come on, Carrasco. This surprises you or something? You know what she is. You know where they found him."

Well, yes, I'd seen the address but it hadn't registered until he mentioned it.

"Her slumming fuck pad over in Playa Norte. Which we had wired from day one, the dumb bitch."

I must have flared up so visibly I didn't need to say anything.

"Jesus, Mundo, calm down. I meant him, not her." He had leaned away from me on the bench, and not comfortably. "You had something going with her? *Hijole*, kid. Talk about getting lost in the crowd. Can't say I blame you though; I'd take a number for that, myself."

I sat there alternating feeling stunned and totally stupid. He tentatively moved closer, punched my shoulder lightly. "I remember hearing you've got a weakness for women."

"Don't we all?" I asked.

"Varedas sure did." He stood up, glanced over towards his headquarters, turned back to me with a sort of big-brotherly commiseration. "You wanted to know what happened to him, I think you know now."

All I could come up with was, "Maybe."

His head bobbed three times, "Sure. You never really know do you? But tell me this, Mundo, do you really doubt that the PAN is the future of this country?"

I stood up too. I said, "What I doubt is that you're the future of me."

He smiled and said, "Think it over," then headed back to his offices, where an aide was motioning him into the door of a double-parked Suburban. Leaving me alone with my thoughts and two cement lions. I was definitely in for some thinking over. But thinking wasn't nearly going to handle it. What I needed was therapy. And I was thinking another bat might be good to have on hand.

One thing that shows how much Mazatlán is so crazy about baseball, why it's a legitimate alternative to *futbol* locally, is that there is no such thing as softball here. Other towns in Mexico play it for industrial leagues, senior leagues, schoolgirls, but in Mazatlán baseball is baseball and *ya muere la cosa.* Even the old men's leagues, the "*Categoría Z*", even the girls. Grown men would walk around in skirts before they'd touch a softball. This is a hardball kind of town.

"*¿Quien Está* on First?" by Mundo Carrasco
Alaska Airlines Inflight Magazine, June, 1998

I get a lot of mileage out of my tough guy act, veteran of drug wars, crawling around the Sierra, Chiapas, Nicaragua, the California frontier. But I never killed anybody before and it makes a difference, even killing an asshole in self-defense. So, screw work, time for some therapy at Wild Pitch. I could feel a creepy recoil in my swing, sort of holding back from a muscle memory of that impact. I kept at it, started picturing the guy. Seeing him holding Mijares, going for his gun, shooting me in the face. I pictured his face on the ball, worked into a fury – knocking him out of the park again and again. I worked on recalling that crunching sound at each hit, trying to remember it better. Slowly I got over it. What I got, actually was hardened. I don't really think of that kind of hardening of the heart towards our fellow man to be a shell, more like a tightened muscle that restricts movement but protects against further damage. Getting stronger but more muscle-bound.

When I stepped out of the box, it hit me that I had gotten my swing straightened out, but not the rest of me. What further actions, lines of inquiry, decisions might flinch away from that impact? I thought about the dead guy for a second and snarled. I realized another reason an organism might get horny after the wingbrush of death, it insulates the experience, wraps it up in something sort of like it but very different. But that kind of protection would only be needed by humans. And the more human you are, the less hardened.

153

The Prof must have sensed something because he didn't come down while I used the equipment of a game for boys to pound out my distaste for killing my fellow man. Sometimes a crowd gathers when I'm in there with the speed turned up; I've even turned it into a spontaneous batting clinic for kids. But nobody watched for long on that morning. I must not have looked like I was having any fun.

Finally I stepped back out of the box and watched the last two pitches on my token sizzle past and clang into the fence. I went out and reset the machine, gave the kid who works mornings their helmet back. He grabbed them and took off without making any eye contact. I got a bottle of Toni-Col from the machine, picked up my own bat, and went up half the staircase. I stopped and said, "*Profé?*" and he appeared at the edge of the stairwell, right above my head.

"Don't see you here much in the mornings, Carrasco."

"Going to work is for people who can't handle baseball," I said and went on up. I nodded a greeting and handed him my bat.

He looked it over closely, raising his eyebrows when he saw the bullet. "Looks like you changed your mind about bunting."

"I also changed my mind about aluminum bats. You have one I could borrow?"

"So that ping ding dong isn't so bad after all?"

"I found out there are a lot worse sounds you can make with a bat," I told him and he nodded very slowly. He stepped over to a barrel and pulled out a long black bat with an extreme taper up to an untapered cylinder at the business end.

"I doubt seriously this one would stop a bullet, if you are going to continue doing this," he said, and flipped it to me.

I examined and hefted it. Nice. Light as fly swatter, but with bone-breaking power.

The Prof said, "Notice the enlarged sweet spot."

I swished it a little bit. "Sweet."

I saw him giving me a stare and realized that I'd been swinging the bat one-handed like a club. I shrugged.

He walked over to his trophy wall and carefully put

my gutshot bat on a pair of pegs. "I was holding this space," he said. "A wonderful bit of memorabilia." He touched the bullet again, then turned it to the wall. "I always said you were the greatest clutch hitter I ever coached."

He turned around, walked over to the window facing the sea, and stood there a minute. Then he said, "But that won't help if you keep taking bats into gun fights."

"So what do you have in the way of guns?"

"A great deal of respect."

I walked over to stand beside him, say something to that – although I don't think there was much to add. He pointed down at his tiny parking lot, where a flashy late model Cougar was blocking Das Boots. He said, "That car got here right after you did. Why isn't he down there taking his cuts?"

I took a long look at the Cougar and didn't like it a bit. "Are you sure you don't have a *pistolita* around the place, *Profe*?"

"No, but I have a telephone."

I said, "Who ya gonna call?" but the Prof doesn't know that much English. Or go to movies. I looked things over a little bit and walked down the stairs, through the shop and out to the lot. Holding the bat in one hand like a hammer, pointing straight out in front of me. Like a huge black hard-on. Maybe I can run this guy off with sheer racial panic.

I was just coming up behind the Cougar when the door popped open and out stepped Tavo, the *pistolero* from the office. I moved up on him fast, hoisted the bat up on my shoulder. He gave me a sort of shy smile and reached inside the car. I stepped up into clubbing distance, my whole body going stiff and jangly. He pulled out a baseball cap and a really expensive Rawlings glove. I looked at him, shivered off a little adrenaline. I said, "I'm not sure you're understanding the concept of Wild Pitch."

He said, "That's a concept I've worked on eliminating."

"Ah, that's right. Pitcher at *Ciencias del Bar*."

"Right. And remember how much I respected your game?"

"I always remember compliments, even if they

make me nervous."

He smiled faintly. "So I hope you won't think I'm, you know, flippant, when I say I can strike you out."

I smiled, probably a little too condescendingly, considering, "Low and inside, breaking away, right? Not any more. I got over that with a little pro coaching in the States."

"At Anaheim."

"Before the Angels dispensed with my services."

He stood up and tugged his cap down, walked over to the nearest cage. He looked at me and said, "Would you do me a great honor?"

I got up and went to the counter, looking through the wood bats. A thirty-six inch Bobby Bonds model looked all right and the kid handed it to me like it was Excalibur. I put on a helmet, tugged on my glove, and stepped into the cage.

He had thought it out. He carried a bucket of balls to the next cage over, separated by chain link for only the first eight meters. He stood so that most of his body was protected by the edge of the dividing fence, but he could easily pitch past it. I turned toward him slightly and we had ourselves a live batting practice set-up. It threw the angle of the plate off a little, but we wouldn't be worrying about that. "If I swing and miss, it's a strike," I said, "We aren't calling balls."

He gave me a fairly predatory grin for such a sweet-looking youngster and said, "I don't do balls."

I laughed. "That's okay, because I don't take walks."

"I know," he said, "I saw that game."

Oh, right. Another of my legendary media moments. My first year with the Venados we needed two straight wins over Hermosillo to squeak into the playoffs and some dorky pitcher was giving me a free base. I couldn't stand it. I stood there with my bat on my shoulder, looking disgusted while he whipped the pitch-outs to the catcher and the crowd gave him hell. Lots of people think it's silly to have to actually throw four deliberate balls instead of just telling the umpire to let the batter advance to first, but I might have changed some minds on that subject.

His third ball was a little careless, a little close to the

plate. Didn't matter, who was going to try to hit a pitch-out? Well, actually, I was. It was a slow floater, of course, and still a long damn way from the batter's box. I had my toes right on the line and suddenly did a sort of dive forward, swinging the bat around with just my shoulders and arms. I've heard how 'it's all in the wrists', but I think that's bullshit. A lot of it is in your eyes, and the rest is in your brain.

If I hadn't hit the ball I would have fallen flat on my face across the plate and the lefty's box. As it was, I was at about a thirty-degree angle when I felt the impact, and I went down on a knee before straightening out and sprinting for first. I could have walked, actually. There wasn't a single player prepared for somebody tagging a pitch-out. I stayed on first for the remaining out, but Jaime Dominquez stole home and we made it to the final inning. Then lost the game. Legends only accomplish so much.

Tavo took a nice, easy windup and put one right across my letters. I pounded it into the netting. He did three more just like it, each one a little faster. The kid could hire out as a machine himself. Then he started throwing junk. One thing a batting machine can't do is mix up really tricky breaking stuff. Which this kid could do, big time.

He repeated the stiff shot across the letters, but then the ball dropped like an orange rolling off a table. I didn't even get a piece of it. I smiled at him, but he was all concentration. The next pitch was a slider, low and inside where I hate them, and with a sick little hop on it. I fouled it away left. Two strikes already. And this kid played at a nowhere like *Mar*? But at least he wasn't going to totally surprise me again. I leaned in and turned on the full radar, the eye-widened focus. He threw to the outside, the ball spinning too slow. But it wasn't a change-up, it was going almost ninety and had a late hop. I fouled it right. Wait him out a little, get his number. I fouled off two more extremely wicked inside curves.

He stepped back, a little relaxed. "Building suspense?"

Damn, he was a fan all right. That was in a television studio in Mexico City two days after we got back from Bogotá. *Don* Estevio asked me about the five pitches I fouled off after reaching two strikes, before connecting with *El Batazo*. I said, "I thought I should build up the suspense a little." For once the old ratchet-jaw had nothing to say, just stared at me. So I said, "You know, make it interesting."

I heard that line come back to me for years, including a lot of times in bed. I got a little sick of it. But it's fun to hear it from a younger generation.

The next pitch was a very sneaky lowball breaking downward. I blasted it right at him. It hit the fence about a foot from the end, ricocheted right by him.

He laughed out loud. "Hey, I was already interested."

We settled down to it. He showed me about six different cute breaks and slides. Then he started mixing up speeds, going for an occasional burner. I'm sure he knew he wasn't going to throw one too fast for me, but it was part of a sequence he was working. After awhile, if I got to two strikes he'd run something new by me. We were sweating in the sun now, both of us stripped to the waist. The Prof had come down into the kid's cage and was sitting there in a white plastic Pacífico chair, studying us both. The kid behind the counter looked like somebody had punched him out and propped him up popeyed. I tapped the plate, but kept the *pistolero* in the corner of my eye. He wiped his forehead with his forearm, ran his fingers through his damp hair. Where there was a bit of grease, unless I missed my guess. Cheating, technically. Good for you, kid. Bring it on.

Sure enough, some of the breaks and skids starting getting suspiciously spectacular. We were both warmed up now, fully engaged. I shuffled my feet and bobbed around a little, he kept looking around non-existent bases before going into his nice, economical wind-up and powerflow delivery. Reminded me a little of films of Sandy Koufax, for those who remember the Dodgers had pitchers before Valenzuela got there and flamed out.

He got two strikes on me by going up inside with spitballs, and I fouled off a really strange hopping submarine and a high insider that dropped at the wrong time. He cut right down the middle with what I figured for a slider, with the stitching turning slow and the wrong way, I was all over it, when it suddenly sunk. I tried to bring the swing down to it, even buckling my knees, but I topped it good and drilled it right into my foot.

I hopped twice, then grabbed the fence and shook my foot around a little. The kid rushed in, solicitous. "Are you okay, Mundo? You all right?"

"Hell no, I'm not all right. I'm fucking out."

"Well, actually..."

"Hit myself with batted ball. Is that a *chingada* out or not?"

"But I didn't strike you out, so..."

"Oh no, you win, kid. I'm very impressed." I put my weight on my foot and it was okay. I tried it, walking around to where the Prof was sitting. "What do you think? Age difference, all that, I still should have outclassed this kid, but I didn't."

"No. He's something else, all right. Where are you playing now, *miijo*?"

"University of Guadalajara. And in the Hospital leagues – I work in one of the labs."

"How are you doing"?

"Really well in both leagues, actually."

"*Hijole*. I should think so."

"Thanks for the contest, Mundo. I'd like to ..."

"Come back and try it when I haven't been up twenty four hours and beaten up?" I said that more for him than for my own ego, and it seemed to relax him a lot. I learned a long time ago that you have to sort of shield true believers from the full force of your legendhood. "We're gonna do this again, right?"

"Oh, I'd love to."

"Maybe next time over in the stadium."

"Hey, great."

"Yeah, fucking wonderful. Let's go get a beer."

The coach shook his head. "They're getting lax on attendance at City Hall these days."

"I finally figured out the proper strategy, don't care if they fire you."

"I like it. And you – come back in here someday. I'd like to talk to you a little about the pros."

160

Americans continually misunderstand the word *macho*, as you might have just done. The word means, simply, "male". A secondary meaning is "sledgehammer." But much of *machismo*, a word closer to what foreigners think *macho* means, is not rooted in the abasement of women, but in keeping masculinity in sharp definition. It's an uneasy balance. For instance, what if women were to become more sexually aggressive, to demand greater amounts and variations from men? They would not only be wresting masculinity away from men, but – since women are basically insatiable – they could be setting up scenarios in which men would be unable to satisfy their demands, thus robbing us of the single most important male characteristic. Who does the dishes, who drives the car, who minds the children, who sits in a cantina, these are secondary considerations, but picket lines that require vigilance.

"I Want To Be Your Macho Man" by Mundo Carrasco
LA Woman, April 1994

I had just gotten my hand around a Negra Modelo when Eusebio looked over my shoulder and exclaimed, "*¡Hijo de la chingada!* Now what?"

I turned to look through the glass wall and couldn't believe it myself. Rocío was reaching for the handle of the door to the Salón Elizabeth Taylor ... and she'd brought Karla Sabelos with her. They came through the door like a moped towing a steamroller. Karla writes for a lot of sections at *Noroeste*; society, women's, entertainment. She also does headlines and can pinch hit on hard news and rewrite. She's written a lot of good stories under the bylines of reporters who were too hung over to come through and everybody knows it. She's enormously fat, but popular, one of the guys. Men don't consider her fuckable, so she can relate normally. She can get ribald and isn't sensitive about being, let's face it, obese.

It's Rocío they don't know how to deal with. She's cute, but has too many balls. *Simpática*, but blood-chilling to guys who hit on her. I once told her that she should tell them she's a lesbian, but she said that would be taking the coward's way out in dealing with men.

"What, a little lie?" I'd asked her.

"No," she snapped, "Being a lesbian."

So it was typical that she had stormed the male citadel herself instead of trying to break in with Karla's support. She looked around the *Salón* for a second, as though she was surprised we hadn't all bolted to another lair, then walked over to a table. Mocho, ever the *caballero*, stood up. With a sweep of his hand, he told Karla, "*Bienvenida, Karlita.* Pull up a couple of chairs and sit down."

"Or I could use half of yours," she replied sweetly. Not the first time Mocho's skinny butt has been, well, the butt of a joke. She grabbed a chair and tested it a little, looking dubious, then gingerly sat. "God, am I ready for a *cervesa*."

Mocho, still gentlemanly, asked, "*Ballena?*"

"No, just pleasingly plump," she replied, batting her eyelashes.

But no, she's not what you'd call *gordita*, she's pleasingly obese. And suddenly there were two presswomen sitting in our midst. Nobody knew what to say next.

"Vicente Fox," Rocío said suddenly. We all looked at her. She said, "Declining popularity of."

Karla put in, "Why?"

Beto didn't have to stretch for that one. Or his opinion of women here in the *sanctum sanctorum*. He said, "Because he's a complete shithead?"

"Or," Rocío mused, "Because we keep telling everybody he is?" I had to admire her tactics. She'd moved the discussion into an area of mutual concern, but gotten it away from the local intrigues of Mazatlán.

"Yeah," Major Tom was getting interested. "Used to be you could tell what each paper was going to say. The *Sol* was pro-PRI-pretense, *Noroeste* liked the PAN, *Adelante* for the lefties. Now you're all gangbanging ol' 'Cente. What gives?"

There was a long pause, marked by inclined heads and shifted gazes, then Karla broke the silence, "He made them quit paying us pimp fees."

Well, she could talk, society writers never pocketed the envelopes of cash that made it possible for reporters to live on the three or four hundred a month the big papers paid. But it was embarrassing for the rest of us to discuss in front of a foreigner. In the corner Eusebio and Andrados, *Licenciados* and not journalists, chortled. Scowling at the 'hot Lics' in their creased *guayaberas* and Ray Bans, Karla went on. "The parties paid off for positive mentions. Lots of it came in the form of advertising, lots of it was sort of pay-per-name. He put a stop to it and now everybody hates him."

"Exactly," Andrados put in, "A great step for non-partisan government."

Tom stared at Karla, thinking. "I thought it was all just subsidies to the publishers. Now I understand why every damned front page story is a list of people who went to some meeting."

"Was," I said. "That's started to change. And there are those who are unhappy about it. And..." I glanced over at Beto, "Some who are terrified."

"Up yours, Carrasco," Beto snapped. "You want to tell *us* about corruption and payoffs, after whitewashing for that coked-out radio moron? Fox is down in the polls because he can't keep his campaign promises."

Carlito shook his head over that one. "Hard to do with a hostile majority in Congress," he said, "And he's not had the best luck."

"You make your own luck," Beto snorted.

"That's not what you were yelling at the race book the other night," Eusebio chipped in. "Hey, he got George Bush talking about lightening up on immigration and what happened? The *muselmanes* crashed-dived into Nuevo York and the borders snapped shut like a virgin's butt." He didn't care for the female contingent being there either, and wasn't a colleague.

"That's true," Carlito said, "So the economy slacked off and tourists stayed home and we got socked by a recession. Now how is he going to bring prosperity with that going on?"

"You can't blame everything on the *arabes*," Beto fumed, "What about civil rights? He talks about safety and transparency, then that *Indio* rights bitch gets bumped off and he can't even get to the bottom of it."

"Digna Ochoa," Rocío rapped out in steel tones. "Not 'that bitch'. She was the greatest female lawyer, the

163

greatest hero of civil rights in Mexico."

Beto withered under her glare, took a sip of his tequila.

Major Tom said, "Hell, how many women lawyers or civil rights heroes *are* there in Mexico?"

"Beto, you eunuch," Karla said, "I read your piece on the Ochoa killing. You were whining about how Fox has to solve the crime or his commitment to civil rights is bogus. What the fuck were you thinking?"

"Really," I said, "What is he supposed to do, hit the streets and find the killers himself?"

Chuy, who'd been leaning in the service window listening, said, "Might make a good TV series."

"God yes," Carlito hooted, "But who would play *El Presidente?*"

"One of the Almada brothers," Karla answered immediately. She did her share of movie reviews. "Maybe both of them. Mumbling and machine gunning hundreds of people into dog food in search of the killers."

Mocho said, "Do you think Clint Eastwood speaks Spanish?"

"Perfect," I said, impressed. "He'd be the perfect Fox."

"And who would be the killers?" Rocío said quietly.

"Well it's obviously going to be the PRI or some of their lackeys," Eusebio said.

Andrados was nodding firmly, saying, "Absolutely. They hated her guts. Threatened her for years."

"You're just saying ..." Beto started tuning up, but Karla said, "Shut up, Beto. Face facts."

"It's the only thing that makes any sense," I said. "They even up their score with Ochoa for bugging them about Indian rights and killing Zapatistas. Then they dump the body on the PAN's shift."

"Exactly. Making trouble for Fox's civil rights profile." Eusebio seemed to be relishing the whole thing at that point.

"And best of all, if they don't come up with any suspects, they're obviously hiding something and their commitment is suspect ..." Karla said, also getting a big kick out of the plot.

"... and if they *do* catch them, it'll obviously be politically motivated to smear the PRI." Carlito was grinning like a cub reporter.

"Exactly," Eusebio crowed. "They'd be saying, 'Our fact-finding investigation found out for a fact it's our political enemies' ... very convincing."

"So why, then," Rocío asked, "Are we doing this to him? Why aren't we writing down what we say in here?"

Once again the embarrassed silence settled. There was no real reason. Just herd instincts, a dot of blood, a big target, the safety of numbers. They weren't even paying anybody to tear him down ... just not paying anybody not to.

"It's the same way back in the World." Major Tom broke the chill, using his term for the United States that reinforced his VietVet status and drove Beto crazy. "You get a honeymoon, then they all start dumping on you every time you burp. He should do like Nixon. Get a dog and make an 'I am not a scumbag' speech."

"He did better than that," Andrados pointed out, "He got a wife and made an 'I'm more popular than Zedillo ever was' speech."

"Should have said he was more popular than Jesus," Mocho said, "It worked good for John Lennon."

Eusebio couldn't believe it, "You call getting assassinated 'working good'?"

"Sure," Major Tom answered, "Getting killed is the best political move you can make. Look at Che."

"Look at Kennedy," rejoined Carlito, "Nobody even remembers he started the Vietnam war."

"Hey, wait a minute..." Tom may be a paratrooper, but he's also a Kennedy loyalist.

Rocío cut in on him, "But what can he do to stay alive? To turn this country around?"

Tom eyed her with a new attitude, detecting a similar eye-gleam. But there is no real answer to the question, really. Except Chuy's. He popped through the window and yelled, "Repeal the *Ley Seca*!"

Actually I'm not so sure the ban against selling liquor on election days is a bad law, it was enacted because so many people got killed discussing their democratic options. But I was a distinct minority.

Mocho brayed, "That would do it! He'd get my vote."

Eusebio said, "I'd drink to that."

Andrados said, "I'd vote to drink."

Karla giggled, "I'd drink to vote," and clinked her glass with Rocío's.

Even Beto could get behind that one.

"A sober electorate is a dangerous, vicious electorate," he muttered. "Not ever to be trusted."

The first switch seems small and inevitable, to act *for* the People, they have to act *in place of* the People. Once that is established, it is also inevitable that they will have to act *upon* the People. In order to do that, they have to act *independently of* the People. Which, of course, makes it possible to act *against* the People. A small series of almost imperceptible shifts to achieve a complete reversal of direction. "They" being, of course, revolutionaries, representatives, spokespersons, organizers, journalists, terrorists, artists, altruists, and saviors. Almost anybody who professes to be acting for any interests other than their own.

"If We Are Them, Then Who Are You?" by Mundo Carrasco
Nexus, October 1997

Alfonso Reyes wasn't in the PRD offices up over Thorny's hamburger emporium in the Machado, so I headed around the corner to the gym. Even if he wasn't there pushing iron, I always enjoyed seeing the ballerinas from The School next door striking impossible poses in their damp leotards. But just as I got to the huge old doors of the Nameless Gymnasium I spotted Reyes down the block in a pickup truck. I walked up on the street side just as Fonseco Amado, dapper head of the local PRD, got out and crossed to the gym. "Don't depress the *Candidato*, Mundo," he called to me. "He's communing with his new toy."

Behind the wheel of the pickup, Reyes lounged, grinning at me – 'El Puma' at his ease. I admired his new truck, a shiny silver Ford Lobo.

"Nobody makes a 'Puma'?"I asked him.

He laughed, motioning me into the cab. "Close enough, close enough." I got in and he started the car, looking at me as I registered the throb of the big fifteen-liter engine. He pulled out and reached over reflexively to turn up the CD player. Ultra-*machote ranchero*, of course. Ultra-macho *ranchero* being what El Puma is all about.

"*Oye*, Carrasco," he yelled over the music, "You know, I never thought anyone could sink any lower than journalism. But you showed me, *que no?*"

167

That was a needle that pointed both ways. He'd always been a tough guy, a real comer as a lawyer – but what kicked him into the headlines and his current candidate status was a gutsy move by Olivia Espinosa y Gannet, whom I worked with on the staff of *Noroeste*. Gutsy on her part, clever on his.

Three years ago General Vargas was being railroaded to silence his accusations of military corruption in the narcotics war and incidentally get rid of a severe critic of the utter sell-out to the money the United States was lavishing on special Army units. They arrested him and whisked him out of Mexico City to a remote military prison in the boondocks – just outside Mazatlán. He was held incommunicado and it was pretty well stipulated that nobody be idiot enough to act as his civilian attorney. Until El Puma took the job anyway and was mentally written off by his colleagues.

It went badly for him. He was only given brief access to the General, all visits heavily monitored and accompanied by embarrassing searches of his person. They had Vargas shut up in a trap and weren't about to let anybody toss him a line. Whatever rights prisoners might have in Mexico, they are non-existent in the military *peni*. So Reyes and Olivia hatched their plot and blew the whole thing so completely open that pieces of it are still falling on people's heads.

Olivia identified a soldier in the prison, awaiting sentencing for selling confiscated heroin. She contacted his relatives and bought her way into a simulation of a relationship that allowed her to bribe her way into a conjugal visit. She came in dressed like a low class hooker and got a perfunctory search, outside of the normal feel-up. The decorated metal cigarette case in her purse had only a few filtertips sticking out, inside it was a transmitting microphone in easy range of the van outside.

Olivia still takes crap about what conjugal liberties she might have allowed the *narco-soldado*, but the scheme brought her into the yard where she shared a beer with him. Sitting directly behind her, at another table, was General Vargas. Under the eyes of the guards in the towers she asked questions, the young soldier drank beer, and Vargas answered into the microphone that was in the purse hanging on the back of her chair. Vargas named names, to say the very least. He mentioned dates, cited numbers, referred to documents, pinpointed witnesses. He blurted out thirty five minutes of extremely condensed, crafted, and inflammatory material that, less than ten hours later, exploded off the front page of *Noroeste* and like explosions in movies, just kept swelling and detonating and burning the asses off everybody involved.

The revelations gave Reyes a laydown on defense. And he played it out like a bridge master. National reporters swarmed into town ... mostly interviewing *Noroeste* reporters – and we got our satisfactions for the offhand way the big cities dudes usually treat us provincials, be sure of that. Then came the wave of international investigators. UPI, Reuters, Amnesty International. Something called *Soldier of Fortune*. The pressure to talk with Vargas mounted; attempts to move him or reconvene the trial ran into a blizzard of highly publicized writs and *amparos* from Reyes. And the political winds started to shift.

Crusty, rigid, old General Vargas refused to accept any compromise except total absolution. He was becoming a folk hero in the tradition of Oliver North. His enemies ran out like chickens to be identified and vilified. Reyes was the most quotable man in Mexico and his quotes were devastating. Vargas was released, restored, and vindicated. Other brass-crowned heads rolled. And the drug war lurched on as usual.

Of course none of this did anything to hurt the Puma's business or reputation. He was acclaimed a hero of courage and cunning. A guy who can get things done. His star rocketed upward in the PRD strata, and now he is a candidate for Federal Deputy. What you would call House of Representatives. With those elections only a year away, he was seen as a shoo-in with coat tails that would drive the PAN and PRI crazy. I could probably get elected dogcatcher just for riding in his truck listening to all these loopy cowshit polkas.

I said, "So you only respect journalists when you can use us to your own ends?"

He laughed out loud, "Not even then, actually. But if you're looking for a job, you're at the right time but the wrong party. We're going to pick up some big chunks of City Hall because of this little disaster, but I seriously doubt anybody the PT brought in this year is going to be around for long."

I hadn't expected anything like that attitude, so I stalled a moment by saying, "Disaster? I would have thought you'd be celebrating Varedas' accelerated retirement."

"His ... untimely ... death wasn't a disaster, his administration was. The Poor bought out wholesale by rich puppeteers, *que bárbaro*. Well, the poor can always be bought up cheap. That's one big reason why they're poor."

It was a more cynical twist on Marx than the social crusader of five years ago would have had, but I was still wondering how they hoped to grab pieces of the government with no elections pending, except possibly for a new mayor. They ran dead last in the mayoral race that brought Varedas to the *Palácio*. And me.

I thought it over while Reyes puttered around the Centro, obviously immersed in the pleasure of his new truck. He missed no opportunity to honk the air horn, fiddle with the air conditioner, or re-contour the graphic equalizer that was giving such perfect reproduction of such trashy music. He was skirting the ferry terminal, heading up towards Cerro Viggia.

I said, "So you think there will be some resignations coming?"

He laughed, "Not resignations, *muchacho*. Dismissals. All those appointees and family friends and supernumerary incompetents. You watch. Those PT clowns are finished."

"Don't you have to be the victor to get the spoils?"

"Actually, you don't. Just don't be the loser. And those guys are fucking losers." He pointed the truck up the street to Viggia and punched the accelerator. The truck leaped up the steep incline like a predator. He threw back his head laughing.

"So it seems you have no solidarity with your leftist

brothers in the Labor Party?" I needled.

He snorted like a draft horse, "They aren't a labor party. They aren't even a legitimate political party. Just a marriage of convenience between the big bosses and the downtrodden. Do you know what PT stands for?"

"It says *Partido de Trabajo* on my boss's desk."

"*Partido de Tontos.* Just a ragbag of people who couldn't make it anywhere else."

"I have to say, that's what a lot of people say about you. The garbage can that all the loose nuts roll into."

"That's because people are anti-intellectual. And increasingly anti-revolutionary. But we're a real party. We have a history; a glorious history for those who think it's better for the Mexican people to own our oil than for gringo companies to own it. How do you stand on that by the way?"

"I think we should sell it to the Arabs."

He chuckled, bending the surging pickup around the hairpin turn to the Mirador. "I've missed those acute analyses in *Noroeste*, Mundo. You are so wasted on those PT *babosos*. But, listen, we have senators, we've had Mayor of Mexico City for two terms, largest city in the world. We'd have won the presidency twelve years ago if the PRI hadn't cheated Coahatemoc and stolen ballots. You know that, everybody knows that."

He idled in front of the Mirador, staring past the restaurant entrance to the steep drop-off into the sea, the looming loaf of Crestón. He pointed to the two old cannons looking out from the heights, two of several claimed to have been the ones that repulsed the French fleet.

"But you know," he mused. "If you want loose cannons rolling into a party, how about your celebrated Interim Idiot? God, he was a Communist, a Priista, then with us for a while. He doesn't know what he is, just that he's in favor of the common man while he sits in his mansion and mumbles through classes at the University."

"See? How can we be anti-intellectual with a Department Chairman on board?"

"I suppose he helped balance out Varedas. One Dean canceling out one junior high dropout. It's just too ridiculous. But it cancels out to zero, don't you see? It does-

171

n't add up to a real political party. The PRI set them up to divide the left, drain off a lot of our support. Now they're using them to keep the PAN out of power, and us too."

"Well, they provide employment for a certain element of the disadvantaged."

"You?"

"Exactly. Listen, don't let this go any further, but I don't really give a shit about all that. I want to know two things that you might help me with. Who ordered the invasion of Infiernillo? Who killed Varedas?"

He started moving again, winding past mansions clustered on top of the hill. "It's refreshing talking to you these days, Mundo. You know why? Because you've managed to put yourself into one of the very few positions where I can say anything to you and you can't do anything with it. Ironic, eh? If you don't realize that yet, think it through."

"This is more or less my own personal curiosity, actually."

"Well, here's a little more irony for you. In case you haven't figured it out yet. We killed Varedas."

That nailed me, all right. He careened around the pointy corner to the Paseo Centenario, heading back towards the lighthouse.

"And here's the ironic part," he said. "We did it by ordering the invasion of Infiernillo."

I was pretty determined not to show how shocked I was he would admit something like that, even if he was kidding. "That's not irony, that's just co-incidence. It's also not very believable."

"I told you you wouldn't be able to do anything with it. Even if you just gossip about it, who is going to take it seriously? Don't you just love this sort of stuff?"

All I needed, a Marxist with ironic whimsies. He pulled into the Paseo's main parking area and nosed right up to the wall, looking down a hundred meters to the thrash of waves on rock. A *V* of pelicans hovered at our eye level. Reyes tooted the air horn and they nonchalantly veered off.

"It wasn't hard to pull off," he was explaining. "We don't have all that many *regidores,* but the ones we have are in places to get things committed. All it took was sending in cops. Mostly yokel cops from out in the *colonias* where we have a little respect. It doesn't take much authority to get guys like that to break up houses and push people around. They'd do it for anybody ... especially with some free tequila beforehand. We didn't figure you could squelch it so well. My compliments, by the way."

I must have still been staring, so he went on, "But you didn't get to the bozo papers, like *Hora!* and *La Talacha*, did you? They're beneath your notice. Those clowns don't drink with you over in there at Lo Peor, do they? And nobody takes them seriously, do they? Except the poor and stupid; they do. Varedas' electorate, in other words. They read that the mayor screwed them, and they would have started believing it. We just wanted to kill him politically, actually, but we'll take what we got. I think I'd rather have run against him next time than whoever the PRI finagles into the position."

Viewed as a murder confession, it had a few holes in it. And I didn't see anything that would add up to anybody going after Mijares. Viewed as a political action, it managed to top my already cynical experience of local politics.

"So you threw all those families out of their homes?" I asked. "The party of The People?"

He shrugged, enjoying a chance to really level for a change. "They were our people in the first place. We sponsored that invasion. We'll take care of them. We already are, in fact. They'll be fine."

"How do you take care of a little boy who's watched big uniformed men break into his home, kick it apart, and hit his mother with a club?"

"They're the poor, they've seen worse. We said there should be no beating, but it happened anyway."

"Think the People's Tequila might have had anything to do with that?"

"I suppose you'd scoff if I mentioned eggs and omelets?"

"You might as well. It's the main thing that puts me off about the Left and the Church, that passion for sacrifice."

"So the PAN and PRI don't break any eggs?"

173

"I guess I'd say that at least they pay for their own eggs."

"A luxury The People can't afford. We have to grow our own. Look, they couldn't have stayed there anyway. We knew that. We sent them there knowing that sooner or later somebody was going to move them out. And that we could make something out of it. But Varedas was such a putz we had to do it ourselves."

So what's the omelet? You get to run things?"

"*We* get to run things. Power to the people means people get sent to the barricade. The chips are on the table for the next presidential, Mundo. You don't want the PRI coming back any more than we do. And the PAN won't last after this term. It wasn't the PAN that won, it was Fox who won, you understand what I'm saying. Just like it wasn't the PT who won here, it was Varedas, the Radio Robin Hood. No substance or structure under their mercenary heroes; it'll all crash back down. Who would the PT have run next term? Name me one single hot PANista candidate? We'll make hay off all this, no doubt about it. All we have to do is keep the PRI from coming back and locking in, and the PAN doesn't want that either."

"The stupid thing about all this is that you think nobody would figure it out," I said. "That the press would just stampede into your version without even any cues."

"Give me a break, Carrasco. Who are you talking to? Who are you talking *about*? You know the press in this city better than anyone – especially since you interned in higher studies with the Head Puppet himself. When do they ever ask any questions? When do they ever get the other side of the story or question the accused when they get a tip? When do they ever actually investigate anything? Especially when there's an inflammatory headline to be had as it stands?"

"I investigate."

"Oh, good, a whiff of sanctity. From the man who sneers at the People and the Church in the same breath. You had the luxury of investigating. You were the one they could point to. The other guys have to feed families, have to make deadlines, have to watch out who they appease and offend, have to live on bribes and subsidies. But mostly, they have to struggle for their fame and glory. Why are they *periodistas* in the first place? Their name in print, impress people, be the Voice From The Mountain. And 'Mayor Fucks Poor' makes more splash than 'To Investigate Causes For Eviction', no?"

"Well, 'People Betrayed by Their Own' has a ring to it.

"Coming from you? The PT lapdog? You sold off your ability to do anything like that when you signed up to pimp for the Carnival Float From Sodom. Besides, you don't have to write anything, do you? That's what I'm getting at. You don't have the needs the press slobs have. Mostly, you don't need fame and glory. You had all that when you were too young to understand it and then you couldn't handle it."

"I just want to find out who killed Varedas and why they're after my woman."

"Your woman, huh? God, you're so naïve and uninformed you'd *have* to be a journalist. I just told you who killed him. We did."

"I don't think there were any *regidores'* prints at the scene of the crime."

"We did him, all right. With help from his own infantile brutality. What good did he do them if the poor turned against him? What use was he to them after that?"

Now that was a drift that sounded promising. "Ah, finally we get down to *Them*. Are *They* on your Rolodex, perhaps? I'd like to get an interview."

"If you can't figure it out, you're not much of an investigator."

"That's why I come to people like you hoping to trick you into giving me hints."

"Hints are just riddles you already know the answer to." He backed away from the drop and started back down towards Olas Altas, saying, "Look, you walk around the city and you hear people say, 'They raised taxes,' or, 'They screwed the tuna industry,' or 'They're handing the city over to the *narcos*.' So who does those things? Who are those guys? You already know. And you're down here trying to find out whether I do."

"Well, whoever *They* are, they're certainly not *Us*.

And isn't *Us* what all this social revolution is supposed to be about?"

"It's about the relationship between Us and Them, Mundo. That's what everything is all about. Let me tell you something. It doesn't require just a free press to ensure transparent democracy, it requires a press that knows what the hell it's doing."

"You mean the kind of press that can see through things like the PRD selling out their people and kicking them out in the mud for their own political advantage?"

"If they were up to that, maybe we wouldn't have to do things like that."

"You *don't* have to do things like that."

"You're missing the point, Mundo. The point is, it worked."

I thought that over as he cruised through the narrow streets of the Centro, waving and tooting. When he stopped in front of the Altazor to roll down his window and chat to some of his *cuates* at the sidewalk tables, I got out. He turned to wave goodbye and I said, "No. It isn't going to work."

He laughed. "All we wanted to do was get rid of the Mayor, Mundo. Now all we want to do is give a break to the poor." I didn't know whether he was talking to me, or the people at the tables. I couldn't even tell if he was intentionally being ironic. He'll probably end up as governor.

Unfortunately, the Drug War in Mexico doesn't fit into the American idea of good guys vs. bad guys, not even the TV version. Not even "Miami Vice", where the Ferrari-driving cops are obviously on the take, is a good model. You see "crooked cops" as a problem, exceptions to be weeded out. I have no idea if the model works in the United States, but it Mexico it's laughable. Here all the drug industry, including the flamboyant "kingpins" and "drug lords" work for the PGR, the federal judicial police. Who also run their errands, guard their parties, and kill their enemies. In turn, the PGR works for the actual owners of the business, the governors and national elected officials. Who finance them and give them impunity. This is a well-known fact of life that for some reason doesn't get known north of the border. PGR, by the way, stands for *Procuradora General de la Republica*. That the Attorney General's office here is known as a "procurer" is ironic, but the riddle is deciding whether Justice is the client or the whore.

"General Anesthetic" by Raymundo Carrasco
Orange Country Reader, May 1988

Just walk into the shabby PGR offices off Avenida del Mar and you are about as close to *Them* as it's safe to stand. The black-uniformed, flak-jacketed PGR cops are the sergeants, muscle and fiber; not only of the narcotics industry, but of virtually every facet of dirty politics and corruption in Mexico. Armed, dangerous, arrogant, and above the law, they are like a dumber, more brutal, in-country CIA. Their offices are the outer pickets of capricious and ultimate power, where you can't help but be aware of the slight flicker of breath from the dragon that guards the treasures, secrets, and bones. There were a lot of people in the lobby – a place nobody hangs out unless they absolutely have to – and they all have a submissive, edgy look. I assume that you would see the same look in the offices of all-powerful secret police in any country. And I assume that those other countries are like Mexico; the Them Police is by no means a secret.

But everything else about them is a secret wrapped in a cover-up, buried under a lie and marinated in betrayal. And guarded by murder. The only thing I didn't like about

El Puma's version of the roust and mayorcide was the lack of shadow of the PGR. I didn't think that Puma's party would actually send people out to rape and murder. For the PGR, that's all in a day's work. I wanted to find out if maybe they had any big agents with shaved heads.

The hard-bitten female cop who manned the desk, wearing boots and bulletproof vest, sent me in immediately. To see Gárfio, of course. His real name is Captain Garza, but everybody in town calls him Capitán Gárfio...you know, the pirate chieftain in "Peter Pan". I don't know if he's the regular gatekeeper – he'd be perfect cast as that three-headed watchdog of Hell – or if they just assigned him for my personal benefit, since he hates my guts.

I don't think it would take much for Garza to hate the particular and God-given guts of any specific individual, but he seems to hold me in special regard for spoiling his only no-hit game in the top of the ninth inning. This was way back when the *burrocratas* and the *Liga Periodista* had a post-season playoff. I actually arrived at the game late, but with an impeccable excuse – held under temporary restraint by the state police pursuant to attempting the seizure of my interview notes with an executive of the narcotics industry. I made it to the game just as we came up, went in for the left fielder, and drilled my usual cheapshot single on the first pitch. They had virtually no bats on the Noroeste team that year, and Garza wasn't a bad pitcher at all. Before he went to fat. And dope. The hit knocked in the go-ahead run, but they came back to win it in the bottom with two outs. So where's his bitch?

I've explained to him several times that if I'd made the game on time, instead of being hassled by idiot cops doing illegal procedures, I'd have clobbered him in the first inning instead, so really all I did was give him the thrill of his career for an hour or so. But that never seems to mollify him.

In fact, he was noticeably unmollified during my interview with him, given to bunching of muscles and clenching of steel-belted teeth. I wasn't being particularly nice or tactful, there is no point in being cordial to the PGR, since they don't co-operate with anybody about anything and any help they give you is totally self-serving and probably some sort of falsehood or rig-up that will blow up in your face if you print it. Not that anybody refrains from using the stuff. What I most wanted was to goad Gárfio into bucking me up to somebody a little more highly placed and dangerous. So I started out with the most obvious question, Since *most* public figures murdered in Mexico turn out to be PGR victims, would he care to decline to comment on their probable motives for doing Varedas?

Garza gave me a long glare, then said, "We're all so sad because of the sudden and totally accidental loss of such a great *alcalde*. And totally embarrassed that it should have happened on our patch. We will bring these perpetrators to justice."

"So, *Yo No Fui*, is that it? Funny, you're the only one I've talked to who didn't do it. What the hell happened, did you all kill him, but you're the only one without the *cojones* to admit it?"

I was just jerking him around, surfing right on the break of his temper, but he surprised me. Downright dumbfounded me, as a matter of fact. His scowl broke into a feral grin without even ceasing to be a scowl, if you follow me on that, and he said that in fact he, personally, had done the deed. It was more than I came for, but I had a deep-seated feeling that I'd have been better off getting less.

In case I had any doubts, he listed details, ending up with, "I brought the soldering iron along specially for the job. My uncle was pissed off when I brought it back to his tire shop dirty. He'd have gone totally *encabronado* if he knew it had roasted *caca de alcalde* on it, *que no?*"

He leaned forward and grinned again, even worse. "So did you hear *that* from all other guys?"

I was thinking it might be time to leave, but I said, "So you're going to get evasive on the possible motives, huh?"

"Why don't you print what I just told you, punk? I hope the fuck you do, I'm sick of your ass."

"I can see why, you're going to have to play *El Debate* this season, aren't you?"

"Fuck you, *pendejo*. You wanted answers; I gave you answers. What have you ever given me? "

"That little tic in your left eye? "

"*Carajo*, the only reason you're still around is you're not a big enough deal to blow away." He was obviously coming to some sort of boil, his forearm muscles flexing and a vein bulging at his forehead.

I was about to make my excuses for a graceful exit when I heard the big glass door behind me open and another cop, as big as Garza but less volcanic, came in to stand beside me. He gave me a warm smile and I stood up to shake hands.

I said, "Oh, finally the Good Cop."

The newcomer smiled serenely while Garza stewed and popped his finger joints. He had the smooth tone of a radio announcer, "Oh that Good Cop/Bad Cop thing from the movies? We don't do that. Well, maybe when *we're* asking the questions."

"Ah, but now I'm asking the questions, right? So you do something else."

He nodded, then unexpectedly swung his fist into my left cheekbone. I tried to duck back, but only cracked my head on the wall, then got knocked sideways. "We call it Bad Cop/Godawful Worse Cop."

I straightened up, touched my cheekbone. Nice and tender; no blood, but it would be a honey of a bruise. "Bad Cop/Worse Cop. It's got a ring. Can I use it for a column title sometime?"

Garza stood up behind his desk, pulled a drawer open. "You can use it for an epitaph, *culero*." He took a pair of surgical gloves out of the drawer and started pulling them on. He'd definitely crossed some sort of line, probably starting to resent getting goaded into a confession, which was not the brightest piece of public relations work I've ever been in on. Snapping the wristband of one of his gloves, he glared at me in a disturbingly final way.

I half turned, facing the smooth cop. "Maybe you could hire an actor to play the good cop."

He gave me another of those social worker smiles and was about to say something pithy, but I spoiled it by suddenly kicking him right square in the *pachacas*. Hard, too. I was fed up with him already. As he doubled over I slammed the heel of my hand into his face, sending him towards Garza, who missed a beat out of sheer surprise, but was going for his gun. I turned and jumped at the door. Kicking at the glass just as I hit it, I shattered it and continued through in the same movement. I remember thinking I was lucky it wasn't some sort of special kick-proof spy glass.

My foot caught on a piece of glass and I stumbled when I hit, trying to duck the flying shards. I hit the opposite wall with my shoulder, looking right into the reception area, where all eyes were on me, including lawyers, reporters, and the general public. I moved towards the crowd, brushing glass off my shoulders and gathering shreds of dignity.

Garza came through the door right behind me, but stopped when he saw everybody staring. He remembered the gloves, put his hands in his pockets. Very quietly, for me only, he said, "Do you know what it sounds like when a red-hot rod goes up your ass, Carrasco? Like frying bacon. *Carnitas de puerco,* crackling in their fat. "

"I'll notify the culinary editor."

"And the smell is something I can't even describe."

"Leave it to me, I'm pretty good at that sort of thing."

The smooth guy stepped through the broken door, shaking with rage and pain. He kept looking at me, then the people in the front. I could almost hear him calculating the cost/benefits of just blowing me away right on the spot. Three years ago he would have done it, but these days that can sometimes lead to prison. Maybe even getting fired.

Garza muttered, "One bad thing about *federales*, asshole ..."

I said, "*One* bad thing?"

He paid no attention, just said, "Yeah. Leaving town won't do you any good."

The Bad Cop gritted, "Neither will staying around."

As happened with Halloween, the sacred origins of Carnival have gotten out of control, overshadowed by exactly the images of wickedness and carnality they were supposed to defeat. On the Catholic calendar and Latinate languages, Carnival is just the festival of meat, an orgy of the incarnate carnality before giving all that up for the forty abstinent, sanctifying days of Lent. Which culminates in the golden resurrection glow of Easter – the ultimate triumph of spirit over flesh. After which, the sins of the flesh start their eternal campaign to engulf and bury the light once again.

"The Rebirth of Death" by Raymundo Carrasco
Mexico Traveler, February 1994

I couldn't drive anywhere near my house. Carnival was starting up for real and the entire Olas Altas area was cordoned off, double-parked, jammed tight with The People, and starting to throb. I had to park Das Boots in a *pension* over behind the Freeman, then walk home through the milling mass of Festival. I had to get a ticket, even though Varedas had declared Carnival free to The People. Cops frisked me for weapons. And bottles, which is pretty ridiculous since I was about to step into the World's Biggest Open Air Bar. The entire Malecón had been converted into a midway of stages and booths strung together by a hundred temporary stands dedicated to practically waylaying people and pouring alcohol down their throats. The booths and stages had been built days ago, and had done some sales and noise, but now it was Friday night and the whole thing was about to break out and run amok.

I bumped into Grady Clevell standing in front of the Puerto Viejo shaking his head and guzzling a *jarra,* a tequila concoction sold in little clay jars that are a signal to Mexicans that it's a party situation. The *jarras* are made with tiny round bottoms so you can't set them down and of the perfect material to smash on the street after they are drained. The Puerto Viejo was definitely not featuring live music that weekend – mostly because there were two enormous sound stages right across the street with stacks of truck-sized speakers two stories high. So Grady was out two nights pay. The bandstand was stacked with chairs, the entry arches across the entire front were blocked by tables, and the entire bar was stacked with cases of beer and tequila. Open for business, cash and stagger.

Grady nodded at me and waved his *jarra* towards the P.V. "It's a filling station for drunks," he said. "More like in-flight refueling."

I pointed to the middle of the street where a traffic circle normally displayed a tile mosaic of Mazatlán's coat of arms, but was currently supporting a giant orange neon sign saying, "Welcome to Carnaval 2002. Thanks for your preference." He saluted the sign and took a swig in one motion. Teo and Lili, swamped behind the table barricades, each handed me a cold Corona. I *salud*-ed them and wandered off with Grady into the milling, shouting, pulsing, obnoxious belly of the beat. It was like plunging into a raging river that couldn't decide which direction to express that rage.

All the stages were operational by then, pounding out basal medulla music at distortion-level volume. The street was already wet with booze and littered with broken glass. Young men were wild-eyed and aggressive, young women were moistened and heaving pneumatically. Jittery spotlights and green laser beams danced around the sky. The gathering rainstorm was whipping waves against the seawall, shooting up sheets of fine spray that caught the frenetic beams then drizzled away to black, leaving the light nowhere to hang. We stood in the middle of the street in front of a big brass *banda* with a stack of keyboards, slightly stunned by the onslaught, letting it flow around us and bring us up to temperature. Grady leaned over and yelled in my ear, "Do they have a word for people who stick around when the refugees take off?"

"Resolute?" I suggested, sidestepping a snaking conga line of Carnival celebraters. "Stranded?"

"How about *loco*," Grady groused. "Everybody else I know split, and I don't even have to work, since the Puerto Viejo is flooded with drunken dipshits from hell and they've turned it into a beer packing house."

Any residents of the areas infested with Carnival usually leave town if they possibly can. With some it's an absolute necessity. Two artists who live on the corner by the Credit Union have one of the biggest sound stages literally right outside their bedroom window – and it keeps it up until 4:00 AM. Up on the hill where Grady and I live it's not quite as intense, but weirder because you hear seven bands at once.

"But you stuck around."

Grady shrugged. "So did you."

I shrugged back. "I like fireworks."

We pushed through the crowds, stopping at some of the bandstands while Grady nodded or scowled at the music. The stores along the Olas Altas had done their seasonal sea change. All week they had been removing their stock and replacing it with beer coolers and crates of booze. Now they had counters across the doorways and shoveled bottles of merriment out to the throngs. La Fonda and Copa de Leche had ditched their sidewalk tables in favor of iceboxes full of beer, it's not a good idea to give drunks a place to sit down. In front of every grocery-turned-faucet were squads of cute girls in skimpy suits handing out flyers touting Bacardi or Herradura or some other liquor.

The crowd had reached that point of wave/particle movement where it becomes a slouching animal instead of a group of individual wills. There must be a critical number when Man becomes Beast – and it is dramatically lowered in the presence of alcohol. And alcohol is the uncrowned King of Carnival, the brute power behind the thrones and dominions. The church has been seared out of the mixture, the state has abdicated control, the dance has broken down into staggers, the mask has been removed, sex is an afterthought, liquor is the order of the day and runs rampant in the street like a conquering army. Grady and I swigged at our drinks, pledging a half-assed allegiance.

The other strike force was just as relentless; the enormous dark wind of sound that mercilessly battered the street into submission, formed up the ranks, and caused them to march. You didn't have to drink the alcohol, but you had no choice but let the sound inside your guts. The bandstands were positioned about every fifty meters, and even one of them had enough sheer kilohertz, megawatts and decibels to make it uncomfortable to talk anywhere

185

along the seawall. The combined effect went beyond songs, went beyond music. It merged into a cacophony that sifted into a bass heartbeat shrouded with random red noise. In front of each stage was an island of coherence, but between them were nodes of interference patterns where everything flowed together, salsa and *banda* and *ranchero* and Britney Spears covers stewed into a bruising static.

I yelled at Grady, "There's no melody, just one big boom."

He waved his *jarra*. "Hell, I don't mind."

I started to notice that half of the bandstands didn't even really have bands, just groups of kids dancing around, either singing or lip-synching to taped techno-tripe.

Grady said, "The boys all look like BackstreetNSyn-clettes. Alien sunglasses, tattoos, and spikydyked blonde hair with more dark roots than Alex Hailey."

"But the girls look good," I shouted back.

"Lotsa yummy nummy tummy," he agreed. "Is this the Navel Combat already?"

"I think it's the Battle of the Brands," I answered. The girls had shapes that did interesting distortions of the names printed on their tight tops. Names like Boots, Corona, Cuervo, Marlboro, Presidente, and that most traditional of all Mexican tequila names, New Mix. The shows were essentially big thundering commercial advertisements. The kids jounced around and trying to whip up mosh while giant monitors and projectors slammed out product placement. Brand names flashed on old buildings, even the overhanging cliffs.

"It's like falling into an MTV commercial loop," Grady grumbled.

I said, "But nobody seems to mind."

"I always hope for something exotic, something poetic, I guess," Grady yelled in my ear. "Something with some Carnival spirit, you know."

I knew what he meant. Not mediation between the *alma* and the *carne*, but exotic animation, wild Brazilian or Caribbean music, Queens and Neptunes from far-off mythologies.

"This reminds me of a state fair midway mixed up with Oktoberfest, a flea market, and the Black Hole of Calcutta," he said. "I want masks and fools, goddammit. Jongleurs, harliqueens, mardipan."

"Okay, you've lost me completely."

"No shit. Instead, there's this frenzy of like, Biz. Like the local cortège industry slapping on the greasepaint for another one-nighter."

"Now that I got. More or less. I think it's because there aren't any masks."

The whole costume thing broke down when they outlawed masks after some masked *sicario* gunned down Governor Loaiza right here in this block. So costumes fell out of fashion and now it's just a big drunken come-as-you-are party in boots and cowboy hats, which probably works just as well to represent the consumption of the flesh. And who knows, maybe Rio and Mardi Gras aren't really as Carnivalesque as we think, you hear complaints of violence and commercialism there, too. In Veracruz they still have costumes, and people complain because of all the whores and transvestites that flood into town. You see TV shots of Rio, with bangled, naked *mulattas* parading down the street and sequined bucks doing the samba. But this is Sinaloa: we get a drunken cowboy wingding and maybe that's just what we need.

We pushed on through the crowds, passing the stairs up to our building. I had a little time and was finding the whole anthill swarm of the street very compelling. As the Paseo rose up towards the cliffs and statues the bandstands were more widely spaced, the space between them packed full of smaller booths and carts and drinking tents.

There were games for plush animal prizes ... but all the same games repeated over and over. A half dozen Kick the Futbol Through the Milk Bottles stands, eight Roll the Marbles Into The Holes. The same *peluche* monkeys and coyotes for the infrequent winners. Well, come to think of, one booth was different, Throw A Softball Through Bin Laden's Head. But same prizes, no stuffed Cluster Bombs or Taliban Talismans. I watched one young couple move along the line, playing the same sucker game over and over for different carnies. No plush, no cigar. They didn't seem to mind.

Towards the cliff-divers' plaza half the booths were selling pirated CD compilations of golden oldies. And various base metal oldies for the truly baffled. Loudspeakers blared the product in small, overlapping circles, while kids and couples moved to the beat of Stones, Credence, Los Flamers, Four Tops, and Tigres del Norte. Except that modern digital technology allows a CD to just play a thirty-second swatch of each song, then switch to the next. So instead of a street beat, what was delivered to the unprotected booties of the boogiers was a jittery mélange like late night commercials for cassette collections. The kids danced to the music, but twice a minute changed to an entirely new beat, stutter-stepping to ecstasy. They didn't, incredibly, seem to mind.

"Why can't they just pick a song and stick to it?" I wondered out loud.

"Nobody has any attention span anymore," Grady yelled. "Look at those Top 100 Videos countdowns on MTV, they can't even play a minute of each vid. It's K-tel without the KY."

"I always wondered how they chose the Top 100 videos. You can't buy a video, so what numbers are they using?"

"Right on. At least capitalism got you something meaningful. Now it's just whatever They decide is tops. They don't even have to give a shit about customers anymore. Once something's free, you don't get any choice in the matter."

"Isn't that what sponsorship is all about?"

"Exactly. They just play what they want to, the hell with anybody else out here."

"But they like it. They're dancing to it."

"That's what really sucks. Let me tell you a secret as an old rocker. Playing dance music is the most fascist living in the world."

The smaller booths had smaller live music. A solo clarinet sounded very jazzy in one taco tent, in another one a huge, fat cowboy was singing sappy love lyrics while playing a stack of a half-dozen keyboards backed up by a bass and drum machine. He was playing a song I didn't recognize, but Grady said the tune was called *Deep Purple*. He'd already pointed out a mariachi playing *Blue Moon* and a *banda* brassing their way through something he swore was called *The Eyes of Texas Are Upon You.*

"Why doesn't anybody play *Carnival of Venice* or *Manha de Carnaval?*" he wailed. "I thought this shit was supposed to be traditional."

I didn't answer him because I thought I'd caught a glimpse of a familiar face dancing N synch on a huge stage hung with Presidente banners. I moved closer and sure enough, it was Palomina, prancing like a pony and leading a troupe of cuties through the song and dance. She was crouched with her hands on her knees, clenching her own yummy tummy while flipping her blaze of ponytail, when she caught my eye and grinned. Her tiny white top, really just a bra with collar, had a red Presidente patch on each sexily sliding mound.

Grady said, "Hey, don't I know her?"

"Sure, she's invited over to watch the Naval Combat tonight."

"Cool." He nodded his appreciation, then frowned. "Didn't you invite that Canadian girl, too? And that newspaper chick you used to do? And Luz, come to think of it?"

"The more the merrier, that's the spirit of Naval Combat."

"Christ, you *do* like fireworks, huh?"

I dumped my beer bottle on the huge midden surrounding a garbage can painted with Presidente colors and wandered away from the blast and jitterbug, down by the seawall in front of the Mermaid Statue. I sat on the rail and looked at the perfect bronze breasts, the motherly hand on the head of the little boy she was sending up onto the land. It's how we *Mazatlecos* like to see ourselves, rising out of the sea in a mantle of foam. But the reality is that we have sent generations of land-born boys out to sea, fishermen who can't swim. It's evolution in reverse.

Grady was casually hitting on some Mexican tourist girls; I just listened to the surf pounding on the rocks below the rail. The whitewater sound seemed highly structured and melodic in comparison to the electronic bellow of the midway. I was thinking about going over for some ice cream when Palomina stepped out of the milling crowd and swung astride my lap. She put her hands behind the nape of my neck and leaned back to look in my face ... her professional stance, you might say, but I always felt it had an affectionate intimacy about it.

"Did they pause for a commercial announcement?" I asked her.

She laughed and flaunted a Presidente-blazoned boob towards my face. "It's kind of refreshing to commercialize the sacred dance by covering 'em up for a change."

"Doesn't seem like it would pay as well as Ramses."

"Except that I'm the one who put the whole thing together for them. They just grabbed those kids out of model schools and hired me to teach them to dance and pretend like they're singing. Cheaper for them than trucking a bunch of kids around the country. Can you imagine trying to chaperone that crowd? They'd have gotten reamed by everybody the first night. Even the boys. Especially the boys."

"Choreographer, huh? You're moving up ... extending your art."

She gave my hair a sharp tug, then went back to running her fingers through it. "Don't talk about art here. This is polite company." I looked at the shitfaced kids staggering around us and smiled.

"It's no different from the lap clubs. A girl finds out she can get paid for flashing her bush and wiggling it in some guy's lap – or bouncing around up here in this so-called blouse. And that's it, nobody tries to con you that there's anything bigger involved."

"Sounds like what Grady was talking about. We're better off greedy than free."

"Grady should know, he's a trouper. This shit, the naked dancing thing, they're both cleaner than that whole ballet scene. In fact, that whole Arts thing is sort of sick."

"Compared to Ramses?"

"Oh God yes. We're just making a living. The dog and pony show. But in The School? And the little schools you hit before you get so wonderfully accepted there? It's boot camp for marionettes. Learning how to do what somebody else wants you to do."

She was starting to heat up, and her grip on my hair

was starting to hurt a little, especially when she tugged it around to emphasize a point. "Do you know how young you have to be to have any future as a ballerina? Or a violinist? They're torturing all these little girls into walking on their toes, all this painful, boring repetition, turning you into some sort of tuned racing machine that nobody admits is a big sexual turn-on. And for what? When you're a little child you do it because your parents want you to, and you learn that if you do these weird things right it makes them happy."

She stopped, soothed my hair down, stared out at the white lines of shore break pushing out of the black water. "That way you learn there are all sorts of peculiar things that you don't understand but make your daddy happy."

She gave a twitchy shrug. "We turned ourselves into an adorable little music box to amuse people. Then it all builds up to some big recital or senior project or the big trip to Culiacán or Guadalajara. They clap, you do a lovely curtsy ... then later you realize it's all over. That was it. It's like half my damn sex life. Some asshole gets his rocks off and I'm lying there going, 'That was it?' What you do, you end up flicking that whole Arts scam off your life like the ass end of a cigarette."

But when she said it, there was a little tear at the edge of her eye. I touched it with my fingertip, then licked it off. She smiled at me, "One of the girls told me another definition of whoring last night. It's whether of not bodily fluids are exchanged."

I thought about the cowboy goon's blood and snot splattering all over my face and decided there might just be something to that one. "It definitely draws some sort of line."

She shrugged. I put my hands behind her waist, supporting her. She gave my hair a quick brush with her fingers, then fluffed her own hair. Intermission over, I guessed.

I said, "You love it, don't you?"

She snorted, but had no doubt about what I meant. "Love, huh? Is that the right word for something you just can't help?"

Well, I thought, that's the nice word for it.

191

She swung off me like a cowgirl, pulled the skimpy top down a quarter inch and flashed me a stage-dancer smile. "But you know the main thing?" she asked. "For little moments there, I can fly."She turned away into the crowd, moving with a flex of fine calves and butt, then spun around and yelled, "Fly, Dammit! Fly!"

Many of my compatriots are still influenced by the starry-eyed national history that I outgrew in primary school. We are taught to think of ourselves as a victorious, warlike country at the same time that we describe ourselves to each other as victims of the Conquest. This leads to confusion in our young men, who flock to American Embassies to enlist in all their invasions. Our national anthem is "Mexicans, To The Cry of War": it says that the earth will tremble at the roar of our cannons. Around age twelve I suddenly said to myself, "What war? What cannons?" But those are questions seldom asked and never answered. Actually, I am glad we are not a country of wars and cannons. And, I have to say, I am glad we are a very patriotic country. We need to be, there are plenty of wars and cannons to go around.

"Bombast Bursting In Air" by Mundo Carrasco
The New Republic, October 2001

Every year they start clogging my street at two in the afternoon, even though the Naval Combat doesn't start until ten. They pull up in old cars and trucks, arrange plastic chairs for granny and all the nieces, set up charcoal grills on the sidewalk overlooking the bay, cook their *carne asada* like clans of gypsies. By seven they block the narrow, curving loop of street. Then the kids can really run amok, fired up with anticipation of the Battle and no longer threatened by maniac drivers. Everybody in my building throws an annual fireworks party. Mine had a long, proud tradition of two Carnivals and got bigger every year as people heard what a great place it is to see the rockets, straight out at eye level and no worries about the hot cinders falling on you like they do down on the Malecón. My invitations had included a lot of City Hall, including a nice note to Hizzoner Varedas, who turned out to be a pretty definite no-show. As in life, so in death.

As Grady and I picked our way through a tangled mass of cars, milling bodies slapped up against the foot of our building like a gentle surf. Pablo's kids hung off their balcony with about a hundred buddies and cousins, waving to us frantically. Neither of us had guests huddled at the iron street door, so we were on time for our own parties.

Some of the hundred plastic Pacífico chairs we'd rented from the distributor were still stacked under the tree in the courtyard, a tarp covering furniture that Pablo moved out to make room to seat his infinitely extended family. There was a very tasty smell coming from the big grill over the cistern. Two hours until blastoff. I was juggling details of my preparations while I jogged up the stairs and wiggled my balky door open. When I closed it I couldn't help noticing that Mijares had been standing right behind it.

She was wearing one of my denim shirts and she looked scared. She kept looking scared after she saw who it was and I'd closed the door. It gave her a very different look, the chrome figurehead suddenly softened into a wide-eyed child. I didn't pause or think, just stepped forward and wrapped my arms around her, kissed her upturned mouth, felt her shivers move through me the way big hidden engines vibrate a ship at sea. She sagged into me, shaking. I wanted to wrap completely around her, shelter her from anything I could think of, absorb her into myself. She broke the kiss, burrowed her head into my chest and murmured, "I didn't have anywhere else to go, Mundo."

I gently tipped her head back and looked into her eyes. They had softened, too. I realized I no longer knew who I was dealing with. But whoever it was, I loved them more than anybody I'd ever met in my life. I felt like I would burst into a star of white light, trail sparks down the sky and disappear into the dark sea with little tendrils of steam. Give the folks downstairs a little preview.

She stood on her toes to look up into my eyes. "So here I am."

I was frozen on my feet, the whole situation sweeping over me like rising tide. I had nothing to help me understand. The night before had been the greatest sexual and emotional experience of my life, and I'm not just saying that to be polite. I'd had the Grail in my hands. And vice versa. But that didn't mean I ever expected to get another shot. The last time had been two years ago and then she'd just disappeared. But here she was, like she said. Here. She. *¡Caramba!* And since she didn't seem to be wearing anything except my shirt, it looked like we were going into extra innings. And it scared her. All I felt was the normal reaction to having all your dreams come true and heaven fall right down into your outstretched hands.

I would have mooned and gooned indefinitely but I heard yells from the street – Grady's friends calling him to throw down the key. He keeps his downstairs key in a big oven mitt for tossing to guests. I stick mine in a slot cut in a solid rubber ball, but there are many chances for errors; the ball bouncing off down the hill and rolling damn near into the surf. I rely on my friends being better fielders than I am. I realized my guests would also be arriving. I looked down at Mijares, still being clasped to my manly chest like the sharp sting of hope.

"You're hiding?" I said.

She laid her head against me. "I've *been* hiding."

I bent to scoop her up bodily but realized I couldn't just carry her around with me all night. Stepping over to the rail, I set her in a ringside seat and said, "I have to do a few things. There are people coming."

She nodded, but seemed as reluctant to let me go as I was to move away from eye contact.

"I'll be back in ten minutes," I said. "We'll catch the whole show."

I snatched up the chairs and stacked them, tottered down the stairs with a huge piles of them, then up to the other roof, which was still open to the sky and used mostly for hanging laundry. I filled the space with chairs, then carried over the table of snacks I'd prepared. Dumping my clothes out of the cooler and filling it with the ice and beer and soda I'd bought for the occasion, I ran sloshing down my stairs and up to the roof of the other tower.
I left a note on the table. "Sorry. Help yourselves. Enjoy. Mundo."

On the outside door I left another note. "Friends. I have been otherwise detained. Please come in, go up the green stairs to the roof, and enjoy the show. Apologies. Mundo." I grabbed Pablo's son and gave him fifty pesos to open the door for my guests, show them the roof, and tell them I had to leave unexpectedly. He was overwhelmed as much by the responsibility as by suddenly being rich. About to run into the apartment waving his wealth, he suddenly stopped and thought it over. Such moments mold our maturation. Smiling conspiratorily, he tucked the bill into his pocket, smiled conspiratorially, and gave me a thumbs-up. Which I returned with interest.

I ran up the stairs and fumbled through the door and she was still there. She had pulled the mattress out by the railing, under open sky. She sat there cross-legged, ignoring the view, just looking at the door like Coyota, waiting for me to appear. I eased up onto the railing and stared at her, almost afraid to touch her or speak. She sat absolutely motionless, just gazing. Waiting. Making it my move. I suddenly blurted out, "You know what I thought when I came in and saw you lying there like a damaged doll?"

She didn't answer, just turned up the luminosity in those silver eyes.

"Well, it's not so dramatic or anything. I just thought, 'She's gone.' Like there was only one 'she' and that wasn't there anymore."

Later she told me that remark had completely melted her, but at the time she just rose to her knees – silhouetted against the sangria-dark sea, posed against the lighthouse on Cerro Crestón (second highest in the world, or hemisphere, depending on which guidebook you believe in), towering above the throng of Carnival (third largest in World, behind Rio and New Orleans) – and pulled off my shirt, artlessly revealing the fourth and fifth most gorgeous breasts in all Christendom. I reacted to that not so much by melting, as by developing a hard-on (seventh hardest in North America at that moment). At which point we began to do what young lovers do while waiting for the fireworks.

At some point Mija gasped, "This! This!" She pounded on my chest, "This is the real thing."

Just like real life, I thought. At some later point, I realized that actually, that's what makes it great, it's *not* the real world. That's what exalts me the most with her, and also freaks me the most ... it's not normal life, can't possibly hold. You don't drink or snort coke or shoot off fireworks to feel normal.

But she's not really much of a screamer. She's like intimacy with a jaguar, a struggle for life sometimes. She snarls, purrs and growls, but no silly screaming or cursing or theological invocations. It's dark with her, all tight and lathered and hot and black and polished. Slippery short fur. Teeth and claws and the scent of blood and fear. Her eyes are metallic and light up in the night. Probably not really, though I'd swear to it. When she's excited and convulsing, they glow like chromium. People see her eyes and think she's from Guadalajara, but the famous *Ojos Tapatios* are a warm gray, like a cat's fur. Mijares' eyes are a silver that's been lying dormant for years in a forgotten mine with a famous name, black history and ancient curse. There is something unique about sex with Mijares that no woman can match. There is a smoldering aspect to it; you can almost taste smoke in your mouth. She has an inhuman body heat, an incandescent stoking released by excitement. Her taste is *picante*, but smoky, like *chipotle* chiles.

I felt like that Italian poet, with Beatriz guiding him through heaven and hell. I think he was the one who said hell is heaven upside down, but I don't think he mentioned sideways, backwards, exploding or strapped down. Bursts of heaven not only in the depth of the pits, but also at the tips of the peaks, hell layered in between, fervent prayers that the suffering won't stop. Pain and pleasure, mastery and slavery, beauty and shame all switching back and forth like they say energy and matter jump back and forth in the black hole of nuclear fire.

I suppose I shouldn't be telling all these private stuff. But what the hell, you're anonymous, right? I have no idea who you are. Since I don't know if anybody will buy this book, I don't even know if you exist. Just a big invisible support group, Mijares Anonymous. You just listen, don't judge. If I'm any good at it, maybe you drool.

We sat entwined in the smolder of the bed and watched the sky light up above us. The show re-enacts Mazatlán's only naval battle, one of Napoleon's warships repulsed by a few cannon shots. The current version had so many batteries of rockets massed on the beach they could probably have repulsed the current French fleet. As soon as the Navy vessel playing the French Bark entered the harbor and fired a salvo, all heavens broke loose. Rockets' red glare, bombs bursting with flair. The whole sky turned into a canvas of the pyrotechnic art. Which I consider the most beautiful of all art forms. The Chinese invented gunpowder to create beauty and we use it for destruction. Printing was probably just a beautiful art toy in Chinese hands, until we got our hands on it and used it for evil. Sex was developed just for making more people, but of course we've also improved that beyond recognition. We watched rockets trace trajectories of glory into the night sky, exploding into heat and light, beauty and cheers, the remnants falling into darkness. Next day the beach would be covered with blackened paper and burnt sticks.

Meanwhile the sky continued to paint our eyes, silvery falls twinkling like fairy dust, bursts of loud-colored flame and shazam, little sizzlers blitzing around the perimeters. They let everything go at once, as fast as they could lock, load, and lift off. At the end, when everybody expected a big finale, the whole thing just sort of petered out. Pauses got longer, the bursts fewer and smaller, shooting off the last few crumbs. Nor really a Big Bang, but a sort of a Big Whimper. I realized the Naval Combat was over. And it was terrific: just should have been run backwards.

Within minutes, six bands on the Malecón kicked back in and we were immersed in the roar of the multitudes. Mijares still stared at the sky, now just scudding clouds of powder smoke lit by the lights and lasers of the Meat Circus. She burrowed her head into my chest and arm and murmured so low I heard it more through my bones than my ears, "Can I stay here, Mundo?"

"Do you have reservations?"

Even softer, she whispered, "Less all the time." And just like that, she was staying with me. Living with me, in my home, my bed!

I was staggered by it, grabbed big fistfuls of it, shook it in my mouth like a dog, sunk into it like a diving pelican. My spirits expanded like a balloon, floated out over the bay, and exploded into bluish fire and white trinkets of stardust. I lay there feeling completely changed, a man with a woman. And it didn't feel strange. It felt usual, ordained, natural. When she caressed my chest her hand seemed to flow like some genetically pre-programmed response, to-

wards inevitable results. We turned to each other like partners in an ancient dance and slid together like two coconut
halves, like the slickest double play of all time.

I gasped twice, then when I was sure I was going to
keep breathing, flopped back and dropped my arms into
the preferred pose for the recently crucified. She sat astride,
arching her back so strenuously her hair brushed my toes.
She convulsed once, totally, every muscle. Coyota started
howling, touching off the other dogs in the neighborhood
into a primal wolf chorus. My light bulb suddenly popped,
showering liquid sparks, then plunged the roof to darkness
interrupted only by the red pulse of the antenna beacons.
Mijares shuddered, uncoiled, and collapsed on top of me,
asleep almost instantly. My final Thought For The Day was
that "This! This! Now *this* is a finale."

SATURDAY
FEBRUARY NINTH

DIA DE SAN NICEFORO

Carnival Calendar

First Parade, Olas Altas, 5 PM
Costume and Fantasy Ball, Valentino's, 9 PM

Some of the anecdotes of my career – hitting the pitchout, for instance – have led people to see me as a bit of a *loco*, a risk-taker. But actually I tend towards the conservative, well-covered, thought-out type of game. I never tried to hit the long ball because there is no percentage in it. And your batting average is nothing more than that, a percentage. It's just a statistic of the number of times you get on.

Mundo Carrasco, interviewed for *Beisbol Hoy*, April, 1992

And your score is just the number of times you're safe at home. All that stuff about playing percentages is true, but only up to a point. Because it turns out that with a woman, or at least with a woman that can affect me the like Mijares does, you're swinging for the fence with no fallback position. Because there is only one to go around. Which isn't fair. I mean, even Babe Ruth was ultimately just a pitcher. A slugger, an outfielder. He retires or dies or whatever, and you replace him from the minors. The replacement isn't as good, but maybe the next replacement will be. You can still win games with the new guy. No record stands forever. But a woman you are in love with is irreplaceable, the only acceptable average is 1.000. So once the First Day of the Rest of my Life got around to the point where I could think, I started thinking about playing safe, protecting Mijares from any possible error. One of my profs at ASU told us, "A man becomes conservative when he has something to conserve."

Starting to think was aided by a cup of instant Combate coffee. I sat on the rail drinking it and reading my free copy of *El Debate* that some poor kid pushing a bike uphill lobs up here every morning. In a lower front page story, a letter had been received from a "Gay Rights Front" claiming credit for killing Varedas to avenge his rapes of young men and serving notice that such attacks would no longer be tolerated anywhere, by anyone. The letter had been tied around a brick and thrown through the lobby window with enough force to shatter the thick plate glass. That Tavo is a quick study, the medium is the message.

But how smart was I being? I could have grabbed

201

Mijares and left town, but then I couldn't have gotten to the bottom of the threat, try to defuse it. As far as staying in town, there are worse places to hide out than my roof. There are no next door neighbors and it's a perfect lookout. It's hard to enter the building quickly, very hard to do without alerting the neighbors. And if we needed to, we could escape easily by jumping over the back wall onto the roof where Coyota hangs out during the day, which leads to a ramble of other roofs, a warren of hovels crammed up behind the view homes. It would take an army to guard all the alleys, ditches and goat paths that run up and down the slopes of the hill. And it's right under the windows of the Channel 7 offices, so anything really wild would immediately get filmed.

But then, somebody with a gun could easily shoot their way in. Which meant, as far as I could see it, that I needed a gun, too. And I knew where I could get one. It was the only thing that could have dragged me away from Mijares. One thing I had learned out of the whole thing, I would do anything to protect her. As the old song says, *Once you kill for her, there is no more escape ever ...*

So I wondered for a moment if maybe she was the best influence on my life. How can you tell? When you take cocaine, you don't feel anything but good. You only feel bad when you need more cocaine. You figure out in your brain ... maybe ... that it's not doing your life much good, but it's not so easy to sell that to the rest of you. When I look at myself *con Mija* I notice this, I have a steady job, I'm around important and powerful people, I move in expensive surroundings, I get respect, and there's talk of a future. So, how could she be some addiction dragging me down the toilet? On the other hand ... well, I don't know. I don't think I'm in a position to judge. If she's in sight or reach, I have no judgment at all.

Which I guess does sound pretty addictive. When I'm with her I'm not curious. I don't want to know how things come out. I don't care when or where, I bask in an infinite date, in a place without dimensions. I blur the who of it, and I sure as hell don't care why. End of story, *punta final.*

But I was having to think things out, and just doing that was rocking my dreamboat a little. The thought of leaving her or losing her gave me a hint of what it would be like if she lost me. Suddenly issues of who and why started to raise their ugly heads. And at about that point, Mijares raised her own beautiful head and blinked at me. She gave me a dirty, sleepy smile and raised her body up, bit by bit, into viewing position. She yawned and stretched and mewed, then studied me a little through a veil of hair.

She said, "A *centavo* a word for your thoughts, Loverboy,"

"Oh, you know. Am I dreaming? Am I out of my mind? That sort of thing." She gave me a sweet look so I went on, "Is this going to get me heartbroken. Or dead? Should we move in here or your place? Do you really love me, too? Will you be true?"

She stood up and walked to the door of my shower, then turned, the full display, with lights lit and flags flying. "I'm too good to be true."

Well, that had sort of been my point in the first place. When she came out of the shower, prancing around the roof naked and wet, she happened to notice that I had my clothes on. Including my shoes. So it came out that I was going to make a little run. Borrow a cup of machine pistols from the neighbors. She didn't object, but she came down off her glow pretty quick, peering out over the rail. She was remembering she wasn't off on a weekend love romp, but hiding out for dear life. She asked me where I was going to find a gun. They are heavily controlled and illegalized in Mexico, only dangerous criminals are allowed to possess them.

"I would think some of your *grillo* buddies would know." I was doing a little fishing. *Grillos* are student rebels, guerilla wannabes. I didn't think UAS had actual armed groups, but many schools are loaded with them. And student rebels in Latin America are different from *yanqui* groups. For instance, the *Sendero Luminoso* that almost overthrew Peru started out as just another bunch of collegiate *grillos*.

She shrugged it off. "They wish. They aren't even very good at striking their own campus, as you recall."

203

"So no help there. Well, I might know a few guys. Let me see your phone."

"Maybe not such a good idea, Mundo."

She had that right. There was an excellent chance that somebody was all over that number, just waiting for her to reach out and touch somebody. I obviously needed some seasoning in hardboiled spy methodology.

"Why don't you just use yours?" She glanced around to find my cellular. Then did a double take, "Oh, no. Is it still in the toilet?"

"Of course not. I had fifty pesos of time left." I found it on the soap rack in the shower area. Before trying to call Uzi's R Us I punched in the number Tavo gave me at La Puntilla. I'd planned to store it, having figured out that Tavo would be a good cutout or emergency number for me. Nobody knew him and he was the one guy I was absolutely sure was not in the Varedas camp. The gutsy little phone lit up and blinked a message that the number was ringing, then was answered, but I could only hear a gargle through the tiny, sodden speaker. Miraculously, the circuits were either waterproof or had dripped dry, but there was still suspicious water in the perforated ear compartment. I tried shaking it, but it just got gurglier.

Mijares took it, snapped it off, and looked around for a place to dry it. She spotted a rusty piece of rebar sticking out of the cement above the doorway and hung it upside down to dry out. She had the general air of somebody taking care of a retarded child's playthings.

I said, "Well I guess we can't call take-out. I'll have to do the driveby window."

She looked at me thoughtfully a minute, standing against me in the shower. I was dressed, but thinking it wasn't the way to go at the moment. "The people you're going to for guns. Do you trust them?"

I said, "Think about that one a second."

She nodded her head and smiled. "Well. I'm not sure I would trust my friends, even if they had anything to help us. Who *knows* who's after me? After us. You're the only one I can trust because you're the only one that got dragged into this, doesn't want anything out of it but me."

I reached around her and pulled her to me, pulled her as close as I could to my heart. "We don't need them. We don't need anybody else at all. All you need on your side is me. And all I need is you by my side."

She threw her arms around me and pulled herself into me, pumping out her animal heat in the small enclosure. Then she let go and pushed back. She was smiling like a cloudless May morning. "Well, I'm not quite by your side, you know."

"Well you're not in front of me, and I'm not so sure you're behind me."

"You'll figure it out eventually."

"You're not under my feet or sitting on my face or anything useful, so how would you describe your positioning. Relative to me, that is?"

"Over your head. Now go get us some guns, lover. And roses."

I could be wrong. A victim of a writer's overactive imagination. But I see these three dots, Borrego pays to elect Limas as Mayor, Limas replaces head of JUMAPAM, then JUMAPAM decides it owes Borrego eleven million pesos. And I start seeing a pattern, like when you were a child and you connected the dots so you could see a picture of a bunny. But this pattern doesn't look like a *conejo* to me, it looks like a *borrego*.

"*Connect the Dots*" "El Mundo Segun Mundo" Column
Noroeste August 2001

A big, black, sinister Cadillac or Packard would have been better. But in Mexico these days the intimidating vehicle of choice is the Chevrolet Suburban. You see a dark color Suburban with opaqued windows and you can assume it belongs to either a *politico* or a *narco*. Not that there's much difference. So if I turn onto the shaded street and see a black suburban with black windows waiting there, and they open the rear door for me, I should be a little intimidated. Especially if it's the same Suburban I saw leaving the scene of my first homicide, full of assault rifles and dirty looks.

My firearm connection was just two doors up, but there was no way to walk around the door that had opened to block the sidewalk. I looked inside, hope springing eternal, and saw the massive bulk and shaved head of the big thug who'd shot up my souvenir of beautiful Bogotá. He had a new, slightly smaller thug driving for him. Probably a job with a high turnover. He gave me a big, merry smile.

"Guess who wants to talk to you, slugger?"

"Well, my mom's always saying I don't call her enough."

"Shame on you. Oh, by the way, *Señor* Borriguín would like a chat."

"Damn. I'd like to chat with him, too. Been trying to for years."

"Your patience is about to be rewarded."

The driver, wearing the standard *guayabera* and Ray-Bans, spoke up, "You learned patience sitting on the bench with the Angels, right?"

"Well, please tell Sr. Borrego I'll pencil him in," I said, trying to see a way to squeeze past the door. "Right after Carnival."

"He's got you down for about fifteen minutes from now. The only chance you'll make it is if we give you a little *raité.*"

"A *little* ride? I'm starting think this is An Offer I Can't Refuse?"

"Yeah," he said thoughtfully, "That's about the size of it." He was beaming. Everybody likes having movie dialog in their everyday life.

"Well, I never turn down a free ride," I said, sliding onto what little seat was left over The driver did a wheel-screeching start that slammed the door shut and pushed me back in the leather seat. At the corner of Belisario Dominguez, he flashed on a siren and ran the red light.

I said, "And I was thinking fifteen minutes wouldn't be enough to get to the top floor of The Aztec."

The bald goon laughed. "No, you're in luck. We're taking you to Valentino's for a drink. He owns that, too, you know."

"Hey, listen, why don't we go somewhere he doesn't own?"

The driver gave a nasty chuckle and peered elaborately at the dashboard. "I don't think we have enough gas," he said. "Barely three quarters of a tank."

Not that much of an exaggeration, my father can remember when the Borriguín family owned the electric company while their partners and neighbors, the Ricardez, owned the water works. These days they merely control those facilities through political interests and naked purchase power.

I turned to the bald hood, who was eyeing me in a friendly way, and said, "I'm Mundo, I didn't catch your name the last time we met."

The driver hooted. "You made a career out of not catching things, didn't you?"

The big guy jerked his shining head at the driver, rolled his eyes up, said, "You can call me Chaco. You don't need any introduction here – I'm a huge fan." He savored the *huge.*

"Big fucking deal," the driver sneered. "The guy led the league in errors every year he played."

That's one downside of a baseball town, everybody always cites the damned statistics.

"*Percentage* of errors," I corrected.

Chaco laughed like a building collapsing. "He's right, Herrera. You screw up the stats so bad you ought to work for the newspaper. Oops, no offense, Mundo."

"*Al contrario*. But speaking of employment. You work for Borrego? Were working for him Thursday night? On overtime, I hope."

"Oh, that's a complex issue. Wow, really complex, actually. I'm sort of a whatyoucall, multi-use infielder."

"And he's a multi-useless outfielder." The driver was starting to get on what was left of my nerves. I gave him a look in the rear view mirror and he smirked. "Couldn't hit it out of the park, but he could *throw* it out."

"Who gives a shit? Who cares if you're a Golden Glove in right field, especially if you can hit?" Chaco growled. He was growing on me, never mind the clutching fear. "And this guy could hit. Don't ever knock this kid's stick. Just ask Aquilar."

"I haven't seen Aquilar lately."

"Which is why you got his job. Wheeling the Big Bopper around. Aguilar's currently filling a new niche in the environment."

"What niche?"

"Alligator shit."

"*Hijole!*" He jerked into the other lane in shock, but everybody gets out of the way of darkened Suburbans. "The estuary?"

"You know the spot. So show a little respect."

"*Rayos!*" He settled down a little. Then, just as he turned into Valentino's, he said, "I gotta admit, he *did* have the highest batting average in league history."

Chaco agreed, nodding. "Man could hit a bullet on the fly. Believe me."

Valentino's is a spectacular tissue of romance and fairy tale by night, a white Disney castle with spires and domes perched on a rock thrust out into a thundering break of ocean. It's floodlit after dark, a gleaming magic kingdom with the dazzle of lights inside the disco towers turning the black oval windows into enchanted opals full of sparks and stars. Unfortunately, patrons of the swank expensive restaurants in the complex have to pass through a court that also serves three frenetic discos, running a gauntlet of spring-break gringo twerps, local punks, and gorgeously trashy girls in search of a cocaine donor – all wrapped in rap music and raucous barker spiel stabbing out of big speakers. So most of the patrons of The Sheik and Mikonos just don't show up. In the daytime, it's even tackier, a cement amusement park across from McDonalds.

But inside The Sheik it's elegant, in a contrived sort of way. Plush circular booths spill down through fountain-draped levels illuminated by skylights, chandeliers, candelabras, and stained glass windows with florescent lights behind them ... down to a frothing, sunlit sea. I've been in Manhattan and Las Vegas and Toronto and it doesn't look too shabby to me: to your average *Mazatleco* it's Fantasy Island. But Chaco ushered me straight through the immense dining room with two hundred chairs and two customers, through a door I wouldn't have noticed, and into a small private dining room. I'd been in the place several times and had no idea the private salon existed. It was cleverly tucked between The Sheik and Mikonos so as not to be visible to either. It was small – just big enough for two tables for six – and hexagonal. One wall had the door and a small bar, two were covered with plaques, awards and trophies, the other three were tall glass doors sliding open to a narrow porch with the surf almost in fingertip reach and a postcard view of the Malecón and Cerro Neveria. The La Paz ferry was just pulling past the islands at land's end, and a vee of pelicans ghosted overhead. It's hard to tell just how much of this stagedressing a guy like Borrego can actually arrange.

He was sitting at one of the tables with a snifter of brandy, looking out to sea. I was brought into his presence, you might say, by Chaco, who stood by the door behind me. Borrego didn't stand up or offer his hand. He looked like I expected, every bit of his seventy-five years, chunky and bald, with white hair and goatee. He had a lizardy look that went beyond the crepey skin. He wore big amber 'Elvis' glasses, and had sunk some of his inherited and otherwise ill-gotten wealth into a lot of gold chains. I don't think it was just my imagination that made him look like an evil gnome, that here was a man who'd scuttled a dozen of his tuna boats with the crews on board in order to cut his fleet and get insurance, a guy up to his tufted ears in drugs, politics, and execution-style murder.

He looked up at me and said, "Pleased to meet you, Mundo. Our first connection since that 'connect the dots' column last year. I liked it, very clever."

I sat down without being bid and was surprised when Chaco came up and put another brandy by my elbow. I took a drink. I have no idea what it was, but definitely not Presidente or *Don Pedo*.

I said, "I'm glad you approve. But I'm sort of surprised you did, actually, since it accused you of buying city hall to scam water and money out of JUMAPAM."

"No hard feelings, I appreciate clever things. Clever people to a lesser extent. Actually, I think you are sort of half-clever. And that could be dangerous ... if you don't mind my sounding like some bad old movie."

"Oh, God no. I *love* bad old movie dialogue."

"So do I. I hope you enjoyed the imperative summons in the dark car. But speaking of those dot puzzles, the trouble is if you don't hit them all in the right order, you end up not getting the picture of the cowboy, you get something else."

"But you're going to set me straight, aren't you? Actually, ripping off the waterworks was the farthest thing from your mind."

"Yes and no. See I'd already ripped it off."

"And you're telling me this? Instead of lying to me? Look, I might be able to get you some sort of special journalist award. We don't usually give them to, you know, the crooks, but..."

"You're being half-clever. Why don't you shut up and listen a minute? Don't they teach you that in journalism school?"

211

"Well, now I'm embarrassed."

"No. Now you're sarcastic. In a minute you're going to be embarrassed. And in two minutes you're going to be totally amazed. And by tomorrow, you're going to be frustrated out of your mind. Ready?"

I spread my hands. "I'm all ears."

"Mostly, anyway." He smirked. "I'll give it to you without the windup. Yeah, I paid to elect Lima. I had to pay a lot more to elect Varedas because he was virtually unelectable, but that's a different issue. Then that fat little buffoon demands the resignation of the guy Lima hired to set the whole thing up. The reason he resigned, then came back three days later to get fired, was because they screwed up in Mexico City and he had to do a few more documents before they could pay me back the water rights."

"It's just like a western, always boils down to the bad guys going for the water."

"See, you're cute, but you are essentially a hick, just a jock. The city stuff is bigger than you think, and a lot more complicated than all your swashbuckling around the narcos. You don't get information like this just by porking that secretary over at JUMAPAM."

"She promised she would keep my shame a secret."

"Hell, I've fucked her myself. No, this is a higher level of arcanery, lad. There is more to politics and journalism than you can deal with by sticking your dick in it."

"I have a hard enough time just avoiding stepping on mine."

"One good way to avoid that is to keep it in your pants."

"I'll just have to buy longer trousers."

"Not from what I hear from our secretary."

I heard a snort from Chaco and looked over to see him purse his lips, shake his head, and measure off an inch between his fingers.

Borrego gave a short, harsh laugh. "Typical male bullshit. Measuring willies. You heard about the two Argentines discussing the British mining of the Falklands harbors?"

In the snotty, Italian-sounding Argentine accent he said, "One goes, 'How big's a mine?' The other says, 'A

212

mine sa twelve inches; a yours, who knoze?'"

I laughed dutifully. But actually I was sort of embarrassed by his informational upsmanship. I'd never be in this guy's league. "Okay, I am embarrassed. But also grateful. You know how often we actually get to find out what happened from the crook's actual mouths? Like never. I'm serious about that special award."

"So here goes phase two, smartass. I invited you out here today because it's come to my attention that you're investigating Varedas' death. And that you have help."

"So are the cops and they don't get free brandy."

"Yes the cops. I'm thinking of just laying them all off." He glanced at me, a serene, humorless face. "A joke. If I started firing people, I'd probably get rid of all the journalists, too."

He does own *Noroeste* outright, and has varying degrees of control of two others. And let's not forget the TV station.

"But when have you ever heard of a police investigation actually nailing anybody?" he went on. "You, however, actually investigate, get actual answers."

"It's a wonder I'm still alive, huh?" I asked.

From behind me Chaco stuck in, "A fucking miracle, really."

"So I'm taking interest in you," he went on, "Interest in what you come up with, what you do with it."

"I'm getting more and more interested myself."

"I would warn you, though, to watch out for other people who seem to be helping you. Like irresponsible, slandering faggots, for instance."

"Ah, now we're in Old Movie Territory. Here it comes, 'Are you threatening me?' No, wait, 'Who are you trying to protect?'"

"You, you nitwit. What do you think warnings are for? And I didn't bring you here to threaten you; I brought you here to find out what you know."

"Well, so far I'm learning a lot more from you, I think."

"I'd hope so, but I doubt it. What I've learned so far is that you don't know shit. So here we go – a curious little *tejon* like you is probably dying to know who killed

Varedas. I mean, that's an assumption, forgive me if I'm wrong."

"You mean Frederico Varedas, the mayor? The one who got tortured to death?"

"The one I had killed." He took a short break to admire my gape. "Are you amazed yet?"

"I think I'll just shut up and listen, if you don't mind."

"See there, you learn. That's always redeeming. You see, *Señor* Populist, after I got him elected, then engineered the last trick of the water deal ... he fires my puppet then goes and tells the poor they don't have to pay their water bills. The guy thinks he's Castro or Perón or something."

"I thought he had a lot of Gandhi in him."

"Who also got shot, no? You know what happens if nobody pays their water bill? It's not like making Carnival free to please the masses, it means JUMAPAM will be broke. For years. So how are they going to take care of me? They *might* have the water; they sure as hell won't have the money. He was an expensive little toy, but he went wrong right from go."

"I have to be frank, that didn't amaze me at all."

"It doesn't matter. We already have what we want. The poor get a saint, we get city hall, his poor wife gets out from under – so to speak – I could just go on and on."

"Well, journalists will miss him a lot. He was the all-time easy target."

"Seems too cheap a shot for a man of your ever-ready sarcasm. But now, what are you going to do about what I just told you?"

"Well, could you pose for some pictures, sort of re-enactments of how you gunned him down? *El Debate* wouldn't run any branding iron up the butt shots, but *Alarma* would kill for them."

"I didn't actually give an order, you understand. I just let it be known that it would be a good idea."

"A well-tempered word or two, dropped in very local bodyguard circles."

"Sometimes you can convey messages with mere shifts of small facial muscles."

"And here we had to learn all those weird, over-acted signals from the base coaches. Pulling on caps, slapping butts, grabbing crotches."

"I thought you just did that one out of bad manners."

"That's what you were supposed to think. See how it works? Now we've both shared some professional secrets. What next?"

"I'll be looking forward to your next column."

I started to say something stupid, then gave it a few thoughts. Finally I said, "You know, I must be learning faster. I think I'm getting frustrated already."

"I sympathize entirely. Knowing secrets and gossip that you can't tell, or won't be taken seriously if you do, is maddening for anybody, but for a journalist ..."

"Well, I want to thank you for your hospitality, and for whatever I'll end up calling your comments."

"Candor, perhaps?"

"Another word for manipulation, I frequently find." Guys like him infect me with stilted speech.

"One other thing you can thank me for. When they shoot your wise ass, I promise it won't be me that does it."

"Just somebody who recently studied your facial spasms?"

"Oh, no. I like your work, actually. And admired your swing. Classic. Like Ted Williams. They should have called you the Sinaloa Clipper. And I have uses for you."

"And here your man was just telling me I was useless."

"No, I think you'll work out just fine. Just do what you would normally do, and I think we'll both be happy."

"No, I think I'll be frustrated. Maybe a little paranoid."

"That's probably healthy." He stood up, indicating my dismissal.

Chaco had moved up behind me without my knowing it, which is a little like having a semi-trailer getting in your back seat without your knowing it. "Aren't you going to ask for his autograph?"

The Man laughed again. "I'll settle for a handshake."

I couldn't refuse, could I? He'd blown me out fair and square.

In last week's column, I noted that the Venados are the only team in the league not named after an Indian tribe or a job title, such as Cottonpickers or Canecutters. I asked readers to submit some tribal or job-related suggestions for renaming the Venados, something that better expresses the nature and economy of Mazatlán. In addition to the obvious ones like the Tunafishers, the Coffeegrinders, and the Brewers, the suggestions included Gringo Wranglers, Busboys, Timesharers, Cokedealers, and Kidnappers.

"The Afternoon Mail", "El Mundo Según Mundo" Column
El Debate, December, 2000

Pepito Moran and I recognized each other immediately. Neither of us was very pleased about it, either. The paintcan-toting little jerk. He was wearing two massive dreadlocks like bull horns, a Mano Negra T-shirt, and an attitude. Like any other nineteen year-old specimen of wildlife from the Bola Ocho, where all the other skateboarding, potsmoking hippie/punksters hang behind the Eight Ball to relate, whine, grope, drink beer, listen to mercifully deafening music, sometimes even shoot a little pool.

He's a pretty decent drummer with a standard Blackshirt punk band with a cool name, *Esos Cabrones*. As in 'Who *are* Those Assholes?' He's also into staining buildings under the *nombre de espraycan* Grünji – don't omit the umlaut – and still resents me for catching him shaking a can by the Casa Romantica one night, taking it away from him, and tossing him like a rag doll while yelling in his face.

He'd come down to see who was in the big black car and was less than thrilled that I'd showed on his street, much less his house. But he overcame his impulse to slam the door and yelled for his father, then stood there squirming a drumstick around his fingers. But instead of his wildman dad, Guilllermo Benavides came into the front room and gave me a polite nod. Stout, balding, calm as banker, Momo is a lot easier to talk to than Pepito's old man, Lorenzo Moran. Who everybody calls Lobo for good reason.

When I told Momo what I was there for, Pepito stared at me a minute and snorted. "Oh, maaaan," and stomped out of the room. I heard a skateboard clatter down the stairwell.

Momo looked mildly exasperated, "Kids."

Of course if it wasn't for kids, Momo and Lobo wouldn't be in their current line of work. They'd still be in narcotics culture and marketing. Momo suddenly yelled, "*Oye, Lobón!* Get your hairy ass out here!"

The wolfman himself blasted into the room in his usual style, Tasmanian Devil on amphetamines. He rolled around the room like a demented ball of hair; looking out the window, making noises, sniffing at me, endangering furniture. He'd actually gotten hairier and worse-groomed in the last few years, an astonishing accomplishment. Finally he settled down to merely pacing the floor while combing his breakfast out of his beard and chest mane as Momo said, "Look who's come to buy one of our guns."

"Oh, a reporter," Lobo grunted. "*Señor Exposé.* Great."

"Come on, Lobo," Momo soothed, "This is Mundo. He's cool."

"Then why does he work for a newspaper?"

"Not anymore, he doesn't," drifted in from the hallway. "He works for City Hall now."

It had to be Momo's son Dario, his voice finally changing at sixteen.

"Not since yesterday, Dario," I yelled back. "Need to update your data banks."

"I don't have data banks," he shot back. "I use other people's."

Lobo kept skulking me, giving me the hairy twiceover. "Going to shoot somebody, Mundo? You're not that kind of guy." But he said it as if suspending judgement.

"Hey, you're the kind of guys who sell guns, why can't I be the kind who buys?"

"We've done worse," said the *Hombre Lobo*. Which was undoubtedly true. Lobo is shaggy as a sheepdog and wild-eyed as rabid boar, but he got his name through deeds, not superficial cosmetics. This is a man that will howl at the moon, suck the eyeballs out of a barbecued goat, demolish a truckload of police, run up walls. He and Momo have been together a long time – brawn and brains – and their career has been not so much checkered as splattered.

Finally, the wolfman stepped back out of my personal space and quit gauging my sweat and sniffing my butt. "Sure, what the hell? We'll fix you up. You can walk out of here blasting people to shit like the Almada Brothers."

"Maybe something a little more subtle. And concealable?"

"Something in a summer weight, perhaps?" Momo had a superior smile. "Look, Mundo. This is Sinaloa. We sell *cuerno de chiva*."

Yeah, the 'goat horn' is the preferred weapon of Sinaloa badasses, far and away. It's a Mexican hillbilly name for the AK-47: hicks think the curved magazine looks like a goat horn. I didn't think a big military machine gun was quite the ticket, but it did sound re-assuring in a way. I decided I'd better not handle one or I'd end up driving it home.

"Nothing smaller?"

"You really need smaller, here? That's your big criterion?" Momo isn't as fast as he used to be, but he's just as sarcastic. 'Look, Mundo. Sit down with us. Come on in here a minute."

I walked down the hall and through a doorway draped with transparent plastic curtains. It was sealed, air-conditioned, and one wall was filled with computer gear. Dario was sitting in front of a big monitor, leaning forward in some Martian massage chair while tickling the keyboard. Momo motioned me over to a pair of comfortable lounge chairs. We sat while Lobo continued dribbling himself around the room. Dario eyed him, but kept on keystroking.

"Look, Mundo," Momo started, "I think we're all agreed on this, you aren't the type of guy to have a gun. But maybe we can help you anyway, somehow?"

I laughed, "Why, times tough in the kidnapping and gunrunning business?"

"You wouldn't believe it," Momo sighed. "You've heard of *Commandante* Simón?"

Of course I had. I'd even interviewed him, if you

can call a voice-scrambled phone call an interview. He was some Colombian the state government hired to combat kidnapping, fast becoming one of Sinaloa's main industries and beginning to adversely affect business and investment. He affected a ski mask, like the Zapatistas, so nobody would know who he was and harm his family. Kidnappers being noted for their lack of respect for the family unit. I nodded.

"Well, those bastards are out of control. They don't go after the big guys like *Mochadedos* ..."

"Wait a minute," I asked, "You mean *Mochaorejas*?"

"Nah, he got forced out, maybe even dead."

Amazing ... the most famous kidnapper in Mexico. And yes, he did *mochar* people's ears and send them to their loved ones. Even when they were already trying to pay. Sort of a logo with him.

"So now there's a copycat who clips off fingers?"

"Yeah. Maybe we should set up shop as *"Los Mochapenes"*, huh?"

Yes. Dickclipper would probably provide an air of businesslike menace. "But you wouldn't really ..."

"Nah," Lobo barked, "I'd have my ex-wife do it for free. She's an expert! But listen, that antikidnap squad is a bunch of assholes. They just come after little guys like us. We're like keeping a guy an hour, taking him to his ATM machine, right?"

"Express kidnapping," I said.

"Exactly! Digital age," Dario put in. "I think of us as 'Kid-napsters'."

"But they're coming around picking up guys like us, torturing us, killing us," Lobo raved. "Shit, they're worse than we are."

"So you wouldn't recommend my hiring them?" That was the unique thing about *Comandante* Simón's brigade...it was privatized. State-funded, trained, and equipped anti-terrorist forces that you could rent by the day to look after you. Or your wife on her trip to the beauty parlor. But Lobo wasn't impressed by private sector economies. He flew into a swirling cloud of hair and gesticulations.

"Hire cops? Cops??? Fuck those cops! They're dirtier than politicians, every one of them. Crookeder than journalists!"

Momo laughed, "Be nice to Mundo, Lobo. But he's right. That's why we quit the drug business, so we wouldn't have to associate with scummy elements like the police."

Dario broke in. "Maybe I can help you out here, Mundo."

Great kid ... a baseball fan before he got swallowed alive by computers. He's a fanatic hacker, reads *Sputnik* and *Wired*, listens to an incredible combination of techno and *ranchero* music called *Nortec*, and believes Bill Gates is the Antichrist. He'd like to move the whole clan over into electronic crime, which in Mexico is one big white underbelly, but it's hard to imagine Lobo or Pepito colonizing cyberspace.

He turned to me. "So who's after you?"

"I don't know," I had to admit. "Maybe everybody."

Dario nodded, "Healthy attitude. Anybody else involved?"

I hesitated, then figured I had nothing to lose. Dario could probably find anything out anyway. "My woman. Mijares."

Dario brightened. "Ahhhh, yes. This would be the Mijares working for the PT, right? Little Miz Jackpot." He clicked keys and a file with her name on it came on his screen. More clicks and it was filled with a grainy picture of Mijares backlit in silhouette behind a gauzy scrim, obviously nude or in tights. I remembered it immediately, her controversial portrayal of the ecstasy hallucination in her theater group's self-consciously hip staging of *Agnes of God*. Wait a minute ... "Why do you have that picture?"

"Oh, I'm an admirer. Let's see, took name of famous revolutionary gun moll, correct name Montserrat Gortari y Guzman. *Licenciada* in Theater Arts at UAS, studying for *Maestral* in Political Science at UNAM, but kicked out for involvement with strike in 2000. Returned to UAS, busted out for major strike activity ... whoa, CGH member in fact. Member *of Partido de Trabajo* for nine months. Currently chief of public relations for the *Palacio* of Mazatlán ... oh, so she was your boss, right? Lessee, arrested for having abortion in 2001, case squelched."

My mouth opened, but he hit another key and popped up another picture, a really beautiful shot of her at her *quinceañera*, surrounded by other little rich girls ecstatic that their friend had managed to accomplish turning fifteen years old. And that they were getting their pictures in the newspaper. He chattered on, "Father *ex-dipudado federal,* currently party secretary for local PRI organization, assumed to be highly involved in the heroin industry. And she needs *you* for protection?"

"Well, I'm hoping to impress her."

"I wouldn't mind doing that myself." He looked at me and suddenly his eyes widened. "Hey wait, *she's* your woman? You *sleep* with her? With *that*?"

"Yeah. Only in real life. I see you're more than a casual fan."

"Well, I got interested in pictures of her. But this is strictly a professional file. She's just so damn nappable, you know. I can't think of anybody I'd rather sequester."

Lobo snorted, "Except you could take bets on who would kill you first. I'd take the narcos over the PGR, probably. Nine to four."

Which reminded me. "Can you look somebody else up on there for me, Dario?"

"Sure. Can't guarantee sexy pictures, though."

"Nickname Chaco."

Lobo went orbital. "Chaco? That same Chaco? Real name Raul Chagón?"

"Huge guy, bald, muscular. Works for Borrego, but I think he's Federal."

"Federal?" Lobo was howling. "He's Infernal! He works for Satan and Dracula! He was around the *narco* thing, was in with *Comandante* Simón at the start."

Dario had been chunking away at the keys and examining the screen. "Nothing much official here. But a lot of rumor and supposition. Newspaper columns, chatroom stuff. Narconews.com."

"And what do they rumor and chat?"

"Yes, *federales*. Also Army. Hmmm, simultaneously ... that's sort of weird. Now a DEA asset, lots of people seem to think CIA, too. Oh look, very close to Caro Quintero and that whole cartel. Was probably there for the Kikki Camarena thing. Ooo, nice picture ... you dig the Mohawk? *Ay chingao*, this is some kickass kind of guy. Very comfortable in black Kevlar eveningwear, it sounds like. A Dirty Warrior. Wait, here he's ranked as a body-building competitor. Last two years. *Sobres* ... says here he popped Colosio. Who knows? He sounds like as good a bet as any."

"You really think some guy banging around Sinaloa did Colosio?"

"Why not? Everybody else did."

"Anything about him doing in Varedas?"

"No. Not yet anyway. I can put something in about it if you want."

Momo chuckled. "Hey, Mundo, didn't you predict in your column Friday that you'd find out who killed him?"

Ah shit, that's right. Well, that will hang over me, even if the rest of the stuff fades out. I don't like blowing it in print. You can write fine for years, but make one mistake and they're all over you. Another reason I like baseball. Fail two times out of three and you're hitting .333, proba-bly a star. I told them I was hot on the trail of the killer, if not vice-versa. And ended up leaving with no gun.

"Listen, Mundo, you should stick to your strengths," Momo told me at the door. "You just don't have the moral fiber to be a vicious criminal asshole."

No problem, I thought, I'll just keep clubbing peo-ple to death. Or more probably, see what I can get from Sgt. Garcia. Out on the street, Pepito was thrashing the cobblestones on his skateboard. He sneered, pulled a can of spray paint out of his pocket, and waved it at me. He sprayed a film of it in the air, then leaned into it and snorted, rolling his eyes in simulated frenzy.

Don't get your ass kidnapstered, I thought; no-body's going to spring for the ransom.

Mexican men say there are only two women that won't betray you; your mother and your daughter. The only safe names to tattoo on your body. But I recently heard a young woman wearing only a *tanga* say that there is another, a whore. "That's why Mexican men are comfortable with us," she said, "They won't get betrayed because there is nothing on trust. "If you think that applies to my previous discussion of confidence in public officials, then you know what I am talking about.

"Names You Can Trust" *"El Mundo Segun Mundo"* Column
El Debate, January 2002

Spending quality time with Borrego and his bunch made my drive home later than I'd planned, so Angel Flores was starting to jam up with vendors and early drinkers. Carnival barriers were up so the closest I could park was Plaza Leones at the bottom of the hill. Which put me right across the street from El Penquino, renters of *Smokin, Frac,* and Fine Men's Wear. Which reminded me of what I forgot in my mad dash to get back to Mijares – to pick up the *frac* I was going to wear to the Masked Ball. Foreigners weird out over a strange word like *frac,* then turn around and call it a *tuxedo.* The forced convenience of my detour fitted right in with what I was thinking over, that Borrego is how the perfect dictatorship works. You do what you want and it turns out to be exactly what they wanted you to do all along. If you rebel, it turns out they wanted you to do that. It makes Big Brother look feeble and clumsy by comparison. But then, hadn't he just caused me to go right where I hadn't remembered I was supposed to? It might cut both ways.

Mijares didn't seem to care that I'd come home empty-holstered, so to speak. I asked again about getting firearms from her *grillo* buddies, but she wasn't interested. What she was interested in, it turned out, was getting my clothes off and variously positioning herself in such a way to get screwed from here to eternity. I quenched my lust, disabled my body, scorched my soul, and snuffed my mind. We lay in the bed, finally, and I sort of burrowed into her.

I said, "This is it. I'm home. I'm just going to stay right here forever."

She giggled. "Right there? You aren't going to come up for air? We're going to the Fantasy Ball, remember."

"As far as I'm concerned," I mumbled, "That *was* the fantasy ball."

She chortled and nudged up against me in approving and salacious ways. She rose to her knees, disturbing my burrow and general worldview. We had pushed the mattress over by the railing and she leaned against it, head nestled on her crossed arms, her butt supported by her ankles and my hands.

She sighed. "I wish I could just do this, Mundo. Just live up here in the sky with you. Fly free of all the dirt and noise and ugliness."

I knelt up beside her, looking down as the afternoon sun broke the clouds and shone on the bay below. "Well, you're definitely invited." I didn't like the idea that sticking around with me was one of those things she wanted to do but wouldn't.

"Would it work out for long?" she asked, staring over at the hill where her family lived. She laughed softly. "Did you know my mother was a Carnival queen? Arcely I, Queen of Flower Games in 1971. I coulda been a contender. Up to thirteen, I was actually being groomed for it. A natural. But it didn't work out."

"Sure, whisked off like Anastasia. By commies. Whereabouts still a mystery."

"Not communists, Mundo. Revolutionaries."

"Of course. Class struggle *aficionados*." As soon as I said it, I knew I'd goofed.

"Let's not get into the class thing, OK? Everyone's born somewhere, and it's up to them to claw their way out of it. That's why the CGH are heroic. Why I joined them."

Oh sure, real heros, the *Consejo General de Huelgistas*. A General Strike Counsel of guerilla wannabes, professional agitpropistas, and thugs, in my humble opinion – voiced less humbly in various publications. I looked for a way out of the conversation and back into Loverland, when she turned around, her eyes pouncing on me.

"Sooner or later this will come up, you know."

"Later sounds good."

"Not really. You know I'm dedicated to those ideals. It leads away from the old corruption and paternalism and into a better future for everyone. I want to see that future, help it happen. And I want to take you with me."

That didn't sound bad. But then she said, "But I need a certain kind of man, Mundo. A man who can smash in and take things, not accept rules and restrictions. I hate the men of my class because they get it all given to them. I want a man who just reaches out and takes it. I'm hungry and I want a man who is also hungry, like a tiger."

"I've played the Tigers. They're hungry because they suck." She started to speak, but I beat her to it. Apparently later wasn't going to work out. "Just kidding. But you do realize there's different kinds of hungry, right? You could say a fat lawyer who missed breakfast and lunch is hungry. But it's not the same as saying it about a family with twelve children trying to live on five dollars a day on a farm with no more water."

She glowered at me, "I've been through a lot of changes since school, Mundo. You can't get to me with that, 'the truly poor' stuff any more."

Too bad, because it gave me an edge on her; not really belonging to the class of people she supposedly championed. "Good. I hate having to remind you rich kids."

"You're not exactly a child of the streets, yourself."

"Nope, I was a railroad brat. Still fairly poor, though." She'd never really asked about that before. Probably afraid I'd grown up as a starving peasant in Chiapas. "But that's not the point. I got out of poverty because of my gifts. I was bigger and smarter and faster. Does that qualify me for a medal?"

"Gifts." She sneered.

"What else would you call it?" I held up my hand, ticking off my fingers. "You've got brains, family, class, looks, nasty habits. What could you possibly need?"

She stood and walked to the mirror, giving herself an objective female scan, like a pilot checking out his plane. Her tone was flat as a damp tortilla. "The 'gift' of beauty."

"Tell me it means nothing to you. That you'll donate your looks to refugees."

227

"Hardly." She scowled. "What it is, it's a tool. A means to an end. Part of a hand of cards."

Right. She'd like to think her demeanor and dress in the office is a sublimation, sacrificing her old radical rags for the good of some cause. But I think she still liked the comforts she was born to.

"A tool to do *what*? You have it all; what could you possibly need?"

"Something to put it in!" she screamed. She turned from the mirror with her fists clenched, startling me with her ferocity. Not to mention giving me another erection.

"I have to do something with it, put it to work," she said in a calmer tone, but still deadly serious and pissed-off. "You sound like my father, saying I have a responsibility to use my gifts. Don't gifts belong to the one they're given to? And there's no reason I can't use them against the ones who gave them to me, is there? Is there?"

I smiled at her – disarmingly, I hoped. "So who gave you brains and beauty? Are you going to use God-given talents against God? Once you get Mazatlán nailed down?"

She gave me a look, then stared out over the rail. "He's definitely on my shit list." She came to stand over me, by the bed. I laid back and put my hands behind my head. Let her take it where she wanted to. Hoping she'd get a hint from the boner.

But she looked down at me very seriously. "Look, I don't get into that whole poor/rich thing anymore. I'm not even in it for the poor anymore."

I didn't say anything so carefully that I might as well have sprayed *Numero Uno* Rules on the wall with imported whiskey.

"Up yours, Mundo," she snapped. "No, I'm continually identifying myself with something a lot bigger than that now. It's not just the poor who are getting screwed, it's everybody really. I just keep feeling my consciousness, and my mission, expanding and including everything."

"Once you become one with everything, will you be able to tell which is everything and which is you?"

She broke into a smile. "I don't think that will be a problem, do you?"

"It might be for me. Am I included in everything?"

"No," she whispered in my ear, "You're an additional ingredient that will cost extra. But I can afford it."

Stroking her into motion, I said, "Maybe after the Revolution they'll have a Red Martyrs Queen pageant. Barbed wire tiaras and little bombs tossed to adoring crowds."

"Physical beauty is not a factor in Post-Capitalist thinking," she muttered. But she's a born queen, no doubt about it.

The main reason I regret that "magical realism" has reportedly passed away and left us "*McOndo*" – the mondo condo, the Empty V, the reality *noir* – is because it's more important now than ever for the people of Earth to keep and respect the objects, rituals, and spirits of the magical arts, because they are sources of both individual and popular power. The United States and Europe have their power, and their versions of reality. But other peoples should hold on to their butterflies, saints, miracles, *quetzales*, dreamtigers, necropolises, talking skulls, flying ships and girls that ascend into heaven. Power is not a dream, of course. But dreaming is certainly power. If we must be realists, we might as well be magical realists.

"*Sur* Realism" by Mundo Carrasco
La Isla de Mediodia, November, 2001

The Fantasy Ball might be the purest vestige of what Carnival once was. It has masks and costumes and a swirl of romantic libido. It pulses with light and sound and movement and nothing is as it appears. Nothing can be phony or heavy or disappointing at a Fantasy Ball. Naturally, it's held at Valentino's – celebrants of their own carnality swirling like flaming butterflies in the white castle above the sea. Life in the flesh lane, the Mask of Dread Death can just wait until Wednesday. I handed Mijares out of our cab into a teeming mass of pheromones and the raw gutwallop of post-industrial disco static. The patios and stairways were packed with a milling mob of young people, mostly Studio 54 wannabes swarming to score fashion drugs, attention and each other. Mijares strode through them like a lion parting dry grass.

CODETUR, the tourism agency that sponsors Carnival, provided some pretty nice prizes for the best costumes, including a trip to Cancun. For two, of course, our saying is, "*Cancun? Con quien?*" But not that many kids wanted to win. Most of them were wearing masks and their usual Valentino's clothes. Not that the fashions of beautiful young *cocodrilos* aren't fairly fantastic in their own way. Cute young women in Mexico generally dress the way Americans might expect prostitutes to dress. But for the fantasy ball they were toning it up – lovely young princesses forced into coke whoredom by evil uncles. They wore flames of all colors, blosssoms from the jungle, schools of reef fish, flushes of parrots, pastel waterfalls and primary volcanos. They showed skin in all the best places, tossed blazing manes, flashed hungry white teeth. They glowed like the pulsating embers of tequila, XTC, and unspent youth. But I like real costumes. The very idea of a costume prize is *muy Carnaval*, a beauty contest for your clothes, applause and gifts for your superficial masquerade. It also made it very feasible for Mijares and I to attend. We stalked in disguise, like the night.

Mijares was wearing a black sheath spangled with silver explosions and made from some clingy material. And I mean clinging desperately. It plunged like a pelican, making her look like two scoops of vanilla in a black goblet. From front or back. She was falling out the top and crawling out the bottom. The dress managed to suggest a nymphomaniac *coca-puf* while hinting at decadent royalty. It had big flounces at ground level that she kicked along like a soccer ball pulling a short kinky train. She had covered her hair and face with a silver mask modeled after something from an Aztec tomb and studded with stones. She'd pulled the whole getup out of my closet; I have no idea how it got there. I was a silverscreen goodguy in white tuxedo with matching boots, Stetson sombrero, and Lone Ranger mask. Just a stunning couple of kids. The crowd opened before us, closed in behind us like open ocean as we swept through the door.

CODETUR had set up manikins at each entrance to the dance floors, dressed in lavish princess costumes and harlequin masks. I won't even bother making subtle commentary on that. Except to wish them a swell time in Cancun, hope everybody is anatomically correct. Inside Valentino's was the most chaotic environment I've ever experienced. It sounded like there were five different pieces of music playing at once – all at distortion levels – and a jetliner taking off. The lighting reflected the mood, disco ball shrapnel, a video jitter of green laser beams, dueling spotlights, deranged slide projectors, little pockets of ultraviolet. I led her straight out onto the dance floor, the heart of the pulsing mystic opal, and led her into a dance with one hand on her waist and the other leading her into a sort of Disney movie waltz. Tripping the blacklight fantastic.

The music seemed to blend into one long number, but I only remember the *tambora*-driven *Papakis* song, traditional at Sinaloa Carnivals. We twirled and glittered, gathering a few eyes, but not speaking to anyone. Clinging to each other, really. Another costumed reveler seemed entranced with us; he quit dancing to move towards us and stare. A big reveler, too, although his gorilla suit and silk top hat probably made him look bigger. Or her, I suppose. If I hadn't been in such a magic, Cinderella-makes-it-to-the-ball sort of mood, I might have let him cut in, he was so fixated on us.

Instead, I waltzed over to a fire exit, bumped it open with my butt, and swung Mijares through like Fred Astaire. The alarm sounded – like anybody could hear it in that madhouse. The door slammed shut, instlantly plunging us from disco inferno to the pounding beat of big waves against the flat oyster shelf that supports the Magic Kingdom. We skittered along a metal catwalk, then down the fire excape stairs to the light skiff of beach sand that hangs on the cratered shelf.

Mijares kicked off her shoes and we moved closer, grooving to the music from Valentino's and the bass thud of waves throwing spray up into the lights to ring us with a curtain of colored jewels. She had her head tucked under my cheek, almost hanging on my hands, as we circled lazily in the sand. She whispered directly into my ear from about an inch away.

"Are you desperately in love with me, Mundo?"

"You don't know? I thought women always knew that stuff?"

"I wanted you to say it, put it in your kind of words."

"*Desfrenadamente.*" Call it 'unbrakedly'. All those curves and me with no brakes, as the truckers tell their honies.

"Good word. Would you take a bullet for me? Risk everything for me?"

"I took your bullet right on the trademark and I've

already been around you long enough that I have nothing left, so what could I risk?"

"How about your life, *estupido?* Or your career? What if it comes to that? You might want to deal yourself out, is what I'm saying."

"I can live without your love ... I've proved that to myself. People kick things, you know. I just don't want to."

"Kicking Mijaddiction. I knew you'd find some romantic metaphor. Maybe there should be one of those anonymous recovery groups like *Alcolicos Anonimos.*"

"*Mejor un borracho conocido que un alcolico anonimo.*"

She laughed. "Would you rather be an anonymous alcoholic or a famous drunk?"

"I want to be right here. With you. Alone. Forever."

"Trite. But all that lovey-dovey stuff always is. What comes through is the sincerity. You almost make me ashamed, Mundo."

"For any particular thing off a fairly long list?"

"For not loving you as much as you love me, you deserve it. For not loving anybody. Or myself."

"I don't think conquerors subscribe to all that love-yourself psychology. They just conquer and get on with it."

"They?"

"You. I don't know if you still think you are a revolutionary, if you ever did or ever were. What you are is somebody who can't handle losing."

"You don't know the whole problem. The thing is, I'm dying to lose. Looking for the chance."

"To lose what?"

"Myself."

I tried to take that lightly, since I couldn't understand it and it disturbed me. "Well, nobody else can ever lose yourself for you."

"No, I think that's exactly how it works. It's the one game you can never throw, no matter how hard you try."

And how hard she could try was damned impressive. We left the ball when I noticed the gorilla leaning on the parapet watching us dance. I thought he might grab Mijares and climb up one of the spires and didn't want to have to go rent a biplane to shoot him down. We cruised back to my place by the seaside route in a white *pulmonia* with strings of little blue lights inside the canopy. She walked to the rail and stared out at the bay for a long time, while I stood behind her, wrapping her in my arms and nuzzling her like a moonstruck saddle horse. Then she turned us around and moved us in front of the full-length mirror glued to one of the pillars that hold up the shed. She leaned back into me, put her hand up to my cheek, staring at us in the mirror. She started to pose, and I could tell it was working on her. One way a beautiful woman can lose herself is through the looking glass.

Watching her reflection was the first time I ever felt that I'm not a bad foil for her. Big, rangy ballplayer in a well-fitted tux with the movie queen on his arm. I hit a couple of poses with her, Gary Cooper putting on the ritz – I'm too tall and clean-shaven to do Pedro Infante – and she got deeply thrilled. She waltzed us over to the railing, looking out on the postcard glamour of the frothing cove lit for celebration. I felt like she wanted to get the background into the mirror, too, arranging angles like a centerfold shoot. She spun in my arms like a dancer, swooned prettily against my manly shoulders.

She pulled off her gown, had nothing on under it but a maddening scent. She started posing again in high heels, long gloves, and her mask, prettily clinging to me, peekabooing the mirror. My tux got a lot less well-fitted. I swept her up in my arms and held her in front of the mirror, then turned and pressed her up over my head like those calendar paintings of Aztec warriors sacrificing scantily clad maidens. I stepped over to the rail, offered her beauty to the night, to the sea, to the town.

She was trembling on my hands like a mare. I lowered her slowly, let her slide down me like a banister, clutching at me in a fever. I don't remember anybody doing any unzipping, but suddenly I was inside her and she was swinging back and forth like a bell clapper; clinging to my neck, then leaning back against my forearms, her hair trailing over the railing. I looked down at my *frac*, at her gorgeous body and queenly accessories, down at the beach lit for the ball.

I whispered, "Bond. James Bond." She snapped back to arms' length, staring at me with a wild, wide-eyed joy. And went just totally, completely wild. One thing I could do for that girl was take her to the movies

I was benefiting from her sudden seizure, but it was a little scary. She was in real danger of lunging out of my arms, off her perch and over the edge. I pushed her up against the railing and got a good firm grip on her hips. She wanted to move freely, and seemed capable of clawing through me to get there, but for some reason I held her down on the rail and tried to hammer her senseless with my entire body. Her reaction to that was explosive and not at all nice. The first time we were together she toyed with me, earlier she'd been exhilarated, then giving. But there on the rail I saw her true sexuality for the first time. I was beyond her beauty by then, but learning a new awe for her libido. I was slipping the curves, trying to pound her over the fence – but there's a lot more to her than curves. She's essentially a southpaw knuckleball from deep left hell. She was hitting on abandon, mad greed, and raving helplessness like a person overdosing on a lethal stimulant. And then the rain broke loose around us.

The storm that had threatened the entire Carnival came in on a cool waft of breeze that made Mijares arch and coo, then a colder lash of low pressure that raised bumps on both of us. Then the immediate driving blast of cold water. Scouring, drumming, deafening rain gushed all over us, dimpled our skin with the impact of hundreds of tiny pellets, tightened our flesh, pasted down our hair, soaked our clothes. She suddenly gave up her struggle and flopped back, her whole upper body hanging out into the air, her head waving from side to side, her hair slashing like a mare's tail in the night, flicking the rain out where it caught the light like white fish flashing off into the depths. When she climaxed, it sounded like she was drowning. Then she hung limp, rain sluicing down her belly, falling from her nipples, cascading off her dangling fingers. I reached carefully down, got a handful of her hair, and drew her back up into my arms. We leaned against the rail with our arms wrapped around each other, cold water pouring across our eyes and puddling up between our breasts, shuddering to the giant tolling of our hearts.

I dried her off before putting her down on the bed, toweling her gently while she clung to my neck. I laid her on the pillow, looked around for a blanket, and covered her up. I looked down at her, curled up like a child. Normally that would have been the point when I started to cool off, wanting to lie down, maybe have a beer. But with her, I was still aroused in a different way. I wanted to bury myself in her. It wasn't over by any means. Sex, apparently, doesn't have to hit a peak and slake off like a burnt-out match. Not if there is something in it that goes beyond skin and muscle and satiation.

I slipped under the blanket with her and she threw herself at me, holding me with fierce strength and sobbing. Then the tears broke. Another flow ran down my chest, this time hot and salty. I heard her whispering and brought my ear down until I could hear her saying, "Don't ever let me leave you, Mundo. Don't ever let me leave."

I hugged her as close as I could, and thought, "She's fallen. She's actually in love with me."

Then I thought, "For now." But didn't really believe it. I only wanted to bathe in the torrent of her tears.

SUNDAY
FEBRUARY TENTH

DIA DE SANTA ESCOLASTICA

Carnival Calendar

Children's Ball, Salon Las Flores, 10 AM
Second Parade, Malecon, 3 PM

Grafitti is an American infection. When Mexicans look to the United States, we are seeing our future. To us it looks material, nameless, faceless, amoral, scribbled on. It looks like Los Angeles. And when gringos look at Mexico, they are seeing *their* future. Hispanic, thirdworldly, crowded, collective. Also like Los Angeles.

Los Angeles is one of the great Mexican cities, like Miami is one of the great Cuban cities, like New York was a capitol of Europe. In Mexico, "Northwest" means what "West" means in the United States, wild, lawless, free, cowboy. But if you go west in the United States you come to a beach and there you are. Whereas if you keep going *Noroeste* in Mexico, you reach the United States. Either way, you end up in L.A.

"Handwriting On The Wall" by Mundo Carrasco
"LA Times Magazine", May 2000

I felt damned good. *Un chingo de* good. I never woke up feeling better in my life, not even after signing with Anaheim or winning the *Serie Caribe*. The sky was clear all around, finches and doves were warbling in the trees, hummingbirds hovered to sip pink hibiscus water from the feeder Luz gave me. I woke up relaxed and happy and suntouched and secured. But above all I woke up lying right up against – practically imbedded in – The Finest Ass In The Known Universe. My nose was full of her odors, the expensive imported kind and the natural variety that grow wild and rude. I remembered waking up earlier, at first dawn, and capitalizing on my position relative to the Finest Etc. to the point that we both fell back asleep for three hours and there didn't seem to be any sheets anywhere. No problem, sleeping by Mijares is like embracing a water heater. I took a deep sniff, got a good look, and got up to relieve myself.

A project that didn't look to be all that easy, except that I have never minded using the sink. It actually requires less water to flush that way, if you need more justification than simple geometry and anatomy. But I don't: this is a male heritage, a convenience that doesn't quite make up for the problems created by a protruding unit. An urban reminder of the way a man should live, cooking over a fire, sleeping under the stars, eliminating in the chill open air, screwing out under the rain.

As usual, I scanned the town while whizzing away. And saw the handwriting on the wall. *¡Putamadre!* That little *cabróncito* MicroBio had sprayed his name halfway up the wall of the Belmar. And a message, for once, *Bin Laden Os Ama.* The little psycho climbed up there somehow and hung by his eyelashes to write, Bin Laden Loves Us, in red paint. *Two* visible smears of his wretched identity across my view, in addition to the damned Beatriz Paredes murals the PRI painted on the seawall.

It pisses me off completely that they make us look at their slogans and colors for *their own internal elections.* Like it matters to us who rules in their party headquarters. But the PRI got their comeuppance in 2000, this little MicroBio bastard has got to be stopped and his whole nasty activity stamped out. Who first called something the 'moral equivalent of war'? Probably somebody totally immoral. But in this case, it was right on, we needed a crusade against this uglification.

It's currently fashionable to call graffiti an artform, or at least self-expression. But it is much less than art, and worse than a crime. Staining buildings reverses the entire order of self-expression, of trying to create something you're proud enough to put your name on. The stainer does nothing but sign his name ... to what? A building somebody else built? The city? Society? Does signing it somehow possess it? In which case, why do the stainers always use false names? What self have they expressed? They are miring our spirit down into a scribble of anonymous noise.

The infection is powered by outside influences, psychology and subliminals, national feelings of inferiority, fashionable attitudes, secret symbols. You can only fight it with those same weapons. On a sudden impulse I slipped Mijares' phone out of the pile of clothes on the floor and punched in the home number for Ibaez Lermanes, my old boss at *Noroeste.* I leaned out over the rail, turning my head and cupping my hands so I wouldn't wake Mijares. I had some ambitious plans for how to do that. He answered himself, didn't seem too surprised to get a call from an ex-employee on Sunday morning. I started raving, hitting him with plans that I was just forming as I spoke.

It would be an Anti-Children's Crusade, spear-headed by *Noroeste* editorials. I would bring other papers on board. Coordinated approach, psychological warfare, shaping of minds. Re-educate people to reject this creeping wall fungus. I was well into a scheme to cut against the artist/outlaw image of stainers, not glorifying them as artists or criminals, but treating them as infantile, unpatriotic brats. Gradually putting out expert opinions that the activity was a symptom of repressed homosexuality. But he cut me off.

"Maybe being around politics too much has caused you to forget," he said, "but we are not propaganda ministers. We are journalists. We observe and report. Reality isn't our fault."

"We just obey the Prime Directive?"

"What?"

"You know, *El Trek*. Don't interfere with local culture and history. So the responsible thing is not to be responsible for anything?"

"Only for informing people about what's going on, Mundo."

"Is that why there are eight pages of opinion columns in each issue?"

"There's a difference between an upfront opinion and trying to run the world by stealth. You're always trying to be the artiste, it's not professional."

"This is no ordinary situation. It's plague, infection. And we can help combat it."

"Look, let's skip the philosophy for now," he said. "Let me point out what seems to have slipped your mind. You don't work here anymore, remember? You quit and went to work for the city and *El Debacle*. Hard to say which is worse."

"Right. And I'd be willing to come back. Go with me on this and I'll quit them both and work for you. What could be a more important civic ideal than keeping it from being turned into a scratchpad for delinquent *drogadictos?*"

"Avoiding the corruption of newspapers by power

plays from hidden interests."

That was a kick in the crotch, hardly my usual self-image. Before I could come to grips with it, he sent me another hot grounder. "Anyway, I'm not sure we'd find that offer as enticing as you might think, Mundo. You're kind of damaged goods these days."

"Not as damaged as some would like."

"You put your finger right on another problem. You're drawing fire. But mostly, you're tainted now, *chico*. We're the New Journalism for Mexico, remember? Transparent, honest, no party agendas, no government carrots."

"I'm not a vegetable. I'm a journalist, remember?"

"It may be you crossed some line, Mundo. Like they say about turning to crime. Something you can't cross back over. It's sort of flattering that you think you can do more to change the world working for me than for the city, but that's not really our line."

"Fine. I thought you'd welcome a chance to accomplish something like this. I'll talk to somebody else."

"My guess, Mundo, you'll get the same answer. You're burning a lot of bridges these days. If you don't watch out, you won't be able to work for any paper in town."

A good Old Movie Line, but clumsily delivered. And, in Real World sense, ridiculous. I wished I'd been in his office so I could laugh in his face. But I just said, "You mean I'd have to go up to Mexico city and write for papers with editors who can read? Screw women that don't cross themselves during foreplay? Or maybe go back up North and play minor league ball, earn about ten times what you paid me? You really know how to intimidate a guy."

"Know what I think? I think you've become one of *Them*," he snapped. "Which reminds me; I have a message for you for some reason. Sr. Gortari y Guzmán himself would like you to meet with you at your earliest convenient. Carrasco, I wasn't your private secretary when you *worked* here." And he hung up.

Leaving a pretty big dent in what had been one of my greatest moods ever, until MicroBio smeared into my life and revealed me as tainted, burned, and corrupt. But it got worse. I turned around to see that Mijares had heard it all. And was grinning.

I said, "I just got some bad news," and the smile went away like an eclipse of the sun. She asked what the news was in a very small voice. From her viewpoint there were all sorts of possibilities, I realized. "I'm as corrupt as the rest of you."

The smile came back, but not quite as clean and shining as before. "I always thought you showed promise."

I sat down with my back to the railing and thought that over for a minute.

"Everybody was telling me I needed something I want so bad I'd do anything for it. And here you are." I could suddenly look at Mijares as a very slippery slope away from the golden idylls of *Juego Limpio*. Somebody wrote that evil is the face of naked need. If it's okay to kill to win, why is it wrong to cheat?

"You're learning that you have to use whatever power you have to work against people's will and behind their backs for their own good," she said. "Haven't you always used your position and talents to bring people around to your way of thinking?"

I'd made her damned point for her, and didn't like it.

"I'm not that smart and I'm for sure not that sophisticated. I made my fame and fortune swinging a club, for crissakes. If I was a musician, I'd be a drummer. Take a simple and obvious idea, pound people on the head with it. Repeat as necessary."

"As long as it's in a good cause, right?"

There was no way to argue. She'd caught me in the cookie jar and approved. Oddly enough, it was her approval that made me so sure it was the wrong thing to do. A very bad sign. I realized that my whole crusade idea was, after all, corruption. But I *knew* it was the thing to do. Graffiti is a contagious infection. We caught it from the United States, along with other spiritual diseases like rap music and automobiles. A lot of Mexicans are afraid the gringos will invade us some day, or kick off some little cleansing war against us, like Iraq or Vietnam. We'd be a cheaper enemy; less travel expenses. But cars kill more of us than missiles. I think gringos do us more harm by impressing us, and we do ourselves more harm by imitating them than by fearing them.

But the whole drift was making me uncomfortable, so I made the mistake of changing the subject.

"By the way, I got a message your father would like to see me. He must have left them all over town."

The subject wasn't all that changed. She went from superior beam to dark hostility instantly, like I'd stepped on her tail.

She snapped, "No!" And she meant it. "The only reason he'd call you is to find out if you know where I am."

"A reasonable question. I'm sure he's concerned."

"You have no idea what his motives are." She was gathering force and darkening like a tropical storm about to be officially upgraded and given a name.

"Well, then, let's find out." I snagged her phone, flipped it open, and asked her the number. She returned a blank, black stare.

"Okay, I'll call around some PRIistas I know and find out."

"No! Are you crazy? What happened the last time you went to the house?"

"The first time I went there. I remember it vividly. It's not every day I win the woman of my dreams. Or kill anybody. First time for that, too."

"Don't do it, Mundo. Don't call him, don't meet him. Don't mention him."

"Look, we can't perch up here forever, we need to find out what's going on. Besides, he's your father."

"So what are you going to do, go ask him for my hand?"

"Well, your hand also has its uses, but at the moment there are other parts ..."

"Don't bet on it."

Which should have been another big warning flag on the road to my blissful future. But I did call Gortari, who said I could come over right then if it would be convenient. I told him I would. Mijares sunk into a defensive huddle, covered with blankets and showing only reproach and spectacularly beautiful glares.

I said, "I am going to see him because he's the only

244

one in this thing that I'm certain doesn't want you dead."

She gave me another dropdead look, but didn't argue.

"Right now all I care is keeping you safe. Not politics, not family feuds, not even if you let me touch you or not. I want you safe and alive. He might be able to help, he might know something. I'm not going to tell him anything."

"Just showing up there will tell him something. Just calling him told him something. Everything you say or do will tell him something. He'll manipulate you, he will win you over, crush you or buy you out. He's out of your league."

"I thought I was so promising at the art of corruption."

"That's the worst. Better if you were as crooked as he is or as pure as a virgin. In between is where he carves his meat."

"Most girls are just dying to drag a guy home to their parents."

She glared some more, then laughed. She threw off the blankets and stood up on the bed, feet spread, fists on her hips. "Do I look like most girls to you, *estupido*?"

I walked over to her and looked up into her face. "You look like no girls ever. Like *all* girls rolled into one. First, last, and total. You're an unassisted triple, a grand slam, no hits, no runs no errors, a 1.000 season, no games out of first. I'm sunk."

She laughed again, then kicked my upper arm, knocking me over on the bed. She dropped down on her knees – on my chest. She started beating on me, showering punches on my trunk and arms. I managed to overcome and contain. To infiltrate and pacify. When I left she was drowsing, sprawled across the bed in disjointed, innocent indecency.

At the door I said, "Trust me. I'm going to pull us out of this." She didn't say anything, just lay there like a strewn casualty.

Last week I was trying to explain to my gringo neighbor the concept of *gestoria social*, the whole system of contact points in neighborhoods where the common people can stop by and complain, request, make contact with the political system. The one he saw was PRI, so he asked if they had always had them or just started opening them this year. I said, "They always had them, but now they have to listen." But I'm not so sure. They'll probably keep trying to figure out some other way to keep control. It's just their nature.

"*Antisocial Science*", El Mundo Según Mundo Column
Noroeste, May 2001

Until I walked up that narrow path to the cross, I never really knew how Mazatlán was laid out. My previous visit to the Gortari mansion had been a bit rushed, and I hadn't had time to pick my way up past the lovely old Zeus and Athena chapel and through the garden that spills down from the odd little rocky prominence where somebody long ago had, this being Mexico, put up a cross. I wouldn't have been doing it this time, either, except that the very competent-looking bodyguards who braced me at the gate made discreet and presumably secure cellular calls and *Señor* Gortari told them to let me in and direct me up to the cross garden. A bit of a tricky ascent, too. I found him on his knees, dressed in old jeans and sweatshirt with an Adidas sweatband, using the flat side of a machete to insert tiny succulent plants into the cavities between crumbling rocks. He greeted me in a friendly manner, but without getting up. As he continued embroidering his private mountain with plants, I asked him if was hard to get good help.

He smiled in a slightly self-satisfied way. "Who should I pay to enjoy myself for me?"

I looked out over the rather startling cityscape below. My house is higher, and the Mirador restaurant and lighthouse on Crestón are higher yet, but neither has the impact you get from the cross. It rises directly out of the slopes of Cerro Viggia, and looks like you could spit right into Playa Sur. As he puttered, I scanned the old buildings

247

and a new vision of progress and order slowly merged with my previous ideas about my own city. I could see the structure and the history of it, slight differences in architecture and colors of materials shading the familiar streets with a contour of time and purpose.

I could see exactly why the original settlement had been planted on the estuary banks, how the middle class would build over towards the beach at Olas Altas, how the civic center would be removed to the north, how the wealthy would climb up Viggia and spread around its slopes for the marine views. I could sense how it was before they built the causeways connecting the Crestón lighthouse to the mainland and Goat Island to Stone Island – easily creating the best Pacific Coast harbor north of Acapulco. To the north I could see the big hotels of the Golden Zone, the destiny that pulled the town into being, emptied the downtown and turned the old buildings to ruins, brought in foreigners to inhabit and restore those old ruins. I got a feeling of predestination from it, the city growing towards a purpose the way water flows into a cavity.

So why couldn't I see some destiny in my own life, something pulling my steps in the right direction? So far the only evidence that I'm inevitably doing the will of a higher power is Borrego. I wonder why it's easier for us to believe that we are controlled by conspiracies of evil than conspiracies of good. And I wonder why I lived in Mazatlán almost my entire life, a *Patasalada* born and bred, making my living knowing the town ... and could only see its perspective from up in a rich man's folly?

Behind me, he stood up and dusted off his trousers. As I turned he said, "Or were you talking about the help at the gate?"

There was no need to mention the obvious reasons for them – ChromeDome and the Cowboy hadn't had to kill anybody to get in and start pawing Mijares, had they? I said they looked American and he nodded, scowling a little. "Yes, it seems a ranking member of this country's majority party has to go out of the country to get reliable help."

"Speaks volumes, doesn't it?"

He gave me a pained look. "They're called Pinkerton. Seems like an unlikely name for instilling fear in the criminal classes, doesn't it?"

I shrugged, "Whatever it takes. Here all we need is three letters to symbolize power and violence and corruption. You know, PGR ... triple letters of that sort."

"Very subtle, Raymundo. It'll be interesting to see how your distaste for the PRI survives the next five years of outside administration. You might end up finding out other parties have their faults and that anybody with power tends to use it the same way."

"You mean have more than one power-grabbing, lying, murdering, conspiracy to repress the people? Not a novelty, you forget I've lived in the United States. But you know, the way you call a duly elected party of Mexican citizens 'outside' explains my feelings towards the PRI very nicely."

"It's *en voga* these days to blame everything on us. Free kicks at the tricolor."

Ay, sore point for Mundo. "You see? That right there. The Tri is the flag of Mexico, not party property. You know how sick I get of you assholes pretending your party is identical to the nation? You had it that way for too long, but that's over now."

"Is it? Has the party disbanded? Are there no PRI-ista governors or senators?"

"Give it some time. You're finished. You've been running this country like your own personal ranch for way too long."

"Then who should run it, Mundo? Some *Indio* from Chiapas? Gringo oil companies? Who should run things, if not people who've shown they're capable of doing it?"

"If anybody ever showed that, I'd be happy to have them in charge. But you're running a sinking ship here. You blew the oil resources, you're fouling up tourism and fishing, you built a government that was a disgrace and embarrassment."

"So should the PAN run everything? With their Christer Cola attitudes? Or those PRD imbeciles, wishing this was Cuba?"

"At the moment anybody would be better. Just because we need to know there are alternatives. If things can change, there's a chance they can get better."

"Especially better than us, the designated delinquents, right? We lose the presidency, and suddenly we're carrying everybody's sins."

"You people are never going to get it, are you? Democracy, I mean."

He pulled off his worn leather gloves and slapped them on his thigh.

A real man of the soil up here, isn't he, I thought.

He pointed out a small stone bench I hadn't noticed, tucked in below the cross on the bay side of the cliff. "There are things more important than politics for us to talk about, Raymundo. Come on, have a seat."

I stepped down to the charmingly carved marble love seat. He lowered himself beside me, reached under the seat and came up with a small plastic cooler. He opened it and offered me – what else? – an expensive, imported beer. I took the can of Coors and popped it open. He took a sip of his own, wiped his face on his sleeve and toasted me. He smiled. "Miller time."

Oh yes, we are sophisticated international types up here. He waved a hand out towards the city view, but what he said was, "I assume she's either hiding with you or those *huelgista* punks ... and naturally I can't talk to them."

I took a deep tug on the Coors. I hate to say it, but it makes Pacífico taste like dirt. "Who knows? Invite them up here to see the sights, have a few high-priced beers, they might rethink their anarchist ways."

He laughed, offered me another toast with his can. "So it's not you hiding her?"

"You don't know?" I asked, "And would I tell you if I was?"

He digested that a moment. "You mean she's hiding from *me?*"

"I think she always has been, actually."

"You could be right. I enjoy those cheap psychojournalistic insights, by the way. *El Mundo Según Mundo,* no?"

"Well, I'd hate to shock a long-term reader."

"Really? No wonder they have you in editorial instead of news."

I took another hit of the Coors. Great taste. Not filling. You could sit here with your butt cooled by old marble, looking down at the municipal creation, with the cross behind you. And call your shots.

"Yes, I know about her little playhouse over in Playa Norte," he went on. "And that she's not there. I know she's not in the Martyrs of April House. And I guess she could end up deciding that I might be one of the people she needs to hide from. Not me personally so much as ... you know."

"None of that is important. She's all right and she's fairly safe, I'd say."

"Then she must be with you. I figure you're good for her."

That took me aback. "Well, that's pretty surprising. I think it also bums me out."

"Why? You're an athlete, a public figure, actually. Decent, clean-living, smart. Certainly preferable to those tattooed, nihilist strikers she runs with or those zombies in her theater group. Or that pathetic bunch of guttersnipes down at the *Palacio*."

"So a personage like you doesn't mind somebody like me having a sporadic affair with your daughter? You just keep blowing my mind."

He laughed. "Then you'll love this. I wouldn't mind you *marrying* her."

"Would you excuse me while I just sort of sit here and gape?"

"What's so odd about that? You're quite a catch. I know she's not going to marry anybody from, you know, our world."

"The Lords. The Rightful Owners."

"I don't know about rightful, consult with a priest. But you see what I mean. And the men she moves with are totally unacceptable. I doubt they could get seated at the Panama. But you, you're for real. And you tame her a little."

"Not that I've noticed. In fact, I've noted the opposite."

He held up his hand in a pained halting gesture. "Please, Raymundo."

251

"I meant ..."

"And I meant, you're good for her. I think someday before too long you might be a substantive person, shall we say. Riches, influence. Maybe live up here on the hill."

"Hey, I can see my house from here." And I could, right across the Old Town, on Cerro Neveria. "And I'd rather live there than here."

It was like he could read my mind. Without even paying for a copy of the paper. "Nice little place. For a man with no family."

Ow, good shot. And perfectly delivered; standing there embedded in soil, in society, in family and wealth and breeding. Handkerchief on his head and machete in his hand like a *campesino* patriarch. Great lighting, no obvious make-up.

He said, "I could get you a job with the PRI right now, but you wouldn't take it."

"No, I don't normally sign on as midshipman on a sinking ship."

"You don't? You're working for a bankrupt administration under a party that doesn't even really exist, with your mayor dead, and your immediate superior evidently kidnapped or fled. And you're worried about jumping to a party with control of congress, Senate, and virtually every local legislature in the country? Oh, sorry, I shouldn't be telling *you* political news, of all people."

"This is different. I took the job to be near Mija."

He sat down and looked at me for a minute, shook his shoulders and looked away. "It's funny, I call her that, but when you do it, I want to say, 'You mean *my* daughter. You mean Monserrat.' Anyway, what if you could work for the PRI and be near her?"

"Unlikely."

He shrugged, drained his beer, and flatted the can in his hands. Then he leaned back on the bench, staring straight out over the town. "You think not. Well, since you're been lecturing me on politics, maybe you won't object if I spin you a little story."

You've always spun us stories, I thought. But this one turned out a little different.

"Look at yourself, *joven*," he said, "As though you

were sizing up a new political candidate. Not bad looking, but not a pretty boy either, perfect kind of sincere face. Big shoulders, good moves, good in front of a crowd. Tall; that's always good. Award winner, champion of justice in print. Athlete, no less! The people's champion. How would you assess the election chances of the guy I just described?"

I just stared at him.

"Fairly smart, speaks well, good manners. Solid working class family with labor connections, but educated. Speaks English. Free of corrupt associations."

"Excellent press relations," I said.

"That's manageable. The press can be led like so many sheep."

"I'll keep that in mind, it should make my job a lot easier."

He went on, "Sense of humor. Shouldn't be hard to make it a little less snotty."

"God knows I've had no luck with that."

"Political seasoning without too much identification with any certain party."

"You mean a certain *certain party*, don't you?"

"Any interested party, actually. All you need is a few years of active membership somewhere, stroking the leadership, solidifying your commitment. I think we could run you for deputy in three years. Certainly for council. But it might be better to give you a good, big job for a few years and save you for mayor, maybe even state senator. Of course, by then you'd be married well and have some patronage built up. Be the star of the *Palacio* team. There's just no limit."

He stopped and let me absorb all that. I was still in shock from the idea he wanted me to marry into his family, now he wants to hand me his political party. I'd have settled for the free beer.

He sat, comfortable in silence. I looked at the city. It already looked different.

"So you've taken me on the mountaintop and shown me the world," I said. "Do I have to do anything? Turn stones into *pan de muerto*? Piss wine? Kneel and worship?"

"You've got it all backwards – typical for a journalist, I'd say. It's you that everybody worships. The adulation after Bogotá, after the Venados pennants even. I wondered at the time what it would be like to be a god-man, to have the crowds adore you for the gifts you were born with."

"I was in constant fear of crucifixion."

"Then you turn out to be the columnist that everybody gets their opinions from. The weekly oracle. Maybe a deeper form of worship, really. Believing you instead of just believing in you."

"I was considering a small, tasteful altar, probably in the Machado. Maybe something coin-operated."

"Then you move into my own personal world, saving my daughter's life. Twice, I suspect. If you had children perhaps you could get a glimpse of the idea that I probably worship you more than any other man alive."

"I'm sorry, I don't usually run out of wisecracks. Or this fake humility. It's embarrassing to me, but I guess I just have to accept your gratitude. Maybe you can accept me telling you that it's not really deserved."

"What do any of us deserve? Do I deserve to live here, in a park full of mansions and riches, while the people who vote us into power live in cardboard shacks in the sewer? I was lucky to be born who I am, that's all it seems to come down to. So were you. People who don't believe that, who talk about how hard they fought for what they have, they're just lucky they were born with fighting spirits. Instead of insight."

"For a revolutionary minion of the State, you sound like you're talking about Divine Right. Or something similar."

"It's a matter of *Categoría*. Family. Class."

"And you're offering me a way to change my class and family?"

"No, I think you already are of our class. You're a leader, a ruler ... a winner."

"I'm a damned *Indio* from the wrong side of the tracks."

"Nobody believes myths of discrimination as deeply as the underclass. It's not all about race – Juarez was Indian. It comes down to class, and you're a classy young man."

When I look back on it, it doesn't seem to change.

254

I really had the opportunity to just reach out my hand and have the world dropped right into it. And it might have been at that very moment that my world was starting to fall apart.

I sat and stared at Gortari, I have no idea how long. He just sat there, waiting to listen to me. I stood up and started walking away. Let's face it, you know and I know there wasn't really any other way it was going to happen.

I climbed up to base of the cross, where the path starts down to the house, and he suddenly spoke.

"Anyway, Raymundo. I wish you luck. And for God's sake, take care of her."

"I hope to." I took a step, then went back down to where he was sitting. I told him, "I'm in love with her, you know. Or something like that. I'm crazy about her. She's the most gorgeous single object ever put together and the most flaming spirit I ever knew. I just want to keep her by me forever and consume her completely and utterly."

He stood up and put a hand on my shoulder. "Thank you, Raymundo. Nobody has ever come to me and told me they loved her. It's very touching and I like you for it. And it's probably going to end up badly for you."

"I know. It'll never work out with her and me."

"How about with her and me?"

"I hate to tell you but I seriously doubt it."

He shrugged, "Rich girls surprise you. Always trying to fight free from what they can't live without. I've seen them fly off, then come back. And the other way around."

He dropped his hands and looked down at them. "You know I love her too, of course, but not how much. I've loved her desperately for her entire life. I also think she's the most beautiful thing alive, the most scintillating soul. It gives us common cause. That makes us a party of our own, in a way. We agree about something more important to both of us than any of that down there."

"Christ, that's scary."

"If you're having an affair with Monserrat I doubt there's anything I could say that would scare you."

Well, at least he didn't confess to any murders.

256

When the police are corrupt, a mafia of some kind is inevitable. And vice versa, of course. Either way, it spreads all over the city through the viaducts of firepower and greed. What you have in a "mafia" is a microcosm of the overall society and economy – a huge structure and a bunch of tiny, disorganized operators. No middle class at all, just those In and those Out. Even a machine or police state is more democratic because they don't leave anybody out.

But the effects are almost theological. People die, people disappear, people prosper – and it's not by fate or random selection. It's sinister *because* there is an unseen hand behind it. It creates its own superstition, its own sacraments and priesthood.

"*La Coma Nostra*" by Mundo Carrasco
La Isla de Mediodia, August, 1997

So the world was transfigured when I came down from the mountaintop. But not as much as they changed when I let myself back onto my roof and realized I had just crashed back down from The Top Of The World. The emptiness in my place was like the echo of silence, a discolored mist hanging on the air. Everything looked too bright, too contrived. The hollow insult of it jumped inside me and took me over. I didn't even have to see the note. She was gone.

Nothing was out of place or broken, but later I found scratches around the lock on my sea chest office. Fortunately it was a serious, American made lock, not like the cheapass one on the door. The note was predictable... Wouldn't have worked out. Better this way. Don't try to find me; dangerous. Thanks. Best ever. So sorry. Barely cinematic. I would have preferred the classic, "We have the girl. Get off the case."

Which brought home to again what my twirl though the Mijares' looking glass had blurred...that I was on a case. A mystery, a murder investigation with the female lead on the line. I needed to get better at it. But there are some immediate problems to living out a private eye movie in Mexico. Especially with a politician dead. In the American movies there's a formula, some dark secret or shocking revelation that was hidden by the murder, buried so deep it takes two hours and a car chase to figure it out.

But in Mexico, what would that dark secret be? Drugs? Racketeering? What's the big secret? Especially in Sinaloa, the major marijuana and heroin producing area in the hemisphere. A Sinaloa politician not being involved in drugs would be like a Texas politician not involved with oil or cattle. Americans play shocked and virginal over this, even though it was the U.S. that originally started opiate cultivation in Sinaloa and provides the market and laws that support the industry. Nothing shocking, nothing worth covering up with more than the usual cynical denials.

Sex? Again, Americans act amazed to find that powerful men screw young women in their employ and power. In Mexico – and the rest of the world, I think – it's pretty much assumed that leaders get a Little Bit of Monica. I think a Mexican politician who *didn't* screw around would be suspicious. Who wants limpdick leaders?

Homosexuality? Old hat. The "closet" is the top drawer. I don't get the impression this goes on in the United States the way it does here: it's a known cultural niche and at a certain level people expect it, just like the second "wife" and family.

Corruption? Embarrassing revelations? Our political system is nothing more than organized corruption, like the Mafia is organized crime—corruption that extends from the very top to the very bottom, everybody bought in and implicated. What could possibly be revealed that nobody already knows? The newspapers pretend innocence so they can appear to be shocking. Again, Americans always seem amazed at it, but however dark it is; it's no secret. Our political events are so multi-leveled and incestuous that there is often no bottom to get to. Looking for corruption and drug influences here would be like trying to run down rumors of sexism in Afghanistan or whiteness in Antarctica. So what motives are left? There's always money, of course. The universal solvent. And family. In Mexico almost everything comes down to family. But where did that leave me?

I stared out at the sky and sea for a perspective, but all I could focus on was the Fortress of Evil. The Bank of Mexico tore down an entire block of beautiful waterfront architecture and inflicted a huge, black, ugly, windowless office tower to dominate the view. Then it shut the damned thing down, leaving a monstrous, useless reminder about governments and banks. I stared at the monument to arrogance and vacancy and realized that it would be necessary to retreat from the western, capitalist world, into my heritage, the Indian world of old Mexico. To take magical measures to deal with reality.

Just kidding. Though I suspect you wanted it to go that way, get back to my Native roots. Eat peyote and go to some *brujo* for a vision. Sorry, but Mexico is a modern country, at least the Mexico I live in. The 'real Mexico' isn't peasants with burros and tribes with funny hats: it's full of webpage designers, inhalation therapists, key grips, marketing consultants, skyscraper painters. Peyote visions are not admissible in court. We are *all* of us part of the world of capital and current culture, like it or not. I wasn't about to handle it by turning the bad guys into a whirlwind of butterflies. So I applied conventional leftbrain logic and came to the concept of asking the neighbors.

Grady was sitting on his porch rolling joints from bright green Stone Island *mota*. He asked me if I had a suspect for Varedas' murder yet. I told him the main suspect should probably be him. "Just watch any bad Mexican narco film. When they get to the bottom of the bad gang, it always turns out to be some gray-haired old gringo."

Grady licked a joint and smiled. "Wonder where they get that idea?"

He hadn't heard anything out of the ordinary, but he did see Mijares leave. "They were parked up on our sidewalk, not across the street."

I looked down. They would have been tucked under the overflowing branches of the rubber tree.

"How do you rate that babe, Mundo? She looked too expensive for our league."

"Women don't have to be good, just have the equipment. But when you say *they* and *parked* ...?"

"Oh, yeah. A couple of guys came in a van. Cool *vocho* van, all covered with paintings and stuff. I thought they might have been Deadheads, but then she came out and they took off. No wait, first one of them went in with her, then they came back out. Sorry, I didn't see much."

"But enough to know she wasn't kidnapped or carried out in a sack, right?"

"Sorry, man. She was more like, in charge." I must have looked pretty downfallen about all that, so he hopped up, dropped the joints in his shirt pocket and said, "Hey look, the parade's about to start. Let's go check it out. Maybe it'll rain on it."

And I couldn't think of any reason not to. Or any reason to do anything particular else.

I stood there shaking my head, but Grady grabbed my shoulder and tussled me a little.

"Come on, let's get out of here," he said. "What else are you going to do? Run around calling her name and whistling? Sit by your phone whimpering and jumping up every time you hear a car?"

I let him tug me out the door and down the stairs.

We had just stepped outside when my neighbor Chema came clambering up over the low wall across the street and ran up to us, obviously outraged. "*¡Mis gallos!*" he was yelling, "My beautiful fighting cocks! You fucker! You piece of bastard pigshit!"

I could see this was going to take some sorting out.

"Your damn dog killed them! I *saw* it with my own eyes! Don't try to deny it!"

"I don't have a dog," I told him, but knew it wouldn't help.

"That coyote, the fucking German sheep dog. She sleeps outside your door. I've heard you tell her to kill my cocks. Many times. Every day. You fuckhead."

"Not my dog," I said, trying to radiate calm and reason. "But you know, a dog. Not somebody who understands jokes, or even Spanish. You understand?"

"Can you deny what you have said? What was done? My beautiful birds! Even the lowest orders get the message sooner or later, you *pinche cabrón*. You can't sneak out of the responsibility for your words!"

I absorbed that one like a hard hook to the gut. I

must have cut a glance at Grady.

In English, he said, "You've got to be completely honest to live outside the law."

I knew it was some song. By some gringo asshole. Who knows? Could have been Dylan or Cobain or that Scoop Doggy Dude. Which probably means it's true. Shit.

What I told Chema was, "Hey!" That stopped him long enough for me to say that if he would shut up immediately and go away, he had my word that I'd come back on Monday and pay him for his lousy *gallos*. He nodded, started to open his mouth, then walked off. Climbed back over the wall and thrashed down through the rubbish jungle to his shack, scattering the goats and cats and iguanas. I saw Coyota slinking around in the trees up past my building, safe from any responsibility or recrimination.

I caught her eye and said, "Great. The one bitch that listens to me."

Grady shrugged. "Hey, they barely listen to me even when they paid cover to get in."

Allowing free admission to *Carnaval* this year was more than just the Mayor tossing bread and circuses to the crowds. The well-off mourn losing Carnival to the masses, but that's who it was always for. The wretched need it more. Their life is a lenten season, they don't have to give up meat because they don't have it to begin with. Do you think the rich invented the Samba?

The poor love the queens and kings and robes and royalty more than the rich do. And now they are trying to wall it off in salons and stadiums where the poor can't go. We need it back in the streets like in the old days; on Carnaval street, in the Machado, parading down the main drag.

"*Free At Any Cost*", "El Mundo Segun Mundo" Column
El Debate, February, 2002

On any day that you lose the greatest love of your life and find out you are just as corrupt as the people you oppose, you deserve a parade. If nothing else, a parade is a great place to come adrift, bob aimlessly in a sea of people, goggle at a procession of things that make no sense whatsoever, surrender to a slideshow of disjointed sensory impressions. My mind was down for the count, my feelings shut off for repairs, my spirits dribbling down the street like a lopsided basketball. And I suppose Grady's *mota* had something to do with it. The way parades work, you just follow whatever's in front of you until it's over. Or just stand there and wave as it all marches by.

The sidewalks were jammed, the streets were clogged, the rooftops were packed. A metal reviewing stand was crammed with VIP's, the Mayor's chair was empty as usual, since nobody could figure out what to do with it. People were renting out chairs on top of their restaurants and homes. In a parade-crazy town, this was the Big Enchilada, one of the Biggest Parades In The World That Doesn't Have Tanks In It. The crowds weren't exactly passive, either. Kids from Mexico City managed to find space to lay out blankets and sell hippie jewelry. Vendors were yelling about cotton candy, donuts, mangos on sticks, coconut clusters, and cheap plastic action figures. There were buskers, firedancers, mimes and musicians. Grady stopped to check out a kid playing an obviously homemade African drum they call a 'yembe'. He was doing all right. Grady said, "Hey, dig. The little drummer boy. I saw him this morning making that drum. Shaving hair off the hide."

The kid smiled and offered the drum to Grady, who popped out a quick beat and said, "Brand spanking new, huh?"

Whatever *that* means. Spanking? But the kid must have caught 'new' because he told us that the goat that provided the drumhead had been alive that morning.

Grady loved it, "Well, he's gone to a higher calling now."

The drummer boy must have known who Grady was, because he gave him a quick riff and yelled, "*Rocanrol*, man."

Grady returned an upraised fist. "Rumpa pum pum, dewd." I looked up from the rhythm and saw horses moving through the crowd.

The parade is always led by squadrons of *charros* on horseback. This *is* Sinaloa, after all. All these musical comedy Mexican cowboys dressed in huge sombreros and elaborate *mariachi* duds – the Sinaloa Tuxedo. They have lassos and machetes tucked into their ornate silver-mounted saddles, and their horses dance in pretty little steps. *Escarmusas*, the *charro* cowgirls, smile sidesaddle from horses immaculately shined, even greased. Later in the parade a trailer from the State Charro Association would show off future cowpokes from grade school twirling lassos and jumping through the loops.

And behind them was a trailer with the first band of the afternoon. A *banda Sinaloense*, of course. First onslaught of the dread *bandas*. Whatever else Carnival is about, it's extremely about music. And the music Sinaloa created, and is famous for throughout Latin America, is the damned *banda*. Take your average *ranchero* band, maybe a *norteño* bunch playing shitkicker polkas about lonely cowboys and faithless women on accordions and guitars. Now throw in about twenty guys with tubas, trumpets, trombones, clarinets and drums, adding some serious oompapa. Now toss in electric bass, synthesizers that can do everything from cheesy organ to dogs barking, and monstrous amplification. And voila. It's a nutty kind of sound, but it's ours. Guys in bars love it, car speakers blare it. It's the official music of the Mexican narcotics industry. And it's relentless.

Grady smirked at the band, pumping out a tuba-friendly version of *Cielito Lindo*, of all things. Every year there is a song or two that dominate Carnival. *Toda La Vida, La Macarena, Mambo #5*. This year it was the idiot repetition of *La Vaca* and the catchy, maddening pop of *Yo No Fui*. It was worse seven years ago when you heard *Macarena* everywhere, all the time. I was delighted when that song went to the U.S. and I saw ballplayers doing it on the basepaths on the World Series telecast. It's not a total payback for the graffiti, but it's a small portion of revenge.

Grady said, "Sounds like Dixieland on steroids. Or Sousa on tequila. They get marching along like this, pacing themselves by swapping solos instead of pumping out beat, and you realize, this could be sort of jazz."

I just stared at him, wondering what the hell he was thinking. But he went on. "You know jazz actually came from Negro funeral parades? If they could ditch the sappy lyrics and four/four beat, get a little syncopation and a genius or two, Mazatlán might end up as a jazz mecca. Create something really unique like Cuba or Argentina." He shrugged, "Or not."

Maybe it's inevitable any form of music that gets popular will draw the best musicians, and they will seek out the abstract perfection of the music. Maybe all music would just evolve into jazz, release instrumental solos to the skies, then die out.

But don't think that *bandas* were the whole show, or the worst or it. There are also military bands. To say the least. Every school and military unit in the area had sent a battalion of drums and bugles, marching along in braids and army caps, pounding out a call to arms for the tone-deaf. There are big contests for this kind of martial art – and most of them practice right below my balcony, marching up and down Olas Altas beating the crap out of their drums and blaring bugle calls. You get used to it.

Comparsas are also competition-honed. These are dance squads, like the samba schools of Rio, dozens of dancers wearing the same costume and drilling in their moves over months of practice. They'd just competed for a top prize of $1500 and got their thing down. They mob the streets between the floats, dressed like harlequins or Rastamans or Egyptians or whatever the theme of the float they associate with. They bop along in rhythm and when the parade lurches to a stop, which it does a *lot*, they perform their synchronized numbers. Another good thing about parades, you keep getting a new audience. If a comparsa doesn't have a float, it has a sound truck, or just a flatbed loaded with generators and speakers blasting out anything from cowboy to reggae to rap.

My favorite *comparsa* was from the *Asilo de Ancianos*, the Old Folks Home. The New Dawn *comparsa* might lack the oomph of the kids, but those old dolls in polka-dot dominos were having a ball. Those not up to The Long March rode in a bus converted to an imitation San Francisco trolleycar, and they knew a thing or two about waving and smiling. You have to clap for the New Dawners, the high scorers in the game of life.

And among all the music/noise, of course, were the big decorated floats – though I personally prefer our term, *carros allegoricos*. Huge motorized stages of flowers and fantasy nudged through the crowds like battleships, carrying their loads of strained allegory, cute girls shaking their booties, and various levels of royalty. Grady said they weren't as lavish or professional looking as New Orleans or Rio or Macy's. "But they have a sort of nice amateur standing. You know, put together by loving hands like something at a homecoming pageant. Just bigger budget."

I told him some were designed by leading artists and he said most looked like they were designed by Liberace. I have to admit there was a lot of gold rococo filigree, Corinthian columns, and neo-classical figures. One had frolicking Oriental dragons, another featured schools of dolphins doing leaps – the dolphins on wheels turned by costumed boys who seemed to be tiring. Many were too tall to pass under power lines so the tops – huge figurines with outspread arms – were hinged so they could pass under, then be pushed up and propped with lumber until the next high wire came up.

The theme for the year was Passion for Carnivals, which made for some fairly vague *carros*. You don't get much more abstract than self-reference. My favorite theme was 1999, a tribute to the movies that flooded the street with vampires, westerns, pirates, and *comparsas* dressed like Charlie Chaplin and Marilyn Monroe. The 2002 version had a different air. I said, "It looks more like Passion for Product to me."

Carros sponsored by tortilla companies tossed out packets of samples, radio stations threw masks with their call numbers. One float was surrounded by shirtless boys on roller skates, painted green, slapping New Mix tattoos on anybody who got in their way. Mexicana Airlines had a float that looked exactly like their TV commercial. I particularly didn't like the *carro* from Gaspasa; just a truck playing their damned jingle and covered with dancing girls in tight shorts. I told Grady their message seemed to be about buying bottled propane.

He laughed. "Maybe pushing gas *is* an allegory."

I told him I preferred the ones that only pushed the benefits of looking at cute girls in gowns, bikinis, and lettered sashes.

He said, "That's the secret of all art, *amigo*, the female form is the ultimate allegory."

So the buffet of young beauties trooped by. And some not so young. By tradition each parade presents Queens of Carnival and Flower Games from twenty-five and fifty years ago. Last year the Queen from 1976 refused to go on because her daughter wasn't chosen and she'd been looking forward to a dynasty. But this year they are up there in their ex-sovereign glory, looking like time has treated them well. Adriana III, from 1977, looked especially tasty and preserved in honey. There's a quality of beauty that goes beyond skin deep ... that lasts. But I didn't like that drift to my thoughts and concentrated on eyeing the current crop of princesses, duchesses and *princesitas* as they rolled by in review. A pretty good crop this year, no doubt about it. Of course, there are barefoot, penniless sweeties up in the hills that could blow them away, but isn't that all part of the fairy tale, too?

Meanwhile, as the *carros* trundled by, the sun was touching the horizon, the February wind was picking up off the sea, and a few drops of rain were starting to fall. By the end of the parade, when it would be full dark with the rising sea wind turning out to be an overture to a nasty storm that would drench the whole scene, they would probably wish they could shake their booties a little. But they hung tough and did their regal thing. Which is, mainly, to smile. For the whole long evening of standing still in shoulderless gowns, or even bikinis, as the wind picked up punch and the temperature dropped, they waved and – above all – smiled. A good queen should be able to turn on an incandescent dental show that knocks you flat without a hint of condescension. Those babes up there on the floats, exposing their young flesh to the elements, did just fine.

Just as the last little red sausage of sun disappeared over the rim of the Pacific, a long flat float appeared, pulled by a Kenworth tractor. Lined up along the decorated flatbed were the candidates for "International Queen of the Pacific". Queens from other nations on parade. Girls from El Salvador and Chile and California. Miss Managua very noticeable, not to mention Miss Twin Palms. I paid close attention because I'd had a long talk and lots of drinks with the organizer in order to make room for an additional candidate. And there she was, waving radiantly in a gold lamé gown and a white satin sash reading, "Miss Tehachapi/Tonapah". Grady had chosen the name and he started applauding as soon as he saw it.

I stepped out into the street, wildly clapping for the Tehachapi Miss, in reality Mazatlán's favorite daughter, the glorious and semi-available Palomina. She saw us and did a regal gesture that presented her gown, sash and treasury, then – supported by a sort of coat hanger for royalty that keeps the girls from falling off the cars – leaned over from the waist, which was quite a sight and drew frenzied applause from males in the area, and blew us two-handed kisses until the International Harem lurched out of sight. I glanced at Grady and he laughed, holding up his hand for a flying high five. Queenmakers for a day.

The last *carro* and *comparsa* was a plain trailer belonging to the Sinaloa State Clown Society. The whole trailer was full of young *payasos* showing off their tricks while the mature members of the Society roamed the curbs flipping out little kids. Something about so many clowns performing together at once sort of cheapened the art. Probably an allegory for politics.

Which reminded me that I had jumped ship from my own Clown Show and needed to go in to the *Palacio* Monday morning. Poke around, clear out my desk, get some closure. Meanwhile, all I had to do was figure out how to get to sleep up there, all alone in my bed. Where the din from The World's Noisiest Pseudo-Catholic Celebration rattled my doors, a cold wind whipped through to rustle my blankets, rain spattered off the floor and clouds hid the stars. I thought about standing naked at the rail, bravely waving and smiling at the crowds below, but just didn't have the heart.

MONDAY
FEBRUARY ELEVENTH
DIA DE NUESTRA SEÑORA DE LOURDES

Carnival Calendar

Bullfight, Plaza de Toros, 3 PM
International Queen of the Pacific Coronation,
Muralla Athletic Club, 10 PM

One of Vicente Fox' greatest maneuvers was allowing the Zapatistas to march across Mexico, and for *"Sub-comandante* Zero" to speak in the Zocalo. It was a turn of the tide for the Zapatista prestige. Suddenly they were in the open, in the limelight they had demanded, open for examination, one more political sideshow. Stripped of their mystique, they plunged out of the headlines and that curious canon of chicness.

Fox proved more than equal to the *"sub-comandante"* and his cyberslick Zapatista image mongers. He neutralized them, beat them at their own game, through mediagenic judo. He gave them what they wanted, and they choked on it. But mostly, he just drew them out of the shadows into the light. Where they disappeared from view.

"Stealing A March" by Mundo Carrasco
Salon Website, May, 2001

I was rudely awakened on Monday morning by the lack of noise from Chema's roosters. And dragged fully awake by the lack of Mijares' body in the bed beside me. It takes awhile to get accustomed to missing components. Then, once I was on my feet, I realized I was pressured by not having to go to work. So I went in anyway, just because I didn't have to. Maybe all the other missing elements would come back if I observed the rituals. Maybe Mijares would be there at her desk. If not, I could clean mine out and say *adios* to City Hall. I had a feeling I'd take one look at the office and wonder why I'd ever set foot in it. And I was right.

In fact, I hadn't even reached my office before getting a nasty shock. I glanced in the window as I approached the door and saw a big, wide guy in an expensive gunmetal suit and spiky bleached hair talking to the *info-chicas*. Loli looked alarmed and a little repelled; Xochitl was all rapt, quivering attention. Then I realized that I knew the guy in the sharkskin suit, had even fought with him. And lost. Then he took off with Mijares, just when I'd first fallen head over heels for her. Ernesto *pinche* Velarde, come back to haunt my office. I was shocked motionless for a moment, then slowly wandered down the hallway, wondering why a criminal, terrorist asshole was back in my life, much less on city property. Hatching possible plots and countermeasures, I stumbled into Sergeant García. I pointed to my office and started to speak, but he was way ahead of me.

"Brought in by Our Brother," he told me. "*Señor Alcalde* Tirado these days. And guess whose job he's got."

"WHAT? *¡No mames, wey!*"

"Would I shit you? After all, you quit, didn't you?" He eyed me like a rat going AWOL from a sinking ship, then grinned, "Hey, does that mean you can play in the Music League this spring? I'm going to be hitting cleanup for Banda Escamillas."

¡Hijole! Nesto! *Comandante* Less Than Zero himself, right in my face. And the worst thing was, it started to make a little sense once I thought about it. It's not really all that long a shot from Brother Mayor to the King of Kampus Kommies, but it's a little hard to explain. Most of the big public universities in Mexico, especially "Autonomous" ones like UAS in Mazatlan, UAG in Guadalajara, or the immense UNAM in Mexico City, have cells of *grillos*. The word means "crickets", but it's a short spin on *guerrillos*—and they see themselves as urban guerillas working to overthrow the system. Most famous was a Catholic-fanatic-turned-Marxist named Salas, who got disappeared back in the seventies. His girlfriend, equally famous, was called Mijares. See?

The *grillos* are university organizations, but not exactly like a marching band or Sig Ep. They are like mushrooms thrust up from a long-standing Marxist, or perhaps Che-ist, structure that also produced the disabling University strikes and the Zapatista rebels in Chiapas. They like brandishing guns, burning flags, wearing ski masks, and functioning as a sort of Mexican IRA, passing firearms to fighters in the mountains.

But they don't just appear out of nowhere, especially in provincial schools like UAS: there are always a few leftist professors around to recruit them and give them status. The welfare dorms like *Octubre Rojo* and *Martires de 7 de Abril*, where poor students can sleep and eat for free, are generally thought of as fertile grounds for future radicals, but my impression is that most of them are upper middle class.

272

And a few years ago, when Prof. Tirado bumbled around campus, you wouldn't have needed to make a very long list of suspected *grillo*-loving professors to come up with his name. Politics was as easy a route to sleeping with students as giving out good grades. He would sit with his black coffee and brown cigarettes, wearing workshirt and beret, and the hoteyed girls and coldeyed boys would flow around him. Mijares was one of his students when I first met her, up to her plucked eyebrows in some very nasty business that almost got her killed. She took me to bed and put her stamp on me, but good. Then waltzed off to UNAM with the smirking strike organizer...one Nesto Valverde. Now he's back with a new suit and minus the shoulder-length hair. Just when Mijares disappeared.

I decided I'd better talk to him. What I'd really like to do is kick the shit out of him, but to be truthful I don't know if I could. He's big, tough, trained, and most of all vicious. So much of fighting comes down to that...to just being willing to do something savage. I'm basically an athlete; he basically likes to hurt people. One thing I will say about the PRI and even the United States' foreign legion, there are lots worse people who could be in charge.

I walked right into the office and told Xochitl I'd come to clean out my desk. She gaped at me, waving her eyes back and forth from me to Nesto, trying to warn me by semaphore that there was a big, unsympathetic guy standing in the middle of the office. Nesto turned around indolently, gave me his bored predator's grin, and said, "I think you'll find your effects in the dumpster."

As a recent dumpee, I took that badly. I spoke over his shoulder, to Xochitl, "Just because the city's hard up for help doesn't mean you can't find a janitor who knows the difference between trash cans and desk drawers." She looked askance, like a trapped hummingbird, so I threw in, "And knows that nobody wears those sea urchin hairdos anymore."

Nesto kept grinning, preened a little, and patted Xochitl's *nachas* in a familiar manner. She was startled, but didn't flinch. The turncoat little slut. He sneered at my cutoffs and worn Leonard Cohen T-shirt and said, "Don't worry, Sr. Fashion Authority, your stuff got tossed in the same dumpster you sleep in." He cupped his crotch and said, "Wanna see what I toss into the broad you used to sleep in?"

Xochitl stepped away from him and picked up some random papers off her desk. Loli blindly grabbed a clipboard and both of them headed for the door in a staccato burst of heel clicking. Their sudden wide-eyed flush brought Sergeant Garcia to the door, where he stood motionless and impassive. Nesto looked at him and snickered.

"Why not call your mama, Mundito? Maybe she can get your job and girl back. But I doubt it...you've served your purpose. And pretty half-assed service at that."

"I seem to remember that you're the one who runs your brave revolution from behind girl's skirts."

"Revolution. You should check into the museum, you obsolete dweeb. One revolution in fifty has ever succeeded. We have to be a little more efficient than that."

I wondered why I was swapping insults and political jive with this dickhead. Forget the ego, get down to it. "Where's Mijares?"

"Where she'll do the most good. You don't understand her, you dumb shit. You don't fit into her private movies. She wants everything perfect on set, larger than life. Perfect bodies doing impossible shit. That's what gets her off. And you're trying to grab her with lace and romance." His scorn was scalding. "You may be a star, but you aren't gorgeous enough to make the cast, see."

"I've hired a gorgeousness coach."

But the embarrassment was relentless. "But what's more important...you can't dominate her. Or at least you don't."

That concept just baffled me. "Who would want to? That's what's cool about her, she's so indominable."

He laughed his sculptured, elegant buttocks off at that one, "That's what you think, hero. Let me take a moment to explain something to you. If you have a moment." He glanced at the Sergeant, who was doing a great imitation of a stone Olmec head.

"Her need to dominate and control, you stupid fuck, is pretty obviously a compulsion, a reaction to her deeper desire to be dominated and controlled. She's the perfect bottom."

"Anybody can see that."

That really cracked him up. I was getting sick of seeing those perfect teeth dancing around and was starting to think they'd look better scattered across the floor. A Louisville Slugger consultation strongly indicated.

But he kept on with the teeth. "No, dipshit, I mean submissive. She runs around pushing men, looking for somebody she can't push, who pushes her over. Don't they teach psychology in gringo jock school?"

"Well, I often wished I had the benefits of your education."

"And I wished I had the benefits of your job. And now I do."

"Why didn't you just ask Mijares for it? That's how I got it."

"That's what you think? You *pendejo*. You have higher angels looking out for you, Bam Bam. Why you aren't dead. How come I know all this and you don't? You're supposed to be the investigative reporter."

"I'm also supposed to be sleeping with the boss. You can't count on anything these days."

"You can't. I can."

"Yeah, the force of destiny and all. Will of the people. Your gilded dick. Your daddys' money."

But I know when I'm beat. Namely when I'm still behind and run out of innings. Because I knew he was right. She'd always prefer a bigger, prettier guy. And she told me she'd prefer somebody who just took without compunction, smashed and grabbed. Well, I could go the gym and have my ears channeled, I supposed, but there was another factor I couldn't overcome...the politics of it. I would always lead her back to home and family. What was I ever hero of anyway? Organized sports, established media. But Nesto led away from all that. To danger, rebellion, to a shot at being in charge on her own terms.

So my ass was out. And if she ever met a bigger guy with a prettier body who's even grabbier and more rebellious, Nesto will be out. Fat chance of that. I just turned and walked out. He'd already won everything important, what did my pride or male ego or the occupation of the office matter? I heard him move up behind me and start to say something, but just then Sergeant Garcia moved by me in a smooth slide, his graceful motion always surprising from such a stocky pug-ugly. I turned just in time to see his gun slide into Nesto's mouth, chipping one of those TV ad teeth.

Nesto's hair got even spikier as he squinted cross-eyed at the gun in the hands of an implacable cop. Who said, "I've thought it over, and I've decided I don't like you. Back in my old *barrio* we mopped out toilets with guys like you. If you ever seriously piss me off, or hurt anybody around here, I'll kill you. I'm dead cold serious." He reached into his pocket and brought out a very wicked-looking switchblade covered with electrician's tape. The blade clicked out and he reached slowly forward until the point touched Nesto's shirt, then slid forward until a drop of blood appeared on the blade. Nesto stood without flinching, staring into his face. Suddenly the blade flicked around and a flap of shirt front fell away to show a tracing of blood underneath. The mark of the "Z". He pocketed the knife and said, "Zerious."

I walked out with him without saying a word. I had lost that encounter, then somebody called the game. I felt like I'd cheated and lost anyway. I felt a real need to get more serious.

Tacticus said that the secret that rocked the Roman Empire was that the Emperor could be made elsewhere than in Rome. The secret that shook the Mexican Dictatorship was that the Mexican President could be made elsewhere than in Mexico City. The secret to our national political paranoia is that we're afraid that our President might be made elsewhere than in Mexico.

"More Revolutions Per Minute" by Raymundo Carrasco
La Mosca, March 2001

We were outcasts, refugees thrust out on an alien world. Our expedition straggled through hostile wilds, suffered untempered elements and an unforgiving sun, flinched at exposure under flimsy shelter. Or I should say that Lo Peor was being fumigated and the denizens were forced to have lunch at a sidewalk table under the Copa de Leche awning, staring across the Malecón at a watery horizon, squinting in the unaccustomed sunlight.

We hadn't taken our exile lightly. When I got to the bar there was an ominous yellow truck with the slogan *¡Adios cucaracha!* painted on its tailgate unloading pumps and hoses while a clump of grumpy journalists sniveled to Chuy. Eusebio pleaded to let us just use the Salón Liz Taylor, the glass wall barricaded against seeping poisons.

Beto, sneering at the exterminators' preparations, asked, "Hey Chuy, do you really think one little fumigation is going to get rid of all the vermin in *this* dump?"

Chuy snapped, "It already did!" And slammed the door on us. We were on our own. Karla suggested the Copa, which she and Eusebio saw as a stimulating, calorie-burning hike, but the most of the other denizens took as a long, parched death march.

As soon as we settled in, getting used to having a view – not to mention the noise and exhaust from passing buses and *pulmonias* – a brisk breeze kicked up off the bay. I found it bracing, but not everybody agreed.

Silvio groused, "Just what I need. A polar expedition."

"Oh yeah, *Señor* Explorer," Lorenzo retorted, "You'd need a *mapa mundi* to find the *polo sur*." More cute Mexican slang, *mapa mundi* is world map, but means a view of the *derriere*. But is that odder than calling it the moon? For that matter, I don't know why the anus would be the south pole, but I remember frat guys at Arizona talking about their girl friends going around the world, so what else is exotic? Meanwhile we brazened the elements with a touch of antifreeze. Time to break the ice.

"Well, you won't have me to kick you around anymore," I tossed out. "Hope you like my replacement." I was amazed at the level of response to that simple opening.

"Yeah, Ernesto *pinche* Valverde," Lorenzo spat. "Ex-CGH! What the *Hell* were they thinking?"

"Not just your replacement, I hear," Rocío purred, "Slated to take over duties of your *huesito*. Or is she already your ex-girlfriend?"

"I never know who's an ex until it's too late," I said, hoping for an abashed, boyish take, "My ex-beloveds are a great bunch, but they go off without warning." She hid a semblance of a smile.

"So now we have to work with that Nesto asshole," Mocho grumbled. "I hope he doesn't start coming here ..." He glanced around. "I mean to Lo Peor."

"There's always the fumigators," I offered.

"Nah, if they killed all the *cucarachas* in that place, it'd collapse." Major Tom drew nods of agreement.

"Can we get back to what the hell they were thinking?" It seemed like a major point to me. There was an embarrassed pause, people avoiding my eye.

Finally Karla reached over and patted my hand in a gesture that was as dismissive as reassuring. "You've been out of the loop, Mundo. Things are moving off into different directions and you have to stay on the ball or you'll miss it."

Carlito nodded. "Try asking the other question." He apparently didn't trust me to come up with it on my own, so he said, "Who are the *They* who are doing that thinking?"

I tried to cover up a little, "Well, that's always the trick, isn't it?"

"Hard to see the wolf from inside its stomach," Ramón offered. "You're still back there thinking it's all Evil PRI versus the Forces of Light. Well, it's a little more complicated these days."

Carlito continued his thought. "Now there are smaller parties darting in to gobble up the carcass. The PRI's playing a waiting game. Why break in a new team when you can wait a few years, work smaller elections, then grab it all back? And in a smaller election, what's to keep somebody smaller from grabbing it instead?"

I leaned back and looked around. Everybody there was staring at me, even Tonio, the mustachioed, motorcycling bartender. I sighed and said, "You people almost sound like real reporters."

"Yeah, maybe you can get back to being one, too," Beto snapped at me. And he was right. Out of the city job and back among them, I could hear what they'd been saying all along. And see what they'd been seeing. Ironic, actually, my closeness to power and influence had cut me off from the flow of information.

"Oh he's back. He'll always be a *periodista*," Karla cooed. "He just tried to cure himself of it and it didn't take."

"I've got an easier question for you, lover boy." Rocío hid another smile.

Uh-oh. "Easier than the 'Who are They?' one?"

"Depends on what you're thinking with. Try, 'Who is She?'" I just stared at her.

"It's where a lot of threads lead, kiddo." Carlito was leaning forward, gesturing with his *medio* of Pacifico. I didn't want to hear it but was going to anyway. He ticked them off, "She was sexually involved with Borrego and Varedas. Also a half dozen *regidores*. She was Tirado's student at UAS, also in bed with him. In the CGH at UNAM, with the strike cadre. Alleged to be sexually involved with Nesto."

I appreciated the delicacy in describing who Mijares had been fucking, but it didn't help much. "Not alleged, definitely. But besides the fact that I wasn't an exclusive, what does it have to do with anything?"

Silvio spoke up, quietly, like he was lecturing a small, not very bright classroom, "Mundo, how would you take over a government?"

That seemed to call for a blank stare, so I came through. When he left it hanging, I said, "You whiffed me on a curve, there."

"Revolutions make good rhetoric, but when was the last time one worked? The way to go these days is a *golpe de estado.*"

That boggled me a bit, A *coup d'etat?* In Mexico? Had things gone nuts in the few months I was digesting the belly of the Beast?

Beto, of all people, chimed in. "It's all swinging to the right and a lot of people want it swung back. Even further back."

"To the left wing?" I asked him. "You guys think it's a coup if anybody but the PRI wins anything."

"The PRI is not a left wing,"Beto scolded, "It is the entire eagle."

Well, not really, but I have to admit it's the middle lane, the mainstream, whatever you want to call it.

"The election in 2000 was a *golpe* from the right, you might say. Straight from the shoulder. What these guys want is more of a left hook."

"And if you can't infiltrate something as big as the PRI, what can you do?" Carlito asked me. "You infiltrate something smaller and then make it big."

"Hijack a party," I said. "Like the PT, for example. But they're nothing."

Carlito was ready. "You look at the PRD. How many votes in the last election?"

"Less than five percent."

"So they're marginal, huh? Except they always have the mayor of Mexico city and control in central districts."

Ramón cut in, "It's like saying, 'How can that drug be effective? It only controls a few isolated cells.' But those cells happen to be in the frontal lobe of the brain."

Carlito nodded. "Disproportionate impact. Like the guy with the big ears on El Trek. He touches you in the right place and *¡Zaz!* Look at the Zapatistas. A handful of posers down there with internet access and funny masks and they end up being more recognizable than any Mexican public figure. A few kids striking UNAM have the whole government by the pubes."

"And one way they do it is by creating powerful symbols, " Eusebio broke in. "Che in a beret, Marcos in his ski mask. T-shirts that people still wear after they've grown up and got jobs, you know. They're like the Beatles or Cobain."

"Lennonists," Carlito grinned.

"But they barely exist. They just got pumped up by the PRI to defeat the PAN."

"And what if, after they sink the PAN, then they're supposed to absorb into the PRI or get out of the way ... but they don't want to?" Carlito leaned forward and stuck his finger right into my face. "Look what they've done here. They allied with powerful business interests who think they can be more powerful than the party. Not a bad idea ... Fox was the Governor from Coca-Cola, right? They prove that they can elect a nobody, a brainless marionette. All on symbols for the masses."

"I'm getting confused about who They is again."

"The wealthy left." Rocío said it with some exasperation, like a disappointed teacher. "And they are using far left students as shock troops. And even in some extreme cases to pussywhip key players into line. Your sweetheart was essentially hijacking Varedas and her buddies were hijacking city hall."

"But *Why*? Why Mazatlán? Why Sinaloa, for crissakes? We're just cowboy hicks in a little town on the outskirts."

"Why Guerrero? " Carlito asked, "Why Chiapas?"

"It's not a bad little laboratory to shake it down, Mundo," Mocho said, "Away from the power center, but not nowhere ... our ex-governor almost beat Fox for president, remember? And you have all the narco money here. Lots of guys who wouldn't mind owning the drug industry instead of managing it for the PRI. And where better than Mazatlán? A PAN-friendly city that's not the capital, but culturally significant and in the international eye. Perfect place to start up the *Sinaloazo*."

The *Sinaloazo*. Perfect. A big burst of cowboy-flavored, rebel-driven, narco-financed grass roots. With a good chance of spreading into the Baja and Northern states where the PAN first showed it's power. Slick and international on top, folksy at the image level, and Marxist dictatorship down where it counts. Make your own Colombia.

As if reading my mind, Carlito said, "And everything misdirected. They've given up fighting for infiltration, but the fighting is increasing and drawing off attention and resources. They denounce the PAN and scorn the PRI, but are playing them off against each other, grabbing chunks from the middle under assumed names. They can flare up the Zapatistas or UNAM students any time they need to.'

"Okay, okay. I can work on getting all this. But I gotta ask. Why did they kill Varedas? And why did they roust El Infiernillo? And don't ask me who They are, if you know that you know why. And if you know why, you know who."

"And we don't know." Rocío was soft-spoken, almost friendly. "We don't know how that fits in. How you fit in. We're kind of hoping you can tell us."

"Meanwhile, you can't print any of this, can you? It's all just speculation and the opposite of what anybody wants to hear. Even if they could understand it. Great."

"The standard torture," Carlito agreed. "Journalists would be the easiest for an interrogator to crack – we think our motivation is to know, but actually it's to *tell*."

I looked around at them. My colleagues, my friends even. I said, "You people make me sick." Everybody cheered and raised their glasses. I lifted mine and we clinked all around. Gossip and self-knowledge, the sickness unto death.

Beto surprised me by standing up and presenting his glass. Without any bitterness or warmth, he said, "It's different now, isn't it? You've been reporting politics like you were calling a ball game. Now you've got some on you. Join the *pinche* fucking world."

Karla giggled, "And welcome to it, cutie."

Then Tonio called me to the phone.

I'm not a proper Latino, I don't admire *futbol*. There is something incomplete about "soccer", something so perverse it's almost inhuman. The use of hands is a main thing setting us apart from animals. Maybe not what makes us human, but where it shows up. Isn't civilization the Hand of Man? So what can you say about a game that denies the use of that gift? *Futbol* is the only ball game that could just as easily be played by burros or cows.

On the other hand, what do I do? Hit things with a club. But there is one thing totally unique about baseball. At the plate you're one man against an entire team and nobody else can help. You're It.

Mundo Carrasco, interviewed for *Beisbol Hoy*, April, 1992

When I saw the van on the causeway, I got the feeling Mijares wasn't going to show. When the Suburban swooped down the Paseo I got the feeling I'd best not, either.

Up to then I'd still had a ragged hope that I'd climbed up to the lighthouse for a reason. A great reason, in fact: Mijares was supposed to meet me there. Or at least that's what one of her girlfriends whispered to me over the phone. And added a few juicy details that made it clear she'd talked to Mijares very recently and had her confidence. You'd think a movie buff like myself would have known better than to fall for it. But you also know a Good Guy like me couldn't even think about refusing the call. No mountain too high, no river too deep, no straw too flimsy.

The girlfriend was there, a shavehead lefty from her old guerilla theater troupe. She'd come to tell me that Mijares was all right and would be there soon. I gazed out at a wraparound marine view almost as breath-taking as climbing up the virtually vertical trail. I could see the hill's points as a rendezvous; a steep island connected to Mazatlán by the artificial causeway, it's as remote as the city gets and has a view of everything for miles around. I asked the girlfriend if that was why Mija chose it for our meeting.

"No silly; for the view and exercise." She smirked. She'd been playing the vapid ingénue ever since I got there, but I didn't much buy it. I'd brought along the binoculars that I hang on the railing of my roof, and on my way over I'd driven up to El Mirador restaurant on the opposite hill, just to see what things looked like. I had seen the girl with her shaved head and flowing clothes, looking a lot like Mijares did when I first met her. So I drove down and across the causeway, then clambered up the Crestón. I could see my house from there, too, but didn't mention it.

"Just look at the view out to sea," she gushed, taking my elbow and pressing it against a breast as she tried to lead me to the westward railing, where the sun was starting to dip towards a bank of fluffy clouds on the horizon. "It'll be a romantic sunset, I think."

I disengaged myself and went back to the inland side. "I like the city view. It doesn't change as much."

She stood behind me while I leaned on the wall with my binoculars, scanning the causeway and what I could see of the trail. Ten minutes later the van showed up, a wildly painted VW with 'Fuck Channel 7' painted on top. Graffiti for news helicopters. I guess it would ensure never seeing your car on TV. I was cheated of the simple pleasure of using a favorite movie line, "Who *are* those guys?" because the third man out of the van was Nesto. I decided to abandon hope and start scheming.

They kept piling out of the van like circus clowns. Three or four came straight up the path, more of them flanked out to make sure nobody slipped by them. The Suburban, back where it could see the peak of the hill and cut off any escape from Crestón, had familiar associations with muscle and firepower. I thought over my next moves extremely carefully. And mentally apologized in advance for the first one.

I took a step backward, capping my binoculars. I didn't know whether to hope I was right or wrong, but I pivoted suddenly, swinging my hand around in a back-handed swat that knocked Srta. Razortrim completely off her feet. The pistol she'd been holding flew up in the air and over the wall, crashing through the jungly growth, bouncing off rocks. Which meant I'd been right, but wished I was wrong. It also meant I was screwed and wished I'd hung on to the gun. Though realistically, what would I have done with it? Probably gotten killed, that's what they build guns for. I was sure she was unconscious – she was never that good an *actríz* – so I scooped her up and in a gentlemanly, caring way, dumped her lying little ass over the wall into the trees. She wouldn't fall that far, and maybe she'd be making noise by the time the hit team got there. I wasn't that crazy about my first gambit, and they were going to get trickier and more painful.

Because the same things that made the hill a good place for secret meetings also made it perfect for assassinations and body disposal. Separated from the mainland by the causeway and isolated by its height, it's essentially remote mountain terrain within the city limits. I wasn't even sure if I could climb down the outside of the hill. After my first step past the safety rail – which dropped me about seven meters and cost me quite a bit of skin and clothing – I was even less certain.

I struck out blind, heading down towards the whatever water I would find. I had originally started down the north side of the Crestón towards my house, but started rethinking that. They had the causeway completely controlled, so I'd have to swim for it. I could tumble down and hit the water by the sewage treatment plant, then swim across towards the Paseo Centenario. If I had to, I could swim all the way to Olas Altas Cove, but it was a long way. And also, I realized, under easy eye of anybody on the causeway.

I started angling around to the south, scrambling on slopes where I could easily slip and roll right down to the rocks at the waterline. I didn't hear anything from the crest, but figured there was somebody after me, they'd only need to get within shooting distance. I crawled through brush and banged over rocks as I worked around and down. On one slip, I caught myself on the lip of a hundred meter sheer drop into breakers. I'd forgotten that the south of Crestón is undercut; the famous sea lion caves. I was lucky I didn't fall into a boatload of tourists. I hung on the upper lip of the caves, breathing like a trapped rabbit, the wide bright ocean view slapping me in the eyes like a sharp wind. I could see that I had to work my way down to the east, away from the bare rock and dropoff, but first I had to climb up to something I could hang on to.

If I went around too far I might be heading right back to them, so I picked a spot on the southwest shoulder of the hill. It's a beautiful little notch that nobody ever visits, since climbing back up would virtually impossible. There are several small, flat reefs just off the shore, separated by channels that funnel the surf in an interesting, violent manner. They're underwater at high tide, covered with some sort of green moss. Each wave replenishes a hundred little waterfalls. A white heron was standing on one of them looking at me. I caught myself wishing for a camera, but I was having a hard time just hanging on to my binoculars. I found a reasonably safe place to enter the water and was immediately rumbled over rocks by a surge, banged up and bleeding before I even got completely wet. I hoped the sewage plant was working properly for once, not discharging untreated waste due to shortage of chemicals. Oh well, anybody who can't swim through shit has no business being a reporter.

I struck out straight across to Isla de la Piedra – destination of the much-pimped 'Stone Island Tour'. I originally planned to cut inside once I cleared the stones of the breakwater, swim down the channel a ways and come ashore at the Isla side. But once I was in open water it seemed easier to just swim across to the opposite causeway, where I would go ashore with the breakwater between me and anybody watching from the Crestón side. It was maybe a two hundred meter swim to the tip of the berm.

Once there, I decided swimming to the shore riprap would be easier than climbing out, then walking on the house-sized rocks of the berm. I kept on thrashing along until I came to a low shelf where, after three false tries on treacherous waves, I managed to drag myself out and clamber up the rocks to the roadway. Stone Island isn't really an island, it's a peninsula. And the river is actually an estuary. But Goat Island, where I was standing wet, tired, and pissed-off out of my mind actually was an island until they tore down half of it to build the berm and now everybody thinks of it as an appendage. I started down the crushed pipestone roadway to the dock.

Which turned out to be worthless. The day trip water ferries had stopped for the evening and a tourist catamaran was loading its last return trip of celebrators. I would have to con my way on board with the happy crowd of drunken morons listening to rap and *banda* at ear-splitting volume, or go to the dock in the village. Normally there would be a swarm of *pulmonias* around the excursion dock, but this late, with all the tourists on package trips, there were none at all and I didn't have the time to walk two miles into the village, much less the energy. I was saving myself for the woman I loved.

The last tourists were staggering and flopping out of a peculiarly *Isla* form of transport; a fourwheeled hay wagon fitted with bench seats and pulled by a huge Japanese tractor. But I spotted another *Isla* special; a chariot. Actually these little rolling photo ops are made from the rearends of ruined pickup trucks. They have a wooden cart body with an awning overhead, two facing benches, and a bored horse pulling them. I hailed the rig, handed the yokel driver a sodden bill and said, "*Vamos al embarcadero.*" He seemed a little insulted at not being offered an explanation of why I was soaking wet and bleeding, but too proud to inquire. He stood up, leaning back against the reins, and lashed the drowsing horse. The reaction was a very impressive acceleration for a one-horsepower vehicle. The road was cluttered with the cattlecars and dithering sightseers, so he took a shortcut along the beach. I hung on to the bench as we tore wildly down a path to the shore, then galloped along the packed sand, occasionally showering spray as waves petered out into our path. He stood erect, slashing wildly, as we careened down the beach, then up through deeper sand to the road to town. The horse plunged along like a lunatic, scattering kids, chickens, pigs, and occasional motor vehicles. The charioteer smelled like extremely cheap *mescal*.

There was a problem at the boat because nobody would sit beside me, even with the *lanchero* pleading them to pack in and make room for more. Nobody spoke or made eye contact with me as we slipped across calm water lit a dusky plum color by the remnants of light in the overcast sky. I eyed the machine gun of the Marine guard as I walked off the dock, it would have been the perfect accessory for my prevailing mood. The guard had no reaction; he'd seen dripping-wet, furious men in his time.

I squished out to the street missing a shoe, enjoying the evening chill in my dripping clothes. The *pulmonia* driver gave me a look. "Don't *mojados* swim north?"

I said, "I'm training for the wetback triathlon," and told him just where to go, because I'd figured out who Those Guys were and where I could find them.

As we passed the Casa de Campesino I had a sudden brainflash, told the *pulmonero* to circle the block while I dashed in to buy a pickaxe handle and some tin lanterns. But they only had one lantern in stock, so I grabbed up a half-dozen *velas*. They looked like standard Catholic candles in tall glass jars with paper saint labels, but actually seemed more like the *Santeria* kind, where the saints and virgins are all symbols for possessive entities that promise all sorts of dubious works. I liked the one that said, "Saint Michael Conqueror protects against evil neighbors". The *pulmonero* asked if I had one that would attract pussy. I read him the label off the one, "Burn for nine days and you will have him tied up and nailed." He didn't seem to like it.

I didn't have to hunt for Red October; we came up behind it on the Zaragoza side, then slid around the flank of the compound and it was right there at the curb; a red VW *Combi* covered with political slogans and warped likenesses of Marley and Che. I paid off the driver and sidled over to the van for a checkup. It was empty; the engine was still warm. But not near warm enough for my taste. I slipped under it with the candles, lantern and a plastic lighter I'd bought off the driver for a ripoff fifty pesos. I had no idea how long it would take for the flames to boil the gas in the tank and make it spill out the filler tube and down to where the fire could take advantage of it. Maybe it wouldn't work at all, maybe it would give me an edge or at least some juvenile satisfaction. I shouldered the pick handle and sauntered into Red October like striding up to the plate needing two runs in the ninth. It might have been nighttime for Mazatlán, but for me it was a few minutes to High Noon.

During the strike at UNAM, when the university strikers got more belligerent and destructive every time they were granted concessions, I read a comment by an American journalist who said it better than I would have. So of course I'll repeat it without mentioning his name. He said what should have been obvious to all of us, but wasn't; that what the CGH *huelgistas* absolutely and desperately wanted was for the government to gun them down. And we wouldn't oblige.

"Three Strikes, You're IN!" by Mundo Carrasco
"Millenio" November 2000

The Red October dormitory is located in the back of the crumbling, graffitied ruins of a huge hospital complex that got built in a welter of national pride and OPEC oil price glory. It always amazed me that a windfall like that could actually make the country poorer, but it shouldn't ... my own finances are an excellent example of the same principle. Big shots of money are like the dancing white flame of cocaine that leaves you more diminished after it flickers out.

Now it's a sprawling, multi-level dorm for UAS, one of several for students too poor to afford their own lodging. Some, like the Martyrs of April Seventh, have communal kitchens to feed the disadvantaged students, but Red October is just an Animal House for the young and underprivileged. The names aren't all that strange in Mexico, where we fancy ourselves revolutionaries: there are grade schools in Mazatlán named after Che Guevara, Karl Marx, Sigmund Freud and *Madre Teresa de Calcuta*. The dorm is a good showing for the attempt to educate every Mexican regardless of background. It's also, predictably, a hotbed of adolescent rebellion and attitude. Not to mention drugs, prostitution, and un-Mexican music. I walked up to a side door, remembering that Grady, a Vietnam veteran, had once said, "I wouldn't go into Commie Martyrs dorm with less than platoon strength, a heavy weapons squad, and a kilo of *sinsemilla*."

I had no search plan, just strolled through the halls of the dorm. Nonchalant guy with a pick handle over his shoulder. I peered into filthy communal bathrooms, chill out nooks plastered with layers of music and political posters like historical sediment. You could peel them off and trace some sort of history of superficial political thought. The constants would be Che and Jim Morrison. Politicians of eroticism.

I started up a short, empty hallway towards several blank doors but two twerps, obvious *grillos* – one even had a CGH T-shirt – stepped out of an alcove and told me I was trespassing. I was in no mood for that crap and started to brush by, but one of them pulled out a pistol. I hampered that action by snapping the pick handle down and fracturing his wrist. Then I knocked both of them repeatedly unconscious. After all, they were just college commies with brand new guns; I'm a professional athlete. And in a bit of a mood. I picked up the pistol and slipped it into my pocket. I walked up to the door of what seemed to be a semi-detached suite of rooms, opened it and stepped through. I might as well have stepped off a thousand-foot cliff with a boulder following me down like some cartoon coyote.

There were a few *grillos* lounging around the room, vague striker types. But all I could really see was Mijares lying naked on the bed with a pillow under her hips and Nesto, also naked, standing at the sink washing off his crotch. That seemed to be enough to deal with for the moment.

The room was steamy and full of rancid musk. I felt like turning around and walking out, but couldn't seem to move. It was all too fucking casual. Mijares turned her head toward me, languid and unfocused. I could almost see heat waves distorting the air around her. Nesto smiled at me, soaping off his unit. "Want to bat clean-up, hero?"

I managed to keep my voice fairly steady as I looked at Mijares.

I said, "Does this mean you won't be home for dinner, sweetheart?" And suddenly it didn't take any effort to control myself. All I wanted to do was go home.

I turned around and headed for the door, but two of the strikers (*cum* gangbangers) hopped up in front of me. I gave them my best autograph-giving smile and smashed the pick handle into the first one's knee. He went down screaming and I stepped back and slammed the other one across the ribs so hard they cracked like a string of fire-crackers. I thought, Hey, I can hit in this league. I turned back around to Nesto, but he was laughing at me. He gave a shrill whistle and the adjoining door burst open and a half-dozen *grillos* ran into the room, carrying guns.

"Go ahead, Mister Clutch," he snickered. "Swing away."

Mijares leaned up on her elbows and looked at me. Something major and radical had changed about her. Her eyes were opaque and shiny, like she was on some drug. But I didn't give myself that out. The room felt close and hot like a stable, the young *grillos* had a familial, hive sort of feel – animals in their milieu. It was a warren, a pile. She lived there and I never would. I felt choked and light-headed, like I was getting the flu. I would have pushed a button to blow the whole scene up in a fireball of white light.

But she rolled to her right and craned her neck to look at Nesto and say, "Please, just let him go. Okay? I'll ..."

Nesto laughed. "Need a woman to save your ass, hotshot?"

He dropped to his knees behind her and stroked her buttocks, running his thumb down into the cleft. At his first touch her head dropped to the filthy mattress and her rear end started to move with his hand. Then slowly lifted up, presenting herself to his attentions. He gave me a flat look that said, It's *you* I'm fucking, isn't it? Then he raised his hand, watched as she arched up for it, and slapped it down hard, reddening her pale globes. She moaned explo-sively and reached back to caress the impact areas, spreading them apart. Nesto laughed again then pushed her away so forcefully she fell off the bed. One of the henchmen grabbed her and hoisted her to her feet.

He snarled. "Beat it, bitch. Old Mundo and us have some things to talk over."

She shuffled towards the door, then turned to me and said, "I'm sorry, Mundo. I..."but she was interrupted somewhat by the door being kicked open with the force of a small explosion, slamming her into a slide down the wall.

She lay there, staring up the length of the body of Chaco – bodyguard to the stars – who grinned at the gaping *huelgistas*.

Strike *him,* assholes, I thought. I was entertaining my usual mixed feelings about Chaco appearances. Mijares also seemed gripped by conflicted emotions.

He smiled around the room, winked at me, then said, "Hey, nice *cuerno de chivo,* lemme see," and snatched an AK-47 out of the hands of the nearest kid. He admired it, checked it out, spun it around his finger, nodded, then yelled, "Hey, drop the fucking guns!"

All of them complied instantly. He rolled his eyes in amused disgust, and motioned to Mijares, who hastily scooped up the rifles. "Just toss them out the window, Honey."

"See, the thing is," he told me. "Guns don't make the man."

He placed the flashcone at the end of his rifle into Nesto's crotch and leered, "Sometimes works the other way, though."

Nesto was impassive, but his disarmed gunslingers were petrified, mostly just college boys, in spite of their tough poses. Chaco stuck the rifle under his arm like a swagger stick, and started marshalling them up. "Right. All of you move over here against this wall. You can stay right there pissing yourself, 'Pesto'."

They obeyed immediately, except one big, tough-looking student about thirty years old, who was showing signs. I saw what Sgt. Garcia had meant, everything about his posture and eye movement was screaming out, "I'm packing a pistol!" Chaco gave a theatrical sigh, reached into his jacket pocket with his free hand and brought out a big automatic pistol with a silencer attached. In the same movement he swung it up and punched three rounds right into the reluctant striker's face. The suppressor muffled the sounds so well you could hear chunks of his head splat into the wall.

In a stage-whispered aside to the terrified strikers, Chaco said, "Won't even wake up your dorm sweeties who actually go to class in the morning."

They became much more eager to please. He lined them up against the wall.

"Okay, one line, shoulder to shoulder. Pack it in there, willya? Good, now lean your heads forward. No, no," he explained by means of cuffs on their heads, "Heads up, chins thrust out. Outstanding. Now turn your heads just a little to the right. But keep the chin out, shithead!"

He reviewed the formation, found it acceptable. "Perfect. Now close your eyes. Don't peek." He stuck the pistol in his belt and swung the rifle, fast and hard, through the arc described by their jaws, knocking all four unconscious. He checked them out, and smirked. "Four-bagger, hey, Mundo? Personal best."

I said, "Best time, too. Bottom of the ninth, nobody on."

He guffawed, then turned his attention to Nesto, standing very naked and alone, but defiant.

Chaco pointed, "*That's* the big cock he's always bragging about? Christ, If I'da got that one, I'da thrown it back."

From the floor, Mijares showed a greater interest in the proceedings. Chaco, hulking huge above her, grinned down at her and pulled off his shirt. He was ridiculously muscular, golden-brown, and glowing with sweat. He had no more hair on his body than he did on his head. He tossed her the shirt, profiling for her, flexing awesomely. He popped his eyes, "Wow, huh?"

Nesto, I've got to hand it to him, snapped, "Big fuckin' deal."

Chaco turned towards him and Nesto flowed into an aggressive martial arts pose. Why do those big, strong guys always learn that stuff? Chaco just walked into him, backhanded his arms away and punched his chest so hard I expected him to barf up his lungs and spleen. Then he grabbed him by the scruff of the neck and said, "Pretty little Pesto. Puffed-up boy playing grownup games. Well, you know ..."

But we never will know because he jerked Nesto's head back suddenly and when he reacted, reversed the movement and slammed a fistful of face into a cement pillar. Nesto made a sound like a cow hit by a truck and went down like a sack of second-hand shit. I had no idea if he survived the impact, but I knew he wasn't going to be bothering anybody for a long time. And would never, ever again, be pretty.

Chaco didn't even look at him, just went over and scooped Mijares up. He cradled her for a minute, then tossed her over his shoulder, holding her with his hand behind her knees. He winked at me and said, "I'm taking a little time off work. Catch me at the Modern Hercules contest in June, though. I've got it in the bag this year."

He moved to the door, looming by me with Mijares draped over his shoulder like a Frazetta painting. He was a huge rounded-off guy, like Fernando Valenzuela or Richie Valens. Also a Valenzuela, come to think of it; those Valenzuela boys are stout. Fernando came back down from the bigs, pitched a few games for the Venados, ended up with the Guadalajara Toros. I'd thought of going up there, getting a hit off him. What a souvenir, huh? I realized my mind was trying desperately to escape the blood-spattered, sex-reeking room and fly off into clouds. I wrestled it back to the present situation.

One reality factor was the gun in my pocket. As Chaco reached for the door, steadying Mijares with his other hand around her knees, I pulled it out and pointed it at him. I was shocked by the surge of power, a sudden ego transfusion as good as any hit of pure coke. I was in control of this *desmadre* for the first time since I walked in. I could turn the whole trainwreck around. No need to be good if you have the equipment.

Chaco grinned, but stopped. "Got the drop on me, Clipper. But see, if you were going to shoot, you'd have shot."

I held the scene there a moment, while three realizations popped into my head. The first was that I was not going to kill anybody over her. Anybody else, that is. The other was that I'd had it with her, before I even walked into the room. And last but not least, that I'd been an idiot not to realize it. I stood there with a gun in my hand, the smell of blood and fresh brains all around me, and the sight of my Most Beloved Ass In The Universe being hoisted and heisted ... and the fever broke. I lowered the gun and that was that, the moment when things were as bad as they could get had just passed. Now things would move in a different direction ... I just knew it.

I started to toss the gun away, then stuck in my hip pocket. See, I was already learning new things. One of them, to hang on to the firepower. Another, that when you hold a woman upside down, with her vagina exposed and her breasts hanging in front of her face, she doesn't look as sexy.

I had to ask. "When you broke into her house, why were you tearing her clothes off? To make her tell you something?"

Chaco laughed, the motion bobbling Mijares various globes like gelatin. "Hell no, I was just curious. And she turned out even better than I thought. Incredible, huh? Little weight training and she could win Miss Hercules in a couple of years."

"Unbelievable. So what was it you weren't trying to get her to tell you?"

"Mostly we wanted to scare her. Tell us about Nesto and his bunch, what they were planning. We were also figuring on shaking you down, since you were working for her and we figured she'd got you involved. Trolled you in by your dick. We were going to let her get away, see if she would run to whoever she was fronting for. Trouble is, she ran to you instead. So we staked you out, scanned your phone, and you led us right to them. Good work."

"For Borrego?"

"Didn't he tell you? But also for her father, of course. The governor. And all of us. To all of you. It's odd, but *federales* on federal business are about as independent as anybody in Mexico can ever be. But we end up benefiting the entire public."

"One for all and all for one."

"Plus a few side bets. Right now I'll settle for the bird in hand." He nodded towards Mijares' butt. "Call it a leveraged takeover. I had my eye on her all along, and things played out right for me."

"Lucky you."

"Yes and no. I have to tell you, I admired you as a

ballplayer, but I really got to be a fan when you bunted that bullet. You don't get to be a real legend without luck, but it's the kind of luck that wouldn't have been there if you hadn't had the reflexes in the first place, you see what I mean?"

I didn't see *nada*, actually. My head was starting to hurt. I looked at him and Mijares a little more and said, "So are *they* going to let you just keep her as a housepet?"

"Maybe even house*wife*. They'll get around to figuring out what to use her for, but at the moment she's my favorite plaything. It's kind of cool having a woman this ruthless who doesn't care about money. Her father preferred her ending up with you – how unbelievable is *that* – but things being how they are, he finds me acceptable. Or maybe I'll get tired of her and she'll be happy to marry some aristocratic dickhead."

He turned to kiss her flank, then shrugged his shoulder up and down a few times. Mijares moaned and seemed to wrap around him a little. He looked at me and shook his head. "What a slut. I think I'm in love."

"I'm having a few doubts, myself."

"Well, don't worry about her." Suddenly he laughed out loud. "And don't worry about me. I think she just met the one guy who can whip her ass into shape.'

"*Provecho, Amigo.*" Good fucking luck.

"You're all right, Mundo. I mean, for an amateur."

He turned to the door, booted aside a striker who was sobbing and holding his knee, and walked out. Mijares looked back at me for a moment and I blew her a kiss, but she was blank, absorbed. I thought, she's in a new movie now. The striker with the cracked ribs moved and moaned a little so I kicked him in the head and felt slightly better. I walked out of the room, down the halls, and out into the night.

I don't know where Chaco went or where he took Mijares, but he was considerate enough to have left the Suburban behind for me. I walked by it a little gingerly, but when the door popped open there was nobody inside but Herrera, so far surviving the demands of his driving job. He motioned me in with a halfhearted gesture, so I shrugged and slid into the passenger seat. He'd just pulled out into the street when the harlequin *vocho* van, up the block across the street, erupted into a magnificent ball of flame.

It bucked up in back like a bull, then tore itself in half, spitting flaming pieces up the street and into the jungly grass around Red October, causing several small fires. Assorted hardware fell from the sky and bounced off cars and asphalt. A patch of street was actually on fire. Che and Marley were distorted, then dripped away. The top had split open and I could just read the word "Fuck..."before it all turned black. Herrera sat still, staring stunned at the mini-apocalypse, no idea what to do about it. He finally decided on the wisest course, which was to get the hell out of there.

As he dodged around debris in the street it dawned on me that my only preparation had worked out too late. Postmature ejaculation.

I sighed. "So much for my legendary timing."

Herrera glanced at me, startled, then turned in the seat to stare, "You did that?"

"Don't curse the darkness when you can light a candle."

He shook himself like a dog, then started laughing. He punched me on the shoulder. "I'm starting to see why Chaco digs your error-making ass."

I spun around on him and blurted out, "Listen! Did Chaco do Varedas? I've got to know, and you're going to tell me."

He shook his finger back and forth, the Mexican *no* sign.

"Not a chance. I was with him when it happened. It was the opposite of what he wanted, really. You still care about the Varedas thing?"

I leaned back in the seat, and fell back into the headache and nausea and general malaise. Worse, I realized I still did care about the Varedas thing. Damn. The big car moved down the street while I watched the flaming van recede in the rearview mirror. San Miguel putting the sword of flame to one more batch of pesky neighbors. And I had to admit that the 'Woman Of Your Dreams In Your Arms' candle worked, though. Just not for me.

297

Beauty is a major obsession in Sinaloa – much more so for women than men – and Carnival is the peak of the fever, the Super-Bowl of glamour. It takes a harmless preoccupation and drapes it over a hierarchy, from the Queens, down through the princesses, the candidates, the singers, the dancers. You can even see that Presidente and Pacífico girls are hotter than the Bacardi, Boots, or Caribe Cooler girls.

It's like when we were boys in school, with an unwritten ranking of everybody's fighting ability. No need to publish it on the sports page, everybody just knew. Any dispute, you'd settle it. But girls don't get to grow out of their ranking system that easily. Contests and crowns are the only way they can slug it out, drag beauty out of the beholder's eye and take it on the road.

"The Queen Gambit" by Mundo Carrasco
La Talacha, March 18, 2001

Palomina is a profesional, so she kind of transcends the whole beauty hierarchy, stands above the ranking system. Or at least outside of it, like a pro boxer ringside at the Olympics. But she can't keep it from eating at her a little.

So when I shambled into the Muralla Athletic Club – burned out, shaky and insubstantial – there she was, dressed like a complete slut to watch the Coronation of the International Queen of the Pacific. I don't know what the hell I was doing there myself. Chaco's driver had dropped me a few blocks away, on the fringe of the Carnival Crawl, and I just wandered in on my way home. I didn't even need to show my city credentials, one of the doormen recognized me and shook my hand, the other seemed intimidated by my torn, bleeding clothes and whatever he saw in my face. I just felt the need for some beauty instead of ugliness, something superficial instead of heavy, dark complexities. Probably I just didn't want to go home. Not without a lot of drinks, anyway.

The International Queen is the stepdaughter of Carnival royalty, not taken seriously. Probably because the girls are from out of town. It's been held in Club Muralla for decades, and isn't so much about *Carnaval Mazatlán* as a symbol of sisterhood. The candidates are from other countries all over South America and the Pacific Rim, Guatemala, Costa Rica, Honduras, California. There was even a girl from Malaysia a few years ago. They come up here at their own expense, hoping to cadge another crown for their collections. They get feted and ogled, but not really thought of as true royalty. They are crowned by the current Queen of Flower Games, which shows them their place in the pantheon.

Since the *candidatas* are all products of the Miss Universe type of beauty pageants, the coronation has always been run like a contest, with judges flashing numbered cards and asking questions. Fading princesses from yesteryear and bloated tourism czars hassle the visiting cuties with questions like, "What does your country need most?" The most famous answer came three years ago, when the reigning Miss East Los Angeles replied to the thought-provoking query, "What does Mazatlán smell like?" by saying, "*Agua, no?*" Which was heard as, "*A guano?*" Which would mean, "Like birdshit," leading to weeks of fun for comedians and the tackier newspaper columnists. I even sunk to the level of a "*No Agua*" column about a smelly deal at the waterworks.

The girls were being questioned as I walked into the main hall, decorated so utterly in Early Carnival Hysteric that it was impossible to tell it's a basketball court in real life. I sunk twenty-seven points here when I was fifteen, my all-time high, Polluelos in a grudge victory over the Muralla hoopsters. I had a tequila in each hand and slugged on them in impartial rotation while I looked at all the fresh young sweetness on stage, painted, posed, tarted up, and hygenically sealed. *Don* Teofilo Megaño had just asked a jutting Miss Managua what she would do about solving world poverty and she was giving it some very serious thought when there was a voice at my shoulder. "She could feed quite a few with just one of those jugs." And there was Palomina wearing a glittering gold mask and apparently a thin coat of red paint. I handed her the tequila with the fewest slugs out of it.

She knocked it back and put her forearm on my shoulder, then leaned her head on it, eyeing the stage from my shoulder. I suspected it was not her first tequila of the evening. "Thanks for that parade thing, Mundo. It was wonderful. Living my lamest dream, Carnie Barbie."

"You were the finest one on the cattle wagon."

"Thanks, *amigo*. I owe you big." Then she stiffened, gagging at the titular princess' answer to a question about population problems. "Or we could all be professional virgins like you, honey, and that would take care of it."

"Now, now." I reached up to pat the cheek that wasn't cushioned by her gold-taloned fingers on my shoulder.

"Now, my ass," she snarled. "Who the hell *are* these idiot little twats? You should have seen the talent competition, Miss Valparaiso was spinning frisbees. They've got their little *tiaras;* one of them will get her *corona* at the coronation. What have I got to show?"

I grabbed a passing waiter and said, "A Corona for the lady."

He handed her a chilled beer with a flourish.

She slapped my ribs, then started giggling. "Still Mister Clutch, aren't you?"

"I think my clutch is getting a little burned out."

"That reminds me. Since you stood everybody up for the Naval Battle, are you going to watch the Burning of Bad Humor?"

I said, "I just did." But she didn't pick up on it.

"You know what?" she murmured right by my ear, "I've got an audition tomorrow. Some *mero-mero* from Presidente saw me dancing, found out I did the choreography. It could mean a commercial. A national shot."

"That's great."

"Yeah, great. Listen, it's starting to sink in through the booze, here. You're messed up, aren't you? Something's in your face."

"You know, worried about work."

"Don't give me work. You're a mess, *mijo*. Hey, where's your bosslady, Miss Gomorrah?" She'd put her finger right on it. Investigators should all be women.

"Isn't going to happen. She just got carried away."

"*Ay, Mundo, pobrecito.*" She came off my shoulder and around in front of me, reaching her hands up on each side of my face, looking into my eyes. "Look. Eventually you'll get over it. Learn to relate to normal women."

"Yeah. You bet. Eventually." I must not have looked very enthusiastic.

"Or," she murmured pregnantly, "you can get over it right now. Right away. Right up the street."

Since she lived three blocks over, above the old cigarette factory, she'd made it pretty clear.

But I tried to blur it a little. "You said you weren't going to ask me again. "

"I'm *not* asking you, *tarugo*. I'm telling you."

Her loft is a hundred year-old niche suspended over the deserted factory floor on pillars of polished ebony worth thousands of dollars apiece and coated in cheap red paint. She lit lots of candles concealed in intricate ceramic shades typical of upland Indian craft. The place was cozy, but the high ceilings and old mud walls would be cool in the summer. The place flickered orange and yellow, disappeared off into shadows. It reminded me of old churches up in the Sierra Madre villages. My fatique from the climb or the swim or the fight – maybe a little shock and disappointment in there somewhere – had made me unable to resist her walking me home. But there, in the fluttering dark, the same factors kept me from feeling like doing much else. Maybe some temporary insanity in there, too.

I said, "Listen, Paloma ..."

She shook her head, reached out and rapped her knuckles on my temple. "You listen, you sap. You think you've figured out what my real hair color is, right?"

What could I say?

"But have you ever wondered what my real name is?"

"*Media Blanca*?" I meant half-blonde but unfortunately it also means White Sox.

"Everything's a baseball game to you, isn't it?"

"God, I wish. You put in nine innings then you go home. You either won or you lost, but you don't have to sit around trying to figure out which."

"My name is Socorro. And that's why we're here."

"To confess to using a *nom du plumed*? I already sus-

pected that strippers use aliases in their work. There could-
n't be that many girls named Yuri and Dulce."

"No, you *pendejo*. I'm here to offer you succor. And
solace. An anatomy to cry on. No charge, no strings.
You've got something coming, and it might as well be me."

"You already *know* about this crap?"

"That *Supercabrona* dumped you? I knew about it
before you did, you simp. Before it happened. Maybe even
before she decided to fuck you over. I know a lot of bitches
like that ... okay, maybe not *that* bad. I could have told you
what, when, who and why."

"No kidding? Nobody ever tells me why. Oh, you
forgot 'where', by the way ... the journalists Pentateuch."

"Oh, let me guess. In a bed with a whole *futbol* team
and you standing in the door with your *chile* curling up?"

"*Ay*. I'm impressed. It was in Red October, by the
way."

"Who gives a shit? Are you ready or aren't you?"

"Ready for what? If you're going to threaten me,
confess to murdering the mayor and pope, or beat me up,
I won't come close to being surprised."

"I'm sure we'll get around to all that eventually. Except the confession; one of those is all you get."

"Thank God for that. I'm way over my quota."

"But the point I keep trying to make here," she
leaned over and put her hand on my mouth. "And I don't
understand how you manage to be a smartass and dumbass
at the same time ... the point is that I spotted you from up
high. I folded my wings, spread my claws." She did a
demonstration of that, a fairly frightening flourish of sharp,
gold, fiberglass-reinforced talons. "I swooped down on
you." She stopped and looked me right in the eyes. "So you
can carry me off."

She made me sit down on her sofa, which I was glad
to do. I just didn't feel like ever getting up again. She said
to wait while she slipped into something more preposter-
ous.

And sure enough. It was the same dress she'd worn
on the parade float, a gold lamé sheath with feathered cape.
She wore a plastic "diamond"tiara and had made a sash that
said, "*Reina de Juegos Plumadas*". I felt honored, there's a

Flower Games queen every year, but she was the only Feather Games queen ever. She had pale makeup, false eyelashes, a quickie coiffure ... every inch a queen. She had a little scepter, which she waved at me like a magic wand. She profiled and gave me the wiper wave. I felt a sudden pride in her, wanted to kiss her hand. Nobody had crowned her, she'd made her own realm.

She said, in a quiet voice like the Blue Fairy in the old Disney Movie, "Mundo, do you know how long I've had the fantasy of being a queen? I want to rule justly and beautifully, enchant princes, have subjects bowing joyfully at my feet, be remembered with a charming bronze statue that cries real tears on feast days."

That provoked a few fantasies of my own, and I said so.

She buried her head in her elbow, her arm thrust down and back. Melodramatically, stricken, shoulders shaking, she wailed in a *telenovela* voice, "I never would have thought you would turn such a moment of grace and nobility into a cheap carnal thing." She whirled away from me in a heartbroken gesture. She'd given the gown's skirt a quarter turn to the side, so the daring leg slit now framed the lower contours of her downy dancer's cheeks. That got me up on my feet, all right.

I walked over to pet her smooth, chiseled behind. She turned, regally, and brandished her scepter. I knelt before her. "Your highness, I am your loyal knight. Ready for a one knight stand."

"Well, in that case." And she tugged the skirt around 180 degrees to offer me a view of curly blonde *peluche* pierced with a small golden coil, "You may kiss my ring."

In Spanish, just by the way, *lamé* means "I licked".

TUESDAY
FEBRUARY TWELFTH
MARTES DE CARNAVÁL (MARDI GRAS)
CUMPLEAÑOS DE ABRAM LINCOLN

Carnival Calendar

Coronation of King Of Joy, Salon Bacanora, 8 PM
The Burning of Bad Humor, Olas Altas Boulevard,
11 PM

The motto of *Los Boiscouts* is *Prepárate*, but I often felt that it was somehow lacking in something. You learn skills, get gear, buy insurance, lock the doors...but there is always something you didn't consider. There is something else involved that is very important, how you deal with things for which you are totally unequipped. It's an area of experience that can persuade us of the advantages of prayer, solid upbringing, and sheer, blind luck.

"Stumbling into the Playoffs" by Mundo Carrasco

Noroeste Sport Page, October 1999

Lick was about all I did, it turned out. I could blame it on the climb, the swim, the fight, the drinks. But mostly I just had an overwhelming drive to be unconscious. First time I ever fell asleep during sex. And I mean *during*. But hey, I said I was sorry the next morning.

"You should be." Palomina had pouted, handing me a cup of moderately hot coffee. "I'd toss you out on the street if I could find an unbruised place where I could pick you up."

"Now there's something wrong with my ears?"

"Too obvious. And there's nothing wrong with your ears, Mundo. Give a girl something to hang onto. And don't worry, I got mine."

"So I did okay? Don't get shipped down to the minors?"

"So you can contribute to their delinquency? Nah, you've got the stuff, Busher. Good enough for the moment."

I sipped the coffee, leaning against the mountain of pillows that landscaped her bed. Big, small, old, new, souvenir embroidered; obviously a lifetime collection. Palomina sat cross-legged, stirring her cup pensively, a cute frown under her tumble of hair. "So what is good, Mundo? I mean in bed? You ever wonder about that?"

"Of course not, I'm a man. If I'm getting it, that's good."

"Yeah, I've noticed how men don't care about their performance ratings. Christ, there ought to be judges with

307

little numbers on cards. But no, I mean ... well, look, every day, all the time, I have men staring at me, reaching for me. I look good, right? So they want me. They want to drag me down on their crotch. Where, like ... what does it matter? I could just be a handful of pork fat. You know?" She paused, sorting it out, "I guess what I'm saying is, I may *look* good, but *am* I good? You know ... when it comes down to it. I keep wondering if I'm just an empty box with fancy wrapping."

"You don't have to be good, my dear, just have the equipment."

She snorted. "Every woman alive has the equipment. And a lot of men give a decent imitation."

I set down my coffee and slid my hand down her cheek. "Ever think that it's not a matter of being good, just of whether or not you're appreciated? There might be guys who would prefer a pile of pork. Does that mean it's better?"

"So quality is in the pants of the beholder?"

"Look, would you rather be good, have some medals from the sex Olympics or have somebody who can see what you're really worth? Somebody who'd rather be with you? Likes your style. Enjoys your humor and ..."

"Mundo, you aren't very good at that sloppy stuff."

"Fine, let your pork fat write you Valentines."

She smiled. "I didn't say I didn't like it."

"So can we consider the discussion resolved?"

"Yeah. I guess. For now."

"Good, let me show you a better use for oration."

Later, I lay on my chest in the big tangle of pillows, while she played idly with my hair.

Very softly, she said, "I know I'm just a replacement for her, Mundo."

I let that one by, went for oblique. "Does that make you feel bad?"

"Should it? Does a transplanted heart or liver feel bad because it came in second behind some dysfunctional organ?"

"Wow, I can see you've thought this stuff out."

"I've had a lot of experience as a surrogate female."

"No, you're the real thing. A handful of pork fat is

a surrogate female."

"You don't have to pretend anything to make me feel better. Ya big lug."

"It's so I'll feel better, actually. But I'm not really pretending here. Not really."

"Me neither. One or two of those orgasms was real."

"Just to keep it interesting?"

"Just to build the suspense."

She settled down, snuggled in and drifted into a doze.

So softly I could barely hear her she said, "But don't we have to try to be good? Try to get better?"

And I have to say it's a question that had been bothering me lately. I'm writing the same column, hitting the same pitchers, swimming in the same little pool. I might be marinating, might be stagnating. How would I know? Maybe we all need judges with cards.

So what with one thing after another it was dark before I got home. I didn't want to miss Palomina getting dressed for work, but I was suddenly in a hurry to get some of my own work done. For a change. I lit my little barbecue in honor of Fat Tuesday, slapped some thin strips of beef on the grill, then stripped to my shorts and got down to finalizing my Friday column for *El Debate*. I thought I had it fairly well boiled down. I'd considered calling it *Talk Show From Hell* in honor of Varedas' radio days, but changed it to *Yo Sí Fui* and just ran through everybody who said, "It was me." And their reasons. It would sound pretty gutsy with the names involved, but boil down to a sort of, "We all killed him. And he was begging for it," sort of thing. I called it an assisted suicide. Euthanasia would have been more to the point.

Informative, clever, and not worth shooting anybody over. It skipped lightly past the fact that I still had no idea who ordered Varedas killed or who rousted the Infiernillo folks.

I was thinking that over a little, staring straight ahead, so I was looking right at the door when the gun came through it. And the gun was looking right at me. It's a heavy steel door with a heavy lock and bars over the windows. But the windows are glass. We have all these psychological barriers around us and one of them is the idea that things are safe behind glass. We lock things for safekeeping in cars that can be opened with a brickbat. We place way too much trust in transparency.

Psychological barriers cut no ice with Capitán Gárfio. He is as free from psychology as a wolf on the pounce. I was on my feet by the time he unlatched the door and managed to slam the trunk shut, locking up my work. I wished I had a gun for the second it took me to realize that it would have been the last thing I ever had.

He sort of bulged into the place, followed by the slim, fey accomplice I knew only as Bad Cop. They did about what you'd expect ... slapped me around, threw me up against the wall, and let Garza take a few very hard shots in my midriff before straightening me out with a smash to my face that slammed my head against the wall hard enough to sparkle the room with bleeping little blips. While Garza was trying to wreck my health and future progeny, Bad Cop wandered around admiring my view and breaking my things. Garza got bored with hitting me long enough to grab my shorts by the waist and snatch them off, ripping their waistband and the skin over my hipbone. At which point the cops turned humorous, smirking at me and making the standard comments about the state of my manhood. Both could have used a lesson from Mijares on bedside manner. They told me to get dressed, but put it in very uncomplimentary terms. Small in front, big in back, that's what they say about you when they've got you by the front, back, and unders.

At that point I realized they weren't going to kill me on the spot. Or question me there, either. Not really a relief. I've seen some of their questioning equipment and techniques. I pulled on the pants I'd tossed on the bed, stepped into a pair of sandals. I didn't bother with a shirt, just snatched a floppy cotton jacket off a hook by the shower. Garza grabbed it from me and searched it, turning up nothing but some old movie tickets.

He tossed it back to me but as I started to pull it on I said, "Hey, I've like *really* got to go to the toilet before we go anywhere."

The Bad Cop laughed and Garza sort of barked.

"No, seriously," I pleaded, "I had to go before you guys even showed up."

"Let's move, *puto*," Garza prodded at me.

"Okay. It's just my pants ... but it's your car seat."

Garza looked at his partner, shrugged and stepped to the bathroom door and looked around. Then he pushed me into the stall and down on the toilet.

"I can't go when anybody's watching." I just said it to see what reaction it got.

Bad Cop's wan't bad, "I think we can make you shit your pants if we apply ourselves."

So I did my stuff and stood up, pulling on the jacket as I walked out of the toilet stall. On the way out, I noticed that the downstairs door wasn't broken. Everybody in town seems to have the key to my building. Not that Garza needs one.

I sat in the back seat hugging my arms across my midriff like a schoolgirl, clasping my elbows, leaning forward, and blattering out nervous chatter. Just trying to kill time, make conversation. "So I'm being 'taken for a ride', I suppose?" For once I didn't feel that old movie phrase magic.

"We're taking you out," Garza sneered.

"You know," Bad Cop explained, "Like 'take out the garbage'?"

"Can you give me any idea of why?" I didn't really want to know when or where, and absolutely not how. Garza gave me the answer that is probably a frequent tradition among fat, ugly, brutal men with uniforms.

"Orders."

"'You mean like, 'just following orders'?"

"No more like, 'place your orders here'."

"You know," Bad Cop chuckled. "Your typical take out order."

"So where are you taking me; the dump?" It was my week for getting dumped.

"We're taking you to The Man. For the time being."

"Wow, The Man. Got his age, profession and address?"

Bad Cop swung around to check my reaction. "580 Golondrinas. Ring a bell?"

It certainly did, but I said, "Not really."

Bad Cop reached back and gave me a slap that bounced my head off the window. "That help, any? Ding a ling."

"Well, since we're going way the hell out there, let's swing by Colonia Javalies on the way. I just wish I could talk you into dropping by Los Mandilones bar, I bet we could work this out. My buddies there, Momo and Lobo, would buy you a drink. They'd do anything for me. We could make everybody happy, save a lot of trouble."

"You are a lot of trouble, Carrasco," Garza snarled.

"But we're going to save you from all that," Bad Cop added piously. "And don't hate us for being way ahead of you. There are worse things in the world."

"Yeah," I said, "Like limp dicks and dead batteries."

Bad Cop shot me a look and shook his head. "You've led a sheltered life."

I looked at the two of them, then thought of reasons they might be hauling me to Ibaes Tirado's house in the middle of the night and knew what Grady would have said. Gimme Shelter.

Mexican corruption rests on a rich, stable base: our legal system. More than archaic and Napoleanic, it's secret. The trials and open operations we see on Northamerican shows don't happen here. You don't see your accuser or your judge. Lawyers file papers, they are examined, a verdict is handed down some time. You couldn't deliberately design a better field in which to reap corruption. And it will not be changed because anybody who could change it has entirely too much to lose. Your system is about people and what they say. Ours is about papers. You see something on a piece of paper and it could be true or it could be false. Where do you go to find out?

"The Truth, The Whole Truth and Anything But The Truth"
by Mundo Carrasco, *Latin America Review*, March, 1994

"I just said I wanted to *talk* with him!" Our Brother sounded petulant, pleading with a Dean over budget cuts in the poetry faculty.

I'd been standing against the wall of his study for ten minutes while he fidgeted in his leather chair, whining at *Capitán* Gárfio and his slick sidekick. Tirado had two bodyguards flanking his desk. They had dismissed me and were regarding the two cops with sullen stares I assumed were hiding stark fear. Neither had moved a muscle.

Tirado still hadn't caught on. He fussed on his desk, turned to his bodyguards for confirmation and got no notice, then stood up and looked directly at me for the first time. "I'm sorry Mundo, this has been merely a misunderstanding. And I think it's time for you officers to leave. Thank you for your assistance."

The Feds looked at each other and laughed their asses off. Tirado goggled at them. Still no clue that they came here to kill people.

Garza cut past the 'what army?' bit and straight to the *neta*, "You expect these guys to protect you? Or even do what you say?"

Tirado blanched and swallowed. The coin had finally dropped. He sat down woodenly and gestured feebly at his bookend *guardespaldas*. They still didn't move.

The Bad Cop motioned at one of them, "Put your hands behind your head and get down on your knees."

Still no move.

Smooth as a seasnake, Baddie whipped out a huge, gold chased, encrusted automatic pistol and shot it right into his face, slamming him against a wall covered with leather-bound books and splattering them with blood and even worse stuff. Tirado looked like he might swoon right out; glide straight up into Labor Heaven.

Garza sneered at the corpse, "Fucking amateurs." He swaggered up to Tirado's desk and glared at him. He frowned, then leaned over to slap his face twice, forward and back. Tirado's head lolled and his eyes bulged.

"Have I got your attention?" Garza yelled. "You have something you want to show us, don't you?"

Tirado's lips were gibbering, but no sound was coming out. Garza leaned over for another cuff, then gave it up. He turned to the remaining bodyguard and barked, "Where is it?"

The guy leaped behind the desk and snatched open a drawer. He pulled out a sheet of expensive watermarked paper and slipped it across the desk to Garza, who snatched it up and read.

"I hope this isn't just about your damn kid being a faggot."

That seemed to rally Tirado out of his shock. He gave Garza a gaze of mild reproof and said, "That's not true. Adolfo was not ... is not a homosexual. That rotten ..."

He got cut off by a voice from the door. Garza spun and drew, the Bad Cop – ever the pro – kept his gun on the surviving bodyguard. Tavo was standing there, looking natty but dogged.

"He means me, Dad."

There was a long general silence after that little announcement. Everybody probably had their private thoughts. Mine were a quick game of connect-the-dots. If Tavo is Tirado's son, then his brother would be, too. Which means that Tirado's boss raped his son. Motive and opportunity clicking right in, and the method would follow pretty well with Garza running his errands for him. A secondary click in the old machine, that's why Borrego didn't want me around Tavo.

"Well I guess that wraps it up. See my column on Friday." I thought I sounded relaxed and breezy, but nobody paid any attention.

It was a little surprising for a man as dry and wispish as Tirado, but in Mexico it's quite common for a man to maintain a *frente segundo*. Action on that second front can be as productive or torturous as any campaigns within the main family. If the secretary or whoever gets pregnant then there are two family hearths, the *casa grande* and the *casa chica*. In fact, to judge by Tavo's clothes, manners, and schooling, the little house might not be all that little. Billable to his wife's fortune, I suddenly realized. Mexican women are doggedly accepting of these second families; conspiring to ignore them, and coping with illegitimate half-brothers suddenly showing up at the door. Mexican wives take a shamed pride in suffering in silence.

Tirado broke into the silence with a low, moaning voice. "Tavito, you could have told me this before."

Tavo stalked over to his desk and leaned on it to glare at him. "Right. You shipped us off to Guadalajara so nobody would even know we existed. You're a real champ at facing up."

I was pretty curious what Our Bro was going to say about that, but Garza butted in. "Enough of this *pinche* family drama! None of this is a shock to anybody and it sure as shit doesn't matter any more."

Tirado even let that remark get by him. He was too busy moving his eyes from the dead man on his marble tiles to his son, now revealed.

I turned to face Garza. "He killed Varedas, didn't he? That matters."

But even as I said it, I realized it didn't. I'd only cared because I thought the killers were after Mijares. Now they were going to kill me and Varedas was irrelevant. If Mazatlán was a kingdom he'd probably go down as Frederico the Irrelevant.

Except to Our Brother. He was all cut up about it. "Yes. I killed him. Put that in your newspaper, Mundo. I stood and watched horrible things done to him, did worse things myself. I wanted you to come so I could make a full confession."

Oh shit, not another confession. The cops seemed to have the same attitude.

"Right. You were about to confess to murder. To a reporter." The Bad Cop seemed to be overcome with the sheer stupidity of it. "Which is why you're both here."

Garza grinned. "Two turds with one stone."

Tirado's eyes ricocheted around the room. He finally decided that the fact that he was going to be killed took precedence over his son's sexual preference and the bloody murder already at hand. Though in an abstract sort of way. "You're going to kill two people? For telling the truth?"

"I count three. At least." Garza smirked at Tavo.

Bad Cop ticked them off. "You for being embarrassing. A murderer with a faggot son stashed away, give me a break. Sissy boy here for sticking himself into Varedas' business."

"His *puto* brother in the hospital, for vice versa." Garza snorted at his own joke and Bad Cop smiled a little before going on. "And Mundo here knows too much. Except to stay clear."

"And because he's an asshole who's long overdue," Garza was quick to add. With feeling.

Tirado looked at me, almost in tears. "I just wanted to make sure he got everything he deserved. And for everybody to know it. You're not going to understand this, but I was sort of acting for the population at large."

"As a matter of fact, I understand that very well. Do you think it will be appreciated?" I really wondered.

"Do you appreciate it?"

"More every day, actually."

He looked at Tavo, beseechingly. "Do you understand what I've done?"

"Killing Varedas? Sure. I went to do it myself."

That seemed to bother Tirado even more. He stared at Tavo and sighed. "I took the sins of all on myself. And for what? I have governors telling me what to do. Publicists tell me what to do. I'm in the power of the police. In the power of agents."

"Welcome to Power to the People," I told him.

He leaned forward, shaking. He picked up the paper from the desk and stared at it. Slowly, he turned to the bodyguard behind him. "You both knew about this. You betrayed me."

Garza laughed. "Don't worry about them. If you find an official murdered and the bodyguards aren't dead, they'll never get hired again."

The guard stiffened and stared, seeing the double-cross he should have known was coming. He was already way behind the pitch, with everybody looking right at him. He ducked behind Tirado and pulled out a pistol, aimed it at his head. Then he froze, realizing he hadn't made the brightest pick for his hostage. Suddenly, with no sound or warning, his head exploded and he seemed to slam himself onto the floor.

Lobo the Wolfman stepped into the room, holding a long-barreled automatic pistol. He pulled a ruptured condom off the end of it and snapped on another one from his pocket. "Like they say on the *tele*, 'Take the time to put it on ... it could mean your life.'"

So how do the Queens and Kings and Thrones and Rainments fit in with the austere Catholic underpinnings of Carnival? Because they are us, just as much as the feasting and fasting and dying and re-birth are ultimately about us. We are each a King or Queen of our own world, and need to rule it wisely and fairly and generously. Like Roy-alty, we all rule as part of a family, and like Royalty, our family spreads all over the world. Life may not always be a ball, but it is always a pa-rade.

"A Personal Procession" by Mundo Carrasco
Viejo Mazatlan Magazine, Feb 1997

Lobo surveyed the scene from under his shaggy thatch and bushy unibrow. He spat in the general direction of the cops. It wasn't quite Red October, but there were still too many guns and unclear motives in the room to suit me. And way too much tension.

"What a bunch of *pendejos*," Lobo growled, "You killed off the bodyguards before the kidnappers even showed up."

Momo and Pepito sidled into the room from behind him with leveled *cuernos de chiva*. Momo covered Garza grimly, while Pepito moved to disarm Bad Cop. Unfortu-nately his inexperience showed, as he came up to the wily cop, he cut between him and Lobo. In the second of being hidden, Bad News reacted with the same snake-like speed. He jabbed the gun up into the kid's face, snatched the Kalashnifoff from his hands, and gripped him by the neck. Spinning the boy to face his father, he punched the barrel of his gun into his ear and spoke in a low, smooth tone. "That's enough of that shit. Drop the guns." As a ironic af-terthought he added, "In the name of the law."

He never even heard it coming. His back was turned to the desk where Tavo stood by his father, feeble geezer and skinny homo presenting no threat. So he didn't see Tavo pick up the paperweight; a gold, engraved baseball with a pen sticking out of it. I'd estimate the solid metal ball moved only four meters and was going 150 kilometers an hour when it hit the back of his skull. No break, no junk, just pure old-fashioned smoke. Bet your ass it killed him. He lunged into Pepito, then slumped to the floor. Before he hit Momo had emptied his *cuerno de chivo* into his body.

I let go of my elbows. Garza stared sullenly when my cellular phone slid out of my sleeve into my hand. I opened it and listened. "It's dead now." Untrue, but I couldn't resist taunting him. "I scooped it into my sleeve in the bathroom. I was scared stiff somebody would call me while we were in the car."

Apparently when I punched Tavo's number he almost hung up, then heard the background conversation and acted. He called the bar, gave Momo the address, and headed over by himself. Alone and unarmed, one gutsy guy. But Garza didn't really need the details to spoil his day.

I picked up Tirado's paper from the desk and sure enough, the real thing. "Signed and even witnessed."

"Witnessed what?" Momo asked while jamming his rifle into Garza's ample gut.

Lobo had walked up behind me, so I just handed it to him.

He scowled at the paper, but took it and fumbled with it , complaining that he hadn't brought his glasses.

I reached for the pair of reading glasses in Tirado's vest pocket. "Here, he can't use them anyway, after you blindfold him."

But as I turned around I saw Pepito shaking his head violently, pointing to Lobo's back. I paused, glanced through the lenses, and said, "Hell, nobody could read anything with those binoculars."

Pepito sauntered up to the table and snicked the paper from Lobo's hands, glanced at it and snorted. "Says he killed Varedas. Says he had it coming." Lobo gave an appreciative rumble and turned to the matter at hand. Pepito gave me a blank stare and I got the picture. The wolfman doesn't want to admit he's illiterate. Hell, he probably voted for Varedas.

"Hey Lobo. Did you vote for these clowns?"

"Not for this nerd, but yeah, Varedas. He coulda made a difference in this town."

"Well, he's sure doing that. Even dead."

"Amen, Mary and Joseph."

I shook my head. "Jesus Christ."

"Him, too."

Tirado broke in with, "What do you mean by blindfolded?"

Which shows literacy isn't the same as intelligence, I suppose.

"Could you wait just a minute?" I asked him politely. "There's an item of business still on the table."

I walked up to Garza, who spit at me. Momo instantly kicked his knees out from under him, slamming him alongside the head as he fell. He rolled over and looked at me malevolently.

I squatted down on my heels to look right into him. I told him I wanted to know about the Infiernillo roust and no doubt about it. "And I mean the whole story. You tell me the whole thing, right now."

Garza gave me a dismissive sneer. "Make me."

I nodded ruefully. "I don't seem to be any good at that stuff."

Garza's sneer became a full-face taunt.

"So it's a good thing Lobo's here."

Lobo loped over to Garza and stood looking down at him out of his distant, lunatic eyes. He was panting heavily like a huge dog, his hands hanging limp and wide-spaced. The bleeding cop sized him up, saw what he was up against.

He shrugged, "Fuck it. What do I care? We were ordered. By a superior officer out of Mexico City." He spat, cleansing his mouth of capitulation. But it wasn't anywhere near enough.

"Who?"

"A guy called Raul Chagón."

"You mean Chaco? Doc Savage?"

"Oh, you've heard of him? Yeah, he came in, directed operations for awhile, called a few shots, then wandered off. It's what he does. Fuck with me and you might get to meet him. God help you."

"Nah, he likes me. I pulled a thorn out of his paw." Or just maybe, I thought, vice versa. "But the point is, who was Chaco acting for? Who was behind it?"

"No idea. "

"Hey, Lobo?"

"Eh!" His ears actually stood up.

"Give him some ideas."

Lobo snorted and jumped on Garza, ravishing him on the floor like an animal. Garza made motions of resisting, but we have no real defense against being eaten by ravaging animals. Our fear of it goes too deep. Lobo latched onto his ear and started worrying it while Garza screamed in rage and pain. When you could hear it turn to fear, Lobo gave a jerk of his head and spit out part of the ear. I called him off and he moved away, but stayed on all fours, blood dripping off his grin. Garza couldn't *wait* to tell me all he knew.

He held both hands over his ear, blood streaming through the fingers, and howled, "Who the fuck you think it was?"

"*Hijole*, do you mean to say ... Them?"

"Who else? You think the PRI just rolled over and died? "

"But why? They elected Varedas."

"Yeah, but he was the short game, you know. They wanted to break him away from the poor, smear the party a little. They were going to set him up for removal later, probably a drug bust. Then the governor appoints a new guy who packs the cabinet with PRI people. The PT assholes come back to the PRI by election time."

"They just used us to get into power?" Tirado was having a night of tough realizations.

"What else, you stupid old fart? But *killing* him? Christ, he'll be a martyr now, probably for years. And *you* get to be mayor. A total fuckup. You people can't do anything right."

Momo stuck his rifle into Garza's bloody throat. "That's enough out of you."

I stood there with the Truth. Running through my hands like sand. I started to say something to Tavo about it, but he was standing by the Bad Corpse, looking sickened. I started towards him, but he bent to pick up the gold baseball. He wiped the blood off with his expensive shirttail and looked at the engraving.

Almost to himself he said, "The intercollegiate championships. You kept this?"

I could barely hear Tirado; his voice was drained and feeble. "Of course, I kept it. I treasure it. I love you boys and I'm proud of you both. I just ... My wife ... " He stopped, then spread his hands towards Tavo. "Can you forgive me?"

Tavo looked at the ball again, then tossed it up, bounced it off his bicep, caught it, and dropped it on top of the body. "Sure, Pops. I forgive you. Let's talk about it when you get back."

"Back?"

Momo was brisk and businesslike. "Yeah, and we'd better get going. Pepito, handcuff the cop. If he so much as spits, blow his kneecaps. Lobo, let's sort 'em out."

"*Andale, pues* ... we've never really taken anybody this big before. We'd better bag him up, take him out to the Esquinapa place."

"You think the city will pay to get him back?" I wasn't very up on kidnapping procedures.

Lobo howled, "Of course not, ya putz. *Burrocratas* get murdered, not kidnapped. Who'd pay for them?"

Pepito stood up from cuffing Garza, added, "Journalists are even more worthless. Who cares if they get killed? Why do you think we never put your head in a sack?"

"Weren't up to the chore of cutting my ears off?"

"Go for the dick, less work. Actually, who'd qualify most is your little Srta. Gortari. We'd love to get our hands on her."

"I'll bet you would. Well, she'd be a handful."

"Who's the Mayor's wife, Mundo?" Momo was busy pulling a heavy, olive-colored plastic bag out of a rucksack. "Do you smell the coffee yet?"

"Oh, right, she's an Osuna. *Café Molino* heiress."

"Exactly. I figure she's good for our biggest payday ever. We considered Tavo here, but his mother doesn't have any money. Doubt his stepmom would pay the freight."

"Besides," Pepito put in, "If you had a faggot son,

would you pay to get him back?"

"I certainly would," Tirado said firmly. He seemed to be coming around a little.

"No way," Pepito snapped. "If I was a fag I wouldn't even pay to get me back. I'd just tell me to kill myself."

Tavo, bland and sincere, said, "Well, if everybody felt that way, we wouldn't have any problems would we?"

"No, I guess not." Pepito seemed glad to have made his point. The little dipshit.

"So we'll settle for bagging *Señor Alcalde* here," Lobo chimed in. "And ol' *Capitán Gárfio* as a little bonus. There's people who'll pay for him, don't worry. Pick his so-called brains, just for openers."

Pepito glanced down at Garza. "Doubt you'll ever be seeing him again, actually."

"If you do," Lobo rumbled, "He'll probably be wearing lipstick and a mini-skirt."

"You're just saying that to turn my stomach."

"So that's it," Momo said. "Everybody accounted for. All the bodies here will make it a very authentic nab. Dead cop will give those pricks on *Comandante* Simón's squad a few things to scratch their heads over. Leave the asshole's gun, too, just to muddy the water."

He stepped over to Tirado, shaking out some manacles, ropes, and the military body bag. "So if you'll just slide into our custody here."

Tirado eyed the restraints calmly. "Wait a minute. Could I ask a question?"

Momo looked at his wristwatch pointedly, but nodded.

"They want to kill me, right?"

Momo thought about that one, glanced at me.

"After you're back from a kidnapping that could be pinned on them?" I asked him. "I'd say it's very likely. I mean apart from them wanting you out so they can run in one of their puppets."

"So you blackmail them," Lobo pointed out helpfully. "Besides, you'll have plenty of bodyguards after this."

Tirado gave a telling look at the dead bodyguards. Momo got his point.

"Well, you know, maybe you should try hiring

some real professionals."

"People who know the napping racket in and out," Pepito added. "Family organization."

The Mayor took a long look at the kidnappers and you could see realignments going on inside his head. "I suppose we'll have time to talk about all this."

"Hopefully not too much time," Momo said. "We like a quick turnaround, and the expenses of keeping somebody hidden run kind of steep."

"Of course," Pepito stuck in, "In your case I'm sure it will be worth it."

"The Poor Come First," Lobo growled, "But the Rich Come Dear."

Momo stayed behind a minute after Lobo and Pepito carried their two victims out, cocooned and limp. He looked around, surveying the crime scene, mentally checking if anybody had touched anything, looking at the positions of the bodies.

I said, "Tirado thinks everything's going to be all right."

He shrugged. "Let him. Once we collect, we're out of the picture. We've got too much pride in our craft to take government jobs." He glanced at me, "Oops, sorry, Mundo."

"No, no, you're right. Anyway, I'd already quit."

"Well, maybe you can work your way up to criminal scum." He shook our hands and walked out. Tavo and I stood alone in a blood-sprayed room, looking after him.

"You know, I do feel a little bad about Our Brother," I finally said. "I mean, your father."

"Don't. He's an asshole."

"Okay, I can see that. Hell, you should have kidnapped him yourself."

"Well, I sort of did. Those guys are going to pay me twenty percent of the ransom."

"*A poco?* You're too much." I didn't know how much I'd needed to laugh, and when I did we both broke up. After a few minutes of overly-enthusiastic good humor I asked him, "But why should they pay you anything?"

"My fee for bringing them over here and turning them on to the job. We worked it out on cell phone while we were tearing over here to see if you were dead yet."

"Well, thanks a lot for that. Just don't tell anybody I had to get rescued by a fairy, okay? The nuns were bad enough."

"Your secret is safe. You can loan me gas money until I get my cut."

"You sure they're going to pay you? Newsflash ... those guys are dangerous armed criminals."

"Not to mention homophobes. But they came through for you, didn't they? They've got a sense of fair play, I think. Besides, you know where they live, don't you? And where their kid crosses the street to reform school?"

"So we could be partners in extorting armed maniacs? Fabulous."

We'd walked out into a sort of family den and Tavo pulled me over to a wall gallery of portraits; from big cibachromes to century-old oils. "Three Carnival Queens right on that wall, two Flower Games. My half-sisters have suffered from their failure to provide the family with another Queen."

"But now they have you."

"They'll be so thrilled. Check this one out, 1971. My wicked stepmother, Yadira III, Queen of Neptune. That's her halfwit buddy Consuelo, Queen of Flower Games. Maybe I would make a fetching Queen."

"You'd have to lose the mustache."

"Oh, really? Take a closer look at Consuelo, there."

"Boy, you're out of the closet twenty minutes and you're already getting catty."

"So will you. When you figure out you can't use anything you heard tonight."

"I have a private collection."

"You'd best keep it that way. This is Chinatown, Jake."

I realized at that moment why Masons have secret handshakes ... the kick of instantly recognizing other members of their cult. I threw my arm over his shoulder and walked towards the door. "Louie, this could be the start of a beautiful friendship."

One of my favorite examples of how Spanish words get fumbled around into different shapes and poses is *paloma*, meaning a dove. We say the sea has *palomas* on it, a lovelier image than "whitecaps", I think. Popcorn is *palomitas*, a bag of little doves. Jazz musicians here don't "jam", they *palomear*, knowing that, listen for hands moving like a flurry of wings. A firecracker explodes into a *palomazo*, flushing feathers of flame. Add the "*-ino*" suffix, meaning "-like" or "-ish" and you get *palomino*, big gold horses named after the soft colors of birds. And there's a hidden cultural meaning, when you hear songs about *palomas*, you know they are about lovers, often unhappy lovers. Interesting, since in Spanish "dove" and "love" make no rhyme or reason.

"Cu Cu Ru CooCoo" by Mundo Carrasco
"Maz Speak" Column *Pacific Pearl*, July 1998

My newfound movie friendship with Tavo didn't mean we went out for drinks to celebate the fact I was still alive. He took off in his Cougar and I drove downtown, ditched Garza's car in a gulch off Zaragosa, and walked home over the hill, not even stopping to enjoy the scene from the top. I walked in, grabbed my bottle of Cabrito and went over to the railing. My *carne asada* was burnt away to nothing, the embers were cold. I blew on them, but no glow answered my breath. Safe at home one more time.

After a couple of slugs of the tequila, I left the bottle on the rail and almost ran to my computer, where I nailed it all, still fresh and vivid. Who killed Varedas, who helped him and why. Who rousted the *paracaidistas* from Infiernillo, and why. It flowed out already structured and sharpened and hard. It's a thrill better than sex when that sort of things happens. Well, not exactly, but you know. I scrolled to the top and typed the title, "Orders of Succession". I went to the rail for another sip of tequila, came back and hit the key to save the story. I have an extensive collection of second thoughts that were never printed, or even submitted. I went back to the rail to think things over.

I was standing there sipping from the *botellita* and staring at the slim slice of moon when a *pulmonia* pulled up below and spilled out a bunch of laughing partiers. Palomina and some music school buddies with bottles, horns, and guitars. She waved to me and I waved the Cabrito at them. One of the *musicos* sang out, *"Las piedras jamas, paloma,"* and they all laughed then started strumming, serenading me with the rest of *Cucurucuru Paloma.* A fine old tearjerker of post-love depression; when they came back to *las piedras jamas* they schmaltzed it up ridiculously. Hey, I might have been dumped and drinking, but I wasn't about to dash my broken heart against the cobblestones. Love songs aren't real life.

I bowed and they clapped and cheered. Downstairs, Grady grumpily retaliated; a Van Halen chorus called *Go Ahead and Jump.* I tossed down the key and they romped up the stairs, still singing. Palomina bounced through the door and into my arms, then produced a bottle of Don Julio, no less, from her bottomless shoulder bag. The rest surrounded us, warbling *La Borrachita.* I like old Mexican songs the same way I like coffee. Dark, creamy, overly sweet, served by pretty women, spiked with fine tequila.

We drank boisterously, tossing the bottles over the rail to startle Chema's newly bought *gallos,* neighborhood *chivitos,* and *gatos* prowling after unwary iguanas. Watching the goats, cocks, and cats scatter, one of the trumpet players said, "Take that, you familiars of Satan."

A long-haired girl with a guitar and a crucifix almost lost in her cleavage sniffed. "Protestants, at least."

They all whooped around and admired the view, then started pointing down at Olas Altas and getting restless. The crucifix girl called across the room, "Mundo, come with us. The Burning of Bad Humor."

I said, "Been there, done that."

This time Palomina caught something. Probably informed by TV news' lust for fires and unexplained explosions ... especially near places where bodies and firearms were discovered.

"Don't worry," she told them, "I'll burn the bad humor off his ass."

They all laughed and trooped down the stairs with a flourish of trumpet calls and *ay-ay-ay's,* then ran down the street towards the hubub of Olas Altas. Palomina kicked the door closed, then wheeled to face me. "I figure we've got about thirty minutes."

"Until we turn into pumpkins?"

"Until they fire it up," she said, starting to unbutton her blouse. "I hope you don't mind if I count my money in front of the needy."

An old wheeze, but eternal. Most women don't understand their own value and power. That a mere movement can be like flaunting food in front of a hungry man. But Palomina understands that very well. And it hit me that when in comes to the *cortitas*, whores might have their motives, but we don't want you to go hungry.

She did a stripper strut to the bed and flopped on her back. "Burn, baby, burn."

Sex with Palomina was sort of like moving around with strained muscles. Like effort against a sort of shadow, unable to get the full burn because of residue that cramps and limits and chafes. The best way to deal with that, of course, is a full deep workout. She could see that she was getting divided attention, not really filling up my sensation. But that's not all that new to her, and she's really good about it.

As though she'd been reading my mind, Palomina whispered in my ear, "No, I'm not her. But is that such a bad thing?"

No, it wasn't. A sip of tequila isn't the same as a shot of cocaine, but you learn to live with it. And the thing is, you *can* live with it.

"She could never understand you. She doesn't need art or love because she doesn't have any flaws."

I raised on my elbows to look at her. "But you can understand me?'

She laughed and squirmed salaciously. "Of course not, *bicho*, you're a man."

I lowered myself beside her. I inhaled the scent of her hair and shoulders.

I asked her, "So how about you? How's your humor level?"

She made a snarling sound and lightly clawed my lower back. "I didn't get that audition after all."

"Aw, that sucks. Why not?"

"I lost out to a handful of pork fat. This business is pissing me off."

"God, me too. I mean, mine too. Politics has been tossing my life like a salad."

"Aren't we old enough to establish our own mastery?"

"I wish. I'm over thirty, right? I've been working newspapers for twelve years, I went to two colleges. I've been around, Columbia, Cuba, New York. And all of a sudden everybody I talk to is kicking my butt, making me feel like a stupid little kid. What's wrong with this picture?"

"I felt the same way when I got out of The School and started working. I think it's called real life."

"That stuff before wasn't real life? "

"Sure it was, but you weren't really living it. What were you doing? The baseball star. The glamorous investigator. You were too busy being a hero, Mundo, not a real human like the rest of us. You had to lose a big one for once."

"So that's what happens after you stop being a hero? I thought you got to live happily ever after."

"Dream on. "

"I've been trying to."

"Well, then, wake up. Quit being a pro and be a gifted amateur. Quit the city, quit the paper, write a book "

"Actually, that's exactly what I've been thinking. "

"Great. I've been thinking of quitting dancing. Maybe teach. I don't know ... what? ... waitress?"

"Christ, what a couple of lying whores we are. "

"Well, as long as we're lying here ... "

All in all, it was thirty minutes well spent.

We could see the tow truck way down in front of the Belmar, the doomed effigy hanging from its crane surround by a bubbling mass of drunks and merrymakers. The Bad Humor Burning is an old Carnival tradition, probably a remnant of something very ancient. It's also a drunken bash, the people's party while the Lifestyles of the Rich and Snotty are over at the Bacanora sporting fashion statements and watching the coronation. The identity of the effigy, made of paper maché and laced with firecrackers, had been chosen by telephone polls open to everybody. Osama Bin Laden was a hot contender, but George Bush and the United States *futbol* team also ran strong for the honor of Asshole Of the Year Goes Up In Smoke. I would have added the New York Yankees and whoever invented spray paint. But the surprise winner was...the envelope, please...the *gasolinero!* The effigy wore a Pemex service station shirt, proof that soaring gas prices generate a lot more Bad Humor than international outrages.

Standing naked, hip to hip at my railing, we could see the effigy twisting in the wind, but couldn't hear the satiric poems and speeches by the reigning King Of Joy. They called him *Rey Feo* for generations but during the reign of Jose Preciado, the *banda* singer, it got changed to *Rey de Allegria.* Preciado is pretty cool. He's a baseball player, a decent hitter, and even started his own team in the municipal league, invited me to play for him several times. He tried to buy the Venados from the Pacífico Brewery, but they wouldn't sell. But I did like the King Ugly name better. It's a lot more to live up to.

We could tell by the cadence of the crowd and music that the currently reigning King of Joy, a fat singer who calls himself El Coyote, was winding up the long litany of "Juan Carnaval's Will and Testament".

Palomina giggled, "I hope he leaves some suppositories to Varedas".

"And to the Venados," I intoned, "I leave a slugging right fielder who can actually field the ball."

The verbal hilarity was over and there was a momentary hush, then the paper gas jockey burst into flame and the crowd roared like a massive sea lion. The fire spread quickly up the paper body, stuffed with thousands of paper slips listing the year's wrongs, peeves, sins, and general bitching. The pump jockey blazed brave in the night, then the firecrackers started blowing him apart. Sparks and ashes shot out over the weaving, waving crowd. Eventually he burned out in the dark, revelers grabbing brooms to sweep the ashes to the seawall then shovel them into the sea, taking away the wretcheness of another year. That's how we deal with Bad Humor where I come from.

As the last ashes were being dumped, a single sky-rocket arched out over the bay and exploded in a huge flower of violet and gold, painting the buildings like an old-fashioned sepia wash and turning the sea to molten bronze. And the music stopped. The silence was almost physical after five nights of incessant pounding. From the islands in the bay several seals trumpeted, probably wondering what happened. It was midnight of Fat Tuesday and Carnival 2002 had just ended with a bang and a simper. It was the split second when the miracle of the entire Catholic world happens, the riot of carnality transforming at its fullest flood into the renunciation of Ash Wednesday, portal to the sacred mystery of rebirth. The party stops, bells toll for Mass, and everything shifts into reverse. Beneath the manic mask of the dance, Carnival has always been about that internal moment when the world transforms from a stew of dying meat to a hymn of deathless spirit.

Palomina said, "So now it's Lent."She picked up the charred *carne asada* from my barbecue grill and tossed it over the rail to the street. Coyota came out of nowhere, sniffed it, then shot us both a dirty look. I shrugged and she slunk off into shadows. Palomina dipped a finger in the charcoal ash, turned around and smeared a streak of it on my forehead. I reached past her for more ash and chalked a line between her breasts. She moved in and kissed me, then licked her lips.

"*Besos de Ceniza,.*"she murmured.

I doubt the old Timbirichi song was about that kind of Ashen Kisses, but it would do as a soundtrack.

She slipped out of my arms and into the shower stall, grabbing her bag on the way. I turned to watch subdued mobs milling in the street. I turned when I heard a tiny cough and she stood there in her feathered cape, arms across her breasts, the glistening wings covering her crotch. She moved into a silent dance that smoldered sexily before suddenly breaking open. She spread the wings wide, nude underneath except for a *minimalisimo* G-string, a nest of bright pheasant feathers that looked completely natural as her pubic foliage. She swayed in front me, her wings making slow circles beside us. She looked into my eyes and said,

"What are you giving up for Lent, Mundo?"

"Not the ways of all flesh, I hope."

"Why not ..." She moved closer to my face, the wings fanning around us. "Give up ashes?"

On one of those impulses we never understand I turned around, grabbed up the barbecue and dumped it over the rail. We watched quietly while the ashes caught the sea breeze and drifted out over the buildings below. I felt Palomina's wing move away but when I turned she was back, holding an old baseball cap from my collection on the back wall. She put it on my head, then the wings brushed down my body. I glanced at the mirror to see an old cap from college with a big sun and "PHOENIX." Well, actually, "XINEOHP."

She swooped to the railing, her plumes carving figures like a matador's cape. She leaned over the railing, her wings spread out into the air. Her G-string was almost invisible at the back, just three threads. But when I touched the little button where the strands met, it fell off and drifted to the floor, a huddle of feathers that reminded me of the loser in a cockfight. She thrust out into the night, open to suggestion. I stepped up to the plate. At her first tiny moan, I whispered in her ear, "Do you want to live up in the sky, like birds without feet?" Then I looked out over the city and nearly jumped out of my skin. In fact I did jump out of hers.

I grabbed my binoculars, not hearing Palomina's protests, and stared at the ugly Bank of Mexico monolith. Somebody was lying on top of it, reaching down with a spray can. Tagging the Fortress of Evil! He had already written three big red letters. "M, I, C,"I yelled, "See you real soon, MicroBio!"

I snatched on a pair of shorts and bolted out the door. "Y? Because, I'm going to kill your ass, you little germ!"

As I went out the street door, I could see him spraying an "R". I looked up and saw Palomina leaning over the railing, not believing any of it. I ran down the street wearing only shorts and a baseball hat. Behind me she screamed, "Christ! *Men!*"

So much for getting my ashes hauled.

335

WEDNESDAY

FEBRUARY THIRTEENTH

MIERCOLES DE CENIZAS (ASH WEDNESDAY)

PRINCIPIO DE CUARESMA (FIRST DAY OF LENT)

Corruption is not the opposite of accomplishment because of any moral symmetry, it's because the genius of corruption isn't about making things happen. It's profoundly about keeping things from happening.

"Dictatorship, Present, Perfect" by Raymundo Carrasco
Siglo XXI, April 2000

There was only one plausible way MicroBio could have infested the Dark Tower, carelessness at one of the fire escapes. They both go down to Calle Venus in the back, so I headed there at full gallop, my feet already burning and starting to bleed. Panting on the Venus sidewalk, I found the gate with the taped-back lock and got into position. I could hear the pitty-pat of little feet on the steel steps. When he burst out of the gate I was right beside him, swinging my arm out to clothesline him off his feet. That American expression, *clothesline* is very evocative. And extremely gratifying to feel his Adam's apple hit my forearm and see his feet swing up off the ground. I dashed him down to the cement with a gesture like snapping water off my fingers. He was shocked and had his wind half knocked out, but he reached in his pocket and came out with something sharp and shiny. I stomped his fingers into it, drawing a squawk. A can of spray paint fell out of his shirt. I realized he had fallen on the skateboard he'd slung across his back. I dropped to his chest on my knees, knocking the rest of his wind out, and picked up the can. I grabbed his gasping face and used my finger and thumb like a surgical spreader to pry his right eye wide open. I moved the nozzle of the spraycan right up to the bulging, staring eyeball and held it there, my finger poised on the button, quivering with internal conflict. He froze, mesmerized by his close-up of the paint aperture. I relaxed my finger, realizing I was not going to spraypaint the little eyesore.

I said, "It's time we talked."

I grabbed him by the armpits, snatched him up, slammed him against the steel rails and frisked him. His wallet said he was Mario Martinez, practically John Doe in these parts. An address in the generic warrens of Infonavit Cochis. The kid was nobody, was Everypunk. I picked up what I had thought was a knife, but it was worse – a diamond scriber pen. I was furious, shaking it in his face, "You little asshole! You know how much it costs real people to replace their window glass?"

He stared back sullenly, his face a flat Indian mask. He had no thoughts or emotions at the moment, had gone into *indio* shutdown. "There ought to be public floggings just for possession of these things." I was still worked up, but it was going sour on me. "I'm going to kick the shit out of you, then I'm going to turn you over to the cops. "

"What have I done to you?"

I doubted he could ever see it. He had no idea of civic pride, of destruction, of value. He was just a mirror, reflecting here what he saw outside his poorly defined boundaries. He paints what he sees, you see what he paints.

But I said, "You're making my city ugly."

Something moved in his face at that, "Your city, huh? It belongs to you? It's already ugly, I'm just making it mine."

I shook my head, suddenly tired and bummed out, "It's not mine, not yours."

"It's got my name on it."

That hit me right in the guts like a line drive. I stared at him, but he wasn't there for it. I knew it was going to come back to haunt me. Maybe I should interview him for my column.

He shot me the other punch in the combination. "I like my name out where people can see it."

Shit. Even this little germ was rubbing my face off. But you know us heroes, never say die.

"But you aren't doing anything with it. You're not signing anything. You didn't create anything."

"*Y a mi que?* I'm just expressing myself. Everybody else can fuck off. You too." He was drawing on his culture now, the magazines and rap of tagger society. "I'm nothing but a paint can with legs."

"Well, you can tell that to the cops. They're fond of nihilist art theories."

He kept shifting his eyes around, anywhere but on

mine. "You got no proof."

What an idiot. "Whose prints are on that paint can and engraver you little fuckhead? Besides, I don't need any proof – I *saw* you, *pendejo*."

He shuffled and snuffled some more, probably running short of paint fumes in his blood stream. He pointed to stained walls up the block. "The place is covered with tags, who cares? I wouldn't do it if everybody else wasn't."

"You're full of shit. You'd be dying to be the first little puppy to piss on the tree."

He shrugged. "So kill me" Rock lyrics promoted better attitudes back in Grady's day, I think. I kept staring him down, but also his comments were buzzing around in my head. Even *MicroBio* was busting my balls!

He gangled around a little, then come up with the only form of entreaty the street permits. "So what do you want from me?"

Like I would have any use for the little scumbag. Then it hit me all at once, like a floodlight. Just maybe I did. Maybe he could end up doing what he wanted, but everything he did would serve my purposes. If I could just give him the right nudge, do the Borrego number on his benighted little ass.

I was letting him sweat before I laid it out. "You know, maybe there is something you can do to square this up. We're going to do a deal. I don't beat your ass or turn you in. You stay *out* of the historic zone, completely. And do me one little favor."

He scanned my face, extremely dubious. I said, "I think you're going to like it."

"I don't think so."

"Oh, no, you will. It's a real challenge. This shit you've been doing is kid stuff. Let me show you the real thing."

It started to drizzle as I walked back up the hill. By the time I reached my building my shorts were soaked and the rain was washing blood off my feet. My lights were off, I was locked out. Palomina was gone. I stood wet and chilled on the sidewalk, wondering about my priorities.

Again.

     I crossed the street and stepped up on the wall, the chill wet stones soothing to my torn soles. The moon was a half circle, a golden arc like a fish scale or half a wedding ring. I looked down at the Malecón, surveyed the wreckage of the Third Largest MeatFest In the World. Then I saw it, scrawled on the sagging black backdrop of an empty sound stage. She'd found the spray can and written, "Fuck Off, Mundo!"in big, lipstick red letters. We all paint what we see. With the materials at hand.

THURSDAY

FEBRUARY FOURTEENTH

EN LAS MAÑANITAS

DIA DE SAN VALENTÍN

My coaches always stressed sportsmanship and character. They said baseball was just like life. Actually I've found it to be the opposite. For one thing, in life you almost never get a raincheck.

"Interview with Mundo Carrasco"
El Debate Sport Page, May 1992

I woke up about five in the morning, slumped over my desk. I didn't remember how I got in the house or why I was at the desk. I looked around at moonlight slashed by the red pulse from the Televisa towers. Something had awakened me, I saw a sudden image of a pistol, foreshortened like an expressionist print by Siguieros, slamming through my door. I shook it off, stepped over to the rail and looked down, expecting to see Coyota staring up like a mooncalf. But it was Palomina, wearing a pale blue shift and sitting on a suitcase. A *pulmonia's* taillights coasted around the curve. She spoke in a normal tone of voice, but I heard her very clearly. She said, "What day is this, Mundo?"

I had to think, I'd slept most of the day. "Thursday?" Yeah, that was it. She just kept looking up at me.

"Second day of Lent." No cigar. "February something."

She shook her head, a shiver of pony blonde under the slim setting moon. "It's Valentine's Day, you dork."

Up on my roof we leaned over the railing, our shoulders and hips lightly touching. I said, "I thought you gave me up for *Cuaresma.*"

"I've got no character. Besides, what would I use as a substitute, those damn Lent tamales with veggies and shark meat?" Suddenly she stifled a giggle.

"*¿Que tienes?*" But I knew what she'd seen.

"If I tell you, will you go tearing off into the night?"

"I'm not going anywhere. Promise."

"Look." She was pointing down to the seawall, where streetlights shone on the recently improved PRI murals. Somebody had been very busy earlier in the evening, the two tricolored murals for BEATRIZ PAREDES now had big blocks of white paint covering all but letters that spelled out "EL TRI ARDE"and better yet, "EAT REDS."

I'd been a little busy myself, photographers had shot the new messages for the morning edition of *El Debate*. Columnists were already speculating about the identity and motivations of the group that took credit for the deface- ment. MicroBio did a very neat job of it. It even looks like he used the masking tape I bought along with the bucket of waterproof deck paint. After all, it was his last tag down- town. It hit me that vaccines are made from tame versions of the microbes they defend against.

Palomina loved the mesages, which were staked out too late by a few cops sleeping in pickups. I told her she might see more such expressions. "I understand the tagging community is taking more patriotic pride these days, hit- ting people who have it coming. Plus it's more macho to stain something that could get you in major trouble."

Palomina eyed me. "You understand that, do you?"

"Well, you know, there was a newspaper item."

"Did you write it before or after?"

"No, I thought this one called for a leak to some- body who needs a byline."

"And she would be ...?"

"Nobody who could hope to compare."

"You muckraking, slanderous scum say the sweetest things."

"Don't we, though." I stood looking at her while she watched the waves and listened to the barking of the seals. Then I did something I'd never done before. "I al- ready sent in my story on Varedas."

She sensed something serious and looked right into my face. "Did you say the sweetest things?"

"It was true, maybe. But not the facts. Good story that covers my ass."

"Everybody has to do that, I hear."

"But not you?"

"Of course not, I rule by uncovering my ass."

I laughed, but she wasn't with me. She kept looking at me. And I felt something crawling up into my head, like the mural idea with MicroBio. Truth, the last frontier. And the ultimate scam.

"I just thought of something, but I haven't worked it out completely."

"Can you give me a hint?"

"CryptoExpressionism."

She pouted. "Why do *periodistas* always use words nobody understands?"

"See what I mean?" I leaned over and kissed her shoulder right at the throat. "How about, journalism as Strip-O-Gram?"

"Like a 'reality TV' show?"

"The opposite, actually. Turn the cameras around."

"Too deep for me, Mundo. I'm just Full Contact Barbie, remember?"

"If you say so. But how about this? I wrote a second version of the story. Tells all, names names. Think I should switch it in? I've got about two hours."

She moved in closer, pressed herself against me, grabbed my ears to pull my head down to hers. There are tiny flecks in her eyes, like the swirl of mica motes that turn the shallows of Isla de la Piedra into golden dazzle.

She murmured, "You're asking a blonde to do your thinking for you?"

I kissed her, then grabbed her bag and pulled out her phone. "I've always wanted to do this."

When the *El Debate* switchboard answered I said, "Get me rewrite."

Palomina chuckled. 'How about 'Stop the Presses'?"

"I'm saving that one. For after 'Follow that *pulmonia*'."

"I knew you'd do it, you idiot."She struck an adoring pose. "My Reporter Ken."

"Reporter ¿quien? I couldn't let you down. So it'll all be your fault."

"Do you think they'll run it?"

"Maybe not. If not, it'll get it out anyway. They'll look bad, I'll look good."

"So we'll see, right?"

"Whether I'm get fired or shot?"

"No silly, how many times we can do it before the papers hit the streets."

I felt an impulse to tousle her hair, but she shook it out in the breeze off the bay, amber waves of mane. She looked really good to me, laughing into the wind. But I realized, in a sort of spasm, that no matter how it is with her there will be times the spell will come back over me and I'll look at her and see only who she's not. Nothing but costume and paint; she and I and everything in the world just meat programmed to slump and hump towards the ultimate indistinction of death. And I'll live with it, because when you strip it of the lies, fantasies, myths and magic that's what life is. It's a living.